THE
BRITISH DEVIL
GREG HOGBEN

Dreamspinner Press

Published by
Dreamspinner Press
5032 Capital Circle SW
Ste 2, PMB# 279
Tallahassee, FL 32305-7886
USA
http://www.dreamspinnerpress.com/

The British Devil
Copyright © 2012 by Greg Hogben

Cover Art by Catt Ford

ISBN: 978-1-61372-619-8

Printed in the United States of America
First Edition
July 2012

eBook edition available
eBook ISBN: 978-1-61372-620-4

For Kenny,
whose love and sheer brilliance
astound me every day.

Thanks to Chris and Randy, Doug and Jen, Kevin, Dee and Katie H. for all your support.

Thanks to Dreamspinner Press: Elizabeth North, Lynn West and Gin Eastwick, all the editors who worked on the book, and cover artist Catt Ford.

Special thanks to Umi, I couldn't have done this without you.

And to Kathy, thank you for being nothing like the character in this book!

CHAPTER ONE

"ARE you ready for this?" Danny asked as he started the ignition in his truck.

"I guess I am as ready as I will ever be," I answered while drawing a breath through a smile.

"Stop looking so nervous! You're only meeting my parents, not going in for surgery."

"I know, Tiger, but it's still a big deal. I want to make a good impression."

Danny laughed. "Well, you may want to control your sarcasm a little."

"I am not that bad."

"Just speak with that gorgeous British accent of yours. But remember not to cuss or blaspheme. In fact, blaspheming would probably be worse."

"When I know I can't swear, that's when I blaspheme the most."

"Okay, probably best that you just cuss!

I looked into Danny's light blue eyes as he smiled at me. I ran my hand down the back of his hair, which had finally started to grow out of its usual military crew cut. Tucking a blond lock behind his ear, I leaned in to kiss him and then settled back into the passenger seat as the truck pulled out of the driveway.

"I promise I will try, but I am as nervous as hell. To be honest, I could murder for a cigarette right now."

Danny looked at his watch. "You still have another three hours before you're allowed another one."

"You're not the boss of me!"

"Hey, these are your rules! I think you should quit cold turkey, but if you think it'll be easier cutting down first then I'll try to support you." He looked sympathetically at me. "Your dad would be proud, I'm sure."

"My dad would be spinning in his grave if he knew I was still smoking after what happened to him."

Duke, the sandy-colored mutt that Danny rescued along the roadside in his last Navy duty station in the Middle East, nestled in the small cabin behind the seats. Danny turned from the residential street onto the highway, and we set off on the four-hour journey from Austin to Baytown, a small city in southeast Texas.

I had arrived from England for my first visit to Texas the day before and had stayed either at Danny's side or in his arms in the house that he rented with Tucker, an old friend from college. Tucker had been kind enough to make himself scarce for the night in order to give Danny and me some much needed privacy. I hadn't met him yet, but Tucker's understanding of the fact that Danny and I hadn't seen each other for months had already put him in my good books.

The night had been perfect, even though I was tired from the journey. The excitement of seeing Danny kicked in, and I caught my second wind the moment I laid eyes on him. For the past few months we had done everything to feel close to each other without actually being together. I spoke to him every chance I could by phone, instant messenger, or webcam and had sent and received hundreds of texts, cards, e-mails, and letters. As precious as each and every communication was, nothing compared to feeling his warm body next to me.

Danny pulled into a gas station just outside Houston. The closer we got to Baytown, the more nervous and anxious I became. I watched Danny pump the petrol into the truck while he sang along to a country song playing out of a car next to us on the forecourt. He nodded politely and smiled good southern manners to the driver, who was looking back at him. He had never seemed so Texan to me. I checked myself in the rearview mirror and wondered for a second whether his parents would see "the British look" that Danny maintained I presented.

We set off again, Danny trying to find a radio station that was playing the country music he'd heard at the station. Finding it, he leaned back in his seat and began to sing to me. He wasn't the best singer in the world and could barely hold a tune to most songs. But when he mimicked country and western songs, his voice was pitch perfect, and he could double for any star on CMT. He twisted his voice into the familiar twang of the singer and added an occasional "yeeee-haw!" for my amusement. I would laugh, but he also knew it turned me on a little too.

"Will your sisters be there?" I asked once the song had ended.

"No, but you'll get a chance to meet them and their husbands tomorrow at the football game."

"What are their husbands like?" I asked, not having really considered what meeting them would be like. I was far more concerned about meeting his parents than anything else.

"They're okay. Slightly redneck, if you ask me. But I get along with them all right."

This only added to my nerves. I had visions of unshaven men in caps and dungarees, carrying shotguns a little too casually. I absentmindedly covered my left ear with the palm of my hand in protection, as thoughts of the scene in *Deliverance* played in my head.

"Do they get along with your parents?"

"They all get along really well. Personally, I don't have a great deal in common with them. But they're nice enough and they treat my sisters well, so that's all that really matters. They're typically Texan men in the respect that they're very much the heads of their households and don't answer to anyone. Mom and Dad don't even attempt to get into their business like a lot of other families might."

"And they're okay with the gay thing?"

"What can they say? They stayed in Baytown while I joined the military and fought for my country. They wouldn't dare let the gay guy shame them."

I paused for a moment before I asked my next question.

"Danny, exactly how religious is your mum?" I had been trying to avoid the question, as the mention of it seemed to quietly rile Danny on occasion. He had told me that she had become more involved with the church as she had gotten older, but often tensed up at the subject, leading me not to ask questions about it. But I thought I needed to know now, to gauge how to adapt any attempt at humor around her.

Danny sighed and looked out over the freeway in front of him. In every direction I looked on this journey, all I could see was flat land with an occasional tree or farmhouse in the distance. It was a stretch of road that I could imagine would force solitary drivers to examine their lives or solve world problems, as there was little, if anything, to catch their attention. Danny tilted his head as though he was trying to figure out the best way to answer, which unnerved me a little.

"I love my mom. She really is a remarkable woman. But you have to understand, Greg, she's not quite the same woman she was when I was growing up. Don't get me wrong; she's still as loving, kind, and generous now as she's always been. But back then she was so funny, so full of life, and I have nothing but good memories of all the fun we had as a family. She's the church secretary now, but then, she was a travel agent and told me all about the different cities around the world, even though she hadn't visited many of them and had only left Texas a handful of times in her life. Truth be told, that was one of the reasons why I joined the Navy, so I could visit all the places she had described to me. She and Dad have always been my biggest supporters." He paused, and, for a moment, a look of frustration crept over his face. "Nowadays her life revolves around the church."

"So she's a newly 'born again' Christian?"

"Well, no, not exactly. She has always identified herself as a Christian, but when I was growing up it was more about leading a decent life and going to church on Sunday. Other than that she was a typical mom who loved life and her family."

Danny chewed on his lip. "I couldn't believe the change I saw in her from when I left to join the Navy to when I got back. She just seemed to morph into this stereotypical Southern Baptist woman whose

4

church dominated her life. I know we kids were her world, but we grew up and left home, and I think she suffered empty nest syndrome. I really thought she would be the type of woman who would go out and embrace middle age freedom by joining bowling teams or taking up country line dancing with Dad. I could just see them drinking beer and two-stepping their way into retirement, but it just hasn't happened that way."

"How does she marry up the gay thing with the church thing?"

"Well, I came out to her years before she became so religious, so by then it was too late. When I told her I was gay, she and Dad couldn't have taken it any better. I had the same sort of reaction that you had with your parents."

"What, they put you in a frock, took you down Brighton seafront, and threw rocks at you?"

Danny laughed. "You know what I mean. They asked if I was happy, and that was it. No drama, no upset, no wailing over grandchildren they would never have. Hell, Mom would ask me in the shopping mall 'Do you like that boy?' and point until I had to pin her wrists down to her hips while she screamed with laughter."

"Hopefully she will point at me."

Danny winked. "You'll be fine, baby. I promise. Both Mom and Dad are, like we Southerners like to say, 'good people'."

It was ten o'clock and dark by the time we reached Baytown. The rain began pouring just as we passed the city limits. By the time we arrived in his old neighborhood, the rain and wind had turned into an almighty storm that made Duke shake and bark at the thunder and lightning. We pulled onto the street where Danny grew up. There was no chance of getting an idea of the area where he rode his bike as a child or where he learned to drive as a teenager, as the entire neighborhood was pitch black.

"The storm must have knocked out the electricity," Danny said as he tried to wrestle a now terrified Duke into a collar and leash. "Duke, come on! You've been here months and you're still terrified of the rain."

5

"Will they mind that it's so late?" I asked, thinking the last thing they wanted was an introduction to their son's new man by torchlight.

"They'll be fine!"

"And you're sure they'll like the hamper?"

"A gift basket from Harrods? What do you think?"

The three of us ran through the rain from the driveway to the front porch of the house, each of us getting instantly drenched in the downpour.

"They're gonna love ya. I promise." He winked at me again before knocking on the door.

As I stood there, half-soaked, I couldn't help wondering how in the world I had gone from my carefree life in England to the front porch of a modest house in Southeast Texas in such a short time.

CHAPTER TWO

DANNY and I had met just six months earlier. The British Ministry of Defense had once again chartered aircraft from the airline that I worked for to transport servicemen and women over to the Middle East, as their own fleet couldn't keep up with the demand for troops. It was the start of the second Gulf War, and Bahrain was the destination for most of the squaddies before they were shipped off to either Iraq or Afghanistan. I had been rostered to operate one of the flights and had been looking forward to the trip so I could catch up with an old friend of mine, Vicky, who was the purser on the flight.

Since we were flying east it was a night flight, which departed at eight in the evening, and we were due to land at five in the morning, local time. The crew and I had started the flight in high spirits, welcoming the soldiers on board with laughter and jokes. The girls shot off a few well-humored innuendos that seemed to cheer the men up, and for the first five hours of the flight all was well. But the last two hours gradually became more intense. Many of the younger troops, who came on board with such bravado and confidence, now sat silently staring out the windows into a black sky as the realization of where they were going and what lay ahead finally hit home. It was obvious that this was their first experience with war, perhaps even their first time being away from home on their own. Though they were in their late teens or early twenties, they still had the faces of little boys who were now plainly scared. Their nervousness became even more apparent as we began our descent. Since we were flying into a military base with a plane full of troops, all of the interior and exterior aircraft lights had to be switched off for landing. It wasn't uncommon to see the odd young soldier desperately trying to hide a tear as we finished our final checks before landing.

We offloaded the soldiers quickly and efficiently, and then boarded the shuttle van to the crew's hotel. Since it had been a night flight, the crew slept for the rest of the day in our hotel in Manama, the capital city of the small Middle Eastern island, and spent the evening at a slightly comatose dinner at the hotel restaurant. After downing a couple of Red Bulls to get us going again, we returned to our rooms to get ready to go out and hit one of the very few western bars in the area. After I showered and looked in the mirror, I was once again thrown by how short my hair was. It had been cut by a butcher of a barber on my last trip, a quick flight to Toronto and back. It was practically a crew cut and made me look somewhat harsher than usual. I threw on a plain white V-neck T-shirt and blue jeans just as the first of the crew arrived at my room for our usual predeparture drinks. We were all well rested and in high spirits and ready, and after a few throat-burning shots of vodka, we headed downstairs for the usual battle with the drivers of the battered old taxis that hung around the hotel. Each of the drivers was ready to overcharge as many gullible tourists as possible. With my freshly shaved head and somewhat menacing appearance, I was immediately pushed to the front and designated the responsibility of haggling the price before we divided up into three cars.

"Oh, Greg, I saw Donna on crossover in Jamaica last week. She sends her love," Vicky said as she tried to position herself into the rearview mirror of the taxi we were sharing to reapply the lipstick that matched her low-cut red blouse. As usual, she looked stunning in her black stilettos and short black skirt, even though it completely went against the guidelines she'd been given by the airline on how to dress in the region.

"How is she?" I asked while half laughing at the Arab driver, who was now looking flustered by Vicky's cleavage, which was in clear view.

"She had a huge smile on her face, so I guess she's okay. Her crew was taking the inbound flight home, so I didn't really have a chance to stop and speak to her. Besides, I think the first officer was chatting her up."

"Oh God, I hope she doesn't get herself involved with flight deck. They're all a bunch of nutcases in uniforms. They'll talk about crosswinds until your eyes bleed."

"This one seemed okay. He was attractive, but a little odd. You know, the type that think that because they're flight deck they're God, and it's their sheer willpower that's holding the plane in the sky."

"They're all a little odd, Vic. Every time they go out drinking with the crew I get cornered and have the same conversation with them. I have no idea why they think it's okay to tell the gay guy about all of their freakiness. 'Hey, you sleep with boys so you'll understand when I tell you I like to pinch my balls hard while a woman stands on the bed wearing ripped stockings and shoves a high heel up my arse.'"

"I can't blame her. I love a man in uniform," Vicky said, settling back and flipping her long blonde hair so half of it lay across my shoulder.

"I dare say you'll be in luck tonight, sweetheart. Half of the Royal Navy and Marines will be out tonight."

"Well, you know I would do anything for our brave, brave boys," she said in a voice halfway between Betty Boop and Marilyn Monroe. She closed her eyes and shrugged, to accentuate her cleavage even more.

"You're like the Red Cross, Vic."

"The Red Cross? Excuse me, I only help one of them out at a time, thank you very much," she said in mock horror. "Anyway, how are you on that front? Have you found yourself a man yet?"

"No, and if all men are like the last one I met, I think I am going to be single for the rest of my life."

"Why? What was wrong with him?"

"After our first date, he gave me a mix CD of love songs and demanded that I tell him which lyrics meant the most to me and expressed the most about our relationship." I shook my head. "I only ended up seeing him for two weeks, and I was away on trips for eight days during that fortnight. I came off one flight and had twenty-seven text messages while I was in the air."

Vicky crinkled her nose. "A bit needy, huh?"

"A bit? Are you kidding me? I half expected to find him wearing a wedding dress with a knife to his wrist on our third date."

The taxi pulled up outside the bar. We paid the driver, who tried to change the previously negotiated price, and then climbed out of the cramped taxi to wait in the nighttime humidity for the other two taxis to arrive. Once our party was complete, we consisted of another four girls and two guys. We settled into the queue of men who were waiting to get in, but were called to the front of the line by the doorman, who immediately let us through.

The local Arab businessmen who owned these western-themed bars were far from stupid. Practically every night was "ladies night," when girls were given free entry and drinks all evening. The owners knew there were only a handful of western women on the island, and looking after them meant that they would attract the thousands of military men who were more than happy to be overcharged for imported American beer, so long as they had something attractive and uncovered to look at.

The blanket of deodorant and aftershave lingering in the air hit us the moment we walked through the door.

"Jesus, I haven't smelled this much Brut since that rugby team lined up in the locker room, drew a pair of tits on my back, and called me Helen," I said into Vicky's ear as we made our way to the bar. It was easier to navigate through the tight crowd of guys with a girl leading, as most of the men made room for her to pass through. Vicky, of course, took her time and made sure to flash a cheeky smile at each one individually as we passed.

The first part of the evening went as I had expected. The girls took full advantage of the free drinks, while throngs of military men befriended us boys. The soldiers bought us drinks and kept us in conversation as long as possible, not because they were really interested in anything we had to say, but because they saw us as a vehicle of getting them closer to the girls. We were possibly the only thing standing between them and the ultimate prize of bagging an air stewardess.

"Greg!" I heard Vicky call, as one group of particularly eager guys was questioning me as if training for interrogation. "Greg, I want to dance!"

She stretched out her hand over the shoulders of the men who had surrounded me by the bar and grabbed my arm. She dragged me onto the dance floor, where two of the other girls on the crew were dancing together, drawing a crowd. Vicky swung herself off my six-foot frame like I was a human stripper pole, and I felt another hand run down my shoulder. I turned to see the other two girls from the crew dancing up against my back. I caught a glimpse of the crowd of men lining the dance floor, taking in the show. With three girls dancing and gyrating on and around me, the faces staring back were a mix of blatant dislike and jealousy as well as good-humored but pained envy.

"I've worked up a thirst. Want to grab another drink?" Vicky shouted over the music. I nodded, and she took my hand as we left the other girls to continue their dance for the audience. Looking for the right destination, I peered over to the rest of the crew, who were on the far side of the bar to the left of the entrance, then to the long bar that ran the length of the room, and then finally to the third bar that lined the back wall behind the dance floor. And that was where I saw Danny.

There was no shortage of attractive, muscular guys in the bar, but Danny easily stood out among them all. From what I could see, he was about the same height as me, but held himself differently from everyone around him. He stood tall with broad, straight shoulders, as if at attention. While I could imagine the other men in the bar standing the same way in formation, they seemed to have a more relaxed posture. Danny and his companions had an air about them that stood out from the others. They stood around a high-topped table slightly apart from the crowd at the bar. All of them seemed in good spirits, but their demeanor didn't match the other, slightly younger guys who were gathered only feet away.

"It's too busy over there," I said, pointing at the bars near the entrance. "Let's go to the other side. It'll be quicker," I shouted to Vicky and beckoned her to lead the way toward the rear of the building.

Although the area in the back was busy too, it seemed a little less crowded. It was also slightly quieter since it was behind the DJ booth and the giant speakers that faced forward, pumping music toward the dance floor. The closer we got to the table where Danny was, the more I could see of him. He was blond, but the shortness of his hair and the various colored lights that streamed around from the dance floor hadn't allowed me to see it before. He was freshly shaven, which only accentuated his square jaw as he turned his head from one member of his party to the other. The three guys with him also had short hair, but they were all dark haired, which made Danny stand out even more. His friends all wore chinos and the same preppy-looking polo shirt. But Danny was dressed smartly in a black form-fitting shirt with the first two buttons undone and a pair of dark blue jeans that were a solid color, rather than the stonewashed jeans that almost everyone else in the bar wore. He and the other men looked no older than us, so I put them in their midtwenties.

Vicky noticed him, too, and turned to raise a cheeky eyebrow. I had directed us toward the table, but I had no intention of speaking to them. Danny was a stunning guy, and all I wanted, or imagined I would get, was a better look to appreciate him at a distance. But as we passed the table a hand came out of nowhere and tapped Vicky's shoulder.

"You're quite a dancer," the voice said in a distinct American accent. I followed his arm and saw that it was attached to one of the three men who stood with Danny.

"Thank you. I try my best to entertain," Vicky said with a wink.

"I'm John." He turned and pointed in turn to each of the guys, whose conversation had stopped while they waited to be introduced. "Casey, Chris, and Danny."

Vicky stopped and nodded to each man before introducing herself and presenting me as "Greg, my bodyguard."

"Hey, good to meet you," I said and stretched out my hand to shake their hands one by one. I deliberately left Danny's last in an attempt to savor the touch for a moment longer. When I took his hand, his grip was firm, but his hands were softer than I expected.

"So, are you boys in the American military?" Vicky said, tilting her head to the side just far enough for her hair to fall forward, giving her an excuse to flick it back like she was in a shampoo commercial.

"Yes. We're in the US Navy," said Chris.

"Well, you're certainly better behaved than some of the other boys in here."

"We're officers," Casey said with an air of pride. "But we still know how to have fun." He added a wink that earned a smile from Vicky. "So what brings you here?"

"We're crew for an airline," Vicky said with almost as much pride. "The others are either dancing or at the other bar."

If the music had not been playing, I swear I could have heard the intake of breath from both Chris and Casey. I silently chuckled to myself at the image of these men, officers in the most powerful military force in the world, being reduced to bumbling fuckwits when confronted with an air stewardess.

"So, are you, like, their chaperone, Greg?" Danny asked in a broad Texan accent.

I laughed. "Chaperone? Yes, I guess in a way I am. I make sure they remain good, wholesome girls all night and monitor their drinking at all times. Like now, for example...."

Chris and Casey both picked up on the cue and looked at Vicky's empty hands, but John made a start for the bar first, managing to get an edge in the race to buy her a drink. "What can I get you to drink, darlin'?" he called over to her.

"A vodka and tonic for me and a JD and Coke for Greg!" Vicky called back. She then gave me a glimmer of a sly smile to acknowledge that, despite her entitlement to free drinks from the management, she also enjoyed our game of getting my drinks gratis too.

I turned to check on the other girls, who were either still grinding on the dance floor or at the other bars, receiving just as much attention. Thankfully, the guys on the crew would be able to look after them immediately should any of the overly friendly militia get out of hand, but I knew I would be expected to step in too. It had never been an issue before, but with so many guys drinking, and the attendant testosterone and cock-blocking, there was always a risk that something could get out of hand quite quickly. I watched for a few minutes as the others chatted, sipping on the drink that John brought back.

"So where in America are you from?" Vicky asked the table.

"John and Chris are from Virginia, I'm from Nebraska, and Danny's from Texas," Casey replied.

"Mmm, Texas, huh?" Vicky said playfully. "Cowboy boots, spurs, and big hats."

"Everything is big in Texas," Danny said with a wink, eliciting general groans from his friends.

"Especially egos!" said Casey.

"You're from Nebraska, buddy, what the hell do you know? The only big thing in that state is the airport, and that's only because of the number of people trying to get out!"

"I am sure Nebraska is lovely," Vicky said kindly, "And I am sure *everything* is bigger in Texas!"

Danny laughed and nodded, but as he did he caught my eye. His gaze lingered only a microsecond too long, but still longer than any straight man would look at another guy unless he was speaking directly to him. My head swirled and my heart instantly pounded. I wondered whether I had imagined it.

"Where are you from?" asked Casey.

"I am from London. Greg is from Brighton," Vicky said.

"Wow, London!" Casey exclaimed. "I've always wanted to go there. Are all of the girls there as pretty as you?"

Vicky pretended to blush. I had seen her receive racier and much more original compliments than this without even flinching. She waved him off and acted as though she was embarrassed. Her shyness was short lived.

"So, Nebraska?" Vicky said, turning the conversation back to Casey. "Isn't that the state that's world famous for vodka?"

Casey looked a little confused. "Um, no, I don't think so."

"Oh, well, if I can't get vodka from Nebraska, where on earth can I find it?" Vicky said, pushing one perfectly manicured nail into her cheek while she looked down at her empty glass.

"I'll be right back. JD and Coke for you, is that right, Greg?"

I nodded and grinned at Vicky, who spent the next few minutes balancing her attention between John, Chris, and Danny.

"So are you guys heading on to Iraq or Afghanistan?" I asked.

"We've already done our tours there. We're actually based in Bahrain now until we head back home," Danny said.

"Do you miss home?" I asked, setting the drink that Casey returned with on the table. It was already half-empty, as I had taken a couple of large gulps to settle my nerves. I decided I must have imagined the look from Danny. But imagined or not, I was twenty-six years old, and I had never had such a physical reaction from even the thought of a man simply looking at me.

"Yes, I miss it a hell of a lot," Danny said sadly.

"It must be tough. I can't imagine there's too much that reminds you of home here."

"It's okay, I guess. We get most of our supplies on base so we have access to American brands of food and drink, which I can pick up and take back to the apartment."

"Oh, you don't live on base?" I asked, kind of surprised. I assumed they all lived in barracks of some sort.

"No, I'm an officer so I have the option to live off base. The Navy gives me a living allowance toward outside accommodation. It's a nice place, just outside of the city, about ten minutes away. It's just far enough to feel like I'm away from work at the end of the day. The cupboards are full of American food and beer just so I can have a small sense of normalcy."

"I can see how that would make things easier."

"It's not the same as having my momma's pies or my dad's barbecue, though."

My brow furrowed from the pain in my heart as I remembered my own dad. The emotional stab hit every day, because in one way or

15

another I was reminded of him every day. Danny noticed my change of face.

"You don't like barbecue?" he said.

"No, I love it! I'm just trying to correct my contact lens," I lied.

"They're a bitch. I wear them too," he said sympathetically. He studied me for a moment before adding, "But I bet you still look just as handsome in glasses."

My eyes darted to each of his friends to gauge their reaction, but soon realized that only Danny and I were talking in this conversation, as the others were focused squarely on Vicky.

"That's very kind of you," I said with a small, embarrassed bow of my head. "So, how much longer do you have here in Bahrain?"

"Not too much longer. I've served out my active duty time and will be heading home to Texas in three months."

"What will you do when you're back?"

"I have three years left on my contract, which I'll serve out on Reserve duty in Texas while I head to law school in Austin. I've been accepted into other schools, but after so much time away I feel like I need to be closer to home for a while."

"I don't blame you. I am away from home a lot of the time, but I have the luxury of returning every few days."

Vicky, who stood on the opposite side of the table, put her hand up and wriggled her fingers to catch my attention.

"Greg, these officers..." she began, clearly loud enough for them all to hear, which wasn't hard since the other three were hanging on her every word. "... I expected them to be all militant and loud. These guys are so quiet!"

I could see where she was going, so I played along, grateful to have a chance to gather myself and for the flush in my cheeks to pale. "I know. In the movies they are usually quite forceful and always shouting orders!"

"Oh my God, they are so damn sexy when they're shouting orders," she gushed.

16

Chris leaned forward eagerly. "We do shout our orders, when we need to."

"Great!" said Vicky as she walked two of her fingers up his chest. "Then can you shout our orders to the barman? Vodka tonic for me and a JD and Coke for Greg."

Danny laughed. "Actually, I think it's my round this time," he said, leaving Chris looking a little crestfallen. Danny looked over to the bar. "It's looking busier. Greg, can you give me a hand carrying them back? I'm most likely to spill that many drinks trying to walk through a crowd like that."

I left Vicky to perform for our generous benefactors, and I followed Danny toward the bar, taking in the sight of his broad frame and what looked like a small damp trail of sweat that made his shirt cling to the contours of his muscular back. We reached the line of people waiting to be served, but Danny made no attempt to squeeze his way to the bar to get the barman's attention. Instead, he waited patiently for a gap to appear, looking forward with no expression. We stood in silence for a moment until he turned his head to show a huge smile spreading across his face.

"My friends are trying to figure you out," he said into my ear. "I think your deep voice is throwing them off."

"And what about you?" I asked.

"I like it."

"That's not what I meant, though you have just answered my question."

"I have to be careful," he said, leaning into me. "The military's 'Don't Ask, Don't Tell' policy is still very much in force."

"Don't Ask, Don't Tell?"

"It's always been against military policy for gays to serve. You could be investigated at the whim of your commander if there was even a hint of suspicion that you were gay," Danny said just loud enough for me to hear but not to be overheard. "Then they formulated a compromise policy that said gay people could serve in the military, but they were forced never to disclose it. But commanders can't pursue an investigation without credible information that can't be ignored."

"What do you mean by credible?"

"Oh, you know, caressing your weapon like it's a male lover or drawing a pair of tits on your back and being called Sally on long nights in the barracks."

I gasped and immediately let out a howl of laughter.

"I know, right? They say that's bad for unit cohesion. They know nothing!" Danny smiled, but his tone changed to one of defeat. "But seriously, it's a mental drain. There are no guidelines on what constitutes 'credible information' so you have to rely on people not calling attention to it for the slightest little thing. So it's best that you just play the game."

"It must be difficult."

He leaned forward. "Sorry, I didn't catch what you said. The music is getting louder."

The bar was busy, so I put a hand on his arm to steady myself as I spoke into his ear. The muscle underneath stretched the material of his shirt. His bicep twitched as if surprised. I thought he may have deemed my touch inappropriate, considering his situation, but before I had a chance to take my hand away he had pressed in closer to me, indicating it was okay.

"It must be tough. You know, to live like that every day."

Danny moved sideways to speak into my ear, also placing his hand on my left arm as if to steady himself. I felt his fingers lightly press down onto my bare skin. It thrilled me.

"It's very hard. When I was on the carrier I used to talk to my sailors about their lives, their families, and their girls back home. They would come to me with their problems and seek advice about anything and everything." Danny's head moved around to my other ear, causing him to shift and rest his other hand on my right arm. The sweat from where his hand had left my arm slowly chilled on my skin in the air conditioning.

He continued. "When they asked about me and my life, I'd have to be vague or dodge the question. We were all in the same boat, so to speak. We were all away from home and missing our loved ones and all living the same life out at sea. Then, as we wrapped up our deployment in the Persian Gulf and were about to head to South Africa for our last port of call before heading home, the World Trade Center towers and the Pentagon were hit. We were held on station in the Arabian Sea for weeks before our carrier was among the first to launch tactical strikes into Afghanistan." Danny pulled away from my ear as if to take a breath before adding, "There are things in life that bind you to people, and this was one of them. I never lied to them. I never flat-out denied who I was, but I had to play a game that left me mentally exhausted every day and full of guilt that I couldn't be honest with the guys who expected nothing but honesty from me."

I nodded sympathetically, still getting a thrill from his touch but also an overwhelming urge to embrace him for his courage. "Do the guys that you're with know?"

Danny nodded in acknowledgement, then after a moment he shook it from side to side as if considering. "Well, I guess they do. We've all been friends for quite a while. I've never come out and told them, as I respect them too much to put them in the position of knowing when the policy is clear. It puts them in an awkward position. But at the same time I think they respect me enough not to ask, since that would put me in the position where I would have to lie to them about it."

"They seem like decent guys," I said, nodding toward the bar to indicate a gap had just opened. Danny stood to one side, allowing yet another guy to fill it.

"They are. But you seem like a decent guy too. I like the way you're looking after the girls. It says a lot about you."

"Well, to be honest, I don't really need to look after them. They have been around the world more times than I can count and put themselves in God knows how many dodgy situations. They can look after themselves better than most people I know. Even when they're drunk, they have their wits about them better than any sober girl," I said, glad that he had lightened the conversation.

"Yet you still check on them?"

"I'm not worried about them getting out of hand. It's the horny militia around them that concerns me. By the looks of things, they are all trying to upstage the next guy, which will probably end up in a fight. I just have to make sure the girls are out of the way before the tables start flying."

"Relax. They know there're officers in the bar, and they know the punishment for fighting in public is harsh, especially around allied forces."

"Good to know, although I have wanted to see a good bar fight since the '80s. There was something kind of hot about the *Cannonball Run* films where all the men piled onto each other."

"Oh, you like it rough, huh?" Danny said with a wry smile.

"And you don't, Mr. Military Man?"

Danny shrugged. "Eh, who doesn't love getting punched in the kidneys while they get a blowjob?" He winked.

"Hey, I have heard of worse American fetishes. Try being British and having someone demand that you speak all the way through sex just so they can hear your accent. Or worse, they want you to judge them afterward, like Simon Cowell."

Danny blushed a little. "Actually, I really like your accent. It's sexy as hell."

"Thank you, guv'nah."

"But I know what you mean. The second a guy knows I'm in the Navy, they almost instantly ask me to wear the uniform. It's so fucking lame."

"You don't like that, huh?" I asked, disappointed.

"I could make an exception. All you'd need to do is smile at me."

"Really?"

"You have the most disarming smile I've ever seen. I've had a hard time looking anywhere else all night," Danny said.

"All night?"

"I saw you come into the bar and whisper something to your friend Vicky." He pointed to the side of my face. "Those dimples made me lose my balance."

"You charmer," I said, instantly blushing and trying to brush off the compliment.

"Charmer? No. That would imply I was being insincere," he said as he moved into the gap at the bar, almost instantly getting the barman's attention. He passed me three drinks and waited for the barman to pour the others.

Over the music, I heard my name being called. I looked over at the table and saw Vicky shaking an empty glass in the air.

"I'm coming!" I shouted back.

Danny moved his mouth back to my ear. "The British are coming! The British are coming!"

"You think that I am that easy to conquer, huh?" I said as if slightly insulted.

Danny turned and paid the barman and collected the remaining three drinks. When he turned he looked genuinely embarrassed and almost ashamed. "I'm sorry. I didn't mean to be so...."

"I am kidding, Tiger."

"Tiger? I like that!" he said encouragingly. "But I genuinely am sorry. Can I make it up to you? Is there any chance I can take you out to dinner while you're here? Tomorrow, perhaps?"

"Sure, I would like that."

Danny gave his biggest smile yet, and we returned to the table just as the rest of the crew came to join us. With all the girls in one place now, Chris and John looked as if all of their Christmases had come at once, while Casey remained on target with Vicky.

Before long it was clear that since Danny was now being pulled into every joke, conversation, or interrogation around our now expanded table, we wouldn't have a chance to speak privately again for the remainder of the night. But this didn't stop him from looking over and catching my eye again and again with a smile.

We knew the queue for the taxis would be long when the bar stopped serving alcohol, so the crew decided we would leave half an hour before last call. Most of the swarms of men lived on base, but since that was still some distance away and they were on a curfew, they would bundle as many of themselves as possible into cabs, knowing full well that the drivers would not obey the passenger limits when they could charge extra for each additional person they could cram in. If we didn't leave earlier, we would end up waiting hours to get back to the hotel. So the girls began the long process of saying their good-byes to their adoring fans before heading out to the taxis.

"It was great to meet you guys," I said as I shook their hands, once again leaving Danny's as the last.

"You too," he said. As we shook, I felt his pinky finger surreptitiously stroke my own. The thrill returned. When I released his hand, I felt a small piece of paper in my own. I slipped it into my pocket.

In the taxi, Vicky laid her drunken head across my chest, leaving me to strap her into her seatbelt. I wriggled to get the paper out of my pocket, and, holding it above Vicky's head so she couldn't see, saw it was a phone number.

"They were such lovely guys," Vicky said into my chest.

"They were indeed."

"You really liked Danny, didn't you?"

I nodded.

Vicky's head popped up and pointed to the bar door just as the taxi pulled away. Men were piling out of the entrance with a look of disappointment, but sound in the knowledge that they would soon be back in the barracks and comforted by the love of a special sock. Chris, Casey, and John were walking out too, with the same defeated look on their faces. Danny, however, who had not spotted me in the car, was beaming.

CHAPTER THREE

BACK on the rainy front porch, a small light bobbed behind the glass pane of the front door and gradually became larger and brighter.

"What do I call her, your mum?" I asked quickly, realizing I had no idea how to address her.

"Call her Mrs. Taylor until she tells you to call her Vivien. I know it's an old-fashioned Texas form of respect, but they notice things like that."

Strictly speaking, this wasn't my first introduction to his mother. Although I had never met or spoken to her, I had been introduced to Mrs. Taylor in another way.

It was a late afternoon in Bahrain on my second trip to see Danny. I had flown out with British Airways on holiday, rather than having a working layover. The dinner Danny had taken me to on my last trip, as well as the rest of night, had been beyond perfect. From that night on we had become almost inseparable by text, e-mail, or webcam. Danny had taken a few days off so we could have more time together. Thankfully, as he had his own place in a small neighborhood called Juffair, we could have complete privacy.

He rolled over in bed, took the last sip of water from his glass, and checked his watch. Jumping up, his feet slapping on the tiled floor, he put on a pair of military exercise shorts and explained that, due to the eight hour time difference, it was the only time of day he could call his mom because it was right before she was due to go to work. I crawled out of bed and threw on a pair of his underwear and walked into the living room as he dialed a score of numbers.

Duke, who was still a very small puppy, bounced around my feet and attempted to chew on my toes as I made my way into the kitchen to grab a couple of fresh glasses of water from the upturned water cooler next to the fridge. As I made my way back with the drinks, I heard Danny's side of the conversation with his mother.

"Hey, Momma!" he said, sounding every bit the respectable southern boy. "Momma, Greg's here!"

I grinned as I leaned over to place the glass on the table next to him. He thanked me with a gentle squeeze of my buttock.

"Greg. You remember, the British guy I told you about?"

I was thrilled that this guy, this incredible, handsome, and intelligent man, had actually told his mother about me. I admit I was somewhat surprised, since our relationship was still kind of casual—though you would never have guessed it from my phone bill in England. I wondered for a moment exactly how Danny felt about me.

"No, he's here for a few days. It's great. It means that we have some time together and I can show him all the good stuff in Bahrain." Danny cheekily pointed to his crotch, which received a frown from me—but I couldn't help but steal another look.

"Yes, Momma. Yes, Momma. I know, Momma."

I stood, wondering what she was saying. Don't fall in love too soon? He lives so far away, it will never work? Don't let your heart get broken?

"Momma, you wouldn't believe how much energy he's got. He never tires out!"

I thought this was a little inappropriate.

"He is so damn cute. I can't wait for you to meet him."

I blushed a little, thinking it was highly unlikely this would ever happen.

"I will, Momma." He paused. "Yes, he's had all of his shots."

Now I was confused.

"I gotta run. He's taking a crap on the floor."

I turned around to see Duke curling a miniturd on the floor tile behind me as Danny hung up the phone.

"Danny, at what point did your mum stop asking about me and start asking about the dog?"

THE door clicked and opened. Mrs. Taylor looked older than she did in the many photos Danny had shown me over the months. She wore her graying hair in a shoulder-length sharp bob that, by hurricane lantern light, made her look quite severe. But the smile she gave Danny was forgiving, and her face flooded with delight. She put the lantern down on a table next to the door and threw her arms around Danny, who returned her embrace with as much affection before standing to one side to introduce me.

"Momma, this is Greg!"

"Hello, it's a pleasure to finally meet you, Mrs. Taylor!" I said, holding my palm out while balancing the hamper in the other arm. She extended a limp wrist that barely seemed to have the strength to grip my own. She seemed a little harassed, but at the time I put this down to the fact that a soaking wet, hyperactive, eight-month-old puppy was jumping up around her heels.

"It's nice to meet you too," she said politely, looking over my shoulder and then trying to get the front door closed as soon as possible. She obviously was concerned about nosy neighbors, so I wondered whether the blackout must have seemed heaven-sent.

I followed Danny into an immaculate living room, which was lit by a handful of well-placed candles that shed light on the many ornamental china cherubs, porcelain praying hands, and plates with prayers inscribed on them in gold leaf. The more I looked the more I noticed the sheer volume of the religious icons decorating the sideboards, tables, and walls. Mr. Taylor rose from his comfortable-looking recliner and hugged Danny before reaching his hand out to me to shake heartily while slapping his other hand against the top of my arm.

"I am so sorry about the late hour, Mr. Taylor."

He stood around the same height as his wife but was much more portly and altogether much kinder looking. Dressed in casual work jeans and an old grey sweatshirt he looked more like the gardener to the lady of the house.

"It's great to finally meet you, Greg." He beamed. "And please, it's George."

We both sat down while Mrs. Taylor fussed over Danny.

"Mrs. Taylor, this is for you," I said, handing her the hamper of typically British food, teas, and sweets that I had picked up in the Harrods shop in the terminal at Heathrow. "I hope you like it. Danny is forever saying that British food is awful, so I hope this will convince you to be on my side of the argument!"

"That's very kind of you, Greg," she said a bit stiffly, as she marched into the kitchen and set it down, only to hurry back as though she was worried she might miss something.

"Danny tells me he's planning to visit you over there in England soon," George said.

"Yes," I replied. "I can't wait to show him around London and Brighton. I am sure he's going to love it."

Mr. Taylor got up to help Danny, who was now struggling into the hallway with bags from the truck. I rose to help carry the bags up the stairs as Mrs. Taylor said, "We'll have plenty of time to talk about how great Britain is in the morning. It's time these boys head off to bed, as we have an early start in the morning." She put one arm out as though to shepherd me out of the room. I stepped aside to make room for her as she passed Danny and me and ascended the stairs with the hurricane lantern held aloft, giving her the look of a solitary lighthouse keeper or horror movie crypt keeper.

As we reached the top of the stairs, Mrs. Taylor turned around and smiled again at her son. "It's just the way you left it, Danny. We still haven't changed a thing." With that, she opened the door of his bedroom and held it open to allow us through.

"I hope y'all are comfortable tonight. Get some sleep, and we'll see you in the morning." She placed the lantern on the bedside table, kissed Danny's cheek once more, and disappeared quickly from the room.

It seemed that his room had indeed not been altered since he was a teenager. An older-looking computer sat on a desk, surrounded by neatly stacked textbooks from his studies. There were no posters on his wall. Instead, framed certificates of various awards and achievements held pride of place above his bed, along with various framed photos of a young Danny with a '90s quiff at the Model United Nations and state mathematics championships. It was very much the room of an overachieving, bookish kid who made it clear from the beginning that he planned to get ahead in life. I knew Danny was smart, bordering on genius, but I was surprised at exactly how much he had accomplished in his youth, especially when such a good-looking guy at that age could easily have had other distractions at hand.

What I hadn't been expecting was the narrow camping bed that seemed out of place in what I considered a kind of shrine to their son.

Danny sighed as his eyes also found the intruding piece of furniture.

"I guess Mom doesn't believe in sex before marriage now either."

"But we can't get married here."

Danny raised an eyebrow. "Yeah, convenient, huh?"

"So no nookie tonight then, Tiger?" I asked, trying to make light of it, as Danny seemed a little more bothered than he was letting on.

He shook his head once more before pulling the sheets back from the perfectly made bed and patted the mattress. "We'll both sleep in my bed."

"But, Danny, don't you think it's a bit soon to be upsetting your—"

"Greg, do you know how many times I dreamt of having a hot man in this bed when I was younger? And tonight—" He pulled me forward for effect. "—my dreams will come true."

"You charmer."

"Is it working?"

"Yes, though you had better grab a towel."

"Now who's the charmer?"

CHAPTER FOUR

WE WERE awakened the following morning by a sharp knock at the door. Before we had time to open our eyes, Mrs. Taylor, who looked like she was dressed to attend a PTA meeting, breezed in unannounced and without a moment's pause. Her face looked as though she had just caught her son with a porn magazine in one hand and his dick in the other. Flushed, she spun around so her back was toward us. She raised one hand to cover her eyes and held the other palm forward in front of her chest, as though she was stopping a car at a pedestrian crossing. She began to mutter, though I managed to catch the words "Jesus" and "strength" as she finished her emergency prayer.

Danny looked up, sighed, and said, "We'll be right down, Momma."

I was mortified. I had only been in his mother's presence for a matter of hours, and she had already made me feel like I had molested her son. What was worse was that I knew I had to go down and face his dad. George had made me feel so welcome the night before. I wondered whether his reaction would be more hostile on our arrival at breakfast, seeing as how I had already disobeyed one of the rules of his home.

Either Mrs. Taylor hadn't told him about the incident, or he just didn't care, as he greeted us with as much excitement as he had on our arrival.

"Hey, boys. The electricity is back on. That was quite a storm last night!" He looked over to me. "At least it's out of the way so we have good weather today. You excited about seeing your first football game, Greg?"

"Very much!" I answered, perhaps a little overenthusiastically, as I spotted Danny giving me a sly smile.

"Has Danny explained all of the rules to you? Come and have some iced tea with me in the sunroom, and I'll go through it with you!" he said, appearing just as excited to convert me into a fan as Danny had been months before.

We left Danny and Mrs. Taylor, and I followed George into the conservatory. As we were about to sit down, George tapped a framed photo of Danny that sat on a side table of the wicker set of furniture. "That's our Danny in his uniform on the Enterprise. His momma and I are so proud of him," he said, not realizing that his face had already said it all. "But I guess you must have seen him in his uniform."

I had, but the smart, crisp white uniform that he wore in this photo was different from the sandy, desert-camouflaged uniform that I had the pleasure to see him wear.

On my third and final visit to Bahrain before he returned to the States, Danny had come home from work early and insisted that I get dressed in trousers and a polo shirt. I didn't know where we were going and wondered why he hadn't changed out of his combat fatigues. He drove us to the naval base, where, after being searched and having my passport inspected by armed guards holding M16 rifles, I was given a visitor's badge and allowed to accompany him onto the grounds.

There were hundreds of men and women in this military hive, all looking every inch of what their government expected of them: professional and very intimidating. Danny and I had spoken many times about the effects of the "Don't Ask, Don't Tell" policy that forced Danny to live a closeted life in the Navy and how increasingly difficult he found it to live with. Any confession of his orientation would have seen him dismissed from his career and shamed out of the force. Knowing this, I was determined not to give even the slightest hint that Danny wasn't simply showing around an allied visitor. I'm sure I must have walked as though I had just marched out of the British Army.

I left Danny to do all of the talking, and he guided me around the various areas of the base until we reached a center courtyard where a dozen guys were throwing around a football on what must have been their break. Seeing that I couldn't be overheard, I whispered to my escort. "Are you sure this is okay?"

Danny simply nodded and winked at me.

Just as we turned toward the mess hall, a group of six loud, uniformed enlisted men walked toward us, jostling with one another. At the sight of Danny, however, they came to an abrupt halt. In unison they straightened their backs and saluted Danny, before being released by a nod of his head and a return salute that crisply touched his brow. It was the sexiest damn thing I had ever seen in my life, and I momentarily lost my breath.

Once they passed, I whispered to Danny, "Seriously, are you sure this is okay?"

"I've never brought anyone here. I wouldn't trust anyone else enough."

"Well, you must trust me a hell of a lot to risk your career to show me where you work."

Danny took two quick strides forward so he could turn and face me directly.

"That's because I'm in love with you."

Without hesitation, he turned as though he had just been given an order and walked away, only glancing back to witness the reaction he hoped for: a stunned, but very happy Englishman standing dazed with a big smile on his face.

AS WE chatted in the sunroom, George opened a drawer on the table standing beside him and pulled out a pipe, matches, and tobacco.

"Vivien only lets me smoke this on special occasions," he said with a wink, "and the Longhorns versus the Aggies is one of them."

"Do you mind if I join you, Mr. Taylor?" I asked, reaching into my pocket and retrieving the packet of cigarettes that I put there just in case I had a chance to nip off for a crafty smoke somewhere.

"Of course not! And please, like I said last night, it's George."

I took a seat opposite him again and listened to the ins and outs of American football as Duke lay at my feet. Mrs. Taylor brought in two china ashtrays, placing one on each table next to us along with two tall glasses of iced tea. She ignored our conversation, instead shouting over us to Danny, who was in the living room choosing some CDs to play in the car on the journey to the stadium. Although she didn't say anything, I caught a look of disapproval as she swept past me and went back into the living room, only to return a few moments later with a tin of polish, a duster, and a spray bottle of water to drench the plants that stood around the tall windows.

I put my cigarette out in the ashtray after a couple of hand waves from Mrs. Taylor, trying to swat away the smoke in the air before she went back into the living room. I settled back to listen to George explain how many points for a touchdown and how to earn the extra point. He seemed determined to make me understand the game, and I was reminded of how my own father would give me a look after explaining something that said "you got it?" As I nodded to show I was following everything, I heard an almighty gasp that made me jump in my chair. I turned to see Mrs. Taylor holding a bag of Jolly Rancher candy, red-faced with anger. I followed her eyes to the ashtray I had been using. There, above the ash, read the words "Jesus Loves the Little Children." Cringing, I moved the butt out of the way with my finger, revealing the face of the messiah, his head half-obscured with the thickest ash left over from where I had stubbed my cigarette out on his face.

"That," Mrs. Taylor said indignantly, "is a candy dish!"

Danny, hearing his mother's tone, leapt to my rescue.

"Oh, Momma, he thought it was an ashtray. It's okay. I'll go and wash it out. No harm done."

"I am so sorry, Mrs. Taylor. I didn't look. I really did think you had put an ashtray down," I said, pleading my innocence.

"Maybe this is a divine sign for you to give it up," she snapped as she stormed back into the living room.

The drive to College Station where the game was being held was a little stressed, to say the least. It was a three-hour drive from the house, most of which backtracked our route from Austin. Mrs. Taylor barely said anything. Danny started to show signs of frustration with his mother, but slowly grew happier as he and George pointed out of the windows at anything of any local, historical, or authentic Texan interest.

At some point, Mrs. Taylor must have taken the opportunity to change the music in the car to her own choice. At first I was confused listening to heavy drums, electric guitars, and the twang of an American man singing, "He knows the truth in what I say, I can't hide it from his heart. He lifts me up in all kinds of ways, he's been there since the start." It took me a couple of verses before I realized that it was a Christian rock band and the man they were infatuated with was God.

By the time we reached the grounds of the stadium I was ready for the day to be over and silently wishing we could start it over again. Mrs. Taylor had arranged to meet Danny's sisters, Kimberly and Tammy, at the entrance to the stadium with their husbands. Clayton, Kimberly's husband, was a contract worker for one of the oil fields in the area and was every bit the stereotypical Texan: dipping tobacco and wearing a cowboy hat. Tammy's husband, Wade, the larger of the two, stood tall and intimidating and looked very much the part of his job as a warden at the county jail. I received hugs from the girls and firm, awkward handshakes from their husbands who, I suspect, had never knowingly met a gay man in their lives apart from Danny, let alone an British one. After repeating almost everything I said, I excused my accent and told them that I knew I spoke like I had plums in my mouth. I then had to explain that was a British expression, as their faces read as though I was saying I'd had their brother-in-law's balls on my tongue.

As we entered the stands I was met with the spectacular sight of tens of thousands of jerseys and T-shirts in either burnt orange for those who supported the University of Texas Longhorns, or dark maroon for those who supported Texas Agricultural and Mechanical. I had never been to an event that held so many people. Whether it was the sunshine or simply their manners, everyone seemed so happy and polite. I must admit the atmosphere was electric compared to the footie matches I had seen as a kid with my dad, where it often felt like there was an air of potential rioting.

We made our way to the appointed row and seats, which were situated halfway up the stands and boasted a fantastic view of the field. As we passed the many spectators, I raised my hand onto Danny's shoulder to steady myself so as not to trip over the people's legs we were passing. Behind me I heard a sharp gasp and Mrs. Taylor's voice. "Oh goodness, look, look at him, George, he's got his hand on Danny's back." Whether it was the noise of the crowd that made her say it so loud for her husband to hear, or whether she intentionally said it within easy earshot of me, I found myself drawing my hand back quickly so as not to offend. I instantly chastised myself.

I was angry that I had so readily withdrawn my hand and let this woman make me feel like I was doing something wrong or something I should be ashamed of, even if it was to keep the peace. The situation in Bahrain when Danny and I were in public had been entirely different. Even with the threat of another serviceman seeing any kind of public affection, or the local Bahrainis—who had very definite views of such things—Danny never once shied away from touching me. It may not have been so obvious, and at the time it was even a turn-on. It had been many years since I had stolen a secret touch from a man in public, and it thrilled me when a handsome American officer did it. But we were in Texas now, and though it was not the most liberal state in the country, it wasn't as though we were going to be sent to prison or lose our jobs if we innocuously touched.

We took our seats, and Mrs. Taylor distanced herself from me, placing Danny and George between us. She laughed and joked with Wade and Clayton in a manner that seemed to show her fondness for her daughters' partners. I listened to her tease and compliment them, and although it felt like a slight on me, I had a glimpse of the playful lady Danny had portrayed her to be. She seemed so much more genuine with them than with me, but I hoped that this was due to their familiarity and that there was still a chance we could have the same relationship. I had only known her for a couple of days, but the chill I felt gave me the impression that warmth would be a while in coming.

The players ran onto the field to deafening applause and fanfare and lined up. I thought the game was just about to begin when an announcement over the loud speaker introduced a local beauty queen who was making her way to a microphone to sing the national anthem. At once, 88,000 people stood in unison and stamped their palms to their hearts as the opening chords began to play.

Danny and his family stood and began to sing. As I slowly began to stand, I noticed Mrs. Taylor looking at me. My arms were by my side, but I wasn't singing. Why would I? I was British.

"Greg, you're in America now. This is what we do here," she called across her son and her husband.

This was said loud enough for the rows in front and behind to hear. I could feel their eyes burning into me.

Danny looked over and winced at me. He knew only too well what torture it was going to be for me to stand up and pretend to be anything other than an Englishman. I had told him of my pride as many times as he had told me of his being an American. I may not have had the kind of pride and loyalty that had been drummed into him by the military, but at the same time I hadn't spent months having people trying to convince me to put my life on the line for my country. Danny held his hands up defensively to those around me, who were now shooting me evil looks, and said, "Hey, he's British! He doesn't know China's anthem either."

I looked at my handsome man defending and excusing me, and I relented. I clamped my hand to my chest. I felt like I was in church, at a wedding or funeral, attempting to sing to a hymn that I'd never heard before. They sang of rockets, flags, and red glare while I thought how the title "Star Spangled Banner" sounded a little camp. Well, until I remembered the name of the British national anthem. I mouthed the words to an Amy Winehouse song and hoped for the best.

I finally managed to follow the game on my own in the fourth quarter, but only after constant explanations of every play by Danny and George. I cheered for the University of Texas team and, much to

Danny's delight, started cheering louder and louder, even hollering a couple of times to make him laugh. But, truth be told, I didn't really know what was going on most of the time and only shouted when everyone around me did.

After the game, we made it out of the stadium's parking lot and met up with Danny's sisters and their husbands at the local Olive Garden restaurant. We'd originally planned to head straight back to Austin after the game, but Danny seemed so happy to be around his kin, I'd suggested that we leave his truck at his parents' to spend more time with them on the journeys to and from the stadium. I couldn't rob him of the chance to be around them for a family dinner, especially as it seemed that having Danny back from the Middle East was still something of a novelty to his sisters.

Mrs. Taylor stood at the end of the table and directed us to our seats, ensuring I was at the opposite end of the table from her. For a moment, I thought she was attempting to work out how to sit us boy-girl-boy-girl so as not to bring attention to Danny and me sitting together. This was impossible with the numbers, so she gave up and seated Danny and me opposite one another at the end of the rectangular table, both with one of Danny's sisters to our right. I was somewhat relieved, as it meant that I had a chance to speak to them a bit more, and they loved asking me to pronounce certain words or phrases while their husbands talked about the game. I didn't think Wade and Clayton were being rude, but rather that they were taking a back seat to let their wives grill the new guy. I made my attempts to make them laugh, which were more than successful, but it brought their mother's eyes to meet mine—mostly with disapproval.

Once the waiter delivered our food, there was a sudden clasping of hands around the table. It took me by surprise when Danny reached over the table to take my hand while Kimberly, to my right, found my other hand and bowed her head. I followed suit, even though I felt awkward and very much out of place. Mrs. Taylor said a prayer that I couldn't hear, so I relied on Danny to squeeze my hand to signal that it was time to let go.

"So, Greg," called Clayton, "did y'all enjoy the game? Better than that soccer y'all play over there in England, huh?"

"It was great. It was more complicated than I expected, but then again I think it was probably the first time I ever really paid attention to the game."

"Ain't nothing complicated 'bout football, buddy," interjected Wade, laughing.

"No, I managed to follow it, it's just that the football we play back home is shorter and a little simpler."

"And a lot less violent," Clayton added.

"That's because all you British are pansies!" exclaimed Wade.

"Perhaps you two should have a proper game of rugby, see how you get on without the pads, helmets, and shin guards!" I retorted, joking back with Wade, who seemed concerned that his tongue had slipped with the "pansies" remark and offended Danny and me.

"So, Greg, do ya like it over here in the States? Are you planning to leave England to come here? Or is Danny coming to you?" asked Kimberly.

"Ah, I am a British boy through and through, so it would be hard," I said, knocking my heart twice with my fist. "But I would do it for your brother, though it might not be so easy. US immigration laws are notoriously difficult."

"It keeps out the unwanted." Mrs. Taylor's voice had an edge to it, and I suspected she said it louder than she intended to. The table fell silent.

"Y'all gonna have a chance to go to church while you're here?" Tammy asked, in a clear attempt to change the subject. This subject however, was one that I had hoped to avoid.

"I noticed you didn't say 'amen' at the end of grace, Greg," Mrs. Taylor called from the end of the table. "Are you a Christian?"

Everyone at the table turned their heads toward me. Wade and Clayton both looked at me with a kind of sympathy, while Tammy and Kimberly looked almost scared. George drummed his fingers on the table and looked down almost as quickly as he had looked up, while Danny's eyes darted toward his mother, then me, and back again.

"In what respect?" I asked.

"Have you accepted God into your heart and know that Jesus Christ was our savior and died on the cross to save you from your sins."

It sounded like a line from one of the late night televangelists that I had seen on American television. I could feel Danny looking at me. I knew what he wanted me to say, but I had already pretended to be American and straight for his mother's benefit that day, and I was as sure as hell not going to pretend to be Christian too.

"I have my beliefs," I said, without even so much as a hint that I was going to expand on my answer.

"So where do you fly? I bet you get to see some great places!" Tammy asked, with a more suitable subject change.

"Oh, all over. Australia, Europe, the Far East, Canada, and Asia. We fly to some destinations in the States too."

"Where's your favorite?" Kimberly asked, hoping to keep the conversation going.

"Oh, America by far! The cities are great, and you chaps are so friendly and welcoming to us British." It was, of course, a stab at his mother, but in order for her to say anything she would have had to acknowledge her hostility.

"So are you going to try and move to America, or is Danny moving to England?" The question was asked again, but I couldn't tell whether it was Clayton or Wade who asked, as I was watching George drum the table even faster.

Danny jumped in. "Well, I still have two and a half years of law school left, so we haven't made any kind of concrete plans yet. Greg will carry on flying while I'm studying, since he gets discounts on airline tickets through his job, which will make it easier for us to see each other more regularly."

The danger from the matriarchal wolf was noticed not only by me, but also by George, who spoke before Mrs. Taylor had the chance.

"Well, I hope you boys get a chance to see each other as often as possible. You must have something real special there to keep going back and forth thousands of miles. I wish you the best."

"Thanks, George." I nodded. I wanted to say more, to tell him how much I appreciated his blessing and his public stance on our relationship. But I couldn't. I was reminded that it was the type of thing that my own father would do and say, and it stung my heart for a moment, knowing that he would never be around to do it again. I also filled with rage as I saw Mrs. Taylor shoot her husband a reproachful look for daring to condone our relationship.

On the way back to Austin, after a quiet journey back to pick up Duke and Danny's car from Baytown, I sat with my hand resting on Danny's leg as he drove. I was trying to figure out if there was something that I said or did to get such an icy reception from Mrs. Taylor. I knew I had broken the rules of the house by sleeping in the same bed as Danny, and I had made a genuine mistake with the ashtray, but her attitude was negative from the moment she laid eyes on me.

"So, is it because you are gay that she doesn't want us to be together? Or is it because I am British and she's worried I am going to take you away to live in England?"

Danny, who had also remained silent, pulled in his lips and exploded them back out with a burst of air.

"Some from column A, some from column B, but also some from column C."

"Column C?"

"C for Christian."

"Your dad doesn't seem to be that fussed about it. How does he cope with her?"

"He loves her."

"What's not to love? Perfectly charming woman," I said, a little too sarcastically.

"Greg, I know she wasn't that welcoming toward you, but—"

"Wasn't that welcoming? I think that's an understatement. That woman would dislike me if I wore a crucifix and holed myself up in a seminary for ten years."

"That woman? *That woman*? Greg, just remember, that's my mom you're talking about," Danny shot back sternly, causing Duke's head to appear between our shoulders, as the rise in Danny's voice had alarmed him. "You don't understand."

I stroked the top of Duke's head to calm him. "Then explain it to me. What the hell did I do so wrong to be treated like that? And I am sorry, Danny. You weren't a great deal of help when we were at the dinner table," I said calmly so as not to rile Duke again.

Danny wiped his face. When he spoke his tone had softened. "I know, baby. I'm sorry. You're the first guy I've ever brought home to meet my parents, and I didn't know what to expect or what to do. Mom would never have behaved like that years ago. If I'd had a go at her, it would've caused such an argument at the table. I wanted to, I really did, but you were getting on so well with Dad, my sisters, and even Clayton and Wade. I didn't want to spoil that by making a scene with Mom."

"Well, for what it's worth, I think the others could see that she was making her feelings known."

"Yes, but they don't view it as harshly as you do. You have to remember they've seen her change slowly in the past few years, whereas the change is that much more apparent to me since I have been away in the Navy. If only you knew what a sweet, funny, and kind woman she can be. That's why they tolerate the religious stuff, because they know she's a good woman at heart."

"Okay, sorry. But I did try."

"I know you did, baby, and I love you even more because of it."

"Maybe I will have better luck with your roommate."

Danny laughed. "Tucker is just as bad!"

"Huh?"

"I have known Tucker since college. He identifies himself as a Christian, but considering his love of *Star Wars*, *Stargate*, *Star Trek*, and anything else science fiction, he should identify himself as Jedi."

"Is he preachy?

"No, not exactly. He says things every once in a while that kind of come out of the blue and go against everything he says and does. It's hard to take him seriously when he has a stream of young tricks passing through."

"So I shouldn't blaspheme in front of him either?"

"It depends on his mood," Danny laughed. "If you don't want to hear a sermon, I'd advise against it."

CHAPTER FIVE

IT WAS evening by the time we arrived back on the outskirts of Austin, where Danny and Tucker lived together while Danny was at law school. Tucker was a Legislative Assistant to a Texas state senator, so he was away for most of the day, giving Danny time to study in peace when he wasn't in class. I hadn't yet met Tucker, but like most of the immediate people in Danny's life, I had been shown a photo and given a description. The love of good Tex-Mex and barbecue had given Tucker a more rounded figure, but at six four he managed to carry it off well. I had also been warned that a childhood operation had left Tucker partially deaf in one ear, which meant that he had a tendency to be quite loud, as he couldn't judge his own volume.

Tucker was home when we arrived and shifted off his well-worn recliner to meet me as *Deep Space Nine* played at a high volume in the living room.

"You must be Greg! Danny's told me all about you!" he sort of bellowed at me as I walked through the door. "Hey, all you British guys are uncut, right?"

"Nice to meet you at last, Tucker," I said, offering my hand, which was taken and shaken so vigorously that my relaxed bicep started to wobble.

"You smoke, right?"

"Trying to give it up." I looked at Danny, who gave me thumbs-up in support.

"Come and have a cigarette with me outside so we can chat. I feel like I already know you, considering I have Danny talking about you nonstop, 24-7."

"Oh, that must be between watching all of your *Star Wars* films, you Wookie lovin' freak," Danny joked. "And Greg, no matter how much he asks, you don't have to prove that you're uncut."

Danny joined us outside and swiped at the air to show his disapproval of the smoke. It irked me a little since it was in the exact same manner his mother had done earlier that day.

"So, Tucker." Danny chuckled. "No concealed weapon, no fedora, and no dark sunglasses."

Tucker chewed on his lip in what looked like embarrassment and ran his fingers through his curly black hair.

"Am I missing something?" I asked, looking at Danny, who was now laughing full-on at Tucker.

"Tucker thought you could be a spy. When we first met he sent me an e-mail warning that I shouldn't tell you any kind of government secrets."

"You were an intelligence officer," Tucker shot back. "It's not that farfetched."

"I love my queen and country, but I have never heard of a guy going to such great lengths to acquire information. I can't imagine James Bond taking one for the team."

"Oh my gawd, I love yer accent."

"Thank you."

"Tonight you are going to be my bait!" Tucker said, getting over his embarrassment and rubbing his hands together.

"No, Tuck, I said we would go out to a bar with you, but you're not whoring his accent around to get laid," Danny said, rather strictly.

"Yeah, yeah. Don't worry, I was only joking. We had better get a move on or all of the good bars will be full and no one will even be able to hear his accent."

As we prepared to go out I leaned against the sink in the bathroom and watched in the mirror as Danny showered as I shaved. I didn't want to go out and be surrounded by people I didn't know or listen to music that made young American men holler and start dance routines that they studied on YouTube for countless hours. All I wanted was to curl up in bed with Danny. Sex with him was mind-blowing. It was a cross between a triple X movie and a Mills and Boon novel. When we were together everything was perfect, without either of us even having to give the other a hint of what we wanted. But standing there watching him in the shower, it wasn't about sex. It was the need to have physical contact and privacy that we had been denied in the previous months because of our long-distance relationship. I silently resented Tucker for making us go out, but Danny had been so determined for me to get to know the people in his life that I didn't have the heart to suggest that a quiet night in was all I wanted.

We arrived at a bar called Rain around 9:30 p.m. and, despite it still being quite early, were made to wait in line. Tucker seemed to know almost every young guy there and frequently stuck his hand out of the queue to stroke the stomach of a passing young twink.

Once we were inside, I was immediately hit by the noise. At bars in Britain you can expect to raise your voice to be heard over the music. But here, it seemed that there couldn't be enough decibels on any sound system to drown out the bellows of young gay Texans, whom I suspected had stored up their campness during the week, only to release it all in a Saturday night ritual. We headed to the back of the main bar and through doors that led onto a large outdoor patio area with two open-air bars. The din outside wasn't so brutal to the ears, as the area seemed to pen the older guys that weren't there to take their tops off and dry hump anything that wasn't bolted down.

Tucker disappeared, leaving Danny and me to order drinks. In England, I was used to having a measured shot of spirit served in a glass and topped up with a mixer, but here, like so many other places in America, the barman's shot was more like machine gun fire, and he only threatened the glass with Coke as a mixer. I took a sip and almost gagged as the practically neat vodka burned the back of my throat. Danny grinned. "You're a lightweight, mister."

As we stood chatting, I noticed that the men around us began to stop talking in their own conversations and started listening to ours.

"They can hear your accent," Danny said, as he looked at the silent bystanders.

I felt my arm being pulled by a muscular stranger who stood with a couple of well-built guys in their thirties, all of whom had used geometry to their advantage when styling their beards.

"Oh my gawd, are you Briddish?" he asked, as if he had just seen a unicorn.

"Yes, I am. My name's Greg, nice to meet you." I bowed a little for effect.

"You guys are all uncut, right? That is so fuckin' hawt!" He leaned back at the waist and clutched his imaginary pearls with one hand while sliding the other down my chest.

I found his question and behavior rude. Had I been on my own I would have laughed it off and not found offense, dismissing it as a guy taking his chance. But Danny was still standing next to me, his arm around my waist and his thumb in my belt, making it obvious that we were together long before the guy even spoke. It seemed so disrespectful. Danny looked at me and raised an eyebrow.

"Yes, but we British tend to leave conversations about the delicate subject of one's cock to lovers only. I hope you understand."

"Oh my gawd, your accent is so fucking hot! Say some more!"

I rolled my eyes and wondered what else I could say to get him to lose interest and leave us alone. Thankfully, he was full-body butted by Tucker, who knocked him sideways to make room for a young, slightly scared-looking guy that he was holding by the wrist and practically dragging to us. Tucker had clearly been drinking more than we had.

"Hey, this is Simon," he said, presenting his captive. The poor boy looked as though he had been abducted from a skateboard park. "Simon, this is Danny, and this is his British boyfriend from England." With this introduction he turned and left, heading straight back into the bar.

"Nice to meet you, Simon," I said, trying to relax the poor kid, who had been left alone and was now looking terrified. "How do you know Tucker?"

"Um, I don't. I just met him."

"Oh, right. Well, I have only just met him tonight too, so you're in good company."

"Hey, I love your accent."

"Thanks, I like yours too. So are you studying at the University of Tex—"

Tucker reappeared and moved Simon to the side so he could present us with yet another young man, this one looking more studious.

"This is Aaron," Tucker announced. "Aaron, this is Danny, and this is Greg. Greg is from the United Kingdom."

Tucker ran his hand over the guy's stomach and began to slide it down toward his crotch. Aaron took hold of Tucker's wrist and moved it away. Tucker shrugged, grinned in defeat, and then walked away again.

"I guess you just met Tucker too?" Danny asked, as this young man looked around and wondered what was going on.

"Yeah, I didn't even know that was his name, but he insisted that I come over to meet his British friend."

"Well, Aaron, this is Simon. The two of you have something in common." Danny winked. "We're just heading back inside, but you guys stay and have a drink on us." Danny signaled to the barman, who had taken in some of what was going on. "You boys have a great night."

Danny left a twenty dollar bill on the bar, and we made our way back inside.

"Sorry about that. He's already had way too much to drink. He used to do that with me because I'm in the Navy, introducing me as his 'military friend'. Somehow he believes it's going to get him laid. It's never worked, as far as I know. Still, you can't blame him for…."

He stopped suddenly, so I looked for his distraction. A handsome, dark-haired guy around our age was making his way through the patio and heading in our direction.

"Hey, Danny!" he said as he stretched out his arms to embrace him.

"Hey, Shane, how are you?" Danny sounded happy to see him, but his body language said otherwise as he lightly patted the guy on the back, barely making contact. "What are you doing here?"

"Ah, I'm just passing through with work. I heard that you were out of the Navy and studying here. I still live in DC, for my sins, but I'm here for a few days. I hoped I would run into you. I tried calling, but your old number is out of action."

"Yeah, I changed my number before I went off to Bahrain. I'm still in the Navy, just in Reserve now." Danny stepped to one side and put his hand on my shoulder. "Shane, this is my partner, Greg."

Shane looked surprised and a little put out as he held out his hand for me to shake.

"Oh, I didn't know you were seeing someone," he said as his eyes looked me up and down. "Well, it was nice seeing you. Have a nice night." And with that, he left—but not before holding his thumb and pinky finger up to his ear and mouthing "call me" to Danny when he thought I wasn't looking.

Tucker appeared from nowhere. "Jesus! No way! Was that Shane?" Tucker's voice boomed through his laughter. "Gee, I bet that was awkward!"

"Who was that?" I asked, looking toward Danny, who began to look a little sheepish. He opened his mouth to explain, but Tucker got there first.

"That was Shane. He's one of Danny's ex-boyfriends from back when we were in college in DC." He sighed as he shook his head from side to side in what looked like good-natured envy. "Man, he was the hottest guy you have ever dated. You were crazy to let him go."

Danny shot a look to silence him, but in his drunken state Tucker was oblivious to it and continued. "Yeah, Danny was a wild child back in DC. Man, you hooked up with so many good-looking guys."

"Thank you, Tucker. I look forward to seeing Danny's monument, should I ever have the pleasure of visiting Washington."

Tucker made it obvious that he hadn't heard what I said, as he was too busy craning his neck and concentrating on a young guy walking past.

"Greg, I wasn't that bad. I was young and in college," Danny protested.

Tucker came back to the conversation. "Yeah, but you saw loads of them when you were in DC and Virginia with the Navy before you went out to Bahrain. Actually, I saw Brett and Mark when I was in DC last. They said they'd heard from you and both wish you luck at school." Tucker looked almost wistful for a second before adding, "Jeez, I thought you were gonna marry both of those guys. Though you may have had a lucky escape from Mark; he's looking a bit haggard."

"Tucker, you've had enough to drink," Danny said sternly.

"I'm good. Besides, I have to stay a little longer since I'm taking Simon back to his dorm after this for some fun. Can you come and pick me up in the morning?"

"No, I can't. And judging by how well your little friend Simon is getting on with your other little friend, Aaron—" He pointed out the two young guys who were now kissing quite passionately by the bar. "—I doubt he'll be going anywhere with you."

"Ohhhh, a hot twink threesome! Thank you, God!" Tucker shouted, rubbing his hands together, only to be crestfallen a moment later as Aaron, who spotted Tucker looking over at them, took Simon by the hand and headed for the exit.

We left the bar soon after, but my mood had changed significantly. I wasn't so naïve as to think that Danny had a lily white past. Who would at that age? And I wasn't exactly a saint. But being confronted with that past by a very real, good-looking guy left me feeling vulnerable and angry that I was 4,000 miles away from home and unable to walk away from the situation. Although Tucker talking about Danny's ex-boyfriends in Washington DC had riled me, they were obviously still living there, so I was relieved there was no chance I would run into them too. I knew I was being a fool and a jealous idiot, but because of my love and devotion to Danny, the idea of anyone else being intimate with him made me want to vomit. I also would never have thought I could feel such rage toward Danny for simply being in contact with these men so recently, regardless of how far away they were.

With Tucker asleep in the front seat of the taxi on the way home, I sat apart from Danny in the back. He reached over and took my hand. I was still livid and could almost taste the bile at the back of my throat, but I squeezed his hand back, thankful that he wasn't talking about my mood, therefore bringing up a subject I had no desire to speak about. It took all my energy not to let my jealousy show. I wanted to even the score and start talking about guys who had been in my life to make him understand how I felt, but the truth was that it hadn't been Danny who had brought up the topic in the first place, and he had done all he could to play it down. I knew I couldn't blame him, so I decided to let it go and not let it ruin the rest of our precious time together.

We arrived back at the house to a hyperactive Duke, who had been barking from the moment he heard the door of the taxi close and the sound of Danny's voice.

"I'd better walk him around the block and calm him down before the neighbors go berserk," Danny said as we went through the front door. He wrestled Duke into a collar while Tucker breezed into the kitchen and poured more drinks.

"You looking forward to the rodeo tomorrow?" Tucker asked, flicking the tickets that were held to the fridge with magnets.

"Yes, it should be fun. I am going to go warm up the bed for Danny. Good night."

"No! You gotta have a drink with me first."

"Tucker, thanks for the offer, but I think I have had enough to drink, and I don't want to be hungover in the morning."

"You may as well have a sore head to go with the sore ass you're about to have." Tucker pushed a glass filled with a dark liquid into my hand. I took a sip, then ran to the sink to spit it out.

"Jesus Christ, Tucker. What in God's name is that stuff?" I put my mouth under the running tap and swilled the vile taste out of my mouth.

As I wiped the remaining throat-stripping beverage from my chin, I turned around to see Tucker leaning against the fridge giving me an odd look. It looked as though he had something to say but was struggling with it, which after the night's events confused me. He looked into his glass and swirled the drink around before knocking it back in one go.

"It's homemade brandy wine. My brother in Louisiana makes it himself. I always bring a couple of bottles home with me after I visit." He set the glass down and took a deep breath and held it for a moment before letting it out, sending a blast of alcohol-infused breath my way. "You know, Greg, you really shouldn't say things like that."

"Like what?"

"Take the Lord's name in vain."

"Huh?"

"You know what I am talking about. 'Jesus Christ'? 'What in God's name is that stuff?'"

I studied him for a moment. It was true that I had momentarily forgotten that Danny had warned me of Tucker's sudden shifts in religious character, but that late in the evening and after a couple of drinks I wasn't so guarded in what I was saying.

"Sorry, Tucker, I don't mean to offend. It's force of habit. But to be fair, I have heard you do the same thing a couple of times tonight."

"If you listen, I tend to use it more as an exclamation than using it in vain."

"I will be honest with you. I haven't ever really given much thought that there's a difference."

"There is," Tucker said in a rather flat tone.

He refilled his glass from the brown bottle that I now noticed wasn't labeled. When he spoke again he sounded lighter. "Hey, I know you don't mean anything by it."

"Good. Right, I am hitting the sack." I turned to leave.

"I just worry about you and Danny."

"Huh? What do you worry about?" I asked, being forced back into the conversation.

"Well, Danny said you're not a believer, and he certainly doesn't have the faith he used to have. So, you know, I worry about you."

"Tucker, I am sorry, I am not following what you're saying."

"I worry about your souls, Greg."

"Well, I don't have one of those, so that's one thing less you have to concern yourself with this evening," I said, only half joking.

Tucker made to add another remark.

"Tucker, I'm sorry. I am very tired and have had a long few days. I haven't had a cigarette all evening, and I need to get to bed and grab some sleep so I can enjoy the rodeo tomorrow."

He backed away and wished me a casual "good-night," and I walked back to Danny's bedroom, leaving him alone in the kitchen. I wasn't too sure whether he was being serious or whether it was just a drunken remark. But for whatever reason, I left the room feeling irked that the comment was made in the first place. The strange thing was that I couldn't actually put my finger on the reason. It was true that I hadn't believed in God in some time, so it really shouldn't have bothered me at all. In fact, if anyone else had said it, I would have laughed it off. But this almost seemed like a personal slight on my character by one of Danny's closest friends, which troubled me— especially so soon after being so harshly received by his mother. It also passed through my mind whether the comment stung because of some residual Catholic guilt that had been so ingrained in me while I was at primary school.

Danny returned, and I heard his and Tucker's voices through the door as I undressed and got into bed. Much of it was muffled, but I caught Danny saying, "Tucker, you can't expect everyone to believe what you believe. Considering you spent the evening telling him about my ex-boyfriends, drinking, smoking, swearing, and showing your penchant for young college men and molesting skater boys, is it any wonder that he didn't take you seriously? Hell, I don't take you seriously when you start acting like this."

"Sorry about that," Danny said as he came into the bedroom and closed the door behind him. "When he's had a few drinks he gets on his high horse about all kinds of things, and you have to rein him in a little. He really is a lovely guy. I am just sorry you saw that side of him tonight."

"Does he really mean any of it, drunk or sober?"

"I think so. He never goes to church and doesn't really follow any organized religion, though he was raised a Southern Baptist like me." He kissed me before adding, "Those people have a lot to answer for."

THE following morning, after a jug of water and a couple of painkillers, Tucker climbed into the back of his car and threw the keys to Danny to drive us to the rodeo, which was another three hour journey back to Houston.

Danny and I made the most of the time together, chatting the way we always had since we met. I tried to make him laugh, while he attempted to teach me something new about American culture or history. Occasionally the roles would change, and I would tell him more about England while he attempted to make me laugh by impersonating the British accent, only managing to sound like Dick Van Dyke in *Mary Poppins*. We arrived at the rodeo, which was being held in the Astrodome in Houston, and attempted to find a space in the parking lot that seemed like the size of my hometown of Brighton. Before I had a chance to get out, Danny tapped my leg and told me to stay in my seat as he jumped out and ran around to the boot of the car. He came back to the passenger's side with a box, and he opened the door.

"This is for you," he said with a smile.

I opened the box to find a shiny pair of dark brown leather cowboy boots with ornate stitching running up the sides in black thread.

"I hope they're the right size," Danny said as I kicked off my trainers in excitement.

I pulled the boots halfway up my calves and felt the soft leather enclose my ankles in a perfect fit. I followed Danny and Tucker through the gates, listening to the sound of the heels clicking on the tarmac, and wondered whether my slight wobble would give me away as an imposter.

I stopped to take in my surroundings. It was as if the Wild West had taken over Disney World for the day. Almost all of the men were dressed in their weekend-best cowboy shirts, tight Wrangler jeans, ten-gallon hats, and large shiny belt buckles that would shame any professional wrestling champion. Their wives hung on their arms, whose outfits only differed by the fact that they wore their jeans so much higher. Three or four steps ahead of the couples, their cute miniclones bounced off people and fixtures as they attempted to navigate themselves with their ill-fitting little cowboy hats slipped over their eyes.

Amongst the fairground rides, shooting games, and apparel stalls stood dozens of food stands serving the typical Texan diet of pizzas, hot dogs, Tex-Mex, gumbo, and barbecue. There were also many other stands that specialized in fried corndogs, fried peanut butter and jelly sandwiches, fried funnel cake, fried Twinkies, and even fried butter—which is as sickening as it sounds. I had to laugh when I spotted the Guess Your Weight stall.

Danny, either out of Texan pride or just to give me a cheap thrill—which hit its target beautifully—wore his tightest blue jeans, a form-hugging black T-shirt, and a black cowboy hat. Just the sight of him in the car was enough to make my jeans tighten, but seeing him stroll among his fellow Texans with such confidence required several more readjustments in the first hour, reminding me of how I lusted over Bobby Ewing every Wednesday night as a kid.

There was an air of masculinity throughout the grounds, but it was much more predominant at the livestock show and rodeo hall. The men showing off their prize steers and studs were also competing in the rodeo themselves. They had spent their lives doing manual labor on farms, and it showed in their size and strength. I didn't think I would find anywhere outside of the Naval Base in Bahrain to be more intimidating, but these guys seemed more wild, and they certainly didn't hold themselves with the same discipline. Tucker, however, didn't seem intimidated at all. Whether it was due to growing up around these kinds of men, or the four glasses of beer that he had consumed since our arrival, he seemed free and easy with his speech, as well as his blatant stares.

"Hey, you as hung as your horse?" he said loudly, directing his catcall at a group of men, each one wearing a holster and trying to corral a mix of livestock into a pen. He nudged me before pointing to a particularly well-muscled rodeo rider walking past with his kids, at whom he directed, "Save the horse. Ride me, cowboy! Will you look at that ass, and I ain't talkin' 'bout no damn donkey." These were not particularly clever or original phrases, but Tucker owned them like he was hilarious.

The rider looked up and around at the people nearby to confirm that they had heard what he thought he'd just heard coming from our direction. Thankfully, they seemed unaware, so he just furrowed his brow as though he must have just been hearing things.

"Tucker, will you knock it off, please," I said as I took his elbow and began walking him toward Danny, who had missed this display as he was bent over a gate and stroking a llama in a gated pen.

"Hey, freedom of speech! These guys are fucking haaaaawt!"

"These guys have fucking guns. You can't say that sort of thing while they have their kids right next to them."

"Awwww, they can't hear me, Greg, and even if they did, what do you think they're going to do? Shoot us? Hey, Danny. Greg thinks we're gonna get shot!"

As Danny walked over to us he saw the look of alarm on my face.

"What's up?"

"Greg is telling me off for telling those guys—" He turned and pointed yet again and raised his voice deliberately louder. "—that they have mighty fine asses!"

"Tucker, are you out of your fucking mind?" Danny said, pulling him back around fast enough that the men didn't have a chance to see the face of the guy that had called out. "Do you have any idea how many people have got off serious violent crimes by citing 'gay panic' as their defense?"

"Hey, Tiger, calm down," I said softly. "I am probably overreacting. You know how I feel about guns. They scare the hell out of me."

Tucker laughed. "Greg! Practically everyone here has a gun on them or in their car!"

"Oh, well, that makes me feel loads better, you know, so long as everyone is armed except us. How fast do you expect me to run in these boots?"

"I have one in the car." Tucker shrugged. "I'll show it to you when we get back. Actually, that ought to be soon. I have a young Mormon boy with killer abs to pound tonight. I haven't met him yet, but his pictures on the website were damn hot."

"Great, you're drunk, horny, and in charge of a gun. Danny, you're driving us home, right?"

WITH Tucker asleep and snoring in the back of the car, Danny pulled onto the highway and began the journey back to Austin. I gingerly started to look around the area of the passenger seat, carefully placing my hands on the dashboard.

"You're getting warmer!"

"Danny, stop fucking with me. This isn't funny."

"Getting hot!"

"So my prize when I find the gun is getting my hand blown off?"

"It's not loaded. The bullets are in the CD wallet in the glove box."

Danny reached under his seat and began to retrieve something. I heard metal clash with metal as he wrestled it out from behind the bar that made the seat slide backward and forward.

"No, no, I don't want to see it. So long as I know where it is."

"You don't want to see it? It sure is pur-dee!"

"Danny, you know how I am with those things. The only time I ever see them is on the belts of police or security at airports. Usually they are in uniform, trained, or in a controlled environment—preferably all three. Having one in the car is a little too gangster for my liking."

"You don't want to hold it?"

"Why the on earth would I want to? I am scared to death of the damn things."

"I've been around them as long as I can remember. I still have three in a case at Mom and Dad's house, but I haven't used them for a long time. Guns are fine so long as you've been taught how to use them properly and you respect them for what they are and what they can do. Dad bought me a gun and taught me to shoot when I was a kid. We used to have great fun, shooting squirrels and deer down by the creek."

"My dad bought me Legos, which are great fun if they're respected and you know what they can do."

"Smartass."

"Doesn't Tucker worry about ever having to use it?"

"No, he's like most other good ol' boys. He's obsessed with the three Gs, though admittedly for different reasons."

"The three Gs?"

"God, guns, and gays." Danny counted them out on his fingers.

After sitting quietly for a few minutes, Danny put his hand on my leg and squeezed. "You okay, baby? Don't worry, I won't let him keep guns in the house, and I don't ever carry them in the truck."

"Do you mind if I ask you a question?"

Danny looked surprised. "Baby, you can ask me anything you want. You know that."

"I don't quite understand Tucker. What with the twinks, the guns, and the vices, how does he still marry it all up with the notion of being Christian?"

"His faith is as much a part of him as anything else. His actions may contradict his faith, but he will always believe that he can do what he wants without guilt because his faith says he will be forgiven."

"How did you lose your faith?"

Danny's eyebrows furrowed for a moment before he raised them, as if surprised that someone had actually asked him the question out loud and he was able to answer it honestly. I could only imagine the number of passive excuses and explanations he had given his mother, who no doubt had quizzed him on the subject.

"When I was a kid I was convinced by Mom and everyone at church that Jesus was like an imaginary friend with magical powers who was always with you. Sure, she let me watch superheroes like Superman on television, but she was always quick to remind me that they were never real. Of course, that was to keep me from throwing myself off the sofa in an attempt to fly. I went to Sunday school every week and listened to stories and fables, filled out coloring books, performed plays, and played games. It was never anything sinister or heavy going. Looking back on it now, it was a great environment for kids. It kept us out of trouble and established morals and taught us how to lead a kind life."

"Then you got older."

"Exactly. And the older I got the harsher the stories became. We were taught more about Jesus's life and God, and we started to learn about the New and Old Testaments. It went from nice stories about kings, wise men, and miracles to stories about God's wrath, plagues, and devils. Jesus was all about love, where God seemed to be about punishment and dictatorship."

"I used to think that too. Jesus always came off better in those stories than God ever did," I said.

"I don't think Mom ever wanted to expose us to that side of things when we were young, but with Dad working and my grandfather suffering from dementia, she didn't really have the help she needed, so I guess Sunday school was a decent option for babysitting. It gave her enough time to go see Grandpa and to give Grandma a break from his care and also time to get other stuff done she didn't have time for during the rest of the week."

Danny took a sip of warm soda that had sat in the car while we'd been at the rodeo.

"I left high school two years earlier than everyone else to start college early, after finding a program for so-called 'gifted' students. I was away from home and exposed to so much more than Baytown could possibly offer. Then when I transferred to Georgetown in DC, I began to learn more about politics and the world in general and found what I had learned as a kid was being twisted. It was a huge eye opener for me. I saw how politicians manipulated people and how people who claimed to have faith condemned others so easily because of what these politicians were spinning. It was the greatest weapon they had, and they wielded it every day. I came out of the closet to Mom and Dad on a visit home, and, as you know, they were both fine about it at the time, although it wasn't something they felt needed to be put on the church's bulletin board. At the time it didn't bother me at all. I was still a kid, and I wasn't ready for the whole community to know, so I almost gave them my blessing to keep it quiet."

He shook his head as if in shame.

"But after hearing what some of the politicians, some of whom I admired, were saying about gay people, I grew to understand how lucky I was to have such supportive parents. I heard horror stories from other guys in DC who had either been disowned or sent away to Georgetown at great expense in order for their family not to have to deal with what they saw as a problem on their doorstep."

I stayed silent and listened to him. He spoke like he was trying to get something off his chest, like he could finally admit the truth to someone that he knew wouldn't judge him.

"Around the same time, the first Gulf War kicked off. The same people I had grown up with were going crazy about fundamentalists in Iraq and Afghanistan, but forgot all about the wars that Christianity had started and all the lives that had been lost in their God's name. I listened to middle-aged, seemingly intelligent people say the craziest things. In one breath they would make a point of telling you how Christian they were, because they gave beans to the local food drive, and in the next breath they said gay people were going to hell and called black people 'niggers', all the while condemning almost anyone in the community who had a hint of individualism.

"The longer I stayed away from Baytown, the more I convinced myself that I never wanted to return there to live. My education had afforded me possibilities that would never exist there anyway. So I stayed in DC, where I got to meet loads of people who worked at the various bases in Virginia or the Pentagon. I saw the military as a good career move, so I signed up as an officer. I also knew there were various programs in the Navy that would help to fund my law school education when I got out. Plus it gave me the chance to keep earning during school, as I would be on Reserve duty.

"It was around that time that Mom started to go to church more. Slowly, through the first four years of being in the Navy, I noticed her mention God more and more. Her letters were filled with things about the church, and on occasion she would even write random Bible verses at the top of the notes in the hope that I might pick up the ship's Bible and read them. She obviously was very worried about me, as any mother would be. But then, after being at sea for eighteen months on the USS Enterprise and finally heading home, 9/11 happened. We were the first carrier to launch strikes into Afghanistan, and it was, of course, reported on the news. Naturally, she flipped out over it. She went to church almost every day during her lunch hour. She got to know the pastor, and he eventually offered her the job as the church secretary."

"Danny, I will be honest with you. I worried all the time you were in Bahrain that you might get called to a combat zone again, and that was only after knowing you a few weeks. Christ knows what your mother was going through."

"I'm sure the church was a source of comfort to her when she was worried. I get that. Hell, I even appreciate it. But she has changed. I hardly recognized her personality when I got back from Bahrain. It's like I keep trying to explain to you. I can see what she's like, but she's still my mother, and I love her. She has said some of the most outrageous things to me since I came back, but I know it's not her voice, but the church's. That's why I give her so much grace with the things she says or does. I'm always so happy to see her, but at the same time I get waves of sadness that she isn't who she used to be. It's like grieving for someone who's still there. She's just not the same woman I grew up with."

Danny let out a breath. "But then again, I guess I'm not the same son she raised."

We sat in silence for a minute and listened to the rumble of the highway beneath us and Tucker's intermittent snoring.

"So, how about you? How did you lose your faith?"

"When that old bastard Father O'Brien didn't give me the Kit Kat he promised for the 'bad man' secrets I kept."

"You were promised a Kit Kat? Wow, Brother Thomas only ever bargained 'a finger for a finger'. The most I got was a Twix." Danny laughed.

"I am not too sure exactly when I lost my faith. I guess it was similar to your experience in the sense that it all started out very nice, with kid's stories about miracles. But now that I think about it, I took my Holy Communion when I was seven years old. We were told to eat the body of Christ and drink his blood." I screwed my face up, shaking my head and realizing for the first time how that sounded. "But it all seemed normal back then. I went to a Catholic primary and high school, so we were taught by nuns and a couple of priests. It was stricter than normal state schools. In fact, it wasn't until the year before I started high school that they abolished the cane as a punishment, and it was probably used in Catholic schools more than anywhere else, so I had a lucky escape. Some of those nuns were brutal.

"Because of Section 28, the policy that Margaret Thatcher's government implemented that banned any kind of encouragement or discussion on homosexuality at school, there wasn't any kind of blatant homophobia or discussion of the subject at all. It wasn't until I was around twelve and I knew full well that I was gay that I began to hear things on the news about the pope and the Catholic Church's stance on gay people. As I became a teenager, I started to rebel against the idea that I should believe everything I was told just because a priest said it was true. I remember being thirteen years old. I had never had sex, worked hard at school, and was a decent kid. Yet I knew I was gay, and these priests on television were telling me that I was going to go to hell, and the politicians all but called me a deviant. From then on I never trusted politicians or the church, because what they said either didn't make sense or was blatant lies."

"Well, sex education must have been fun, at least." Danny winked.

"Yeah, the nuns did a great job of that. I think they must have explained it wrong to both me and my brother Craig. I ended up gay, and he ended up with seven children. What were they thinking allowing celibate nuns to teach teenagers about sex?"

"Well, you did get it back to front, so to speak."

"Yeah, but in their defense, they did improve my sex life eventually. I enjoyed it all the more when I was doing it, knowing that I was going to suffer the guilt afterward!"

Danny nodded into the rearview mirror at Tucker, who was still fast asleep. "Hmmm, some people have never felt that guilt."

"So, how does he keep his faith? You had similar upbringings, and you both went to DC at the same time. What makes him still believe?" I asked, winding my neck around.

"Well, apart from me, God is the only one who will listen to his bullshit!"

CHAPTER SIX

THE first flight I had to work after returning from Texas was to Vancouver, which gave the crew a couple of free days in the city before having to return to London. I was particularly looking forward to this flight because four close friends—Jackie, Donna, Steve, and Lee— were also on the flight, which guaranteed a good day in the skies and a couple of great days on the ground. It was our annual request trip together, and although we hadn't gotten the destination we wanted, it could have been a lot worse. I called my mother, who lived in a granny annex at my sister's home since my dad's death, and promised I would see her as soon as I returned.

I felt guilty that I hadn't had the chance to visit her in between my trips to Texas and Vancouver, but after all the years of flying, she understood that my lifestyle took me away most of the time. I still hadn't told her about Danny, but I knew if I had, she would have fretted instantly that I might leave to live in America, and that would just add on to the grief she was still experiencing over losing her husband. Mum had grown to rely on me for many things that my father would take care of, such as helping with her banking, bills, and odd jobs around the annex that my sister's husband didn't have the time to do. The arrangement of the annex was perfect and a huge weight off my mind to know that she had the security, protection, and company of my sister and her family just yards away. She had returned to her job as a matron at the local hospital too, so thankfully her time was occupied, but I know she had found it difficult not coming home to share her day with her husband.

I had only told people at work about Danny four months into our relationship. It was still so special and new that I couldn't cope with the idea of people voicing their opinions or questioning why I would want to go through the hell of a long distance relationship. I knew that if any of them met Danny, they would have understood straightaway.

I went through the safety briefing with Jackie, who was the Cabin Services Director, asking the usual evacuations procedures questions that we were expected to answer before each and every flight. With such a good crew on board and her eagerness to get away from the prying eyes of the managers, she hurried through the briefing, leaving us enough time to stroll down to the aircraft at our leisure.

While Jackie dealt with the flight deck and Lee and Steve went to the back of the aircraft to prepare the galley, I stood at the second set of doors with Donna, ready to greet the boarding passengers. Donna started at the airline the same day I did, as did Lee and Steve. We quickly all became friends, confidants, and accomplices during our mock evacuations, drinking benders around the world, and countless scrapes and injuries. Both Steve and Lee were gay too, but like me didn't tend to wear their sexuality on their sleeves. On more than one occasion we had been accused of us all being brothers. Donna, being a beautiful brunette and petite girl, could turn every head on any aisle on every aircraft she worked. It was only when she spoke that you realized her innocent looks didn't match her not so innocent mind.

"How are things going with First Officer Todger?" I asked, knowing that Donna had partaken of a down-route fling with one of the flight deck on a Cancun trip the month before.

Donna dropped her head in mock shame, a slight smile emerging. "They're not. The bastard is married. He took his ring off when he went to work. I just finished a Barbados flight with one of the older captains who told the crew that they advised the younger first officers to take their bands off before they went down-route if they wanted to get some 'hanky-panky'. After a few more drinks the old guy named all of the younger first officers he had told and the girls who they have scored with. Thankfully, my name wasn't mentioned or I would have had to of put a bottle of rum around the fucker's head."

"I'm sure you would."

"I don't know what made me feel dirtier, him being married or knowing that he took advice from a dirty old bastard who still says 'hanky-panky'." She shuddered and took a sip of lemonade from a miniature can that rested on top of the crew seat next to her, as though she was washing a bad taste out of her mouth. "He was a freak, anyway. Can you believe that he wanted me to dress up—" She paused for effect. "—as an air stewardess? He works with the bitches all day! And if that wasn't bad enough, he wanted me to stand at the end of the bed and do the safety demo because 'I never get to see it because I am always in the flight deck,'" she ended in a whiny voice.

"But you still did it, huh?"

"Of course."

"Okay, so how do we go about defending your honor? We cannot allow this cad to take advantage of you in this way!"

Donna gave me a mischievous smile that I knew all too well. "Already taken care of. I printed out his name, rank, sexual kinks, and marital status on a sheet of paper and pinned it to the flight deck room wall and the incoming and outgoing crew rooms. And for good measure, I put a hundred copies in random drop files of the crew. I knew he wasn't going to be in for a couple of days, by which time the damage will have been done!"

"Ouch."

Donna straightened her scarf. "The picture of a pinky finger and the caption 'Big Plane, Little Cargo' may have been a step too far, but I felt it brightened up the page."

"Good girl. I am a little disappointed that you didn't include me in your plans."

"Well, you were off gallivanting around Texas knocking boots with your cowboy! Anyway, how is that going? You got any spur burns?"

"Oh, Donna, I had the most perfect time with him. Well, almost perfect."

"Almost? Why, what happened?"

"Well, his...." I trailed off as I saw the army of passengers descend the air bridge toward us. "I'll tell you later."

"Okay. Ready for them?" Donna asked as the first passenger approached. "Meet, greet, and seat. Tits and teeth!" Donna jutted out her bust and gave a wide smile. "Welcome on board!"

After the aircraft leveled out at cruising altitude, the crew was released from their seats to prepare for the service. Donna set out the beverage cart for the right-hand side of the aircraft, while Steve prepared one for the left.

Jackie sauntered over. "Lee, it's okay, my darling, you can give the rest of the crew a hand in the back today. I will be working the drinks service today! I want to have a little catch-up with Greg." Lee looked at me with a hint of sympathy as he turned to walk to the rear of the aircraft.

Jackie had worked for the airline for many years and was my favorite supervisor to fly with. She was in her early forties and beautiful, even though most of her face was expressionless due to frequent Botox injections. She wore her long black hair in a tight bun for work, but always released it at the end of a flight, like a geisha clocking off. Well educated at private schools in Surrey, she had the accent of a woman with an affluent background, very posh and sometimes unforgiving. She was married to a wealthy, but older, hardworking banker in the city and maintained that she was only flying because "It's nice to have a hobby."

In the seven years I had been flying I had never seen Jackie not immaculately dressed or speaking with the clarity of a finishing school graduate. Unless, of course, she was drunk, then she seemed to develop the mouth of a fishwife. Years of good living had fostered a sense of humor that showed no great hardship in life. She was easygoing and available to joke with, but if you took advantage you would be on the receiving end of a razor sharp tongue that left a mental scar that would never heal.

"So, my darling," she began as she collected the glasses and drinks for one of the very few passengers that she would be serving, "how is the dashing young sailor?" She turned her head but kept her eyes on me. "Very well done, my love."

"Actually, he's not in the Navy anymore. Well, he is, but he's on Reserve duty. He's at law school at the moment, training to become an attorney."

"Oh, bravo, Mr. Stephens! You've found yourself a young stud muffin who can shag you in the true military position and get you off a life sentence. How marvelous!" she added before setting drinks down in front of a young couple that had their headphones on and was engrossed in the in-flight film.

"I miss him like crazy, though. It's a killer being so far away from him."

"I am sure it must be absolutely horrid for you, so in love and being on the opposite sides of the globe." She drew a deep breath. "I, on the other hand, have to go on little excursions like this just to get away from my husband. Good grief, you know he actually mentioned the word 'adoption' the other day? I swear, he must be going senile." She stopped to hand me a couple of glasses of ice for drinks I was preparing. "I will sponsor a dog, perhaps. Maybe one of the ones on the television ads whose owners used them as an ashtray. But only by direct debit. I don't actually need to see the creature. Honestly, adopting a child? What on earth was he thinking?"

"But you're so maternal, Jackie!" There was no point in hiding my sarcasm.

"I like kids, but only the ones I can walk away from."

"Hey, I remember you in the orphanages in Mombasa, lady. I know there is some good in your heart when it comes to kids. You were close to tears."

Jackie sniffed as she whipped her head around. "I was only upset that we were going to be late back to the hotel, and I wouldn't get a chance to see Sambuki."

"Sambuki?"

"Yes. Oh come now, you remember him. He was the local Masai warrior who the hotel employed to take photos with the guests. He was an absolute dream lover. He could go for hours and hours with only a cup of rice and a glass of mango juice for sustenance. And for two pounds extra he would carve me a giraffe, which is always nice."

"Say what you will, but I bet you have thought about it."

"Warrior sex?"

"No, Jacks, children!"

"I would be an awful mother. No, no. I am far too uptight for such nonsense."

"You couldn't be any worse than Danny's mother."

"You've met the mother already? Crikey, it must be serious. What's wrong with her? Too overbearing?"

"Too overbearing, and too Christian," I said as I bashed clumps of ice cubes a little more aggressively than needed to separate them.

"You know you could always grow a beard and buy a nice pair of comfortable sandals. Maybe that would endear you more to her. Though, to be honest, I can't imagine any mother not being thrilled to have a son-in-law like you who…."

Jackie's voice trailed off as she spotted a passenger waving his hand in the air.

"Oh Lord, please don't be a stroke. The paperwork is such a bore," she said as she opened the nearest stowage to retrieve the first aid kit, just in case.

THE following day, Donna, Jackie, Lee, and Steve and I sat on the patio of a restaurant after a long bike ride around Vancouver's Stanley Park.

"I knew it," Lee called from across the table. "I know you have a love of seamen, but going so far as to find a sailor is a bit much, isn't it?" He laughed at his own innuendo.

"I'm in love with the guy. It's mad; he lives in Texas and I live in England. But he is amazing, absolutely amazing."

"Oh rah, rah, rah. My boyfriend is just *sooo* terrific," Steve mocked as he poured himself another glass of red wine. "He's just *so* fucking wonderful and dreamy, all I could ask for and more!"

"Don't listen to the evil queens, Greg. I think it's sweet. Though, he can't be that perfect. There has to be something wrong with him," said Donna.

"Nope, he's perfect," I said as I poured myself and Jackie another glass from the bottle of white wine sitting on the table. "But his mother, she really doesn't like me. I think she sees me as 'a heathen that needs to be stopped'." I added the last part in my best Texan accent, which for some reason always came out sounding Australian.

Since I met Danny I had spent much of my time explaining to friends why I was with a man who lived four thousand miles away. I had to give examples of how caring, generous, attractive, intelligent, and loving he was. It was the only way I could explain how it was all worth it. Although I had no need to defend my decision to be in a long-distance relationship, I actually ended up cherishing these explanations, as they were a constant reminder of the man who was so far away. I didn't want to speak harshly about his mother for fear that I might blemish his story, but I was among friends, and I felt like I needed to get it off my chest.

"I don't understand," Lee said. "Why doesn't she like you?"

"She's a Bible basher, and I think she believes that I am not holy enough for her son." I said it as if a dirty secret had just been released.

Donna cackled. "Greg, I can't see your problem! Just get drunk and speak in your best British accent. Americans can never understand what we're saying when we're drunk, so she'll think you're speaking in tongues. And if that doesn't work, explain how you love wine and that you have already enjoyed the company of twelve men."

"Donna, I had no idea that it was that sort of club when I went in there. And you promised you'd never tell."

"So long as you love each other it shouldn't matter what the mother thinks," Jackie said.

"Gay love against the odds!" cried Lee. "It could be worse. She could be some chavvy tart from a council estate who tries to steal your wallet."

"How is Damon, by the way?" Steve asked Lee.

"He's okay. More than I can say for my arse. Those sovereign rings sting like a bastard. I had Elizabeth the Second's crest imprinted on my right arse cheek for a week. Still, it's amazing what he'll do for a couple of cans of Stella and a pack of duty-free cigs."

"She could quite easily become my mother-in-law, and I have already gotten off to a bad start with her," I said, attempting to bring the conversation back around.

"Mother-in-law?" Lee spluttered, just catching the wine from his mouth back into his glass. "You really are serious about this guy!"

"I would marry him tomorrow," I answered honestly.

"I am sure his mother would love that. The walls of the church bleeding would make a terrible mess of her shoes," said Jackie, topping up our wine yet again.

"Has anyone ever thought Jesus was sexy?" Lee asked out of nowhere, bringing the table to complete silence. "Don't look at me like that! Every time I saw him up on that cross he had the most amazing abs. Oh, and the beard! It was all so very manly. I bet he had rough hands too, from working with all that wood. Hands with calluses that leave welt marks on your arse after you've been spanked."

"Am I the only one who is beginning to see a pattern here?" I asked as I looked at Lee and grimaced.

"I know what I am getting you for Christmas now," Donna said, licking an imaginary pencil and writing on her palm. "One carpenter. Can I get a crown of thorns at Claire's Accessories? Or will I need to go to a garden center?"

"Is she like one of those dreadful women you see on television in the States who are forever standing next to the creepy evangelical preachers hawking their 'Pray your way to a better life!' DVDs?" Jackie asked, spreading her arms in a great impersonation. "My name is Talulah Baker, and I buh'leeve in the power of Gaawd to live a good life, and the skill of a good drag queen to do ma' hair!"

"They always remind me of Stepford Wives," said Steve.

"Yes! That is exactly what she is like!" I said with appreciation, thinking that it was the perfect comparison. "She's just had the Jesus chip put in too."

"How do you know she doesn't like you?" asked Donna.

"She pretty much made it obvious. I feel awful about saying anything bad about her because Danny clearly adores her, and she worships the ground he walks on. She just doesn't like any other footprints in the sand."

"Well, does she at least make an effort with you?" Lee asked.

"Well, she has refrained from throwing holy water over me, so I guess she shows some restraint."

Steve dipped his fingers in his wine and flicked them at me. "Burn! *Burn!*"

"Well, you have only met her once, right? Once she gets to know you she'll love you, I'm sure. What's not to love?" Donna said in consolation.

"Other than the fact that what you're doing to and with her son is an abomination?" offered Lee.

"I also think she doesn't like me because I am British."

There was an audible gasp, and all four faces clearly took umbrage with the idea.

"Excuse me. She's American, and she doesn't like you because you're British?" Donna was clearly offended.

"I think it has more to do with the fact that she is worried I am going to take Danny away from her. I can kind of understand that. He was in the Navy so long, so she couldn't see him since he was either on a ship or in Bahrain. Now she finally has him back, and I pitch up and threaten her with the idea that I am going to take him away again." I chewed on my lip and went on. "God only knows how she would have reacted if I had been from New Zealand. Come on, guys, it's important to Danny. What can I do to make this woman like me?"

"Walk on water," Lee suggested.

"Cure the blind," offered Jackie.

"Come back from the dead," said Steve.

"Feed the starving in Africa," Donna ended the round before adding, "No, wait. That was Bob Geldof."

I put my face in my hands and spoke through my fingers. "Okay, I will get straight onto it. Thank you for all of your sage advice."

CHAPTER SEVEN

I LIT up a cigarette on the drive over to see Mum on my return from Vancouver, cursing myself for the thousandth time. Giving up smoking should have been the easiest thing in the world to do after watching Dad die from lung cancer at only fifty-seven years old, but I just kept breaking. The shame I felt after each cigarette was eased by yet another promise that it would be my last, even though I knew in my heart that wasn't true. I had cut down a tremendous amount, but with each attempt to kick the habit cold turkey, I always found an excuse to light up another one.

The three months between the discovery of a shadow on Dad's lung after an X-ray from a fall and his eventual death at home with us by his side were agony. The world seemed to spin faster on days that we thought about the time we had left with him, only to slow down to a crawl on his particularly bad days, when we could see his suffering from the chemotherapy and medication. All the while Dad was still coherent he managed to keep his sense of humor, which only added even more pain to the idea of losing him. I witnessed his bravery as all concern for himself left with the news that his cancer was terminal, and he was left to deal with what would happen to his wife and children. Mum and Dad had been married for thirty-five years, and, while I knew they loved each other, I hadn't realized the full scope of their love affair until they knew they were going to be separated.

I tried to remember all of the good times I'd had with Dad, everything from how he made me laugh as he spun me on his shoulders when I was kid to screaming as he faked fear in an empty supermarket car park while teaching me how to drive. But with each happy memory came attached a darker one, as I remembered his last days when his mind became addled from the medication, and he asked the same questions he had asked a dozen times earlier the same day. I never dreamt that I would have to answer some of those questions even once, let alone so many times, and each time was just hard as the first.

"You know where I want to be buried?"

"Yes, Dad, I have already arranged it." I hated saying it as much as I hated doing it, but it seemed to reassure and calm him knowing that things were in order.

"You will look after your mum, won't you? Take care of her."

"I promise you, I will make sure she's okay."

"And make sure you kids all look out for one another. Craig's going to need help with all of those kids."

"We will."

Dad paused and took a breath to fight a stab of pain.

"Who will look after you, Greg?"

"I'll be fine."

"Your brother and sister each have someone. I worry about you the most."

"Honestly, Dad, I'm all right."

"You'll meet someone someday." He smiled. "I just hope he looks after you."

"Dad, please, you need to get some rest."

He went silent for a few minutes, as though he drifted off somewhere.

"What can I do to stop this? Greg, help me figure out a way to sort this out."

This was the worst question. He had always been such a practical man who thought things through carefully, and I had yet to see him fail to find a solution to any problem any of us had. I stayed up with him all night in the living room, where we had brought his bed, as he was too weak to manage the stairs. Mum and Natalie were in the spare rooms

73

trying to rest after a long day of caring for him, and Craig and I took turns keeping watch at night. It was three o'clock in the morning three days before he died. He had attempted to get up again, only for me to softly tackle him back onto the bed for fear that he might fall and injure himself. I knew what he was doing. He wanted to pace around the room like I had seen him do so many times before when he wanted to think, but this time it was to find a way not to leave. Instead, he sat up in the bed and buried his face in his hands, deep in thought.

"Dad, don't worry, we'll sort it out," I lied. "Try and get some rest so we can get our heads around it in the morning."

"Yeah, we'll sort something out, won't we? We always do."

The smile and look of relief on his face that I was there to help him find a solution to the problem forgave my lies, but I knew that he would drift off to sleep, only to wake and ask the same question again in twenty minutes.

The day Dad died was the most painful of my life. My moment of relief for him, that he was no longer suffering, was replaced by anguish as I watched Mum's grief knock her to the floor. She wailed and refused to let go of Dad's hands when the funeral home came to collect his body. I waited for Craig and Natalie to have their last moments with him before I took my place alone at his bedside. I kissed his forehead, told him I loved him, and said good-bye, before I turned and nodded permission for the awaiting funeral director and his assistant to prepare his body for removal. I watched closely as they positioned his body to be wrapped and moved onto the wheeled trolley, but turned away as they covered his face. I helped my brother get Mum into a chair and then stared out of the window until the funeral director said it was time for them to leave.

"Remember, that's my dad," I said, almost in a threatening tone, as if they were going to somehow mistreat him or handle him without care. I steeled myself before adding more kindly, "Look after him."

I pulled up outside of my sister's house and sprayed aftershave over myself before grabbing the mouthwash I kept in the glove compartment. I gargled until my throat burned, hoping Mum wouldn't detect any smoke on my breath. I jumped out of the car with a bag of duty-free goods and went around the side of the house to the annex where Mum lived.

"Hey, mother dearest!" I called as I swept through the living room.

"Greggy! What's in the bag? *What's in the bag!*" she cried out as she got up from the sofa and playfully snatched at the sack. Mum was in her midfifties, and while still a handsome woman, she had not given in to our pleas to have her hair cut and colored by a professional. This time her hair was a reddish brown color, which suited her face so much more than the almost black color she had opted for a couple of months before. Although her abilities with a pair of curling tongs and lacquer were amazing, she still managed to look like a washed out Italian widow ready to beat on the lid of a coffin.

"Authentic maple syrup, a dream catcher, and a snow globe of Grouse Mountain for your Christmas collection."

Mum never cared what was in the bag. She was just excited to get something from another country, the same way she had when Dad brought her gifts from his voyages in the Royal Navy.

"How are Craig and Natalie?" I asked as I took a seat on the sofa and poured out two cups of tea from an old-fashioned teapot that sat on the coffee table.

"They're both fine. Natalie is still running around after the little ones, and Craig is working hard, as usual."

"And how are you?"

"I am fine, love. Don't you worry about your old mum," she said cheerily. "How was your trip?" she asked as she dangled the dream catcher on her finger. "Your Dad would have loved this."

"The trip was good, thanks!"

Mum studied me for a moment. "You're very lively. You're usually tired after one of your trips."

"I'm happy, that's all!"

"Well that's good. So what's making you so happy?"

I drew a breath. It was time to tell her. "I've met someone."

Mum smiled. "He must be nice if he's making you smile so much. So, who is he? What's his name?"

"His name is Danny. Mum, he's amazing."

"He must be. You don't impress easily," she laughed.

"He's American, lives in Texas, and is studying law."

She looked at me with a mixture of concern and alarm.

"I met him while he was in the Middle East."

"What was he doing there?"

"He's a big Navy boy." My joking tone didn't make her face change, so I added quickly, "Mum, don't worry. I'm not leaving anytime soon. He's got another two and a half years left of studying to do, and there is no way I can move out there. You're stuck with me for the time being."

"Move out there?"

"No, I'm just saying that I am not going anywhere."

The smile returned to Mum's face, and she seemed to relax. "Okay, tell me all about him."

I spent the rest of the afternoon telling her about Danny, but conveniently left out the part about his mother's reaction to me. Although Mum was a soft woman, still in the throes of grief, she had the ability to turn when anyone attacked her children. I knew if I had been truthful she would have stopped listening about how great Danny was and concentrated on the fact that his mother hadn't been so kind. Although I wished he could have been around to make a great first impression, I think I did him justice, even to the point that Mum was beginning to think that he was Superman.

As I left I gave her a hug, which she returned by almost crushing my ribs, another habit that she had picked up since Dad died.

"Love you! Drive home carefully. Make sure to call me when you get there." These words still made me chuckle. She never seemed to bat an eyelid of worry when I was on a trip to Africa, the Middle East, or a city with a particularly bad reputation. But she was always overly concerned about my short drive home.

"When do you think I will be able to meet Danny?"

"I am not too sure, to be honest with you, Mum. I won't get a chance to see him for another twelve weeks, and that will be in Texas. Hopefully he will make it out here sometime soon."

"Well, send him my best, and let him know I am looking forward to meeting him."

"I will do. Love you, Mum."

I got in the car and slid a packet of cigarettes that I had carelessly left on the passenger seat onto the floor and then under the seat. Mum watched and waved as I pulled out of the driveway and headed back to Brighton. Just as I arrived back at my flat in Kemptown, I felt my phone vibrate in my pocket. I pulled it out and read the text message.

G, I have been rostered a week trip to Orlando in 6 weeks. You wanna swap so you can go see loverboy? Love Donna x.

CHAPTER EiGHT

"I CAN grab a cheap flight with American Airlines with my concessions, fly across from Orlando on the Monday, spend four days with you, and then fly back!"

"Baby, that's fantastic!" Danny sounded as thrilled as I was that we were going to have a chance to see each other sooner than we'd expected. "Ah, hang on. I'm supposed to be in Houston that week for Reserve duty. I can't cancel because it's also Mom's birthday, and I promised that I'd have dinner with her and Dad while I am there."

"Damn," I said, not believing my luck.

"It's no problem. I can grab a hotel room in Houston instead of staying on base, so we can still see each other. You can come to dinner too. It'll be a nice surprise for them."

"Yeah, it will be a surprise, all right."

"Look, I know you didn't get off to a great start, but if you turn up at the dinner too, it will show her that you're making an effort. We can have a nice meal, maybe even get her a present from the two of us. Come on, baby, it would mean the world to me if you two got along."

"But…."

"Greg, are you seriously going to pass over this chance for us to see each other because of my mother?" Danny asked, sounding a little more frustrated.

He was right. The only thing I wanted was to be with him, and with such an opportunity landing in my lap I would have been stupid to give it up. If it meant that I would have to go through a couple of hours with the matriarch of his family, it was a small price to pay, especially if it meant that I had a break from the wall-scratching celibacy.

Knowing that I was going to see Danny again cheered me up significantly, and the six weeks went by faster than I could have imagined. I arranged the flight to Houston before I left London for Orlando, ensuring that I had enough time on either side to account for possible delays. I had visions of standing in front of the crew managers at the airline, trying to explain why I was a thousand miles away from where I should have been when I was due to work the flight back.

Once I arrived in Houston I ran through the arrivals gate, almost tripping over my suitcase. I scanned the hall for Danny but couldn't see him anywhere. A wave of disappointment washed over me, feeling that our reunion was going to have to wait even longer. I slowly walked through the opening of the crowds of people who were hugging loved ones and others holding banners and signs. As I looked for the exit I saw a cardboard cutout of my face staring back at me with the words "Welcome home, Greg!" arched in colorful block writing above. I ran into Danny's arms and buried my head in his neck.

"Thank you so much! Thank you, thank you, thank you."

"Whoa, baby, it's only a sign," he said, laughing as he took a step back so he could get a better look at me.

"I know, but I have walked through Arrivals halls over a thousand times, and I have never once had anyone hold up a sign for me."

He smiled and pulled me back into an embrace. "I'm glad you like it and you're happy, because I don't think you're going to be too pleased with me."

"Why?"

"Mom changed the reservations at the restaurant, and they're coming into town tonight instead of tomorrow."

"That's okay. We can get it out of the way and have the rest of the days to ourselves. It may actually work out better this way."

Danny chewed his lip. "She changed it to tonight because she wants me to head back to Baytown with them tonight so we can all go to church in the morning."

"Danny...."

"I know what you're going to say, but they still don't know that you're here, since it was meant to be a surprise. Please, baby, just this once. And it will give you a chance to get to know Mom better. You know how much that means to me."

"It's not that I don't want to see your mum, it's just that I want to spend time alone with you and Duke. Where is he by the way?"

"Tucker's taking care of him while I'm here. Look, I know what you're saying, and I want to be alone with you too. But I promise, we will leave straight after church and come back to the hotel, where it will just be you and me."

THE restaurant was an upscale steak house in the middle of downtown Houston. Since Danny and I hadn't seen each other for a while, we had spent the afternoon in bed and were ravenous by the time we arrived.

"Table for three under the name of Taylor," Danny told the hostess as I looked around at what would have been considered a themed restaurant in the UK. "We actually have someone else joining us now, so is it possible to have a table for four?"

The girl checked her computer screen. "We do have a reservation for Vivien Taylor listed, sir, but it's for a table of five."

"Ah, maybe my sisters are joining us. Well, in that case, do you have a table for six available?"

The waitress showed us to the table, and I placed a wrapped box containing an Elizabeth Arden gift set that I had bought from the Duty-Free on a recent trip to Dubai. I had asked Danny's advice on what the best birthday gift would be, and he gave me the safe bet of creams and lotions that he knew his mother used. Danny drew a card out of his jacket pocket and wrote, "Happy birthday, Momma! Love, Danny and Greg." It was simple, to the point, and screamed the fact that we were now to be considered a couple.

"I hope she likes it," I said, slipping the card under the ribbon of the box.

"Of course she will! She told me she loved the Harrods hamper," Danny said, and he reached to tousle the back of my hair. But he whipped his arm back at the sight of Mrs. Taylor and George coming through the door, closely followed by two people I didn't recognize. A heavyset man wearing a grey suit and cowboy hat that edged his grey hair stood with a petite younger blonde woman who wore a black pencil skirt and frilly white blouse. His mother stopped dead at the sight of me. Flustered, she redirected herself and the others toward the bar.

"What's going on?" I asked Danny, who looked as confused as I was.

"That's Tim Mayer with them. I haven't seen him in years."

"Who is he?"

"He's a friend of the family. He and Mom go way back. His parents and my grandparents were best friends. He left Baytown about twenty years ago to come to Houston and now has a very successful and wealthy career in the oil business. He spends a lot of time in Baytown on the weekends since he still has a house there, so Mom says."

"So the young lady that's with him, is that his wife?"

"I think it's his daughter, Marylou. I can't be sure. I haven't seen her in years either."

"Marylou Mayer? Does her mother know she's missing from the prairie?"

"I don't know why they haven't just come and sat down," Danny said as he rose from his chair. He caught George's eye. "Dad, over here!"

George turned as if to look surprised that we were already there and walked over. His expression changed to one of sheepishness as he reached the table.

"Hey, boys, um...." I saw George nervously drum his fingers on the back of the chair on which he was leaning, causing his shoulders to raise. It gave him the look of a young boy in trouble, about to give an explanation.

"Did you want us to join you at the bar?" Danny asked, tapping my elbow to motion to get up with him.

"No, no, it's okay. Tim is just showing off his knowledge of expensive wine. You know how he is." George winked at Danny, but still looked a little anxious. "Greg, it's great to see you. I must admit, we weren't expecting to see you both here tonight."

"You okay, Dad? You seem a little odd," Danny said, furrowing his brow.

"To be truthful, and I can't tell you how much I hate to say this, but Tim, doesn't, um, *know* about you boys."

Danny looked around his dad to see Mrs. Taylor looking nervously over at the table. "He doesn't know that we're together, or doesn't know that I'm gay?"

George's look of shame said it all. "Danny, your momma…."

"It's okay, Dad," Danny said, raising his palm. "Don't get me wrong, I am beyond pissed about this, and I will have something to say to Momma tomorrow, but for the time being we'll just let it go. So long as she remembers that Greg didn't fly thousands of miles to pretend that he's just a friend of mine," Danny said, making it obvious that he didn't blame his dad.

"Well, son, perhaps you should say something this evening and let them know that Greg is your partner. Get it out into the open. Tell them straightaway so there's no…."

"George, really, it's okay. It's not a big deal. We'll just say I am a friend visiting for now. I would rather not make a big deal out it tonight, especially as it's Mrs. Taylor's birthday."

George made to say something but was cut off by a booming voice.

"Daniel! Why, stand up. Let me see you, boy!" Mr. Mayer said as he and his daughter arrived at the table with Mrs. Taylor. "Why, Vivien, he has turned into a fine young man!" He shook Danny's hand and walloped his shoulder with the other, grabbing Danny's bicep like he was testing the strength of a bull. He stepped aside to introduce his daughter. "You remember Marylou? You kids ain't seen each other since you were knee high to a grasshopper. Let's get you two sat together so you can have a catch up."

"Mr. Mayer, this is my buddy, Greg. He's visiting from England." Danny eyes narrowed when he said "buddy," but Mr. Mayer didn't catch it.

"Well howdy, Greg. Good to meet ya. You ready for some proper meat?"

Although the table was round, Mrs. Taylor still managed to seat everyone at her direction. However, on this occasion she placed me in between herself and George, while Danny sat to her left and next to Marylou, leaving Mr. Mayer next to his daughter and George.

After studying the menu for what seemed like an awkward eternity, the waiter finally arrived to take our orders. I made the mistake of asking the table in general for a recommendation, and Mr. Mayer immediately made the decision and ordered me the biggest steak on the menu. The waiter delivered our orders to the kitchen and promptly returned with baskets of fresh rolls. But before anyone reached for one, we all joined hands and, at Mrs. Taylor's request, Marylou delivered a long thankful grace.

"So, Daniel, your momma tells me you're studying to become a lawyer?"

"Yes, sir. I'm at the University of Texas."

"Well you know my Marylou is a paralegal here in Houston now." He pointed his fork toward his daughter and raised it to signify that it was her turn to talk. "Go on then, tell the boy."

"I'm at Mason, Flory and Golding," she said shyly, barely looking up at Danny. "I started about six months ago."

"Are you enjoying it?" Danny asked.

"Yes. It's hard work, but I enjoy it."

"Nothin' wrong with hard work," said Mr. Mayer, smearing an obscene amount of butter onto a roll. "Ain't that right, Daniel?"

"No, sir," Danny replied.

Mrs. Taylor was yet to speak and, because of the arrangement of the table, had her head turned away from me to listen to Mr. Mayer.

After a brief conversation between Danny and Mr. Mayer about company law, she finally spoke.

"Wouldn't it be nice for Marylou and Danny to get together while he's here on Reserve duty so she can show him around the area and perhaps some of the law firms here in Houston?"

"Fine idea, Vivien. What do you say, Daniel?"

"Well, I know that Momma would love to have me working in Houston and be closer to her, but I'll probably be looking for firms in New York."

"Well, that doesn't stop you from looking here too, boy!" Mr. Mayer bellowed as the waiter arrived with our meals. "Your momma and daddy want you around, son. You can't blame them for that, and you never know, you may have something else to stay in Texas for." He then winked at Mrs. Taylor.

"We're just happy to have him back home and safe," said George, not looking at anyone in particular.

"So, how long are you here for, Greg?" Mr. Mayer asked, turning his attention to me.

"I'm only here for a few days before I head back to London."

"And whaddaya think of Texas? Is this your first time here?"

"No, I have been here before, but I have only seen Austin and Baytown. This is my first time staying in Houston."

"I bet you drive the gals here crazy with that accent of yours." He chuckled. "You stay lucky, ya hear?"

I laughed, though it was more at Danny's face, which looked at me as though he concurred with Mr. Mayer.

"So, Daniel, what do you think of my Marylou? She's grown into a pur-dee young thing, ain't she?"

Marylou looked away in embarrassment, but I could tell she was eager to hear Danny's answer.

"Yes, sir. She has turned into a beautiful young lady."

"She does a lot of work for the church in her spare time too," said Mrs. Taylor, who smiled and nodded to Marylou, encouraging her to carry on.

"Well, I try to when I can," she said bashfully before adding, "I'm a group leader in the Young Christian Fellowship of Texas."

"And what exactly do they do there?" Mrs. Taylor asked, though I was sure she already knew the answer.

"We run a Bible camp in Waco during the summer, which is, like, so much fun, and the rest of the year we spend fundraising for charitable organizations throughout Texas."

"Isn't she a sweetheart, Daniel?" Mr. Mayer asked Danny for his approval again.

"Yes, sir. Her efforts are very commendable."

I took my chance to mouth "David Koresh!" to Danny when I saw all eyes were on him, but only his eyes on me. He began to laugh, which brought his mother's attention to me, and I received a filthy look.

We finished our main courses, and, after a series of badgering comments from Mr. Mayer that I should "Man up, boy" and finish the half cow that was on my plate, we finally raised our glasses over dessert to Mrs. Taylor for her birthday.

"Thank you all so much for coming, especially you, Tim. I know you live over half an hour away. I really do appreciate it," she said to Mr. Mayer, who nodded politely. "And Marylou, it was an absolute pleasure to see you again. You make sure you arrange a time to meet up with Danny before we leave to head back to Baytown tonight."

"Actually, we're staying in Houston tonight and driving down to Baytown tomorrow morning," Danny said. "Greg had a ten-hour journey over from Great Britain to be here, and I don't think it's fair to ask him to drive another couple of hours now after such a long day."

"You're right," agreed George, who had remained relatively quiet most of the evening. "You boys head down when you're ready. Your momma and I will see you tomorrow."

"Make sure you both wear shirts and ties for church in the morning," Mrs. Taylor added as she signaled to the waiter for the bill.

I turned to Danny, who stubbornly refused to meet my eyes.

"Now, let's get you two organized now, shall we?" Mr. Mayer said as his head turned between Danny and his daughter.

"Vivien, may I please borrow your pen to write my number down for Danny?" Marylou asked sweetly.

"Hush now, girl. Don't you know that it's the gentleman that is meant to give you his number?" Mr. Mayer said as he took the pen from Mrs. Taylor and handed it to Danny. "Now, Greg, I know Vivien and George are heading back now, but will you join me for a brandy while these two organize their date?"

"Thanks for the offer, Mr. Mayer, but I am dead on my feet. I am going to head back to the hotel now." I retrieved the present from under the table and placed it in front of Mrs. Taylor. "This is for you, Mrs. Taylor, a very happy birthday to you."

She looked a little shocked, and for a brief moment I thought I glimpsed a look of shame on her face. She accepted it and gave thanks, but didn't open it.

As we made our way back to the hotel I slowly shook my head and laughed in disbelief.

"Crazy, huh?" Danny said as slung his arm around me and pulled me into a half embrace.

"I didn't know whether to laugh or be offended."

"Offended?"

"You have to admit that it was bizarre. Your mother was trying to set you up with someone else in front of me. I know it was with a woman, but it was still weird."

"I don't think it was Momma. I think it was more a man trying to marry off his spinster daughter."

"Oh, come on, Danny. You're not that naïve. It was your mum's birthday dinner. You can't tell me that it wasn't planned between the two of them."

"Greg, she knows I'm gay. She's hardly going to try and hook me up with a girl," Danny said, laughing and digging his fingers into my ribs to tickle me. "And even if she was, just imagine what we could do with the dowry!"

"What the hell am I going to do with a hundred head of cattle and a nodding donkey?"

THE following morning we dressed as requested and made our way to Baytown. Once we reached the city, Danny took a detour around the area to show me where he went to kindergarten and where he and his friends hung out as kids during the long, hot summers. As we headed toward his parents' house, Danny must have noticed that I looked a little anxious.

"You okay, baby?"

"Danny, it has been a hell of a long time since I have been to church. In fact, I can't remember the last time I went to church for anything other than a wedding or a funeral."

"You'll be fine," he said, trying to reassure me. "It's only for an hour or so. Just bow your head when I do and put your hands together when they tell you."

"I said it's been a long time since I have been to church not 'I have never been to church.' I just can't remember the things that you are meant to say back to the priest."

"Pastor," Danny corrected me.

"Or when to take communion."

"No communion. That's Catholic."

"Or how the Hail Mary ends."

"No Hail Marys either," Danny laughed.

"See! I am going to get it all wrong and be shunned."

"Greg, that's Amish!" Danny laughed even harder.

"Fine, but I am leaving the second they bring the snakes out."

As we reached the house, George and Mrs. Taylor were waiting outside for us. Danny had agreed to leave the discussion about the fact that Mrs. Taylor hadn't told Mr. Mayer that he was gay until after I left to return to London. The conversation needed to be had, but since it was only the second time I had met them, I insisted that her second impression of me wasn't as a troublemaker.

Mrs. Taylor barely lifted her hand, presenting it to me like a monarch waiting for her ring to be kissed. Danny, however, got the full welcome treatment with kisses, cuddles, and a joyous face. George, on the other hand, looked happy to see us both and pulled me in when he shook my hand and whispered, "Sorry about last night." I waved my hand as if it was nothing, only to notice Mrs. Taylor looking over Danny's shoulder giving George a look of disapproval, as though he was speaking to an undesirable.

We got into separate vehicles, George and Mrs. Taylor into their SUV, and Danny and I returned to Danny's truck. Since the back of Danny's truck was empty and we had another pair of hands, George had asked if we would pick up some fence posts from the local home improvement superstore on the way back, and we agreed before we all headed out.

After making a couple of turns, Danny looked a little confused. He dialed his mother on his cell phone and spoke to her through the Bluetooth that came through the truck's stereo speakers.

"Momma, where are we going? The church is that way, isn't it?" he asked with his finger pointing toward the exit we just passed.

"We're going to a different church today, dear. I thought since Greg was in town we could go over to Beaumont for a change of scene, and so he can see a little more of the area."

Danny looked at the back of his mother's car. I could see he wanted to protest, but he accepted his mother's excuse without argument. Everyone in both cars knew that we weren't going to their regular church because of my presence. Too many questions would have been asked, and his mother clearly didn't trust me enough not to go skipping down the aisles announcing my penchant for man love.

Once again, I could see Danny was smarting a little, but he remained silent on the subject, not only to protect me from a row with his mother, but also to protect Mrs. Taylor's reputation, even if that meant denying who and what we were.

We followed a stream of cars to the church, where a manicured lawn stretched out in front held a large sign near the road. The message read "Jesus is in your heart," and was spelled out on individual white cards with each letter, in the same way that "Free Cable In Every Room" was advertised outside the local motels.

Generations of families, young and old, gathered outside catching up, all with the most impeccable manners. As I looked around I noticed that there wasn't one person who wasn't smiling or looking bright and cheerful. I wondered whether I was being cynical thinking that this was all an act, or if these people were truly this happy to be there. I remembered when I was a kid I thought of church as a harsh chore for which I was occasionally dragged out of bed on grim and rainy Sundays. But here, with the sun shining and everyone dressed in their Sunday best, it resembled more of a summer tea party social event than a religious duty.

We parked next to George and Mrs. Taylor, who joined us to walk toward the crowd of people, only for Mrs. Taylor to stop and rifle through her handbag as though she had lost or forgotten something. She motioned for us to continue while she and George returned to the car. We were shown into the church and waited by the door for his parents until a man asked us to take our seats as the service was about to begin. The room was almost full, and there was no block of seats that would fit four people together, so we sat at the end of a pew. I turned to see George and Mrs. Taylor enter just as the doors were closing and take two seats across the aisle from us at the back of the church. Her plan of pretending to look for something so that we would be seated separately was executed perfectly.

I had never been to a Southern Baptist church. I had visited and toured mosques in Bahrain and Dubai, temples in Thailand and Kuala Lumpur, synagogues in New York and Paris, as well as countless Catholic churches or cathedrals all over the world, including St Peter's in Vatican City. Throughout my travels these places were more like photo opportunities than anything else, and their architecture was some of the most incredible I had ever seen. I had been inside many of them, obviously never to pray, but to see parts of the culture of wherever I was. I always left a donation at the door as payment, like it was an entrance fee to an attraction where they left it to the visitor to determine how much they wanted to pay for a ticket.

This church, however, was different from any I had ever seen. There was nothing significant about the architecture. Like most of the other structures I had seen in Texas, it was a basic wooden frame, clad on the outside with sheet metal siding that was painted brilliant white. The inside was just as plain, with plaster walls painted a muted shade of beige. There was a single aisle down the middle that led to a slightly elevated stage at the opposite end of the heavy wooden front doors. On either side of the aisle there were wooden pews with small shelves in the back of each that held hymnals. There was no padding on the pews, and after just a few minutes I could feel my rear end falling asleep from the hard wood.

The stage held a simple wooden lectern, on which a bound Bible rested. The stage was flanked on the left by a small old-fashioned piano and on the right by an organ. Behind the lectern, on a slightly raised platform, about fifteen men and women stood in white robes with giant scarlet crosses across the front. I knew they were the choir, but there was something sinister about the way they swayed in unison as the piano played, like they were just a pointed white hat and burning cross away from a Klan rally.

The walls on either side of the pews were adorned with satin banners that looked as though they had been pieced together from scraps leftover from the high school's latest theatrical production. They were stitched together to form the words "Joy," "Faith," "Hope," "Love," and "Praise." Each banner was gilded with glitter and sequins, which only made me wonder why these people had the reputation of hating gay people so much. Surely our love of all things sparkly had to amount to something.

I was drawn from this reverie by the sudden silence. A man walked forward from the rear entrance, stopping to shake hands with whoever was sitting at the end of every other pew. Thankfully, Danny was sitting on the aisle and had to take the man's hand.

"That's the pastor," Danny whispered, but no explanation was necessary. He was the embodiment of every stereotype of a televangelist. In his late forties, he stood about five ten with a stout build. He wore a light grey suit that had probably once been fashionable, but had obviously seen better days. His tie was a silk print of a black background with tiny silver crosses that made a thatched pattern. His hair was styled in a bouffant and looked as though it was held in place by a gallon of lacquer. But it was his smile that stayed with you. It was wide and blinding white, and seemed to concentrate all of its energy on whoever was shaking hands with the pastor. It wasn't fake, but it wasn't quite genuine. It left me with the unsettling feeling that he really might care about the people in his congregation, even though he clearly didn't know them all. I didn't really know what to make of him. I glanced back at Mrs. Taylor, who was eyeing me cautiously, and it was clear she was enjoying my discomfort.

Just as the pastor made his way to the stage, the piano and organ started playing and the choir began singing. Everyone in the pews stood.

"Thanks for the warning," I whispered to Danny. He winked slyly and sang along with the choir to a random hymn that I'd never heard before. I have always enjoyed choir music, and though the surroundings were a little creepy to me, I enjoyed their beautiful voices. By the end of the hymn I was even humming along, much to my chagrin.

At the conclusion of the song, the church took their seats and the pastor introduced himself as "Brother Peter." He welcomed everyone, made a few announcements about plans to expand the church, and led the choir in another hymn, this time without audience participation. This was followed by a twenty-minute sermon, which Brother Peter kept referring to as "the message."

The message this week was about the evils of alcohol and the temptations of modern dance. Brother Peter started his sermon by saying, "Across this great state, in the nightclubs and bars of the cities, young people dance with the Devil." I almost sniggered out loud but managed to stop myself, as I knew that anything I did other than sit there like a good Christian would give Mrs. Taylor cause to berate me.

Danny looked at me and mouthed, "He's talking about you!" My shoulders bounced as I tried to stifle my laughter again. I managed to compose myself by closing my eyes and biting down hard on the side of my finger until the pain took all amusement away. I looked around, marveling at the way the congregation nodded their heads in agreement or occasionally voiced an "Amen!" to show their support. Though the whole point of the message—that we were going to burn in hell for an eternity if we had more than two beers and a boogie—was patently absurd, I was fascinated at how convinced and convincing the pastor was. I began to understand how these charismatic pastors could whip up a following, though it troubled me to see young children of eight or nine years of age hanging on his every word. I watched their rapt attention to the man in the suit and wondered if Danny ever looked the same way at their age.

After the message concluded, we all stood again to sing yet another hymn. We were asked to remain standing as Brother Peter stepped down from the stage and stood at the end of the aisle for "the invitation."

"If any of our brothers or sisters here need guidance, need the love of Jesus, this is the time that I would invite them to come forward," Brother Peter said solemnly. The choir sang in muted voices, and the piano played gently. It was peaceful, but again I felt uncomfortable at the overt show. An elderly man ambled to the front and spoke in hushed whispers to the pastor. There was brief nodding, eyes closed in prayer, muttering lips, then tears slowly falling from the pastor's eyes. It was either the most moving and compassionate display I'd ever witnessed or the most overacted piece of amateur theatre.

The old man slowly returned to his seat, but the singing continued. Brother Peter announced that the offering would now be taken.

"I know times are hard, they're hard for all of us, but if you have a few cents or dollars for Jesus, your fellow church members would appreciate it." Then, from what seemed to be out of thin air, men appeared at the end of the aisles passing large wooden bowls from one end to the other. I started to panic, as I had left my wallet in my bag in the truck, and I knew Mrs. Taylor would be watching me and judging how much I contributed. Thankfully, Danny intervened in time by slipping me a ten dollar bill to place in the bowl.

Once the bowls from the last aisle were collected, there was yet another hymn sung, this time with all of the congregants encouraged to hold hands with the person next to them. I grabbed Danny's hand and that of a slight, but sweet-looking old woman next to me. Danny reached across the aisle and took the hand of a six-year-old boy, who stretched as wide as he could to be included. Even though I didn't have their faith, I could understand the sense of community that these services would bring.

The song ended, we released hands, and Brother Peter thanked everyone for coming before concluding with a prayer for Jesus to fill the souls of all those present and to watch over them in the coming week until God could bring them together once more. I don't think my soul felt any fuller, but the whole experience hadn't been as bad as I had thought it was going to be. We were just turning toward the door when the little old lady whose hand I had held during the last hymn tapped me on the shoulder. I turned to see her kind face looking up at me. She held my hands together, raised herself up onto her toes, and gave me a simple peck on the cheek before grabbing her bag and shuffling out. I was confused, but Danny was beaming. At least I had won over one local.

As we joined up outside, Mrs. Taylor suddenly smiled at me—a huge smile that for a moment I took as genuine warmth, until I saw she wasn't looking directly at me. I looked over my shoulder to see a small older woman around sixty years old hobbling faster than her hunched posture should have allowed her to. She wore a bright pink suit and skirt, with a matching large brimmed hat, a white frilly blouse that matched the petticoat that peeked out from under her dress, and a large, gaudy glass broach of a yellow rose pinned to her lapel. Mrs. Taylor ushered us back to the truck and told us to meet them back at the house, tapping on the window in farewell and attempting to hurry us along.

I lowered the window of the truck just in time to hear, "Vivien! Puh-rayz Jee-zus! What are you doing here?" The old woman was flagging Mrs. Taylor down with an old arthritic hand holding a long lit cigarette.

"Mrs. Anderson! We were, just, um, visiting Tammy and working at the food bank this morning. But we couldn't miss church altogether, so we decided to come to one a little closer to my daughter's house here in Beaumont."

Danny was watching this scene too, as we were only crawling out of the car park in the truck because of the volume of people attempting to leave at once.

"Now, Vivien, tell me, are you heading back to Baytown now?" the old woman asked.

"Yes, yes. We're going straight home. Lots to do today. But it was lovely to see you!" Mrs. Taylor said, making it obvious that she couldn't get away fast enough.

"Puh-rayz Jee-zus, I thought I was gonna have to get the bus. Could I get a ride back with you, please? My dear sister has been so ill recently, and I had to stay over here until her daughter arrived this morning." She threw her hands up in the air. "I damn near missed church, myself!" Without waiting for agreement from Mrs. Taylor, she opened the back of the SUV and climbed in with all the expertise of an old Texan girl.

"WHO was that, and why did your mum want us gone so quickly?" I asked Danny as I checked behind the truck to ensure that Mrs. Taylor wasn't too close behind. I opened the window and lit the cigarette that I had bargained with Danny I could have as a prize for making it through the church service.

"That was Mrs. Anderson, Mom and Dad's neighbor. She's another person I haven't seen in a long time, though by the look of her she hasn't changed at all."

"And the hurrying along?" I asked.

94

"She tends to talk."

"She talks a lot, or she gossips?"

"Both," Danny said

As we told George we would, we drove to the local home improvement superstore and wandered around looking for the fence posts. Among the big, burly workmen, small Hispanic laborers, and families whose children used the shopping carts like go-carts, Danny stopped frequently and asked my opinion on different types of appliances, lighting fixtures, and even garden furniture.

"You like this, don't you?" I asked, nudging him as we walked.

"Of course I do. I can't wait to set up a home with you. Maybe even have a couple of those." Danny pointed to a cart that held an infant who was looking around like he was in Oz.

"Dammit, I thought you were pointing to the workmen."

Danny playfully chastised me with his eyes.

"You'll make a great dad," he said.

"You think?"

"I do. So long as you are the one who teaches them how to talk. I want a kid with a British accent."

"Why on earth do you want a kid who speaks in a British accent?" I laughed.

"One too many Disney films as a kid, I guess. I think they sound cute."

"Great, I will make sure they're fluent in chimney-sweep."

We arrived back at Danny's parents' house and got out of the truck to unload the posts. George came out of the front door and hurried toward us.

"It's okay, George. We got this," I said as I slid the first post out and waited for Danny to take the other end.

George leaned in and whispered, "Leave that for a minute, Greg, Mrs. Anderson is inside. She saw y'all leaving the church and insisted on coming over to see Danny."

We followed George back to the house and into the living room, where Mrs. Anderson sat on the sofa, her legs crossed to one side like a girl in an etiquette class. She rose to her feet at the sight of Danny, who stood at least a foot and a half taller than her.

"There he is!" She reached up like a small child signaling that she wanted to be picked up. Danny stooped down and gently hugged her.

Mrs. Taylor stood by the window watching with a nervous look on her face. She was obviously stationed as a lookout, as the net curtains had been disturbed and hadn't been re-adjusted.

"Now, stand back and let me look at you, boy," Mrs. Anderson said, patting Danny's chest as if to push him away so she could take all of him in. "Oh, puh-rayz Jee-zus! Look at you, all growed up. Oh, Vivien, he has become a fine lookin' man."

She spun around with the same agility I saw as she climbed into the SUV. "And you must be Danny's friend, Greg. Why, I do declare, you are just as fine lookin' as any prince I evah saw! Vivien tells me you're visiting. How long are y'all here for?"

"I'm only here for a few more days before I go back to England."

"Well, I hope y'all get to see ev'rythin' here. It's a shame you're not here to see the blue baw-nets. They are so pur-dee when they come out."

"That is a shame," I said, with no idea of what she was talking about.

"Now, Vivien tells me that you two met when Danny was out fightin' in the war. So that was Eye-rackee? No, Sow-dee Rabia? Oh, puh-rayz Jee-zus, I forgit the name."

"Bahrain, ma'am," Danny corrected her, rolling the *r* in the accent in which it was correctly pronounced.

Mrs. Anderson playfully slapped Danny's chest. "Now you stop that, ya hear? You sound like one of them there sand niggers!"

I didn't know where to place myself. If I hadn't seen it with my own two eyes I would never have believed that such a character existed outside of *The Color Purple*.

Mrs. Anderson turned back to me. "Now you boys, you bee-yoo-dee-full Briddish boys, you came out and you fought with us." She raised her fist in exclamation. "You helped us when we were attacked by the Telli-ben! Oh, puh-rayz Jee-zus, you boys were with us all the way!" She was elderly, but the old pioneer spirit and attitude was alive and well in her expressions.

Even though she was racist, and I expect a little senile, I didn't have the heart to tell her that I was serving tea and coffee while other men were putting their lives on the line. But Mrs. Taylor wasn't letting her think otherwise either.

"I see your Momma ev'ry day at church. She is just so proud of you. Hell, we're all proud of you, puh-rayz Jee-zus!" she said, turning back to Danny.

I studied Mrs. Taylor for a moment. She was proud, but also seemed alarmed. She loved that her son was being told about how much she spoke of him and in what high regard he was held, but she could also see I was a potential bombshell. Separating us, Mrs. Taylor insisted that Danny sit on the sofa with Mrs. Anderson so they could catch up, relying on Danny to play the game. I, on the other hand, was instructed to sit with her on the other side of the room. All the time Mrs. Anderson was around, Mrs. Taylor fussed over me and kept me in conversation about everything from the correct way to cook barbecue to stories of how things had changed in Baytown since she was a young girl. I would have found her quite engaging if she hadn't been looking over my shoulder after every other sentence. I turned and saw Danny looking over at us, happy to see us chatting away like two old friends. But I knew his mother was desperate for me not to talk to or join in any conversation with Mrs. Anderson, as I could blow her cover.

Once Mrs. Anderson left, the atmosphere changed almost immediately. Anytime I began to talk, Mrs. Taylor spoke over me, starting a new topic of conversation. If Danny asked my opinion on something, she again sliced through my words with her own opinion, even if it matched my own. Danny didn't seem to notice and seemed to relish the appearance of Mrs. Taylor agreeing with me.

George requested help moving the fence posts from the truck to the backyard. I welcomed the opportunity of a change of scene, even if it was only a few feet away. But Danny had other ideas and insisted I stay in the kitchen with his mother, probably because he wanted to encourage what he believed to be a happy turning point of his mother's acceptance of me.

Alone for the first time with her, I waited for the first shot. I didn't know what shape the bullet would take, but I knew it was going to be fired.

"Would you like a drink, Greg?" she asked. Her voice wasn't harsh, but it wasn't friendly either.

"That would be great, thanks."

Mrs. Taylor walked over to the fridge and pulled out a can of cola. Silently, she poured out barely three inches into the glass and filled the rest with ice cubes, so by the time she delivered it to me it had already changed color from dark brown to something that resembled watered down tea.

"It's a company that stuffs animals that people have hunted," she said as she saw me looking at an advert on the back of a magazine that was on the kitchen table. "They skin them and mount them on plaques or stands."

She saw me grimace. "You don't like that sort of thing, Greg?"

"No, it turns my stomach. I don't understand why anyone would want a trophy like that, and the idea of skinning an animal myself, even for food, revolts me." I had already scanned the room to be sure there were no such objects in the home.

"Well, this is Texas."

We sat in silence for a minute before Mrs. Taylor spoke again.

"The church doesn't know about Danny," she began, sitting upright at the table with her hands clasped together so her fingers interlinked.

"Okay," I said simply, not really knowing whether she was making the statement to inform me, or for me to question.

"Do you know why they don't know?"

"Well, I understand that you work at the church and the church has its own position about our type of relationship. I understand that you would perhaps be more secretive about it in order to protect Danny." I said it kindly, making an effort to let her know that I understood the situation in the hopes that she might be less harsh on me and give me a break.

"Were you raised a Christian, Greg? Do you know that Jesus died for our sins?"

I tried to choose my words as carefully as I could, but I wouldn't lie to her. I felt like my attempt to show her a bit of understanding had backfired, and I was now being led into some kind of ambush. In that moment it became more about principle, but I still wanted to keep the peace.

"I believe that what Jesus said and what he preached are good templates on how to live a good life."

"You know that the Bible says that being gay is a sin."

"I think I have read that somewhere," I said jokingly, trying to break the atmosphere.

"Have you accepted God into your heart? Do you even believe in God?"

"I am not too sure what I believe, to be honest with you, Mrs. Taylor. I believe that someone named Jesus existed and that he taught love and peace."

"You haven't answered my question, Greg."

"I am undecided. I find too many questions unanswered to believe."

"So you have no faith?"

"Let me put it this way: I am not a bad person, so if there is a god I would hope that he would judge me on what I do and who I am, as against someone that does believe but still doesn't live a good life."

She studied me for a moment. "You know that God doesn't condone your lifestyle," she said, and at that moment I saw a trace of sadness on her face. "I have forgiven Danny for this, but I will not forgive you if he loses his faith."

"Excuse me?" My heart started racing with rage. "You forgive him? Forgive him for what? And what is it that you think I am going to do to him that will make him lose his faith?"

"I have long accepted that Danny is gay—"

"Yes, that's evident by the way you tried to marry him off to a Laura Ingles last night," I interrupted and was ignored.

"—but I believe that any sins that he may commit will be far outnumbered by the many great things he is destined for and the love that he has in his heart. I do not judge Danny—"

"No, it doesn't sound like it," I interrupted again, my voice rasping with sarcasm. "You so obviously accept him for who he is."

"He is my only son, and I love him with all of my heart, and I will not lose him to a nonbeliever who will take him to the other side of the world and turn him into something he's not."

I laughed with disbelief. "I don't understand why you are saying this to me, Mrs. Taylor. First of all, Danny is one of the most intelligent people I know. There is no way that I or anyone could convince or persuade him to be something—" I raised my eyebrows to deliberately indicate her. "—or become someone that he's not."

"When the Christians set sail on the *Mayflower* from Britain it was because they were being persecuted—"

"Seriously? You think this is the same thing?"

"I think there's a good chance that you have been sent here to test my son. Your smooth British accent may fool some, but it doesn't fool me. You may have charmed Danny, but I have met people like you before, Greg, and I will be keeping my eye on you."

"People like me? You barely know me! How have you developed such an opinion of me, and who is it that you think 'sent' me?"

"My son has told me a great deal about you and some of the things that you have spoken about. You seem to live a carefree lifestyle and have a very dark-sided sense of humor."

"That doesn't make me evil, Mrs. Taylor."

"I will be the judge of that, Greg."

Mrs. Taylor's haughty face disappeared in an instant and turned into a smile. I turned to see Danny walking into the kitchen.

"Everything okay?" he asked

"Of course! Greg and I were just getting to know each other a little better." She smiled in my direction as if she had just made a new best friend. "Daniel, dear, are you looking for a drink? You sit down and let your momma get it for you."

Danny took her seat at the table and beamed at me. He seemed so excited that his mother and I were getting along. I decided to go along with the façade so Danny would stay in the room longer and not leave me to have yet another uncomfortable conversation. Mrs. Taylor emptied the remains of the nearly full can of Coke into a glass and added just a couple of ice cubes and passed it to her son.

"Take a drink out to your dad too. With Greg's help you boys should be finished in no time," she said, indicating that she had no intention of being left in the room on her own with me again.

After unloading the rest of the posts into the backyard, Danny and I were ready to leave and head back to Austin. Leaving the house, Mrs. Taylor said her good-byes to me in a cheery tone the moment Danny turned to hug his dad, giving him the impression that she was hugging me at the same time, he just couldn't see it. The truth was, she was staring directly at the ground while she said, "It really was so lovely to see you again, Greg!" in a chipper voice.

As I turned to shake George's hand, he put his arms up and hugged me the same way he had embraced his son. I felt an overwhelming urge to thank him for the gesture, but also to apologize to him, because I knew the moment they closed the door Mrs. Taylor would punish him for it.

On the drive back to Austin, I struggled with whether or not to tell Danny about the conversation I had with his mother. He seemed so happy that we had "gotten along" so well that it seemed cruel to rob him of it. If I were to say something to Danny about her grilling me, I would look like the bad guy causing trouble, especially after her stellar performance on the doorstep as we left. I wondered whether this had been her intention all along.

For the rest of the journey no mention was made of the awkwardness of the dinner the night before, other than Danny shifting all of the blame for the setup onto Mr. Mayer's shoulders, which I thought was either a tad naïve or too generous a benefit of doubt to give his mother, especially since she had not informed Mr. Mayer of Danny's current relationship. Instead, Danny spoke with joy as he recounted his youth and the things that they did as a family together. Most of these tales revolved around his mother's actions or sense of humor. Listening to the stories, I thought I would have liked the woman he described. She actually seemed like my kind of person. But, as it was, I had never met this past personality, only the one that made me feel like I was some kind of obstacle to overcome.

CHAPTER NINE

"I DON'T understand why they are doing the interviews when you're only in your second year of law school," I said to Danny over the webcam. It was 3:00 a.m. and I was at home in Brighton, jetlagged after a flight from Thailand. I looked at my handsome man and the fully grown sandy dog that was flopped in his arms as though he was still a puppy.

"The law firms come to the university campus and set up interviews so they can have their pick of students. Then, if they like you, they interview you in their own offices a few weeks later, wherever that may be in the country. If you're successful, they'll offer you a job as a summer associate during the months between the second and third years of law school. If you prove your abilities while you're there, they extend it to a formal offer to start fulltime work after graduation."

"Have you looked at the firms that may be of interest to you?"

"Yep, most of them are coming in from New York."

"Are you nervous? It must have been a long time since you went for a job interview."

"No, not really. They'll be interviewing me, but at the same time I'll be interviewing them. They want the students with the best experience and the best grades, so they'll be trying to impress me as much as I'll be trying to impress them."

"Well, you're at the top of your class, so I dare say you'll be in demand."

"I'm not really thinking about it at the moment, to be honest. The only thing I'm thinking about is seeing you."

"You'll be here in England in less than two weeks."

"I know. I can't wait!"

The two-week wait couldn't have ended quickly enough for me. This time it had seemed like an eternity since I had been with Danny physically. We had spent the past few months apart, since his study schedule, exams, and Reserve duty had kept him constantly busy. Almost all of my flight schedules seemed to go east, not allowing me to even steal a few days with him as I had managed to do when I was in the States. On these occasional but precious trips, we had no more than a couple of days together, but we made the most of them, knowing that his two week trip to England was still some time away.

Because of the time difference and his school attendance, most of our time together was spent over the webcam in the evening or in the early hours of the morning. Danny would e-mail me an electronic version of his study cards, each with a question and answer on opposite sides, and I would quiz him for hours on end. At the time it seemed like a pointless exercise, since Danny never once got one wrong. I found it unbelievable how much knowledge he could retain, and I accused him on several occasions of having the answers on a board out of sight of the webcam. But it made me feel like I was helping him in some way, which made every moment worth it.

The only times that Danny and I ever argued during these chats were when he elected to join the Capital Punishment clinic to gain more experience and earn credit toward his degree. Most of his time was spent working on an appeal for a convict who was on death row after being found guilty of the torturous rape and murder of a young girl. Even though Danny was working on the appeal, and looked at the case with an eye toward educating himself on the various legal implications of the death penalty, he still maintained that he believed that it was the right punishment to hand out—a view that he shared with the rest of his family.

The idea of Danny meeting this man chilled me to the bone, but the debate on whether he should die for his crimes continued for weeks. Since the death penalty hadn't existed in Britain during my lifetime, it was hard for me to comprehend the idea of it being as entirely acceptable as it was to him. Most of my arguments against it were hammered back by Danny simply saying "an eye for an eye" in a tone that echoed his mother's religious voice. This led to discussions about abortion and Danny's pro-choice views, which seemed to render the biblical punishment null and void. Tucker often appeared on the screen to side with his roommate and throw even more related topics onto the fire. By the end of one particular discussion, I summed up their views back to them.

"So, the loss of innocent lives in war is not considered 'murder', but rather the regrettable outcome of retaliation of threat or attack on innocent lives. Abortion is not considered 'murder' because it's the woman's body and her choice, and the fetus is not 'legally' deemed a life in the early stages of gestation. Hunting and shooting deer or any other animal is not 'murder', since they are just animals and we are carnivores and they exist for us to eat, not taking into account that many people do it purely for sport and to get their jollies. But if you shoot someone in the street and they die, that is considered 'murder'. And when you put that person into an electric chair and flip the switch, that isn't 'murder', it's just punishment. Have I got all that right?"

"Yep!" they said in unison.

It's not that I didn't agree with some of their views. What bothered me was that they seemed so unfazed by the contradictions. I, like most people, struggle with my views on such topics, but I at least acknowledge that they don't make sense and openly admit it. Danny and Tucker seemed not only to consider their principles completely separate from one debate to another, but refused to acknowledge that their moral high ground on one subject cut square across another. I wondered whether being this opinionated and strong willed to the point of pigheadedness was more of a Texan trait, or whether I was being excessively British by calmly pointing it out to them.

AN UNUSUALLY warm end of spring had arrived in Brighton, and at long last, so had Danny. We had two weeks together planned and arranged with military precision, the first two days of which were struck off the list almost immediately, as we spent them together in bed in my flat in Kemptown. I met him at the airport with a "Welcome to England" sign and a lukewarm steak and kidney pie that I picked up from the local petrol station just outside Heathrow. He smiled at the sign and then pretended to vomit at the sight of the pie, which I held up toward his mouth as a form of punishment for mocking British food for so long.

On our first day out, we walked along the shingle beach and the promenade that leads toward Brighton Pier. I laughed at every little thing that he noticed that I had taken for granted and had been blind to for so long. Since it was only late spring, the area was full of Brightonians, as opposed to the usual swarm of tourists that flock to the beach every year from around the country and the thousands of French students who all seem to arrive on the same day at the beginning of summer.

Among the locals, Danny's accent seemed magnified ten times and was so much more noticeable to me. It had been over two years since we'd met, and I simply didn't hear it anymore. But now, in between the posh accents of Hove and the Deans, the more common accents of Brighton and the occasional cockney throwback from London, Danny sounded as if he was from the Wild West.

We walked onto the pier together, where we stopped by a small concession selling seafood. I bought a small cup of cockles and drenched them in vinegar.

"Have a taste. They're good!" I said as I handed him the cup and a wooden toothpick, the traditional eating utensil for the dish. Danny shook his head and clamped his lips together. "Come on now, you made me eat fried chicken neck and God-knows-what other stuff in Texas and I didn't complain. Come on, it's only a cockle. Be adventurous!"

"What the hell are they? They look like tiny human organs," Danny said with a disgusted look on his face.

"They are kind of like baby clams, but blue, and meatier." He dangled a cockle from the end of the toothpick and inspected it warily.

He almost looked like a caveman testing a new fruit for poison as he stuck out the tip of his tongue to take the smallest taste, then yanked it back like it had attacked him.

"That's just the vinegar," I laughed. "Just eat the damn things. They're not going to kill you."

Danny slid the cockle off the toothpick, popped it in his mouth, and began to chew. After just the second clamp of his jaw he spat it out over the side of the pier into the sea and wiped his now fully extended tongue with the back of his hand.

"How the hell do you eat that crap? It tastes rank and it's full of sand!"

I speared five cockles and munched on them. I opened my mouth, exposing the mush. "Come on… gimme a kiss!"

Clearly unimpressed with seaside cuisine, Danny sprinted down the decking of the pier to escape me, as if I had just pulled the pin of a grenade with my teeth.

Since the weather was fine, we boarded an open-top bus that took us on a tour of the city, including the West Pier, the Lanes, Hove, Brighton Marina, and the Royal Pavilion. As the tour guide's voice came out of the speakers of the bus, informing us of the history of each landmark or attraction, Danny added his own running commentary. He had read up on the area and taken so much interest in where I lived that he had more knowledge of the history of the city than I did. I felt slightly ashamed but more than comfortably loved.

The one place that I had never told Danny about was Devil's Dyke, which was a fifteen-minute drive outside the city at the top of the downs. The view around the isolated pub that sat atop the highest hill was possibly the best in the whole of Sussex, as it overlooked the rolling farmlands and countryside and ended with a panoramic view of the city that edged onto the English Channel.

I ordered a pint of cider for each of us and took them outside, and we sat on the grass, taking in the scenery.

"This is what I imagined Britain to be like," Danny said, taking his first sip of Scrumpy Jack and smacking his lips together in appreciation. "It really is very beautiful. Very Jane Austen."

"It's a veritable banquet of delights to the eyes, my dear. Yes, most diverting from the education and pursuit of the title of 'an accomplished gentleman'."

"You are so gay." He took another sip of cider. "It is so good to be away from law school for a while."

"Sir, please do not be sour that you must toil for your title of 'esquire' whilst I was bestowed it at birth."

Danny laughed and nuzzled closer into me, raising his glass in a toast.

"This is the Britain that I know. Can you see why I commented how flat Texas seemed to me? I grew up exploring these downs, building camps and tree houses with my brother in woods. We always lived near the sea, but it was so exciting when we actually went to the beach in the summer, as it meant that the weather was warm enough that you could explore the rock pools and actually go into the water without suffering hypothermia."

"So, two weeks a year then, huh?"

"It's not that bad! I always remember the school summer holidays lasting forever back then, and along with it the sunny weather. On the odd occasion that Mum and Dad got the day off work together during the week, they would bring us down to the seafront with Lilos, towels, a windbreaker, and buckets and spades—"

"But there isn't any sand!"

"No, but when the tide goes out a little further along the coast it becomes sandy. It may be wet sand, but that just makes it easier to build castles!"

The memory brought my father to mind. "At the end of the day we would all wrap ourselves in towels, sitting on the beach and trying to keep warm, desperately getting the last ounce of sunshine out of the day. Natalie would shiver with long, damp hair; Craig would pick knots out of his, which curled in saltwater like he'd had rollers in all day. I would be cold, too, but none of us wanted to leave. Dad would disappear and come back a few minutes later with cans of pop and white polystyrene cups of cockles or winkles." I took a sip of cider and smiled at the thought. "Somehow we always managed to find a pin or a badge somewhere in Mum's purse or Dad's car to get the winkles out of their shells."

"Winkles?"

"Don't ask. The summers here are fantastic. I miss home so much when I am away during the summer that coming back after a trip is almost like a reward now. I love my job, but sometimes I crave the comfort of being in just one place that I know and somewhere I call home."

"You know, I could always move to England. I can take the Qualified Lawyers Transfer Test and start practicing here. It's not too difficult since most US law is based on old British common law anyway. I can just imagine us here and Duke running across these hills."

"What about New York? You have to admit it would be amazing experience for you."

"It would be, but I want you to know that I would move to England in a heartbeat if it's something you truly wanted. I would move to the moon for you."

I leaned over and pecked him on the cheek. "I know, and I do appreciate it, but let's get you finished at law school before we figure all that out."

The following afternoon after a lazy morning in bed together, we made our first trip to the supermarket. As we walked down the aisles, I watched Danny as he stopped at almost every box, package, or sleeve of food, examining them as if they were of alien origin. He had traveled a lot in the past with the Navy, and I could imagine him conducting the same inspection in any other country around the world. He smiled politely to everyone we passed, some of whom smiled back, some of whom looked at him with suspicion. Finally he found a brand that he recognized and held it high. "See? You Brits do love the Americans!" And I suppose in cookie love, we do.

As I transferred the food from the cart onto the belt at the checkout for the girl to scan through, Danny stood beside me and inspected the chocolate and gum. By the time I noticed, the food had piled up at the end of the counter and was beginning to resemble a primary school harvest festival. Danny looked puzzled at the mounting boxes and vegetables before I nudged him and whispered, "We Brits enjoy packing our own shopping. We don't have bagboys to do it for us."

Excited, like he was experiencing yet another brand new aspect of my culture, he ran down and began piling things into carrier bags as if he was playing Tetris with our groceries, happier than a happy thing on a happy day.

Back at the flat I had a brief glimpse into what life would be like in England with him. He unpacked the bags and put food in the fridge and cupboards and emptied the dishwasher. He looked so handsome and relaxed, but above all he looked like he was home. Our lives when we were together had revolved so often around other people and their plans that this was one of the first times we felt like a regular private couple at home.

The following afternoon we drove over to see Mum and Natalie. On the way over I took Danny on a brief tour of the neighborhood where I grew up, the local park where I rode my Grifter bike as a kid, and the primary and high school that I attended. We also passed the cemetery where Dad was buried, which I pointed out as we drove by.

"Hey, why don't we go and get some flowers?" Danny suggested as he twisted around, following the entrance gates of the cemetery with his eyes. "I know I never got a chance to meet him, but I would like to pay my respects since he's your dad."

"Maybe next time, Tiger," I said, appreciating the gesture but hoping he wouldn't continue.

"It wouldn't take too long. We passed a florist a little farther back. Turn the car around and we'll go get some. I'm sure your mum will understand if we're a few minutes late."

"No," I said a little too abruptly.

"Oh. Okay. It was just a thought. Sorry."

"Danny, I will be honest with you, I have only visited Dad's grave once, about a fortnight after we buried him."

Danny looked puzzled.

"I went up there on what would have been his fifty-eighth birthday. I started talking out loud to his headstone as though he could hear me, wishing him happy birthday and telling him everything that had happened with Mum and the rest of the family since he died."

"That's understandable," Danny said, resting his hand on my leg and giving it a little squeeze.

"A couple of people walked past and heard me talking. I was so embarrassed I stopped speaking. Two minutes later I felt guilty that I felt embarrassed and ashamed that I let two strangers make me feel that way for chatting to my dad. I just thought if there was anywhere in the world that he would be able to hear me, it was there."

"I am sure he could," Danny said kindly.

"Anyway, that I could cope with, but afterward I sat on the grass next to his grave and just stared at it. Before long, horrific images of how his face would look after two weeks underground flashed through my head. I didn't want to think about it, but I just couldn't help it. It upset me so much that I never went up there again."

Danny squeezed my leg again.

"Now I tend to just talk out loud to him wherever I am, whether I'm in the car or at home. I don't think of his last days or funeral so much anymore, but they still creep in. I find it easier to cope with when I concentrate on the good times."

MY BROTHER Craig traveled down from Epsom, Surrey, where he lived with his family. He had thrown his seven kids in the mini bus that doubled as family transport and headed down to meet Danny at the same time as Mum and Natalie. His wife, Diane, was left alone with a house full of blissful silence, giving her a much-needed respite from the children.

I knew Danny was slightly nervous, as he complained that he had a lot to live up to after the glowing raves and reviews I had given him. But like a plaster that had been left on too long, I dealt with it with one good yank. I hadn't told any of the family of Mrs. Taylor's reaction to me, as I believed, as with most parents, Mum would only jump to my defense and not give Danny a chance. I hadn't mentioned it to my brother or sister, as they were still in defense mode when it came to anyone in the family since Dad died. I was eager for them to make their own decision based on Danny being himself. Besides, Craig was the type of person who would have said "What the fuck is the deal with your mother, mate?" while shaking Danny's hand for the first time.

We pulled into the driveway of the house and were greeted by a swarm of nephews and nieces running over and hugging me. Their little faces spied Danny, and at first they kept their distance, but the second they heard his accent their faces lit up like they had just communicated for the first time with a friendly monster or alien. Up to that point, none of my brother's seven, or my sister's two, kids had met a boyfriend of mine, although they knew I was gay, as from an early age they were told by Craig that "Uncle Greg likes boys and thinks girls are yucky."

Mum and Natalie were in the kitchen alone, as Natalie's husband, John, was at work, and Craig had gone out to get the nine children some sweets to keep them quiet for our visit. Craig was very much of the opinion that children, in company, should be seen and not heard and had prepared for this by buying the latest Disney DVD. Ever since Dad died I had heard his voice come out of my brother's mouth so many times that, on occasion, I looked around to see if Dad was in the room with us. Even the expressions on Craig's face mirrored Dad when he was telling off or praising the kids.

Danny took a deep breath and followed me into the kitchen. He carried with him a bag containing Kool-Aid, Whitman's chocolates, Twinkies, and Ding Dongs on my advice, as Mum requested them every time I went to the States on work trips.

"Well, this is him!" I said as I walked through and presented Danny.

Mum's face broke into a wide smile, and she rushed over to him. She clasped her two hands around the side of his ears and pulled him down to plant a kiss on his cheek before giving him a hug. Natalie followed suit after Mum released him.

"Danny, it's so nice to finally meet you!" she exclaimed before looking him up and down and adding, "You're right, Greggy, he is a handsome chap!"

"It's great to finally meet you too, Mrs. Stephens!" Danny said as he was ushered onto a stool.

"Mrs. Stephens? Don't be daft! I'm Angela," she corrected him quickly over Natalie's laugh. "How was your flight over? Have you settled in okay at Greg's place?"

"Yes, ma'am. I love what I've seen so far."

Mum chuckled and turned to Natalie who continued to laugh. It had been a long time since anyone had called her "ma'am."

"Craig will be back in a minute. He has just nipped down to the shops," Natalie said, walking over and flipping the switch on the electric kettle. "Can I get you a cup of tea?"

"I would love one, thank you. I have been here for days, and Greg hasn't made me a proper cup of English tea yet." Danny looked at my mum as if this absence of care was typical of me.

"Jesus, Danny, all I do is make tea all damn day at work. The last thing I want is to do it when I am at home," I joked as Mum slapped my arm at my apparent rudeness.

"How's law school going, Danny? Greg has told us all about your studies. Is it as hard as it sounds?" Natalie asked.

"It's okay. It's taken some getting used to, but I'm in my second year so I only have one more to go."

"You're in the Navy too, aren't you?" Mum said as she pulled open a tin of biscuits and offered them to Danny.

"Yes, ma'am," he replied, though I don't think he realized how much pride came out in his voice.

I knew what was coming. Mum had recently taken to talking about Dad at every opportunity. For the first year of heavy grief, the mention of his name upset her so much that it was to be avoided, even if it was a happy memory. Now she spoke of him constantly, even to us kids, as if we had never known him. Each time I'd seen Mum in recent months, she told me what Dad would have made of the weather, what news in the papers would have made him angry, what programs on TV would have made him laugh, even what his opinions would have been on sports events that I knew she never followed. On the odd occasion, I disagreed with her and argued that she may have gotten it wrong. I wasn't being unkind, but rather proving to her that I hadn't forgotten exactly what he was like, which is what I think she feared the most.

"Greg's dad was in the Royal Navy," she said. "Hang on, I will just go and get a photo of him." With this, she disappeared from the room.

Danny, of course, had seen many photos of Dad, most recently the ones that were framed on my mantelpiece at the flat. But I didn't have the heart to tell Mum, as I knew that showing a static image of Dad was the closest she could get to actually introducing him to Danny.

Just as Mum went out of the room I heard the front door slam shut.

"Right, you little buggers, here's your sweets, and here's your DVD. Now sit down and shuddup!" Craig shouted to his and Natalie's kids in the same playful, harsh gruff voice that Dad used to use.

He walked into the doorway, stopped, folded his arms, and stared at Danny like a defiant convict in a courtroom who had nothing but contempt for the judge.

"So, you're the guy that's messing around with my little brother, huh?" He may have stood the same height as Danny, but with his shaved head and laborer's build, he could look quite intimidating if he wanted to. "I hope you haven't told my kids what you're doing to their uncle." He spoke with a mixture of a sneer and revulsion.

Before Danny could take the stunned look off his face, Craig marched forward, his hand extended. "Only kidding, mate," he said, obviously pleased that his introduction had gone the way he'd planned. "Nice to meet ya!"

Danny raised his hand but still looked slightly wary. This surprised me, considering some of the men that he worked with in the Navy. If nothing else, Danny knew how to stand his ground.

"I could barely hear you as I walked in the door. You're a hell of a lot quieter than the usual Americans. I was stuck in the London

Underground with a load of them the other day. They were shouting and screaming at each other. They were so loud they sounded like they were in the Channel Tunnel and needed rescuing."

Danny looked at Craig, expressionless.

"Crazy fuckin' Yanks," Craig said absentmindedly as he went to the fridge and pulled out a bottle of water.

Danny, who was yet to speak, brought himself up to his full height and, standing tall, he faced Craig head on. "You know I am one of those 'Yanks', don't you, Craig?" Danny spoke in the same authoritative tone I heard him use with enlisted men at the naval base. "I am proud to be an American and don't appreciate people speaking disrespectfully of the people in the homeland for which I fought." Danny took one step closer and almost squared up to Craig, whose eyes darted between Danny and me, hoping for some reaction. "I may be in your sister's home, but don't think I will put up with your attitude. I am your brother's partner, and I am due a little respect."

Craig now studied Danny, a little dumbstruck. After four painfully long seconds, Danny said, "Only kidding, mate!" Danny slapped Craig's shoulder playfully.

"Well done, Danny," Craig said, finally smiling and shaking his head. He jabbed his thumb in my direction. "I can see why you're with this wanker."

Mum came back in with the photos of Dad and started going through them. She kept them in a metal box that locked with a rubber seal, fearing they could be damaged in the event of fire or flood. This was despite the fact that I had scanned them all and put the images on three separate disks that Natalie, Craig, and I each kept at our own homes, for fear of earthquakes. She found her favorite picture and passed it to Danny, who held it carefully at the corners.

"This is Derik. Doesn't he look handsome in his uniform?"

"Very," Danny said kindly, "I can see the resemblance in Greg and Craig."

"Really?" I asked, in mock surprise. "I have always thought that Craig looked much more like the man who drove the ice cream truck."

Mum slapped my arm again.

"Oh, Mum, we all see the look you get when you hear that music. You start sweating and are out the door quicker than the kids!" Natalie teased.

Mum took the photo back from Danny and stroked it with the back of her hand. "From what Greggy has told me, the two of you would have gotten on really well."

All Danny could do was smile and nod in agreement.

My eldest niece, Elizabeth, who turned fourteen that month, came through the kitchen trailing her angelic, blond-haired little brother behind her by his hand. Josh was four years old and had been diagnosed with autism just a few months previously, which wasn't too great a shock, as there had been signs that his development was running in a different direction to that of the other children.

"Danny, this is Joshy," I introduced the little man, who was looking in any other direction than Danny's. He had been painfully shy around strangers ever since he was a small toddler, and the look of anxiousness on his face could easily be mistaken for terror.

Craig walked over and scooped him up in his arms and nuzzled into his face. "You all right, son? You want to say hello to your Uncle Danny?"

Josh finally looked over and, shocking us all, he raised his arms out to be taken by Danny onto his lap where he sat and played with the collars of Danny's shirt, looking perfectly happy. Danny, after being bestowed the title of "uncle," beamed at him while Craig stood back in awe at how well his son had taken to him.

"How far away are you from Dallas?" Mum asked as she made another cup of tea. "We used to watch that show all of the time. It was one of Greggy's favorites."

Danny winked at me. He knew that I was mentally picturing Bobby Ewing riding bareback across Southfork Ranch with an opened shirt.

"Well, at the moment, I'm in Austin, which is about three hours from Dallas. But I grew up in a town called Baytown."

"Do you like it in Austin?" Natalie asked. "What's it like?"

"Well, out of the whole of Texas it's probably the most liberal."

"Your mum must be so proud of you, going to law school. She must be thrilled!" said Mum.

"And is there something wrong with being an air steward?" I asked in mock anger. "Are you saying you're not proud of me because I'm not a lawyer and only serve beef or chicken for a living?"

"No, Greg, she's not proud of you because you sleep with men and haven't given her any grandchildren," Craig chimed in.

"Well, it's not like you haven't made up for it, is it?"

Craig hunched his shoulders and put his balled fists together. "That's because I am a real man! Grrrrrr!"

"Craig, I am off to Barbados for a week a couple of days after Danny heads home. Do you want me to get a cheap ticket on my concessions so you can…. Oh, no, sorry, you can't, can you? You have to work and look after your army of kids, don't you? It's a shame. I know all of those twenty-year-old air stewardesses would love you. They are forever asking me if I have a straight brother." I exaggerated a sigh. "They get so lonesome in their hotel rooms after a day of tanning their perky little breasts and going to the gym to tone up their petite little bodies."

"I hate you."

"I know," I said simply.

"Do you have a big family, Danny?" Natalie asked, trying to steer away from the battle of sarcasm that we all knew would only get worse.

"I have two older sisters, and Mom and Dad. My grandmother was one of six girls, and my mother is one of five girls, so we have a pretty large number on her side. I was the first boy to be born to her line in sixty years, so they're a bit overprotective of me."

"Danny is a mama's boy," I teased.

"You're a fine one to talk, old golden balls over here," Craig said pointing at me. "Mum is forever going on about what you're doing or where you're going. 'Greggy's doing this, Greggy's going there.'" Craig did a terrific impression. "Greggy's *such* a good kid."

"That's because every time I speak to her I don't utter the words 'she's pregnant' into the phone. Besides, Craig, I don't speak to her that regularly because I am always off to another new exotic destination getting sun kissed while lying by a hotel pool." I stopped long enough to act as though I was reminded of something. "Oh, and I get paid for it!"

"I hate you."

"I know."

"Oh rah, rah, rah," Natalie began. "Can't you for once at least pretend you have bad days? Maybe you just get a flat tire on the motorway."

"At 3 a.m. with no phone and no spare," added Craig.

"In torrential rain with a madman on the loose," Natalie continued.

"Who has a knife, a balaclava, and a twenty-inch black dildo that he's been itching to use," Craig ended, releasing his cupped hands from around Josh's ears.

"No," I replied blankly while Mum slapped at their arms.

With the kids finishing the DVD in the living room, Danny was sent in to execute a joke devised by Craig where he would call each of the kids by the wrong name. It was silly, but it amused them tremendously, and they seemed thankful that they were being included in the foreigner's visit.

As we were leaving, Mum took Danny into a bear hug next to the car, almost knocking him over. "It was so nice to meet you, Danny. You two really do make a great couple. I'm sure his dad would have approved."

"Yes, he would," Natalie confirmed as she took her turn to say good-bye.

Danny was released and turned to Craig and smiled. I instantly recognized this particular cheeky grin. He opened his arms out wide like a toddler waiting to be picked up, and walked slowly toward my brother. Craig considered him for a moment, then opened his arms, mirroring Danny. In a bizarre game of chicken, they reached each other and stopped only a few feet apart. Danny leaned forward ever so slightly, forcing Craig to buckle and sling his arms down by his sides before raising a hand out to Danny. "Well played, mate."

On the way back to Brighton, Danny sat beside me, grinning like a Cheshire Cat.

"Okay, okay, the family loves you," I said, laughing. "I must admit, I am pretty impressed with the way you handled Craig."

"He's a good guy. I've never had a brother before."

"I am glad you feel that way, as it means that you now take half the responsibility of buying all of his kids' Christmas and birthday presents."

Danny turned his head and looked out of the window. "I know what you're thinking, Greg."

"What's that?"

"Your mom gave me a much warmer welcome than mine gave to you."

"That's because you are a charming military officer and a learned scholar that shows respect and works hard," I replied. "And I am Satan!"

"Well, thankfully you and Momma are getting on better now. I must admit, it killed me when you two didn't hit it off straightaway."

"I knew you were concerned about it, but I didn't realize it had upset you that much."

"Of course it did. You're two of the most important people in my life. How would you have felt if your mom and I hadn't hit it off, and we disliked each other to the point that it was awkward?"

I nodded in agreement, but didn't comment for fear of bursting his bubble.

CHAPTER TEN

IN THE summer between the second and third years of law school, Danny headed to New York to begin his "summer associate" job at a firm in Battery Park in Manhattan. He had been invited to, and had attended, many interviews with large firms around the country, most of which were in major cities. He had been successful at all of them, each firm offering him a position. After much research, Danny decided on Buddle & Darcy. It was one of the most reputable firms in New York and had higher standards than most, but it was still a standard that Danny easily surpassed. Danny was a particularly attractive candidate for the firm, not only because of his grades, but also because of his experience in the military, and the fact that he was gay would earn them marks on their record as the top firm when it came to the diversity of their attorneys.

During these three months, Danny worked with various attorneys in different practice groups. They kept his schedule busy, giving him a taste of what was to come and the hours that were expected to be worked if he chose to work there full time. On the odd occasion that he wasn't working into the evening, he and the other summer associates were expected to attend functions and events designed for them by the firm's partners. These evenings were an attempt to woo the summer associates.

As with the visits to the university, the firm was still interviewing, as well as being interviewed itself. But this time they were not only interested in making a good impression on the star students they had already attracted, they were also hoping to secure the good favor of the students' wives, husbands, and partners, who the firm knew would influence any decisions to be made. My flight schedule permitted me to grab the odd night in New York to be with him, but my visits never coincided with the firm's social events, which left Danny to attend them all alone.

I felt like I had been away nonstop during these months, as my trips were often long and to places I had been a hundred times before. Since Danny was so busy with work, I didn't have my usual outlet and was unable to speak to him as often as I would have liked. Nights went by and the dark thoughts slowly crept in.

Danny was in one of the most exciting cities in the world, meeting new and interesting people and being wined and dined and introduced to a new way of life. I had momentary lapses in faith, wondering whether I would still be a part of this new life or whether he would conclude that our long distance relationship was just too hard. I never doubted that he loved me, but I was sure that he had the same kind of moments when we were down or missing each other, thinking how much easier life would be if we were with someone who at least lived in the same country.

We were always there to support each other in any way that we could, but I sometimes wondered if that was enough, when sometimes the only thing you need is a hug or physical contact to claim the comfort you desire. As with most long distance relationships, texts and e-mails were taken out of context, and hours of not knowing where the other one was led to feelings of suspicion. The mind can play games that can lead to days of unnecessary foul moods and trails of thought that lead to all sorts of visions and insecurities.

Danny's parents had made a trip to New York to see him, which also gave his mother a chance to visit a "megachurch" that was touring the country and was due in New York at the same time. The sight of these mass gatherings of tens of thousands of Southern Baptists was, to their credit, very impressive. Not only did it give them an opportunity to reach huge numbers of people at one time, giving them much more of a feeling of a national community, but it also portrayed a definite image of what had been called the Jesus Army. If they all took up arms and walked out of some of these gatherings, it would have taken a hell of a lot more than the National Guard to stop them.

It had been a few weeks since I had seen Danny, and I could tell that he was beginning to feel the pinch of working such long hours and being in the city with so many people, but at the same time being alone. Sure, he had the company of coworkers and the other associates, but he complained that it wasn't the same as sharing experiences with a partner. I heard the phrase "I wish you could have been there" on so many occasions, I expected it after every story he told.

I was pleased that his parents had made the trip up to New York, but at the same time I was beginning to fret that his mother might use her time with him to try and drive a wedge between us. Of course, she wouldn't be blatant about it; she'd just feed him seeds of doubt big enough that she could cover her back if he confronted her. I began to worry, because during the past few weeks, my conversations with him had changed.

Danny would often ask me for my advice or opinion on many different things, which he still did. But I noticed that he began to add "that's what Mom thinks," or "that's what Mom said too," showing me that he had sought his mother's counsel before my own. This may have been because we hadn't been able to speak as often as usual because his work kept him too late into the night, and the time difference meant I would have to be on the webcam at 4:00 a.m. just to say good-night to him.

When Danny left New York to return to Texas for his third and final year of law school, our relationship changed. Up to that point, any plans or scenarios for our eventual future together were always discussed in years, a seemingly never-ending countdown. But now everything was discussed in terms of months and semesters. Our casual chats about the future were being replaced with definite plans. I knew that the time was coming when I would have to tell Mum that I was leaving. I would also have to put my beloved flat in Kemptown up for sale, as we would need the money to get started in New York. I would also have to think about handing in my resignation at the airline, which was one of the hardest things to think about, as it meant my sense of security and independence would disappear.

During the first few months back at school, Danny was tied up with a busy study schedule, as well as attending his Reserve Duty for the Navy. I was rostered a few trips to the States, but once again our timing never seemed to fit. While on these trips, however, I began to notice the influence of religion throughout the country more and more, and I realized for the first time that I was actually looking out for it. I had never been so blind that it went entirely unnoticed in the past, but when I took in my surroundings a little more carefully, there was evidence of religious influences everywhere.

Bumper stickers on cars told of the faith of the drivers, and were plastered next to yellow ribbon magnets that read "I support the troops." Some cars had boxed stickers that read "I am pro life," and "Abortion is murder," next to "Proud member of the NRA." There were even ones that read "If you don't support the President, you're a traitor." They all made me cringe. I had no issue with what they said, but rather the fact that they were so intent on letting anyone and everyone know their stances on such personal beliefs. Anywhere else in the world, these topics would only be brought up in a debate of some kind. I wondered whether British people just seemed more reserved or private about such matters, only discussing their views with friends or family in a private environment, or whether Americans put on these declarations of their beliefs to provoke a debate.

I also saw young kids, particularly teenage girls, wearing T-shirts printed with various Bible quotes across the chest. Again, I had no problem with this in theory, but the T-shirts themselves were always fashionably tight and practically begged men to look at their breasts—and the scripture printed across the shirt gave them an excuse! Then there were the T-shirts generally worn by somewhat larger teenage girls that featured black and white images of Jesus's face that were airbrushed to give him smoky eyes and model features, as though David Beckham had posed as the messiah himself. The same thing always appeared above the images: "He loves me." These shy-looking girls, who seemed awkward in their own skin, broke my heart. They were convinced that this sexualized Adonis of a man loved them. Maybe it made them feel better about themselves, but to me it just seemed that they had given up on boys that were actually alive.

Every day on the news there were more and more politicians that crowbarred Jesus, God, or faith into any discussion or interview, often as a diversion when they were challenged for something that could have been deemed discriminatory. But more than anything, I was troubled by the "Christian Broadcasting Network" on cable TV. Any time I was jetlagged, I could flick through the channels on the hotel television and inevitably land on an elderly gentleman giving his opinion on the day's events. I would go into a trancelike state as I watched and heard a kindly looking granddad in a suit say some of the most wonderful things about good deeds that people had done, the benevolence people had shown to others in their hours of need, and how people were not alone, as their lives were filled with love—even if they had no one. He looked and spoke so serenely that I could understand the comfort that he provided. But within minutes I would be snapped out of my stupor by bizarre statements that undid every kind word.

The pleasant old man turned into a growling lunatic when he turned to condemn people and target a group that was no longer promised salvation: "the hommah-secks-shulls." It was mind blowing to listen to straight people remark that being gay was a choice, as if they had some authority or qualification to make the declaration. It was even more confusing when this "choice" was discussed in the same breath as reports of yet another gay teenager taking his own life because he couldn't deal with the torment and ridicule he faced every day at school. It seemed like they couldn't see the connection between the two things. If it was a choice, why not choose to be straight and carry on living? Instead they blamed the older "predatory" homosexuals in society that were "likely to have abused them," and it was the shame of this abuse that drove them to suicide. Gay people were blamed for countless wrongs in the world and, since 9/11, were even being branded "the real terrorists in America" by far right-wing Christians, who believed homosexuals threatened the "American way of life."

"YOU'RE finally here!" Danny shouted as he squeezed me tightly at the arrivals hall at the airport in Austin. "I've missed you more than you could possible know." After three long months of not seeing each other, Danny and I finally hammered out our schedules and managed ten days together during the break between semesters. I managed to beg, barter, and blackmail other crew to get them to swap rosters with me so I could get the time off.

"I have so much planned. I have tickets to a hockey match, tickets to the symphony, a weekend hunting trip in Baytown, and I thought we could go out to the Rainbow Cattle Company, a country bar where I can teach you how to two-step!"

"Whoa, back up a little, Tiger. A hunting trip?"

Danny winced. "I know, I know. But I haven't seen Mom and Dad in ages either, so I agreed to go down there. Tucker is coming too."

"Danny, have you only just met me? You know how I feel about guns and hunting."

"I know, but it was such a big thing from my childhood that I want to share it with you. It's okay. You don't have to shoot anything if you don't want to!"

"So I just have to creep around the woods for a while, and then witness you killing an animal?"

"Deer."

"Oh, well, so long as it's Bambi, that's fine," I said, waving my hand around.

"Please, Greg. Dad's really excited about taking us. He's rented a cabin in the woods so we can all stay there overnight." Danny gave me his big blue doe eyes. "Please, it's been a long time since I have spent time with just Dad."

My ears pricked up. "You mean your mum's not going?"

"No, she's taking my nieces to some church fundraiser on Saturday, which is a shame, since I know she was looking forward to seeing you."

"And if you had told me about this trip to Baytown, I would have looked forward to seeing her too," I lied.

"If you really don't want to go hunting we don't have to. You know I wouldn't make you do anything you didn't really want to. We'll just spend some time at home with Mom and Dad."

I thought about it for a moment. Should I dress up like a bush and stalk poor, innocent woodland creatures that will be brutally gunned down as they frolic in the glade? Or should I spend more time confined to a room with Danny's mother?

"Okay, we'll go hunting if it really means that much to you."

The first few days at Danny's house were blissful, despite the occasional awkward morning conversations with young men who hadn't been there the night before, and who were waiting for Tucker to get out of bed and take them back to their dorms. Duke obviously hadn't gotten used to these strangers. He would lie on the sofa and growl at them as they made their way to the door. I fretted a little over going to Baytown and hoped that Mrs. Taylor would have already left by the time we got there. Unfortunately, that wasn't the case.

"No, Danny, I will hang on here until you arrive," she said over the speakerphone as we made our way to Baytown. "I haven't seen Greg in so long, and I have a little present for him."

The drive was as long as ever, but more comfortable in Tucker's car. Danny kept us all engaged in conversation about various aspects of law that he had learned, while Tucker told of his recent sexual conquests. Duke nuzzled his head into my lap in the back seat and then demanded attention by head-butting my ribs until I began to stroke him. The subject eventually turned to the reason we were heading to Baytown.

"You mean you have never been hunting before? Like, ever?" Tucker asked in astonishment.

"No, it's not really my bag. I don't agree with it, to be honest with you."

The second I said it I knew Tucker would begin to argue, and he would bait me until I finally gave in.

"Foxhunting. You Brits love foxhunting!" Tucker said, as if my opinion on blood sports was now null and void.

"Actually, Tucker, they are in the throes of banning that at the moment because too many people recognized it as a barbaric way to get your jollies."

"But they have to kill the foxes that kill people's livestock and affect their means of making a living."

"They are doing it for sport. You can't deny that. They are doing it to get their kicks. Why else would they send a dozen men on horses with a pack of hounds chasing through the countryside? There are many ways to control the fox population, Tucker. I just tend to think that terrorizing the poor little bastards for miles beforehand shouldn't be one of them."

"But you're not a vegetarian, Greg," he said, as though declaring victory.

"That's true, Tucker. But I think you're missing my point. I accept that animals are killed for food. I can only hope that the laws require that it's done humanely. I don't understand going out and killing something for the thrill of it, whether it's in America or Britain."

"So you have never even shot a gun?"

"Greg didn't grow up like us, Tucker," Danny interrupted. "We had BB guns and shot rabbits and tin cans when we were kids. We went out hunting deer with our dads when we were just children."

"And that doesn't happen in England?" Tucker asked, as if what Danny was saying was both absurd and untrue.

Danny saved me from responding. "It does happen on large, private estates of wealthy families, on their own grounds. But everyday Brits don't see it as the recreational pastime in the same way we Texans do. They could get arrested for even having a gun, since their firearms laws are so strict."

"Ah, so they can't do it," Tucker said, as if this made much more sense.

"I don't think it's so much that we can't do it. I think it's more that we wouldn't want to. We are a nation of animal lovers, and even the idea of slaying a defenseless creature for a laugh would turn the stomach of most British people." I said as I reached down and took hold of Duke's muzzle and gave it a playful shake before resuming the stroking of his head.

"You Brits, you're so nelly. My niece shot her first deer when she was nine years old! What do you think about that?"

"I worry about her soul."

WE PULLED up to the house and were greeted by George, who was loading equipment and supplies into the back of a truck that he rented for the weekend.

"Y'all ready to get some buck?" George asked as he rubbed his hands together. He was grinning widely, and it was obvious he had been looking forward to this for a while.

"I am always ready for some buck," Tucker said, winking at Danny as if George couldn't understand the innuendo. "Not too sure about Greg, though. He's refusing to hunt."

"Thanks, Tucker," I said, as I watched the smile fade from George's face to be replaced with a look of crestfallen confusion. "George, I am excited about going hunting, but my visa doesn't allow me to handle a firearm while I am here. Danny said I need to get a license to actually hunt, and I don't have any US-issued ID."

George perked up. "Hey, no one will know!"

"George, to be honest with you, I have never shot a gun. Plus, if I was caught it might affect my visitor's visa, which would mean I would have problems coming back into the country. And with Danny training to be a lawyer, it's probably a bad idea for him to be around anyone breaking the law."

George pondered this for a moment. "Yeah, I guess you're right. But we'll have fun and you can still do everything else!" he said happily before turning to Danny. "Glad to see someone is looking out for you."

Mrs. Taylor came into view from the side of the house and placed a picnic basket into the back. Spotting Danny she rushed over and hugged him.

"Danny, you look tired," she said, taking him in with a look of concern on her face. "Make sure you get some rest this weekend. I know how hard you've been studying. I put all of your favorite foods in the hamper, including my pecan pie, which I know you love."

"Thanks, Momma," he replied. "And thanks for looking after Duke while we're gone."

"Hello, Greg. It's so lovely to see you!" She sounded genuine enough, but her hug consisted of barely placing her fingertips on my shoulders while she air kissed my cheek from a foot away. Tucker was greeted much more warmly and received a full-on embrace and a compliment of how well he was looking. "Now, you boys come inside for a minute. George wants to leave soon, and I want a chance to give Greg his present."

As we walked into the kitchen, I saw one of the large cupboards next to the fridge was still open. It contained various supplies for eating outdoors, such as Dixie cups and plastic knives and forks. This obviously was where our picnic basket was stored. Mrs. Taylor rushed over to shut the door, but not before I saw the unopened Harrods hamper that I brought her on my first visit, which sat alongside the unopened gift wrapped box that I gave her on her birthday.

"This is for you," Mrs. Taylor said with a smile as she presented me with a black rectangular box.

I felt awkward. Could this be some sort of peace offering, a genuine attempt to make nice and to show that she was making an effort to welcome me? I felt sad for a moment that I had judged her so harshly, and in that moment I began to almost feel affection for her, realizing that it must have taken a lot for her to show a sign of truce and a new beginning. I decided there and then to forget the past and make more of an effort myself.

I opened the box to find a black handled knife with a six inch curved blade.

"It's a hunting knife. I bought it for you so you have something to skin your first squirrel or rabbit with."

"Mom, that is so thoughtful of you," Danny said as he leaned in and gave her a side hug. She patted his arm and gave him a smile.

"Thank you so much, Mrs. Taylor. It's very kind of you."

She looked directly into my eyes and held my gaze long enough to tell me that she thought she was winning a game. "I look forward to seeing your handiwork, Greg. I am sure Danny will show you how to use it properly." She then turned to her son. "It's very sharp so you be careful now, you hear?"

We heard George call to leave so we all made our way back outside. Tucker and Danny said their good-byes and headed toward the truck. I turned and walked toward Mrs. Taylor.

"Thanks again for my gift." I said as I raised my arms and held her in a hug that she wasn't expecting. "That was just damn aggressive," I whispered in her ear.

She patted my chest hard enough to show me she was struggling to get free from my hold but not hard enough that her family might notice. I released her and tilted my head to the side and pretended to laugh as if we'd shared a joke. Danny looked pleased through the window of the truck.

Mrs. Taylor walked to the truck with me and poked her head through the window to kiss George on the cheek. "Bring back a big one!"

"SO HOW does this whole hunting thing work, George?" I asked as we unloaded the truck and began taking our gear into a wood cabin that sat alone in a densely forested area about an hour's drive from the house. George hadn't lost his excitement and regaled us on the journey with stories of his past hunting trips as a young single man with his friends. Hunting was obviously one of his passions, and he became quite animated when spinning his tales.

"There are different seasons for different animals. November to January is white-tailed deer season, which is what we're hunting tomorrow. The owners of the land in this area lease their grounds for hunting. They make some money out of that and the rental of the cabin, and in return the culling of the deer is taken care of." George looked over and saw a look of concern on my face. "Don't worry, there won't be anyone else hunting in the area we're in. It's private property, and only me and a few of my friends have the lease on this land, and I know my buddies won't be here this weekend. Besides, the game wardens patrol the area checking licenses and know who is authorized to hunt around here."

"Good, I did wonder about that."

"I headed up here couple of days ago and set the feeders, which are essentially barrels of feed that are turned upside down with timers that periodically release food. They're elevated about three or so feet off the ground. Gets 'em used to not being so nervous in the area. Ya' understand?"

"Yes," I nodded.

"Then I built a blind, which is like a small open faced shed on stilts, 'bout fifteen feet up so the scent we give off ain't so close to the ground. I covered it with branches to camouflage it to look like part of the trees behind it. It holds three or four people and is about twenty yards away from the clearing that I set our feeders in. We'll head up there early in the morning, and we'll just wait for the bucks to come to us."

"So you don't actually stalk them?"

George laughed. "Boy, you ever tried to run after a deer? Those sonsabitches run like the wind and could hear you coming long before you ever spotted one."

"So once you've shot it, what do you do with it? It must weigh a ton."

"You tie off their back hooves and then slit—"

I shuddered. "Sorry, I mean what do you do with the body? Do you cut it up for the meat or do you keep their pelts?"

"You can do it yourself. But we usually take 'em to a processing plant where they'll do all of that for you. We just return and pick up a whole lot of steaks. You can imagine how much meat you can get off a full grown buck." George paused. "Danny tells me you're not entirely happy with the whole idea of hunting."

"It's just alien to me. I know it's part of your culture, so in that respect...."

"But you're not happy about actually killing something."

"No, to be truthful, I'm not. I am also terrified of guns."

I expected some kind of explanation for why they did it or perhaps an argument to convince me to try it, but George simply nodded. "Don't worry. I'll keep you safe."

That night at the cabin I saw a very different side to George. We sat outside by an impressive fire that George seemed to magic out of nowhere and drank beer and talked. But mostly we laughed. I had never seen George so relaxed or have such a boom to his laugh before. He took great pleasure in telling stories of what he had caught Danny doing as a kid or proudly spoke of how Mrs. Taylor could cut a rug when they were young and still dating. His stories of what she had done as a young woman when she was drunk again reminded me that she was the type of woman I would have gotten on quite well with. He spoke with such affection for her that I could begin to understand that his love for her outweighed any problems he had with her newfound Christian life. In fact, he even managed to joke about it a couple of times, but soon reprimanded Danny when he did the same thing.

The similarity between Danny and George was much more apparent as they sat side by side. Even their mannerisms and speech patterns seemed to mirror one another, especially as Danny's original accent slowly crept in throughout the evening. When Tucker showed no shame in informing George of his recent exploits, George was good humored, asked questions, and even offered relationship advice. He was fatherly without being condescending, and very much reminded me of my own dad.

Early the following morning, about an hour before sunrise, we arose a little hungover from the night before and began to kit ourselves out with the necessary equipment. My outfit was made up of spares from Danny's, Tucker's, and George's, all of whom were different sizes. I looked like a teenager wearing secondhand military surplus that I either hadn't grown into or already had grown out of. Along with the green was a bright orange cap, which confused me for a moment until I was informed that we were required to wear "hunter's orange" on our person to ensure that anyone else that could happen into the area, or maybe the warden, could identify you as a hunter. The deer can't see the color, so to them it essentially blends in with the rest of the gear.

We took about a fifteen-minute walk through a densely wooded area before we came to the clearing where George set up the feeder. It was still dark, so I left Danny, Tucker and George to set up our gear in the blind since they were such old hands at it, while I searched the ground for suitable branches to camouflage the front of it with. Every once in a while I looked up at George giving directions and was reminded of my own father and how he helped Craig and me build tree houses. It made me smile, and rather than feeling sad, I was happy to see that my Danny still had the chance to spend time with his dad.

Once everything was assembled and ready, George climbed down the thin ladder that led up to the blind and unlocked a large metal box that he carried from the cabin. Inside it were four gleaming rifles that were obviously well taken care of. He removed three of them and relocked the box. He passed one each to Danny and Tucker and gave them instructions on how to load and fire them. It was clear that they both already knew how, but I suspect George continued the safety briefing for my benefit.

One by one, we clambered up the ladder. Tucker was last, and had a bit of difficulty maintaining his balance. Once inside the blind, we took our seats on the wooden floor. It was about four feet long, ten feet wide, and four feet from floor to roof. On the broad side, there was an opening that traversed the length, with an unobstructed view of the feeder and the surrounding woods. Danny explained that this blind was a lot bigger than usual, since most are made for only one or two people. But George built this one from scratch just for this trip. Seeing all the effort George had gone to, I began to feel a little guilty.

We settled into our places, Tucker on the far end, then George, then Danny, with me to Danny's right. Since I wasn't holding a rifle, the cooler and snacks were packed in the corner behind me. We lowered our voices to a whisper.

"Be vewwy, vewwy qwi-et. We're hunting wabbits," George whispered in a great impression of Elmer Fudd, hunched over his rifle.

"Wait a sec, we're forgetting something," Danny said as he reached into his pocket. He pulled out a small bottle of liquid and sprayed it on himself, then on Tucker, then George. "You're gonna love this," he said as he squirted my jacket.

"What the hell is that?"

"Deer piss. It disguises your scent and attracts bucks, since they think another buck might have invaded their territory."

"Lovely," I said as I breathed in the stench.

We looked out onto the clearing and watched the feeder again.

"We should have brought some antlers," George whispered to me.

"If you think I am going to put on a pair of antlers and start running around a forest pretending to be a deer, George—"

George laughed. "No, Greg, you knock the antlers together as loud as you can. The noise makes bucks in the area think that other males are fighting, so they follow the noise to fight and defend their territory."

"And that's when you get them?"

"And that's when you get them!" George exclaimed.

For three hours we sat huddled together, only one of us speaking at a time in a whisper. We stifled bouts of giggles over George's continuing stories, until I couldn't contain it and finally let my laughter break the silence. I began to understand that the purpose of these hunting trips was less about the prize and more about the fellowship.

George suddenly put his hand up and pointed to an area to the left of the feeder. It took a moment for my eyes to focus, but eventually I saw it. A magnificent twelve-point buck had wandered into the area and was heading toward the food. Danny's and George's faces showed that this wasn't a normal buck and its size took them by surprise. The grace with which the creature moved his huge body was breathtaking, and I had no choice but to stare in awe at it. George loaded his rifle first, putting him in position to be the first to bring the deer down, leaned forward, and took aim. Danny and Tucker stopped loading their guns for fear of the noise alerting the animal to our presence.

I couldn't bear to watch. I closed my eyes, lowered my head, and turned away. I held my breath and prepared to flinch at the rifle being fired. I stayed clenched for about ten seconds.... But the shot never came.

I opened one eye and, still wincing and expecting the shot, turned to George. He was still staring through the scope, but the intense look on his face had left. He chewed on the inside of his cheek for a moment before looking at me. With the rifle still resting under his chin, he winked at me, turned forward again, and yelled, "Go on! Gitouttahere!"

The echo of his voice alerted anything that might be breathing in the area, not just the buck. The huge deer bolted and was gone before the first syllable bounced back to us.

"George! What the fuck?" Tucker said loudly, bouncing an inch off his seat. "What are you doing? That thing was fuckin' huge. I've never seen a buck that size before!"

"Calm down, Tucker. So we didn't get the deer. We still had a good time, didn't we?" George said as though he wasn't at all bothered.

"Are you crazy? You let it go!"

"Tucker, it's no big deal. We'll get it another time."

"But...."

"Tucker, I didn't want it today, and that is the end of it." George's words were edged with finality. He looked at Danny. "He's right, though, that thing was fucking huge." Then he nudged playfully before adding, "There was no way I was going to be able to lift something that size with my bad back, even with you boys helping me."

I mouthed the words "thank you" appreciatively to George and made my way down the ladder. Tucker followed, still looking like he was on the verge of throwing a tantrum.

"Well, at least you got to see some nature," Danny said as he jumped down the last two steps of the ladder. "I honestly have never seen a buck that was that...."

There was a loud bang to my left that caused me to physically jump, lose my balance, and tumble into Danny. I looked to see Tucker lowering his rifle from an almost vertical position. He pointed up at the treetop with his free hand and smiled. I watched as the squirrel he'd shot tumbled like a furry little acrobat off each branch until its lifeless body landed on the ground with a small thud before bouncing and landing in a pile of leaves.

"Well, at least we got a squirrel for you to skin with your new knife!" Tucker said proudly.

George walked over to the animal and began kicking leaves over it.

"You're burying it?" Tucker said, astonished.

"It's what its mother would have wanted."

"But that was a damn good shot!"

"Gun back in the box please, Tucker."

When we arrived back at the house, Mrs. Taylor was there to greet us. She walked down the driveway as we pulled up and peered into the back of the truck.

"No luck? Maybe next time, darling," she said to George as he got out of the truck. She patted his backside and waved to us through the window.

"You should have seen the size of the one he could have had, Vivien." Tucker called. "It was massive."

As we helped George unload the equipment, Mrs. Taylor brought out a tray of iced tea. After giving the first one to her husband, she joined Danny and me on the front lawn, where we were folding a tarp that covered the gear as we traveled. Tucker stood over us, watching but not attempting to help.

"It's unlike your dad to miss," she said, looking toward George as he ferried the rest of the gear into the garage. She looked genuinely concerned, almost as though this could be a symptom of an illness, or that her husband could be losing his sight or reflexes as a result of growing older.

"Miss? He didn't even take the shot!" Tucker said. "It was right there in front of him."

"Oh my God, Tucker, are you blind? Dad didn't take the shot because he didn't want to shoot the damn thing in front of Greg! Now will you please stop banging on about it?"

"Please don't blaspheme, Danny," Mrs. Taylor said, a lot more casually than she would have if I'd said it. "You mean he could have brought home a buck?"

"Yes, Momma, he could have, but he decided against it. It was damn good of him to do it, too. That would have been one hell of a prize. I am so damn proud of him."

Mrs. Taylor began to get red faced.

"What's the matter, Mom? You look angry."

"We agreed that if he shot anything we would give the steaks to the church to distribute to some of the poorer families in the area. Do you know how many mouths that would have fed? Now they are going to have to go without," she said sharply, looking at me like I had just robbed a charity box.

I started to defend myself, but Danny stood before I had the chance.

"They didn't have venison steaks before; they don't have them now. How are they going to miss something they never knew they were going to get?"

"That's not the point, Danny."

"Momma, if it means that much to you I will go to Safeway and buy a load of meat for them now. Please don't give Dad a hard time over this. His heart was in the right place."

Danny's tone was bordering on harsh, but it seemed that his point hit home.

"You're right. There are other ways to help, and I am glad you boys had a good time."

She tousled Danny's hair like a child that had been forgiven and headed back into the house, but not before turning at the last moment to give me an icy glare.

On the way back to Austin, Tucker still seemed to think that the chance of a lifetime had been ripped away.

"The head of that buck would have filled a wall."

"Tucker, please, enough about the deer!" pleaded Danny.

"Fine, but this was the last chance I'm gonna have to go hunting for a while, so I hope you're happy."

"I am elated, Tucker," I said, my patience beginning to wear thin. "Anyway, why is this the last time you can hunt for while?"

"I'm going to be too busy. I planned to take some vacation time next month, but my boss was just elected to Congress and now I have to head up to DC to scout areas for an office. Still, at least we'll get to see some *bucks* up there, eh, Danny?" For emphasis, Tucker added air quotes when he said the word bucks.

Danny jumped in before I could ask. "Tucker wants me to go to Washington for a long weekend while he's there. You don't mind, do you?"

The fact was, I did mind. I hated the idea of Danny being dragged around to every bar and club in the district while Tucker searched for his next victim. It also immediately stirred up my jealousy of his ex-boyfriends and lovers who still lived there. I already had one experience with an ex of Danny's who made it only too clear that he wanted to pick up where they left off.

"Of course he doesn't mind," Tucker interjected.

"No, you go ahead and have a good time. I am away most of next month, and I have my request trip again with Lee, Steve, Donna, and Jackie to Vegas too. You should go out and enjoy yourself."

Danny didn't seem entirely convinced of this answer but left it alone, knowing that any discussion would be heard—and commented on—by Tucker.

CHAPTER ELEVEN

"HOW the hell do you expect me to react, Danny?"

"Well, I don't expect you to ignore my texts and e-mails for three days. That's just passive aggressive."

"Don't give me that American therapy bollocks. I was mad with you and didn't want to talk to you until I had calmed down. End of story."

"So how the hell are we meant to sort it out if we don't talk about it?"

"We're talking about it now. So go on, how did you expect me to react?"

"Greg, it wasn't like I had arranged to meet up with them. They were in the same bar as we were. We bumped into them. They weren't even out together. They were in the bar separately with other friends."

"So you thought, 'Hey! I know, l haven't seen Brett or Mark for a while, let's all arrange to head out for dinner the next night and then go to a club afterward.'"

"It wasn't my idea. It was Tucker who suggested it. I had already said that I wasn't in DC for any particular reason other than visiting, so they knew I had nothing planned. Even if I had made something up, Tucker would have thrown me under the bus."

"So why didn't you tell me that morning?"

"Because I knew you'd be upset about it."

"Right, so don't pretend like you don't know why I am mad, Danny. If you knew I was going to be this way about it, don't act as if you have done nothing wrong."

"Okay, what did you expect me to do?"

"Make excuses so you don't spend the night with two of your exes, one of which Tucker said that he was sure you were going to marry. How did you think I would feel whilst being stuck here in the arse end of India?"

"Greg, that was a long time ago, and we weren't as emotionally involved at the time as Tucker thinks we were, and you know that there isn't anything even remotely emotional there now. How do you think I felt about it? I had to sit there with the two of them all night. It was damn awkward. Ask Tucker. I talked about you all evening."

"Yeah, that's an idea. I will chat to Tucker about it. That won't wind me up at all!"

"Oh for fuck sake, Greg. You're letting this wind you up."

"Of course I am. Not only am I pissed off that Tucker thought it was appropriate to suggest such a thing, you thought it was okay to go along with it!"

"Anyone would think you didn't trust me! Look, I know I feel absolutely nothing about them, so I didn't think it was that big of a deal."

"But you knew I would be angry about it?"

"Yes."

"And you still did it, Danny."

"Yes, and I told you about it. It's not like I've lied to you, Greg. I understand why you're mad, but not why you're *this* mad."

"It wasn't just one ex, Danny, it was two! Two of your old flames got to spend time with you while I couldn't. And one of the fuckers made a pass at you."

"Yes, and I was honest with you about that too. I told you that I walked away from the situation."

"You shouldn't have put yourself in that situation in the first place! If you were talking about me all night, why on earth did he think he stood a chance?"

"He'd been drinking. He chanced his luck. Greg, don't tell me when you're out at bars you don't get hit on."

"Yes, I do. But not by ex-boyfriends who I had arranged to have dinner with."

"Again, it was Tucker who arranged it."

"But why? Why on earth did he do it?"

"Because he assumed we were all still friends. And when you consider the fact that when we split up it was amicable, I suppose we are."

"So Brett thought that since you were still friends it would be okay to try sleep with you?"

"Well…."

"Well what? If a 'friend' knows that you're in a relationship, what kind of 'friend' still makes a pass? That's hardly friendly, is it?"

"Greg, I only dated the guy for a couple of months. And it was years ago. I've been with you for three years! You're blowing this all out of proportion. It was an awkward moment brought on by too much drink and passed in two seconds. He probably doesn't even remember doing it."

"Oh, thank heavens for blackouts! I would hate to think that prick's day was ruined by feeling any kind of shame."

"Greg…."

"Fine. Okay, okay."

"What does that mean? Are you still mad with me or are we back on track?"

"Danny, I am thousands of miles away from you, stuck in a hotel, and driving myself up the fucking wall. I appreciate that you told me about it, but you should have said something before you even went out for dinner."

"I could hardly have called you. It was the middle of the night where you are."

"You know you could have sent me an e-mail."

"And you know that you would have accused me of copping out of the conversation by not telling you one-on-one over the phone, which by the way you have complained about not having any reception whenever you're in India, and leaving it to an e-mail. I told you as soon as we spoke on the webcam. I kept nothing from you."

"I know. And I really do appreciate you being honest about it. It's just that… I know how hard it is. I know we go through weeks and months of celibacy until we're together. I know how much I love you, and I know it's worth it when we're together, but I also know how hard it is to dismiss an easy fumble when it's so readily presented to you on a plate. So I try and stay away from the plate! Sometimes I am just reminded exactly how hard it is."

"But we get through it."

"We do."

"So, it's been a few days. Tell me what you've been up to."

"Not much. I have been running around haggling over tuppence to get Mum some saris. I have no idea what she's thinking or where she thinks she's going to wear one."

"But it will make her happy."

"It will. Speaking of mums, I got a Facebook friend request from your mother today."

"Really?"

"I have declined it. I hope you understand, there are far too many photos of me in various states of inebriation and undress. Plus, the comments on the wall aren't exactly what you would consider 'Christian'."

"No, but it's nice she's considered adding you. But I'm sure she'll understand that you wouldn't want her to see anything that could offend her."

"And I am sure she will once you have explained it to her."

"Why do I have to explain it to her?"

"Are you serious?"

"Give her a call. I know she'd appreciate it."

"I am in India, Danny."

"Fair enough."

"Anyway, what about you? What have you been up to?"

"Well, I had so much more time on my hands since you were being a whiny little bitch and weren't talking to me. So I attended and was the guest star at the university swim team's orgy, which was fun. It took a while to get through them all, so it killed a few hours. Other than that, just studying!"

"From your mouth to God's ears, Tiger."

CHAPTER TWELVE

"… AND we have a new captain in command today, by the name of Adam Cooper," Jackie said in the safety briefing before our flight to Las Vegas. She looked directly over to Lee and Steve and smiled. "You boys will like him. He's as cute as hell and he's single. I grilled him last week on a little Montreal flight."I could just picture her interrogation over drinks in the hotel bar. She then looked over at the girls. "Sorry, ladies, for the first time in living history we have an attractive captain, but unfortunately he is of the homosexual variety." Donna groaned, causing Jackie to smirk before she addressed me. "And you, Master Stephens, you are taken so he is strictly off limits. You are up at the front with me today, so I shall be keeping an eye on any galley or down-route flirtations from either side, and I shall pounce should I spot any indication of wrongdoing!"

"Greg? Wrongdoing?" Donna protested as she gathered up the flight's paperwork and stuffed it into a folder. "Greg is an angel, an angel, dammit! I have never seen or heard of him doing wrong."

I chewed my lip and waited for the punch line.

"That glory hole in his front door was made to make the delivery of his world maps easier for the postman and nothing else."

"Thanks, Don."

"And I don't care what anyone says, I know Greg wouldn't have gone in those bushes with that man while his kid was strapped into the child seat in the car, waiting for his daddy to come back."

"Again, thanks, Donna."

"And it's unfair to blame Greg for that gimp's injuries when it was him that was holding the lighter and…."

"Yes, my love, he's an absolute angel," Jackie said, stopping anymore abusive insults that were heading my way. "Time to fly, my pretties!"

I MUST admit, when I first saw Adam I was taken aback. Most of the captains who worked for the airline were tired-looking older men who seemed to be grumpy more than most of the time or else embarrassing themselves after a couple of drinks, trying to charm the girls. Adam, however, was in his early thirties, had jet-black hair styled just short enough that the five o'clock shadow he sported at 10:00 a.m. ran seamlessly into his trimmed sideburns. More handsome than Jackie gave him credit for, he looked dashing next to the awkward, youth-training-scheme-looking first officer that accompanied him into the flight deck.

"So what's he like, Jacks?" I asked as we began the service.

"He seems like a nice guy, albeit a bit quiet," she said, snapping the brake on the cart to roll forward onto the next set of waiting passengers. "He seems a bit nervous of me, though," she added with a comical expression of surprise.

Just as we stopped, the overhead galley call bell sounded, sending a high-low chime into the cabin.

"One of them wants out," Jackie sighed as she nodded to the illuminated light above the curtain.

Since 9/11, there had been countless changes in the way the area around the flight deck had been controlled. New procedures seemed to come every couple of months. This time it was the rule that if one of the flight deck needed to use the bathroom, one of the crew had to remain in the galley area and ensure no passengers could enter and the area remained "sterile."

I walked up and picked up the interphone and called into the flight deck. "All clear," I said. I waited for an "okay" and the clicks from the door, which was now reinforced and sounded like a bank vault opening.

"Thanks," Adam said as he walked out of the flight deck. "You must be Greg?" he raised his hand to shake mine. "To be honest, I don't need the lav. I just had to get out of there for a few minutes. The first officer is talking airport trivia, and it's sending me into a coma."

"No problem," I said as I peered through the gap in the curtain for a moment to enjoy watching Jackie work on her own. "So you're a new captain?"

"I am. It's crazy, but I am slowly getting used to it. Have you done many of these Vegas trips?" he asked as he rocked backward and forward on the balls of his feet, trying to stretch out and resembling an old-fashioned bobby on the beat.

"I have done a few. It's an interesting place with plenty to do so at least you won't get bored. The crew will show you around all of the best places to go and the best shows to see."

"Great! I was hoping so. The airline I have just come from was in Germany, and the crew and flight deck didn't really mix that much," he said, almost relieved.

"I don't think you'll have that problem here, fella. So long as you remain blind to what you see down route you will get on fine," I said, laughing.

"I had better head back in." But he paused before he turned to leave. "The, um, boys at the back…," he said, looking a little nervous, "will they be heading out to any bars or clubs?"

"Sure, we are planning on heading out tonight if you want to come out with us."

"Well, I was kind of hoping to see some of the"—he began to whisper—"gay nightlife."

I started to laugh. "You know everyone knows you're gay, don't you?"

"It got around that quick, huh?"

"Yep!" I nodded. "We are heading out with a couple of the girls to a gay club tomorrow night, if you want to come with us."

Adam looked at me and narrowed his eyes for a split second in confusion. "You mean, you're…." He finished his sentence with a raise of both eyebrows.

I laughed again. "Yes, I am…." I raised my eyebrows back and wondered whether all German crews were straight. I may not have been camp, but I was still in a uniform and was employed to point out the exits. It couldn't have been that much of a shock.

"Oh, right. Okay, well, I had better get back in my seat," he said turning back toward the door. "I'll look forward to it."

Joining Jackie on the back end of the cart, I started to chuckle.

"I hope that's not a school girl's giggle I hear, Greg," Jackie said as she let out the long breath of a person who had been working in a field all day, rather than one who had been left alone to serve two drinks over four minutes.

"Of course it isn't!" I said in mock horror. "I have just outed myself to the captain, who didn't seem to know I was gay."

"That's because I told him you were married," Jackie said, a little smugly. "I didn't mention it wasn't in the traditional sense. I didn't want him to get the wrong idea about you."

"Shucks, look at you trying to protect my honor," I retorted. "I don't think you will have a problem with my behavior, Jacks. I am a good boy, I am."

Jackie simply smirked like she had heard this protest before in the past. Unfortunately, she also knew in the past, when I was younger, that what I said wasn't strictly true. Although her reaction was comical, it kind of stung too, as it seemed to question my devotion to Danny.

After a few hours of sleep, Jackie, Donna, Lee, Steve, and I met by the hotel bar and waited for Adam to arrive. We had already seen three of the crew looking miserable as they walked out of the hotel, an awkwardly dressed first officer trailing in their wake looking like a nerd at a comic book convention.

"Hey, guys," Adam said as he arrived, looking more unlike flight deck than I had ever seen. The usual civilian clothing of the captains and first officers were a uniform of chino shorts, polo shirts, or cheap

Hawaiian shirts that were typically bought for one pound off the beach in Thailand. Not only did they think they looked young and "snazzy" in such clothes, they never seemed to be abashed at telling you they had snagged a bargain. Adam escaped such an apparel trap by wearing a plaid shirt and well fitted jeans that not only added to his handsomeness, but also made it obvious that he liked showing off the work that he put into his body.

He took a seat next to mine and glanced over at the waitress to get her attention to order a drink. Lee and Steve were practically drooling into their own drinks, and I saw them look to each other. It was the kind of look that was joking, but hinted at acknowledged competition.

As the rest of the crew chatted, Adam leaned over to me. "Jackie tells me you're married. Was it a civil ceremony?"

"I think that Jacks just meant that I am with someone. I am not actually married," I said, taking a sip of beer.

"Oh, right. So is your boyfriend crew too?" he asked.

"No, he's at law school in Texas. He was in the Navy when I met him."

"Wow, so you live in England and he's in Texas? That's got to be rough," Adam said, raising his eyebrows and nodding his head for a reply.

"Yeah, but we are doing what we can to make it work." I shrugged.

At this point Jackie announced to the table to drink up as we would be late for the show the concierge had arranged tickets for.

"Hey, are we still heading out tomorrow night?" asked Adam.

"Sure," I said, "it's just a bit heavy the first night we arrive so we tend to take it easier."

"Great. I'm kind of new out of the closet so I'm looking forward to seeing what I've missed out on," he said, but in a way that showed he was excited about seeing a whole new world. He looked innocent. The kind of innocence that you know full well will be preyed on by the knowing masses. It almost made me kind of sad for him. Goodness, how I had changed.

The evening was fun, though I had sat apart from Adam all night, at Jackie's insistence, who maintained she could see trouble coming. I laughed this off, as the only thing on my mind all night was Danny at home in Texas, studying through his books and making the reference cards on which I often quizzed him when exams grew closer. I wished I could have been with him.

Despite the nap earlier, we returned to the hotel straight after the show, which was a performance of energetic, acrobatic brilliance and completely wasted on us as we were all so knackered. As we walked through the lobby I saw the first officer sitting alone in the bar and pointed him out to Adam.

"I had better make sure he's okay," Adam said. "Thanks for a good night." He smiled kindly, and I nodded back as he walked over to the bar.

"He wants to ravish you, you little tease," Jackie said as she threw her arm around me for support while she balanced on one leg and readjusted her stiletto.

I rolled my eyes. "Jacks, believe it or not, not all gay men are after one thing. Besides, he's just excited because he's only come out recently. He's still a baby gay. It's probably nice for him just to talk to another gay guy."

"Oh dah'ling, he could barely take his eyes off you during the show. Every time he leaned over to speak to me he was looking over my shoulder at you."

"He was probably avoiding your gaze in case you turned him to a pillar of salt, babe," I laughed, feeling a little awkward.

"Okay, my naïve little chum, but I feel it's only right to warn you."

"Jacks, I love Danny more than you can imagine. There is no way I would fool around on him," I said a little sternly. The conversation alone almost made me feel like I was cheating.

"Oh stop it. I am going to cry," Jacks replied, pulling her finger down her cheek, chasing an imaginary tear.

THE next day I slept in most of the morning as I had been up late the nights before the trip chatting to Danny. After even more catch-up sleep I spent the afternoon by the pool with the crew. Adam had taken a sightseeing tour with the first officer so was spared the conversation we had been having about the state of the Americans who were staying at the hotel and who were screaming around the pool.

Years ago there were many comedy sketches on British television mocking overweight, fanny-pack-wearing, Hawaiian-shirt-sporting, Rascal-riding American tourists. At the time, they seemed to be an over-the-top parody. But now it seemed they were all realistically based on the tourists in Vegas. I find nothing more ridiculous than seeing a tourist wearing a T-shirt emblazoned with the name of the city that they are still actually visiting. Well, apart from the T-shirts of Jesus or Bible scriptures being worn by middle aged men and women staring like hypnotized idiots at the flashing lights of slot machines. "Sin City," where else would a good Christian go for a holiday? To top this all off, there were thousands of students everywhere, randomly shouting *"Spring break in Vegas, baby! Wa-hoo!"*

By the time the evening came around, we were not as relaxed as we usually would have been after an afternoon at the pool. Rather than face the tourists in the hotel bar, we had decided to use my room as the venue for pre-departure drinks before we headed out for the night. Danny was due online, so I got myself ready to head out an hour before everyone was due in my room so I had the time to chat to him.

"Hey, Tiger!" I said as I saw his face appear on the screen. No matter whether he was tired, sleepy, fresh-faced, or dopey, he always looked so handsome.

"Hey, baby! How's Vegas?"

"Hot, sticky, and loud!" I moaned.

"That's Vegas, baby! Wa-hoo!"

I groaned.

"How was the show?" he asked.

150

"It was good. Well, as good as it could be. A revue is no more than a bunch of ostrich feathers and shiny legs after a while. How was school?"

"It was okay. The professors made a point of calling on me today, which was fine, but it got a little annoying toward the end, since they are meant to be a little more random than they were being," Danny said, sounding bothered. "Then the damn truck was acting up on the way home so I have to take it to the garage in the morning. And now Tucker is stomping around the house because he was stood up by a trick, which is driving me mad. I have to concentrate on a paper I have to write that has to be in by next Monday."

"Sorry to hear you're having a hard time of it, Tiger."

"That's okay. I have you to vent at, and, as always, you make me happier." He smiled and leaned his head to one side.

"How are the crew?"

"They're all fun. We even have decent flight deck. Well, the first officer is a little hard work, but Adam, the captain, is gay and seems like a laugh."

"Does he look like Biggles?" Danny asked, impressed with himself that he remembered the name of a character I referenced so often when describing flight deck.

Before I could answer him there was a knock at the door. I excused myself and opened the door to Jackie and Donna, who were holding hotel bathroom glasses, vodka, and mixers. As usual, they were early when drinking was involved.

"Hey, Danny's online. I will just be a minute."

"Hurrah!" shouted Jackie as she shoved past me and presented herself on the chair in front of the webcam. She threw her palm up to the side of her head like an old Benny Hill salute. "So you must be the dashing young naval officer who has wooed the ever so professional yeoman that stands beside me, yes?"

Danny laughed and returned the salute. "At ease, ma'am," he said, making Jackie swoon.

"He called me ma'am. An American called me ma'am, and I am not even offended. What a delight!" she squealed.

Donna leaned over her shoulder and introduced herself as I answered the door again to Lee and Steve. "Hello, Danny! Show us your cock! We can pay! I have a PayPal account!" she demanded. It seemed Donna already had a cheeky drink in her room before her arrival. "Greg says that you fell out of the big dick tree and brought a big ol' piece of wood with ya!"

"Oh, boys, come and see Greg's dandy boy," Jackie said, waving her hand to beckon Lee and Steve.

Lee and Steve introduced themselves before I pushed them to one side. "Okay, okay, let the man be," I said, scooting Jackie off the chair.

"Okay then, Tiger, I am going to head off. Have a good evening. I love you!"

A chorus of "I love you" echoed from the crew behind me as I heard yet another knock at the door.

"I love you more, baby. Have a great night, and I'll text you later," he said, as he waved his good-bye. But before he signed off his eyes shifted to one side. I turned around to see Adam sitting on the bed and being handed a drink.

"Hey, Adam, this is Danny," I said, pointing to the screen.

Adam leaned to one side, showing himself, and waved at the screen, giving a sheepish grin.

"Hi!" Danny called back. He paused, "Right, I have to go. Take care tonight, and I will speak to you in the morning," he said flatly. And for the first time, the screen abruptly went blank. No cheeky wave, no smile, no hint of a warm farewell, and no waiting for any answer from me. No one else noticed. But I did.

We got to the local bar and began ordering drinks. I went to one side and texted *"You okay?"* to Danny.

I waited for a response. Although I wasn't too concerned, his instant webcam departure niggled me. I knew he was home, and he very rarely had his phone more than a foot away from him. An hour later, I still hadn't heard from him.

"Hey, Tiger, we're at the bar. Hope you're having a better evening than the day you had." I closed my phone and waited. Still no response.

"You seem bothered by something," Adam said, moving himself around the crew to talk to me.

"Me? I am fine," I said, waving past any chance of a conversation about Danny. I wasn't in a particularly good mood at this point and didn't want to make it worse by whining that I hadn't heard back from him.

"How was your sightseeing tour?" I asked, flipping a smile and consciously trying to better my mood.

"It was good. It's a lot more garish than I had imagined, and the strip is smaller. But other than that it's pretty much what I expected." He shrugged as if it wasn't that big of a deal. "I was looking forward to seeing the club."

"So you haven't been to many clubs?" I asked as the barman handed us two more drinks that Jackie ordered.

"No, I only really came out in the past few months. I decided to come out as soon as I joined this airline. It would have been tough in Germany, but here it's been a breeze."

"That's great, really great. It must have been a load off your shoulders," I said while actually looking directly at his muscular shoulders, which were silhouetted by a form-fitting white T-shirt. It wasn't the typical "tight gay T-shirt," as it wasn't clinging to his stomach. Instead, it hung off his shoulders to cascade off his chest. "At least you can be yourself now. And trust me, there will be no shortage of admirers." Even though it may have sounded flirty, it was meant more as a genuine compliment.

Adam laughed and playfully tucked my chin with his fist. "Thanks, I guess I will just have to get my head around it all."

"Yeah, but for now just enjoy yourself and have some fun. We'll go see if we can find you a little blackjack dealer whose arse looks good in a pair of tight black trousers."

For most of the evening, Jackie and Donna were dancing and being flung around the room by various muscle Marys who were overjoyed they had discovered a British fag bangle and had bought the girls all of their drinks most of the night. Adam and I spent most of the night laughing, as I had discovered that he had never cruised a guy in a bar in his life and was just awful at it. He joked at my lessons and laughed until one of his targets looked back with a smile. He took the whole thing lightheartedly, and for a guy who was getting so much attention, he didn't seem at all bothered by it.

By the time we finished at the club we were two short of our party. After giving up entirely on Adam, who kindly and respectfully dodged their advances all night, Lee was still at the bar chatting up a drunk frat boy who we assumed had found himself there by accident, and Steve had disappeared all together.

In the taxi on the way back to the hotel, Adam and I jumped in the back and sat on either side of a very drunk Jackie, while Donna sat in the front passenger seat and questioned the driver about the various tacky items he had stuck to his dashboard.

"I am horribly intoxicated. All I can hear is bells and whistles. Am I… am I having a stroke?" Jackie whined.

Adam wound the window up on his side, drowning out the noise from the Vegas strip.

"Ah, that's much better," Jackie said as she laid her head on Adam's shoulder. Adam raised his arm to make her more comfortable and slung it around her shoulder, resting his hand on top of my arm. He didn't move it, and instead acted like it was innocent. Which it could have been, but I was very conscious of it.

When we reached the hotel, Jackie stirred, and Adam released his hand. Jackie attempted to get out of the car unaided, but failed miserably. I took her arm once again and led her to her room after wishing Adam a good-night, leaving him at the elevator. Donna and I spent the next two hours attempting to get Jackie into bed. Each time we thought we were successful we had to run back into the room and prepare to hold her hair back as we heard her make a run to the bathroom to throw up again.

The following morning I jumped online to see if I could catch Danny before I headed out to breakfast. It bothered me all night that I hadn't heard back from him, and I was beginning to worry. As I opened my e-mail account I saw a message waiting for me from Danny.

Greg,

I hope you had a good time last night with your new friend. I tried calling your room at 3 a.m. but there was no answer. I'm heading to school early this morning so am just on my way out. I'll be busy most of the day.

Danny

I immediately got on my phone and texted back. *Danny, what is the problem? Just so you know, I was with Donna in Jackie's room until 3:30 a.m. as she was vomiting half the night.* I waited for the response, which came a minute later.

Greg, my problem is that you have a go at me for being out with gay friends in DC, yet you don't think I should have an issue with you spending the evening with a hot pilot?

I responded, my hands shaking with anger. *Daniel, he is at the same airline as me. Would you like me to ignore him? If I ignored all of the gay guys at work I would be doing the fucking safety demo on the aircraft wing. You know you went out and saw* ex-boyfriends *in Washington. This is not the same and you know it.* I waited for the snarky answer, but it didn't come until I was sitting in the restaurant of the hotel with the crew. I was quiet from the moment I joined them and sat there stabbing at my breakfast steak like it was still alive.

Fine, enjoy yourself as much as you want.

I responded: *Anyone would think you didn't trust me.*

It was a cheap shot. I turned off my phone and left it in my room as we made our way out to the strip. I was livid that he had the nerve to practically accuse me of some kind of wrongdoing when he had bleated on at me for having an issue with him going to Washington.

And again we played the game of not answering text messages or phone calls to spite each other.

Over the next couple of days there was no communication with Danny, which only led me to becoming angrier with him. I got annoyed and was determined to enjoy myself to switch my temper off. As it was our request trip, I didn't want to spend the time with my friends with a face like a slapped arse. Most of the time I was with the crew, Adam joined us in whatever we were doing. We chatted about various things, and I got more of a background on his story. He had been in the Royal Air Force at the start of his career, and only left his position at the insistence of a girl he was seeing for many years. He spoke of his life like each day was another lie and another hardship. He spoke of the guilt he felt about lying to his family and the humiliation he felt he had caused his ex-girlfriend when he made the leap and came out of the closet. Throughout the talks and chats there was a sense of anguish that was extinguished by the simple phrase that often ended the conversation: "But that was all before I came out." He always said it a smile and a sense of sad relief.

It was late afternoon by the hotel pool on our last day and Adam and I were alone, as the rest of the crew had already retired to their rooms. We sat chatting, drinking beers, and watching the color of the sky change behind the concrete jungle of statues and casinos. I hadn't mentioned Danny for the past day or so, as even the mention of his name made me feel angry.

"You're a good guy, Greg," Adam said, holding a bottle of beer up to me. "Thanks for a good trip. I hope they are all like this."

"No problem. Glad you had a good time, although I think Lee and Steve are a little bitter that they didn't get a chance to be a flight deck floozy."

Adam looked over at me and cracked a half smile. "Yeah, they were pretty intense and unashamedly flirtatious."

"Of course they were. You can't blame them for trying."

"Wow, do I take that as a compliment from you, Greg?"

I saw him sheepishly grin.

"Can I offer you a few words of advice, for what they're worth?" I asked, looking at him seriously.

"Sure!"

"We work for a great airline, but the gossip is unbelievable. Do me a favor: if you end up messing around with any of the crew, just be warned that it's more than likely going to get back to everyone else. If they realize you are the type to screw around with crew down route they will be knocking on your door on every trip, and you will have to go through the embarrassment of rejecting them. Then you have to work with them the next week, the next month, and the next year. Fly for a few months and you'll be able to gauge who you can trust." I nodded slowly to make sure he understood what I was saying, before quickly adding, "Hey, I am by no means suggesting that you are that kind of guy. It's just that flight deck have a reputation, and there is good reason why they have that reputation. You're a nice guy, so I wouldn't want to see your name bandied about."

He took a deep breath and considered what I said.

"I appreciate what you are saying, but after living in the closet for so long I don't think that my automatic distrust or wariness of people will go away that fast. I am a pretty good judge of character, so hopefully I will be okay."

"I am sure you are," I said as I gathered up my towel and iPod. "I am heading up now, as the flight home tomorrow is going to be a long one, and I need a full night's sleep. Have a nice evening, fella, and thanks for the beer."

I shuffled my feet into flip-flops and walked toward the entrance of the hotel when I heard Adam take a deep breath in. I looked around.

"I would have trusted you, Greg," he said, not even attempting to catch my eye. Almost immediately his face showed regret for the confession.

All I could do was smile and nod my head in what I hoped would look like appreciation. I walked up to my room cursing myself that I shouldn't have felt so pleased to be complimented by such a guy.

I slept badly that night. Being on bad terms with Danny was awful. I hated when we argued. It played on my mind, and I struggled with my own thoughts, from "I was completely in the wrong for not considering his feelings," to menacing thoughts about Adam and how much easier life would be if I was with a man who knew my lifestyle and lived in the same country as me.

Late the following morning, I packed and got back into bed to try and nap before operating the flight home. I knew that my mood was lousy when I was tired on night flights, and the row with Danny wouldn't help it at all. I set the alarm on the clock and took the phone off the hook.

Just as I drifted off there was a heavy knock at the door. I shouted out, "No, thank you!" to the chambermaid, who I assumed had come to clean the room, before flipping over and closing my eyes.

"Greg, it's Adam," a muffled voice said through the door.

I jumped up and threw on a pair of jeans. I walked to the door hoping that this visit to my room wasn't going to become awkward. However, when I cracked the door open I could see that he looked rather disturbed.

"Is everything okay?" I asked. I knew there had to be something wrong. It was unheard of for the captain to disturb you during your rest time before a flight.

"I have just had a call from the head office of the airline. Apparently, your mum has been trying to get hold of you, and it sounds like it's important. They put her through to me because your phone is engaged, and I told her that I would get you to call her as soon as possible." He looked at me with some unknown pity. "I hope everything is okay."

"Oh, Jesus, I will call her straightaway. Thanks for letting me know," I said as I was closing the door, ready to run to the phone. The faces of my brother, sister, nieces, and nephews shot through my head.

"No problem. Hey, I didn't know you're an American too."

"Huh? I'm not," I answered, reopening the door a little wider, puzzled by his statement.

"Oh, I just assumed you were since your mother is."

"She's not, she's… wait, was it an American woman who called you?"

"Yes, very strong accent. She said it was important that she speak to you, but she didn't offer the reason why, and I wasn't about to ask."

My heart skipped a beat. Something was terribly wrong. Danny must have been hurt, or even worse. At least I was already in the States. How quick would I be able to get a flight to Texas? I dashed to my phone to get the number off my contacts list and dialed his mother's number, leaving Adam to close the door and return to his own room. It took three attempts, with my hands shaking and near crying, terrified of the news I was about to hear. First, I got the outside dialing code wrong, then lost track of the stream of numbers that I had to prefix before even entering hers. Finally, I got through and the call was answered.

"Mrs. Taylor, it's Greg. What's happened, what's wrong?" I asked, my voice shaking. My head was spinning. The last contact Danny and I had had been an argument.

"Thank you for calling me back, Gregory," she said calmly. "I just wanted you to know that you have really upset my son with your argument. I think you are being very mean and very unfair to Danny. Perhaps the two of you should—"

"Mrs. Taylor, is Danny okay? Has he been hurt?"

"No, of course not. He is, however, very upset that you are arguing. I have just spoken to your mother, and she said—"

"You did what?"

"I have just spoken to your mother. She said that she wasn't even aware that there was a problem. I guess you're not as close to your mother as Danny is to his."

"Are you kidding me with this shit? You've called my work, who put you through to Las Vegas, disturbed my captain's rest to come and get me, put the fear of God into me that something was wrong, troubled my widowed mother, and you are telling me that you did this because Danny and I had a row? Are you out of your mind?"

"My son is upset because of you, and I think I have the right to tell you that you should leave him alone for a while." She paused and took a deliberate, theatrical breath. "I am warning you—"

"No, you have *no* right, Mrs. Taylor. And you don't 'warn' me about fucking anything, lady. *Never* do this again. And let me make it quite clear, if you even consider worrying my mother with such things again I will be at your church within a day and declaring your son's sexuality so loud that every last person in Baytown will hear it." I slammed down the phone with such force that it bounced back off the receiver, so I slammed it down again.

For the next two hours I paced in my hotel room, swearing and wishing evil things. This was getting beyond a joke. I knew Danny had given his mother my mother's number as another contact when he was visiting England, but I never dreamt she would ever use it. As I packed the last things into my bag, I grew angry at Danny. I couldn't understand why he would want to put me in such an awkward position, knowing that I would at some point have to deal with his mother again face-to-face. I threw the toiletries into my wash bag as I muttered, "Fucking mama's boy, running to mama. 'Mama, Greg's being mean to me'," under my breath with venom. Of all the people he could have spoken to, he went to her? Why? Was it because if he spoke to someone else about our argument they would have told him it was ridiculous? Or was it that he knew full well that, out of everyone in his life, his mother would agree with him one hundred percent, and therefore validate his notion that I was going to cheat on him.

But the guilt slowly crept in and I eased up. After Adam's comment to me as I left the pool, Danny obviously did have something to be concerned about. But if he realized this, why did he make such a huge deal about the way I felt about him going to Washington? Why was it okay for him, but not for me? How was this so one-sided? And if I had gone running my mouth off to my mother about our argument about Washington, he would have been mortified. Yet he put me in that position without thinking.

Getting on the crew bus to head toward the airport, I sat stone-faced while Donna and Jacks mouthed "Are you okay?" at me. I separated myself, and my mood, at the back of the bus. Jacks got up toward the end of the journey and sat next to me.

"My dah'ling, Adam said you had a bit of a distressed phone call. Is everything okay? Would you like to position home?" she asked kindly while rubbing my knee.

"I am okay, babe. It wasn't so much a distressed phone call as it was a telling off."

Jackie looked confused.

"I have had an argument with Danny, and his mother tracked me down and, well, made her feelings clear."

Jackie began to laugh. "Thank God for that! I thought someone died! You put that smile back on your face and don't let the mother get you down, sweetheart. Although disturbing the captain's rest, regardless how cute he is, is a huge no-no."

I nodded in agreement, although I was still seething.

By the time we took off to return to London, my mood had done nothing but get steadily worse with my fatigue and was made even worse by an uptight middle-aged woman with graying hair travelling with her more placid friend, who did nothing but demand something every time I walked past her. Usually I humored these types of passengers, most of whom were returning from Vegas in a bad mood from losing a great deal of money. However, this particular woman resembled Mrs. Taylor in age, face, and attitude, so I had to make a concerted effort not to take her demands to heart.

"The plane is too cold," she barked at me after gripping the side of my shirt and pulling me back. Passengers who poked, shoved, or grabbed for my attention were one of the only things I hated about my job.

"Okay, madam, I will turn the heating up," I replied as I made a point of re-tucking the side of my shirt back into my trousers.

I returned to the galley, turned the cabin temperature up, and then sat down to one side on my own to calm down and drink a cup of coffee. I hadn't even got halfway through it when the bell called. I got up and made my way down the cabin to find the same old dragon pressing the call button repeatedly.

"Now you have made it too hot. Can't you turn it down? It's like an oven in here," she said, fanning a safety card in front of her face for effect.

"Madam, it takes more than two minutes for the temperature to change in the cabin. I can assure you it's no warmer in here than it was moments ago when you asked me to turn it up."

"Just do as I ask," she said, waving her hand to dismiss me.

Menopausal old hag, I thought as I marched back to the galley to take my seat. Before I even took another sip I heard a series of continuous chimes, and once again I saw the arm of the demanding woman pressing the bell above her head in rapid succession.

I looked around the galley and saw that I was the only one available to answer. Reluctantly, I walked down and faced her again.

"Will you turn this air conditioning down? It's making the air dry and affecting my throat," she said, stroking her neck like she was gasping for water.

"Certainly, madam," I said a little too casually, making it obvious that she was becoming tiresome.

As I turned to walk away, she grabbed the bottom of my shirt again, pulling it clean out of my trousers.

"And get me another pillow, as well. My back hurts," she demanded without so much as an apology.

Once again, I completed her request while muttering under my breath about wanting to hold it over her face, before returning to the galley to help prepare the dinner service.

I didn't smile at all during the flight. In fact, I had a face like thunder from the moment we boarded. I couldn't believe how mad Mrs. Taylor made me, and it was made even worse that I now suspected that, for once, she had a good reason for it. I hadn't done anything wrong, but it was almost as if she somehow channeled extra guilt my way, like she had a sense and ability to make it worse. I was so enraged that she was on my case even in other countries and while I was at work. Surely she must have known this was going to make me angry, or was that part of her plan? The more I thought about Danny telling her about our argument, the madder I became at him for putting me in that position in the first place. I hung up on his mother, and that was only going to make things worse. I played out the coming argument in my head as I mindlessly handed out the meals to the passengers. I didn't realize that I had reached the ever-demanding woman until it was too late.

"You don't like your job, do you?" she asked, with a satisfied smile on her face.

"Actually, madam, I do. I enjoy it very much." I forced a smile, even though I was livid that she would say such a thing out of pure spite.

"My throat has become very sore with this air conditioning."

"Well, since we have to consider the comfort of the other 300 passengers onboard, I am unable to adjust the air conditioning any further. Perhaps a little water may ease it," I said as I laid her meal in front of her, trying with every ounce of my being to remain calm.

"Silly boy, that's not going to work. Get me a lozenge for my throat."

"I am sorry, madam, but we only carry special medicated throat sprays in a sealed first aid kit, and they are only ever opened in situations where a passenger is in real need and on the advice of Medlink, which is a service that connects us to a doctor on the ground who tells us to administer it. I simply cannot open a sealed, fixed first aid kit just for a sore throat."

With this, she turned to her friend to ensure she was watching, then spun her head back to me and said, "This is your job. If you don't like it you shouldn't be doing it. Now get me something for my throat." She leaned forward and snapped her fingers. "Now!"

It was as though I was in a dream, or having some kind of out of body experience. I calmly opened the wrapping on the cutlery kit that was on her meal tray. I slowly drew out the plastic knife and presented it to her on a napkin and whispered, "Something for your throat, madam."

The moment I said it I knew I had gone too far.

She leapt out of her seat and began shouting at the top of her voice, all the other passengers around her taking off their headphones to hear what she was saying.

"Where is your manager? How dare you! How dare you! Get me your manager now!"

Donna, who was across the aisle, looked over at me, confused and a little scared. The woman looked as though she was possessed.

"Madam, I am the Cabin Services Director," came Jackie's voice behind me. She obviously had been alerted to the commotion. "I would be happy to hear anything you have to say, if you would just follow me down to the galley so I can hear you a little better. You see, your seats are over the engines, and I would prefer to be able to give you my full, undivided attention," she said in an authoritative tone, as if this was normal procedure.

I moved the cart back so the old hag could get out of her seat and watched her stomp down the aisle toward the back galley. I turned to Jackie, who was preparing to follow her.

"Jacks, I am really sorry," I said honestly.

"Good grief, young man," she whispered back, "what on earth did you do to make that woman act so wild?"

I winced. "I messed up, Jacks." I bowed my head in shame. I knew that Jackie was going to be in for it, and there was nothing I could say to defend myself.

Reaching the other end of the aircraft, I decided to remain at the front while Jackie dealt with the passenger in the back. I sat on a jump seat with my head buried in my hands and cursing Mrs. Taylor for getting me in such a state that I had just held a knife, albeit a plastic one with no real intention, up to a passenger's face. Without my job, which I was surely going to lose, it would be impossible to keep flying back and forth to Texas to see Danny or get the time off to spend with him. I also had a mortgage to pay on my flat. Would I be able to fly with another airline with such an appalling reference? My mind began to wander. Perhaps this was a good thing. Maybe this wasn't going to work out anyway. Mrs. Taylor was hell-bent on doing what she could to make Danny and me split up, the distance was hard enough, and the arguments were only making matters worse. My head was spinning.

After an hour and a half I got up and poked my head through the curtain to the sleeping cabin and watched the passenger leave the galley and, strangely, wobble back to her seat.

I sat back down, waiting for Jackie's arrival and shouts, with Donna rubbing my shoulder.

"Greg, can I have your ice tongs when you leave? Yours are so much sturdier than mine and it's unlikely you'll ever need to use them again since you won't be crew anymore and the unemployed can rarely afford to have dinner parties," Donna said in an attempt to make me smile.

"Jackie is going to go crazy at me for this," I replied, sorrow etched on my face.

"Would it be awfully wrong if I got my camera out of the crew bag so it's ready for when the police arrest you on the air bridge?" Donna clicked the make-believe camera in her hands. "Psycho Stephens: Stabbing Steward's Sad Story, only in today's Daily Mail."

Jackie entered like a Broadway star through the curtain.

"You are a very naughty boy, Mr. Stephens!" she said, smiling and laughing. I looked at her, not quite believing what I was hearing or seeing.

"You would have been in a world of trouble, young man, if I hadn't found that little stunt so wildly entertaining!" She winked and sat on the free jump seat next to mine. "I must admit, I never thought you had such a wicked side to you. I quite underestimated you. There's a jolly old evil streak in you!"

"Jackie, I am so sorry. I didn't mean to do it. I am just overtired, and I had to deal with Danny's mother again today."

"Oh, my love, don't you worry about it. I just sat her in the galley and plied her with free drinks and convinced her to say the most horrid things about you, which wasn't hard. That way, if she does make a formal complaint, I can say she was saying terrible things and she'd had far too much to drink. Such accusations against you were never brought to my attention! But I did see her sloshed and almost on the floor complaining that she lost all of her money on the slots." She gave me a sly smile. "Dah'ling, no one is going to believe her over me, I promise you." Jackie raised an eyebrow. "Having said that, as humorous as it was, I wouldn't repeat that story to a soul. You, that is, not me. I will retell that story at every dinner party and soirée from this moment forth. Fabulous!"

"I owe you one, Jackie, I really do," I said as I gave her a hug.

"Just you stay with that gorgeous man of yours. One day I may need to call in a favor to get out of some trouble stateside."

Each time I went into work in the following weeks, I opened my drop file carefully and peered inside like there was going to be a poisonous snake coiled up inside ready to strike. I dreaded the thought of finding a letter informing me of my dismissal or at least a meeting to discuss my behavior, which in turn would lead to my dismissal. An offer of tea and biscuits in the office with a manager was like being marked for death. Despite Jackie's insistence that the matter would go no further, I was still convinced that it was only a matter of time before a letter from a solicitor seeking damages would arrive. Thankfully, it never did arrive, but I served out my own punishment by fretting over it so much.

My mood at the time wasn't exactly helpful when it came to Danny and me trying to work things out. We spoke when I returned, and he said that, on reflection, he overreacted. He told me that he thought about it long and hard and concluded that I couldn't control my environment, and even if I could, I had given him no reason not to trust me. He also finally admitted that he completely understood where I was coming from about the Washington trip.

As I silently sat and listened to him, I waited to hear his opinion, or at the very least an apology, for what his mother had done. Within five minutes, however, it was clear that Mrs. Taylor hadn't told him about our phone call. We ended the conversation with a lingering chill between us. But Danny, having said he was in the wrong, was confused why we didn't immediately go back to normal.

Once again, Mrs. Taylor had gunned for me and hadn't told Danny about it. Why did she trust that I wouldn't do the same? Was this a test? Was she trying to goad me into arguing with Danny about her, therefore proving that I was trying to cause trouble between them? Did she think that by keeping quiet I was confirming that I knew I was in the wrong? What she didn't foresee was that Danny was so happy she and I seemed to be getting along that I couldn't bring myself to smash that image. I saw the way that Danny reacted when I criticized her in any way, so I knew that if I tried to talk to him about it my anger would get the better of me and all hell would break loose. Mrs. Taylor would have spun it that she had only called me out of concern anyway, so what would be the point? By the end of the month any arguments that Danny and I'd had were forgotten, and we resumed our usual relationship. However, the memory of what Mrs. Taylor did stuck with me firmly.

CHAPTER THIRTEEN

"TIGER, are you sure you want to do this?" I asked as I looked into the webcam.

"I'm sure. Five years ago, the thought probably wouldn't have entered my head. But back then I was young, and I was blinded into thinking that my service outweighed everything else. I can't live like this anymore, and it's not fair to you," he replied, looking sad.

For a few months, Danny had been battling with the idea of "coming out" to the Navy, sooner rather than later. He only had a matter of weeks left on his contract, but had, with each passing month up to now, seemed more and more intent on contacting his seniors at the base in Dallas, where he was on his Reserve duty while he was at school.

"Danny, this is not my decision, it's yours. I will stand behind you whatever you decide to do, but it will all come down to what you want. Not what I want," I said, making my feelings clear.

"I know," he said, "this is entirely my choice."

"I won't lie to you. The idea of you being called to go back in and fight somewhere has always scared the hell out of me. But you're so close to the end of your contract. Is it really worth it?"

My fears had grown even more recently, due to steadily increasing reports of terrorist attacks in the world. With Danny's qualifications, it would only be a matter of time before he was called back from the Reserve. He knew this himself and remained steadfast.

But now he was due to finish his contract and weighing things in his own mind.

"Greg, if I hadn't met you, I probably wouldn't. But the fact is, if I don't, I'll be just another person who comes out of the military service and nothing more. Why not become a statistic and a number for a report of how many people the policy affects and how much knowledge, money, training, and good men they're losing to it? It might help others in the situation if they have to deal with it."

"Danny, what are the repercussions to this?" I asked, worried that he would somehow be in trouble.

"Well, the worst they can do is give me a dishonorable discharge from the Navy, but in order for them to do that they would have to prove that I performed my duties dishonorably. The discharge is a characterization of your service, not the circumstances under which you left. My service has been impeccable, so there's no worry of that. I would still receive an honorable discharge. It's not like I've done anything criminal, and it's unlikely to affect any résumé that I put forward. If anyone should ask, I'd just tell them the real reason: I was discharged because I am gay." He said the last sentence in a matter-of-fact way, although I knew he was covering his sadness. "If any employer had a problem with that, I wouldn't want to work for them anyway."

"You have changed, Tiger. When we met, you were all about serving your country and being a good officer."

"I still am! Of course I am. There's no way I'd have joined up and spent two years on a ship and the years in the Middle East if I wasn't The Navy is still one of the greatest military forces in the world, and I loved being part of it and serving my country. I took a lot of pride and dignity in that. But since I met you, they don't seem to want to show the same respect to me. I just didn't realize how big a deal it was before you came into my life."

"Have you spoken to your family about this?" I asked, meaning *Have you asked your mother her opinion?*

"No, and quite frankly it's none of their business. None of them have served in the military, so none of them are in the position to judge what is right and wrong. Obviously, I expect them to support my decision, but they won't alter it if they don't," he said defensively.

"Just remember you have great memories from being in the Navy, and you have made some great friends. Don't let all of this sour you."

Danny shook his head. "I won't. I'm just older now and look at things differently. Maybe one day they'll overturn the policy, but I don't think it'll be anytime soon."

Danny signed off, and I knew he was getting straight on to writing his letter to his commanding officer. Danny had proven he was a person who, once he set his mind to something, he would see it through. It seemed like such a personal statement that I felt I shouldn't have any input into the way he went about it. He was due to go to his Reserve unit the following day and decided he would deliver the letter by hand but would stay in person should there be any kind of discussion or questions.

It was impossible to sleep that night. The idea of Danny being on his own while he handed in his confession, and therefore his notice, worried me. I was concerned that there would be an immediate backlash, that whomever he handed his "coming out" letter to would inform everyone else immediately and leave him in a position of danger. I didn't know his comrades in the unit, and I didn't know what their reactions might be to discovering there was a gay man in their ranks. These were not the same men he was on active duty with. My head filled with horrible scenarios of him being ridiculed or, even worse, injured or set upon.

I never understood media commentators or even military personnel of all ranks in America who got on their high horses about "gays" in the military. During the war in Iraq, the American military made it clear and announced they were so thankful, so glad, and so honored to fight alongside British forces. Yet not one of them mentioned the fact that some of the men and women they fought alongside, who took bullets and were killed by IEDs, were, in fact, gay troops. The UK opened its military services to gay people many years before. It seemed that it was okay for them to put their lives on the line, so long as the Americans didn't have to share a base, or as long as they went home to England afterward.

Yet, amazingly, all their right-wing morals and values disappeared when they needed shared information. It was a travesty that higher-ranking American military leaders shared secrets and operational information openly with gay British intelligence officers, while their own were confined to the dark spaces of closets. I know that the British once had a policy against gays in the military too, but like so many other injustices toward gay people, they all seemed to be resolved by the time I hit any age of activism.

Since I was six hours ahead in the UK and it was my day off, I spent most of the day trying to occupy my time and not to fret too much over it. I drifted off into a daytime nightmare once that morning and began to panic, and considered calling Danny to get him either to change his mind or at least hand the letter in as he left after his duty and was returning home.

Around 7:00 p.m., I received an e-mail. I knew it was going to be difficult to call me, since Danny rarely called from his personal phone while on duty. In the scheme of things, that was probably wise, considering the personal text messages I had sent to his phone, so I checked my laptop regularly for any kind of update.

Hey, Baby,

I just spoke to the captain and handed in the letter. He seemed to take it okay, although he seemed more bothered about the amount of work it will cause for him. He suggested I leave now and miss the rest of this month's reserve duty while he processes the paperwork. He hasn't had to handle anything like this before, so I think he's kind of on a learning curve. It was a strange conversation. It seems like I was hiding this from them for so long, I never thought it would be me that brought it to their attention. It feels good, though, and I'm sure I made the right decision. Below is a copy of the letter. I'm leaving now but will call you on my way home.

All my love

Danny

I opened up the attachment.

Captain Burholt:

I have given the United States Navy more than six years of my life, and am very proud of the service I have provided my country. The Navy's core values of honor, courage, and commitment are an important part of my life. But the military's "Don't Ask, Don't Tell" policy prevents me from truly living up to those standards, because I am homosexual. Instead of honoring my right to love whoever I wish, the military criminalizes it. Rather than having the courage to accept service members as they are, I am discouraged from being myself. And instead of committing to support those who are willing to sacrifice their lives for their country, I am told that revealing who I am is grounds for dismissal. Where are the core values in that?

I have known of my sexual identity for many years, and I knew of the military's discriminatory policies when I joined. But my patriotism and desire to serve my country overcame any doubts I had. I am first and foremost an American, and my sexuality is secondary. But I have repeatedly seen how the military's policies toward homosexuals denigrate not only my dignity, but also my contributions to the country.

My partner of three years is a British national, and in his country homosexuals in the military are entitled to the same rights and privileges as their heterosexual counterparts. Just this week, the first homosexual couple moved into military housing. It has not caused the breakdown in unit morale or cohesiveness that the Pentagon has used as an excuse for the "Don't Ask, Don't Tell" policy. On the contrary, British service members are not as suspicious of one another, and recruiting levels don't suffer the way they do in America. The "Don't Ask, Don't Tell" policy simply does not make sense.

My partner does not receive the same respect and would not be afforded the same support as my colleagues' spouses. I cannot, in good conscience, continue to hide my sexual orientation from a military that will not value my partner or my relationship in the manner to which they are entitled.

I understand that this admission may end my naval career, and that genuinely saddens me. I have met and worked with some of the most extraordinary people during my service. I worked hard, learned a great deal, and experienced the world from an angle very few get the opportunity to see. But I also struggled with discrimination, hid my life from the service, and lived in constant fear that everything I worked so hard for would be taken from me. For the past three years, I have been fortunate enough to have a partner who supports me and has endured the travails by my side. I owe him and our relationship the honor, courage, and commitment that the Navy has taught me to embrace— even if the Navy will not embrace me for who I am.

Very respectfully,

D.M. Taylor

LT USN

Driving back to Austin, Danny called me.

"How are you feeling?" I asked.

"Actually, I feel pretty damned good. It feels like a weight has been lifted off my shoulders. I forwarded the letter to a few friends and Navy colleagues over e-mail, since I don't want them to find out from anyone other than me. It's probably best they know I did this on my own before the gossip starts that I was found with my cammies around my combat boots in the mess hall screwing a fellow officer."

"How do you think they will take it?" I asked.

"Well, I've already received five e-mails back saying that they didn't feel any differently toward me, that they never agreed with the policy in the first place, and that it was a shame that the Navy was losing me as an officer and wishing me luck. So, so far so good!"

I could hear the relief in his voice. I knew he had great respect for many of the people with whom he worked on the ship and on the ground. Many of the e-mails were to the people who served with Danny on the USS Enterprise when they were directed toward Afghanistan immediately after the events of 9/11.

"Hang on, baby, I have another call coming through. Can I call you straight back?" Danny said as I heard his phone beep in my ear.

"No problem," I said and ended the call.

I was so happy that he received a decent response back to his e-mails. I thought for a moment that I had been stupid not to give these people the benefit of the doubt. These were not silly people who would take issue with the matter of sexuality. Would a straight mountain climber think any less of a fellow crewmember who climbed to the top of Everest and then came out? They made the same journey, and that kind of respect far outweighs anything else.

I felt a little foolish that I had been so nervous of Danny coming out, and felt that, for once, my views on Americans in general had been way off. But on this occasion I was more than happy to be proven wrong.

The phone rang again.

"That was Mark on the phone," Danny spat.

"Mark who?"

"He was a fellow Navy officer I used to date when I was in DC, the one Tucker told you looks haggard now," Danny said, sounding furious.

"Okay," I said, though I could already feel the monster of jealousy writhing in my stomach. "What's the problem?"

"He was included in the list of Navy contacts in my e-mail folder."

"Okay, Tiger. Again, what's the problem? Danny, you sound really mad. Can you at least pull over while you talk to me? I hate it when you drive and speak on the phone."

He didn't respond, but I heard the wind echoing in the receiver die down and eventually the sounds of tires slowing to a stop on the gravel.

"He's just gone off like a bomb at me. He said that it was 'a betrayal of my oath of office'. He said that I knew the situation before I went in and shouldn't have expected it to change and that I made a huge mistake," he ranted. "He said I was naïve to think that I was making any kind of difference to the cause and that, if anything, I had just made it worse, and I was using it as an excuse to get out!"

"Is he in the Navy now?" I asked, hardly believing what I was hearing.

"Yes."

"And this guy thinks he has the right to judge you on your decision? I hope you told him to shove it up his arse, Tiger. What the hell has it got to do with him anyway? If he wants to live his life like that then that's up to him. And how the hell can he call it an excuse when you only had a few more weeks to go?"

"I know. I'm just so angry——"

"Why?" I interrupted. "Why are you mad at a fool like that? The only reason he is mad with you is that he is jealous. He is jealous the e-mail said that you had something more in your life than military service or career, and that he can no longer count you in his little group of closeted friends when he wants to whine and bitch about hiding. You made the break, and he's pissed because he probably wants to do it but doesn't have the balls."

"I'm not sure it's quite like that, Greg."

"It is exactly like that. If he wants to serve in the closet, that's up to him. But to go off at you for coming out is fucking outrageous!"

Danny's breathing seemed to slow as he calmed down and recomposed himself.

"Maybe you're right," he finally said. "Maybe I shouldn't take it to heart."

"Take it to heart? Why are you letting this bother you at all? You knew there was a possibility someone may have something negative to say about your actions, and you prepared yourself for it. Why are you letting this dickhead get you down when you had five other e-mails wishing you luck?"

"Seven now."

"There you go! Don't let one guy, who frankly should know better and should be supporting you more than any other person you know in the Navy, get you down. Fuck him! Or better still, give me his full name and rank. I will report the fucker for being gay. Fucking self-loathing little prick. Seriously, give me his surname. I will call the Navy myself and tell them he's had his arse occupied by more American military men than Fallujah."

Danny started to laugh and eventually relaxed. I on the other hand, remained furious and would have gladly boarded a plane to DC to rip this bloody guy's head off his neck.

CHAPTER FOURTEEN

AFTER three long years of studying, exams, question cards, papers, and lectures, the day finally arrived for Danny to graduate from law school, and, of course, his parents and family were coming to town for the ceremony. Danny was a mixture of fret and excitement when his parents' SUV arrived, closely followed by his sisters and brothers-in-law. Tammy and Kimberly were thrilled to see their little brother and, despite a look of betrayal on Mrs. Taylor's face, threw their arms around me and embraced me as one of the family. It seemed that they hadn't bought into Mrs. Taylor's brand of private persecution.

Even in their late twenties and early thirties, the three of them teased each other the way I imagined they did when they were kids. You could tell they were immensely proud of their brother, but were determined not to let him get above his station, continuously mocking his choice of career. He was to be a hotshot New York City attorney, as he had accepted the offer from the law firm where he had worked the previous summer.

"Oh, Danny, you look so smart and handsome. You become a lawyer today!" Mrs. Taylor exclaimed as she got out of her car, arms outstretched for the waiting hug.

"Not quite yet, Momma, I still have to take the bar exam," Danny said into her shoulder.

"Well, Tiger, I think if you managed three years of law school, you can manage the exam. You're far too smart not to ace it," I remarked as I walked clean past Mrs. Taylor and held my hand out to shake George's.

"Of course he is," Mrs. Taylor snapped, like there was some kind of doubt in my voice or as if I were just paying lip service. "He has always been very smart...." She paused long enough to release Danny into George's handshake and looked me up and down like a piece of dirt on the street. "Well, about most things." Even though it was one of the most important days of Danny's life, she obviously was not going to even pretend to like me while in sight or earshot of her golden child.

As Tucker walked out of the house, Mrs. Taylor made her usual over-the-top, high-pitched greeting, once again making it blatantly obvious that she was more pleased to see him than me. Tucker responded the same way, especially when he saw a tub of what looked like homemade cookies in her hand. I had to let the resentment go, as I was determined not to let anything ruin the day for Danny. He worked so hard and studied for too long to let this day go without absolute family perfection.

I drove alone with Danny to the ceremony held at the University of Texas. He was overexcited and kept singing along with the radio station, only occasionally stopping to turn the music down to ramble about what I should expect from the event. He was a bag of nerves and energy, like a kid who knew he was going to get a new bike but had to wait for his parents to get up on Christmas morning before he could take it for a ride.

As we reached the graduation hall, Tucker, Danny's sisters and brothers-in-law, and I began to search for our seats in the auditorium. As we made our way down the steps to the seats that Danny reserved for us, I noticed Mrs. Taylor stepped down a little faster to catch up with me. I tried to quicken my pace to outrun her, as I wanted to be a few seats away from her, but the next thing I knew there was a searing pain at the back of my arm.

"Oh, Momma, are you okay?" I heard Tammy cry as she caught her mother's arm. Mrs. Taylor had begun to fall, far too slowly, backward. As she pretended to fall she reached out to my arm to "catch herself," driving every last white-tipped acrylic nail into my flesh. Even though it was Danny's graduation, she seemed determined to get some attention today.

"Good thing Greg was there or else I would have gone all the way down, but I think I twisted my ankle." She smiled like I was her savior just to drive in the excuse that it had been an accident.

I rubbed the five arced wounds in my arm, two of which were now raised and bleeding in a trickle, and just for a moment imagined her tumbling down the rest of the stone stairs like Crystal Carrington, her head barely protected by her lacquered bob.

"I don't think I can make it down the rest of the stairs. There are two free seats here. George and I will sit here, and you guys go down to the seats," she said, wincing and acting like a wounded soldier asking her troops to leave her on the battlefield. She chose the only two seats in the area that were free, leaving no possibility of us joining them.

"Mrs. Taylor, we can't sit separately during the ceremony. Danny expects to see us all where he reserved us seats. We'll carry you down if we have to."

"I am sure my son will understand, Gregory," she said, using my full name again. I hated when my own mother did it when I was being chastised as a child. But listening to Mrs. Taylor use it just put my back up more than it already was. "I don't think he would like to see his mother in the hospital."

"No, I am sure *he* wouldn't," I said flatly and deliberately. Once again, visions of her in the hospital on life support (and me denying I flipped the switch to a jury) popped into my head. "We will all sit up here together, so he has his crowd." I looked higher in the auditorium.

"No, no," she protested, "There aren't enough seats for us all to sit together here, and besides, if Danny has gone to the time and the effort to reserve seats I think we should use them. You go ahead," she said, as if it made sense, even though she was doing the opposite to his wishes.

"Fine, we'll go down there, and I will text Danny to let him know where you are sitting. I will be sure to text him about your little accident and reassure him you weren't too injured. I wouldn't want him worrying on his big day." I turned my back and headed back down the stairs, fuming.

George looked at me. I could tell he was torn between wanting to pull me up on my tone, but at the same time it was clear that he disapproved of his wife's plan.

We all took our seats just in time for the ceremony to begin, and I texted Danny just in time to tell him his parents' new location and received a simple "ok" back in response.

The ceremony was as dignified as one would have expected for such a prominent school. The Mayor of Houston delivered the commencement address, as well as many other speakers, all of whom offered advice for the newly graduating lawyers. They spoke of their responsibilities, their own careers, the way law was changing, and encouraged the people, all on stage and spellbound by the speakers, to continue their commitments.

Once the speeches were done, it was time for the dean of the school to present each student with his or her diploma. Each name was called alphabetically, leading that student on stage to be cheered on by the crowd of family and friends in the auditorium. About half an hour passed before the time when Danny would be walking across the stage.

"Sarah Taplock," said the voice of the announcer. "Sarah would like to thank her parents for their love and support, her husband, and God." There was a mini-eruption from a group of people in the seats a few rows below us.

"David Tartly." Another young man rose and began his walk across the stage to the sounds of hollering, briefly looking up at his group holding banners with his name and waving flags. "David would like to thank God, his parents, and his friends for all of their help while here at The University of Texas."

The volume on the speaker was set louder than it had been at any other time during the ceremony. The echo was so loud that I am sure it was what many of the people in the auditorium imagined the voice of God to sound like.

I looked over at Danny, who was next in queue. There was no way you could tell he was nervous. He exuded all the confidence that a military background brought. Straight back, chin up, and a stride that was effortless. But I knew he was nervous by the way he wouldn't let his eyes shift off the person in front of him for fear of being out of step.

"Daniel Taylor." Our applause was deafening. As we all rose to our feet, screaming, Tucker, Wade, Clayton, and Danny's sisters shouting his name, I looked at him. He looked so handsome as he made his way toward the stage, glancing up toward his parents. I looked up and saw his mother, miraculously back on her fully healed ankle, nudging the man next to her and pointing out her son to the stranger.

"Daniel would like to thank his family and friends for all their help…," said the booming voice. There was a slight but noticeable pause before the announcer continued, "… but mostly his partner, Greg, for his continued love and support over the past three years."

I was stunned. His declaration meant more than most people in that auditorium would ever know. He looked over to us, bowed his head in thanks, and smiled. I was thrilled and so happy for him. Secretly, I was overjoyed that not only had he put me over his mother, he had announced his sexuality and his priority in general public. But most of all I was in awe of his bravery. Announcing such a thing among thousands of Texans was one hell of a courageous thing to do. As I stomped my feet, shouted, and clapped my hands over my head with joy, I could feel the heat from his mother's eyes, burning a hole in the back of my head. So, turning slowly enough for my moment of glory to be held a few seconds longer, I faced his mother, smiled, and cocked my head to one side. But my eyes only rested on her for a moment. It was George's face that caught my attention. He was smiling and nodding at me as if he was not just proud of his son, but incredibly impressed.

I was still beaming at the end of the ceremony as we all waited for Danny to return to us from the stage. Mrs. Taylor stood away from me in a sour mood, not even responding to Danny's sisters.

"All done!" Danny shouted as he bounded toward me. He grabbed me and kissed me on my lips and drew me into a hug. His mother looked appalled at his lack of social awareness. His sisters moved toward him and congratulated him while their husbands held their hands out from a fully extended arm, as if they feared they were going to get the same hug as I and his sisters had received. His mother smiled sweetly in his direction, then, eyes darting toward me for confirmation, she embraced her son.

"Well, I guess it's off to New York for us!" Danny said, rounding back on me, lifting his embrace from his mother far too soon for her liking, since it appeared that she was trying to hold onto him for dear life.

"Yes! It all seems a bit unreal, eh, Tiger?" I smiled back at him. "Danny, really, well done. You're a star." He leaned in and kissed me.

Danny threw his arms over his sisters' shoulders and walked toward the door, followed by Clayton, Wade, and George, who patted him on his back as he strode away.

"You've done well, haven't you, Greg?"

I turned to see Mrs. Taylor standing alone in front of me. She raised one eyebrow and took a step forward.

"You've landed yourself a New York lawyer. That must be nice for you."

"Sorry?" I said, furrowing my brow. I knew what she was saying, but I was still slightly astonished that she wasn't even filtering her comments anymore.

"I am just sure that Danny will give you a very nice lifestyle. One which you haven't had to work for."

I was awed by her nerve. She was doing nothing short of calling me a gold digger, which was odd since she knew I had met Danny when he was still in the Navy.

"Yes," she continued in a snobbish voice far above her station, "Very well done."

"Thanks, Mrs. Taylor!" I said, holding my voice in jest. "Perhaps one day we'll be able to afford to buy you some manners. I am British, so I'm lucky enough to have them taught to me for free."

She looked taken aback, but then composed herself once more. "Thank heavens you still can't marry my son."

"No, but I can in England. It may not be called marriage, but since I don't go in for all that religious stuff, a civil partnership is just as good!"

"You think you are very clever, don't you, Gregory?"

I sighed and dropped the smile from my face. "No, actually I think Danny is very clever, which is the reason why we are here. So, if you can, please just leave the nastiness alone for today? This is about your son graduating, not about you having the opportunity to try and make a fool of me."

She pursed her lips like she had bitten into a lemon, calculating what she was about to say next.

"I mean it, Mrs. Taylor, if you upset Danny today you will have me to answer to," I said flatly.

"Is that a threat?" she shot back through gritted teeth.

"No, that's a promise."

I looked over and saw Danny waiting at the door, looking in at our direction with a slight look of concern on his face.

I walked over to her, smiled, raised my arms, and placed them softly around her shoulders and hugged her. I spun around with a massive smile on my face, one arm attached to a very stiff and startled Mrs. Taylor. I drew her into me and waved at Danny. I dug my fingers into her shoulders firmly to keep a grip on her arm that was struggling to be free of my hold. But for Danny's sake it was picture perfect. Then I leaned in and kissed her on the cheek, lingering just long enough for it not to be a peck, but not so long that it could be seen as an act.

"One day you will show your true colors, Greg," she said like a ventriloquist.

"You can shove a broomstick up your arse, you old witch," I said, throwing my own voice back.

I jumped into the truck with Danny, and we made our way to the restaurant that he booked, as it was one of his favorite places in Austin to celebrate. Danny was so happy, and I loved seeing the relief on his face. I knew more than anyone how hard it had been for Danny to go to law school. The actual classes and paper writing were a breeze for him, being so intelligent. But going back to school at a later, more mature age after the Navy would have been hard for anyone. He went from having a career in the military and earning a good wage to living like a student again in his late twenties. But finally, it was all done.

We arrived at the restaurant in time to see Mrs. Taylor directing everyone to their seats. I was sent to the opposite end of the table to sit with Tucker. Danny was to be placed next to his mother, who arranged things so she sat at the head of the table with George to her left and Danny to her right. Upon seeing this, Danny leaned over and asked everyone to move down, shifting Tammy out of her seat and beckoning me over to the now vacant chair next to him.

Despite the occasional filthy look thrown my way from Danny's mom, it was an enjoyable meal, which I spent talking mostly to George and Danny. As usual, Mrs. Taylor spoke over me on subjects on which her opinion differed from my own. She was like a lioness waiting for her prey to make that one wrong move, or in my case, remark, before pouncing. But after Danny's declaration at the graduation and our heated exchange, I simply let her speak, occasionally looking at Danny, who rolled the side of his lips in sympathy and gratitude that I was letting it go.

After we finished our desserts, the waiter filled everyone's glasses with wine and left the bottle next to George, who the waiter assumed would be leaving the tip. Mrs. Taylor rose from her seat and tapped her glass like she was the emcee at a lavish hotel wedding, demanding everyone's attention.

"Daniel," she began, looking down at her son with pride, "the family is so proud of you today. I have always known that you would go on to do great things, and here you are, on the eve of your new adventure of being an attorney in Manhattan. I hope your dad and I have given you all of the guidance and support that you need to make the right choices in life, and that you have taken our advice carefully." She didn't hide her shift in glance at me. I didn't understand how she could play the game of being friends one minute, then make it so obvious that she disliked me the next.

I stared at my glass like a movie was playing in the wine.

"I brought my camera for us to take a family photo to commemorate this special occasion, so if I could ask you all to rise and follow me."

Without pausing, she turned her back and walked away, correctly assuming that the family and Tucker would follow her immediately.

She led us all to an unlit fireplace on the back wall of the restaurant, which, in the heat of Texas, probably had never been used since its construction. Overlooking the mantle was a huge stuffed and mounted deer with a blank look of death as its artificial eyes looked over the bibbed patrons chowing down on its species. Once again, Mrs. Taylor organized everyone and their poses for the family picture.

"Tucker, dear, you at the back as you're so tall. Tammy and Wade next to him, that's right. Now, Kimberly and Clayton at this end next to me and George."

I waited to be directed into the portrait as she pulled Danny into the middle of the group.

"That's perfect," she declared. Then, breaking away from the pose, she reached over and handed me the camera. "You don't mind taking the picture, do you, Greg?"

"Momma, Greg should be in the photo too," Danny said, moving forward.

I held my hand up. "No, no, Danny, it's fine. I will take this one—" I shot his mother a look. "—with *just* the family." I then glanced over to Tucker. "Then I will get the waiter to take another one." He gazed at me and sighed.

"Okay, just make sure you're in the next one."

I could have been in a thousand other photos after that one, but we all knew that since it was his mother's camera they would never be developed. Only this photo, sans the foreign object, would be hung pride of place in the family home. His sisters looked over at me and tried a compassionate expression, which only confirmed that I wasn't the only one who noticed the blatant attempt to make me understand that my position was outside of the family. I took the snap and signaled to the family that it was all done.

"Excuse me, would you mind taking a quick photo?" I asked the waiter striding past toward the kitchen empty handed.

I took my place behind Danny, and we prepared to take another photo. Just as the waiter counted down to from three to one, I leaned forward and put one arm around Danny's waist, with my head rested on his shoulders and my smiling cheek pressed against his. It would have been a nice picture if I hadn't been making bunny ears behind his mother's head with my other hand. Well, to an American it would have looked that way, but to a Brit, the two fingers jutting up would have had an entirely different meaning.

CHAPTER FIFTEEN

BY THE time Danny was ready to start in New York, I had put my beloved flat in Kemptown on the market for sale. I spent much of my spare time over the years renovating, painting, tiling, boarding, carpeting, sanding, and furnishing the place. It was a labor of love to get it exactly the way that I had wanted it. Now that it was finally finished and I had to put it on the market, I felt an overwhelming sadness. It wrenched my heart out to sell, but I knew we would need the money for the deposit and furnishing of a new place in New York as well as some back-up cash should we fall short.

Although Danny was on a fantastic starting salary at the law firm, which was more than sufficient to support us both, it would have taken at least a year to save for everything we would need, especially at New York prices. I wasn't prepared to wait any longer. It had been over three years, and I was desperate to put the limbo behind us and move forward. Although I tried to help as much as I could, Danny had lived like a student the past three years and deserved to have a nice home and the peace of mind of money in the bank.

I called the local estate agent in Brighton, who came along to value the flat and take details. It was awful to stand there and listen to her say how nice it was and how comfortable and homey it felt and what a good job I had done. I was ready to take her clipboard and slap it around the back of her head by the time she left. I also had to decide what to do with all of my furniture and possessions. The property market had dropped, and hardly anyone was buying at the time, so I didn't think much of it. I expected the flat to take months to sell, which

I was secretly happy about, as I could spend a little more time there knowing that I was doing everything I could to sell it.

Two days after it went on the market, I was away on a trip to Ottawa when I received an e-mail from the estate agent telling me that she had found a buyer who was paying cash. She was prepared to give me the asking price if I would leave the furniture, as she was buying it as an investment and planned to rent it as a furnished flat. I simply couldn't turn down such a great offer, especially considering market conditions, so I e-mailed her back accepting the offer.

Upon returning from my trip, I drove up to see the Sold sign posted outside the flat. It made me shudder with panic and nerves. Still tired, I walked down to the estate agents and the solicitors and signed the initial paperwork. I had a brief glimpse of what it must be like for any parent to give up their baby for adoption for someone else to look after.

I had just a few weeks until the completion of the sale, and most of that time was spent away on trips with work. I was close to tears when I loaded up my suitcase with my last bits and pieces and handed the keys to the new owner. She already had a doctor lined up to rent the flat who had just transferred from a hospital in London and was keen to move in right away. She was already renting out my home. It felt like property prostitution.

Selling the flat was the first big step, so when the discussion of giving up my job arose, Danny and I agreed that it would be better for me to take a part-time contract at work that allowed me to work one month on and one month off. I would spend my months off living in New York with Danny. It was one thing to sell my flat, but giving up my job entirely and, to an extent, my independence was something entirely different.

I couldn't work in America without a visa, and after eight years of flying as crew, my CV hardly read: "Would be suitable for a corporate position in a Manhattan office." Danny was understanding about my disdain for becoming a "househusband" and supported my choice to continue flying. We both knew that as a first-year associate in a big law firm, he would be working ridiculously long hours, and so for the sake of my sanity, and his ability to work those hours without the guilt of knowing I was at home alone in a new city, we agreed it was the best thing to do in the circumstances. Donna offered me a room at her place for the months that I was flying back in Britain, which enabled everything to work out perfectly.

Danny was due to start his new job in the middle of September, which fell on the first month of my working contract. He looked around Manhattan with a realtor, and after many phone calls and e-mailed photos, we decided on a high-rise building at the top end of Chelsea, overlooking Herald Square and the world's largest Macy's. It was a brand new building, and the management offered special rates for new residents, which made it more affordable to live in such a building in the heart of the city. The first time I saw the corner apartment that we were to inhabit, I was taken aback by the floor-to-ceiling windows that framed a spectacular view of the city, only partially blocked by a very tall Empire State Building. Danny and I both stood there, barely believing that we were signing the papers. We were finally somewhere we could both call home.

Every night for the first month, Danny, Duke, and I gazed out onto the scene below us and were coated in different colors, as the Empire State building changed the colors on its rooftop lights that flooded our apartment. Each and every day I was greeted into the building by the doorman and given parcels by the reception team, who would arrange everything from post to grocery deliveries, which were stored in massive refrigerated units at the back of reception until residents got home and could to take them up to their apartments.

New York seemed to be a different city every day, depending on which route you took to get to your destination. It is the only city in the entire world that reminds me of the melting pot of London, but there is a difference in their attitude. For the first few months I seethed over the general lack of manners and blatant rudeness I encountered every day on the streets or in the stores. Any "thank you" I offered was continually answered with a curt "Uh-huh," void of eye contact, as if they were intentionally pointing out their dislike for helping in any way. I began to actually come to expect it and almost started to enjoy their cultural brashness. Like London, you could never say that New

York was typical of the country, although in London there seems to be a constant flow of foreign tourists from all over the world, whereas New York primarily is bombarded by American tourists. This, of course, made an already loud city even louder.

Each day I jumped on the subway and headed down to Battery Park to meet Danny for lunch, where I met his colleagues. They all seemed very nice, despite their constant looks of worry and concern, as they seemed unable to switch their minds off during that precious hour during the day that they weren't dealing with work.

I then spent part of my afternoons at the local gym in Chelsea, which was originally the home of the YMCA that was made famous by the Village People. However, these days it was less about young Christian men and more about the porn stars, male escorts, and trust fund babies who spent time ripping up their bodies to keep ahead of the game. The men were ridiculously attractive, with the bodies and vanity of Greek gods. They went from shamelessly cruising each other across the room, to staring each other down like feral cats in an alleyway when they wanted to use the same machine or set of weights. Although they were near perfect to look at in the gym and fully clothed, the changing room revealed their extreme body acne, the telltale signs of steroid abuse. But any kind of fantasy about their ripped physiques would drop the instant they opened their mouths. No man who gives the world the impression of supreme masculinity should have pink glitter spill from his mouth when he speaks. How the hell they held up those heavy weights with such limp wrists remains a mystery to me.

I had been to Manhattan a couple of times before, but only as a tourist. Nothing could quite prepare me for actually living there. There was no need for a car, as the public transport system saved me from numerous inevitable car crashes at the hands of the death-wish taxi cab drivers. But getting to and from the local grocery store was a pain in the arse. After being shoved all over the place by bolshie shoppers and then laden with heaving bags of horrendously overpriced food, I realized why usually mild-mannered people might open fire in the street. Suddenly the luxury of online grocery shopping and delivery to the apartment building became a way of saving lives. Though I was well aware of the stereotypes about New York, it was still unnerving when men and woman barked at me on the street and all I had to defend myself was ten-dollar paper towels and bars of bitter-tasting chocolate.

I went from being quietly cautious about my personal safety to laughing out loud in the street as I saw the scores of women who had seen far too many episodes of Sex and the City. They looked unsure whether their ridiculous "couture" dress sense clashed with the ten-dollar knockoff neon-green handbag they just bought from one of the local bootleggers in Chinatown. At least once a day, when I returned from lunch in Battery Park, I would stop and marvel at the whole thing and pinch myself that I was actually living there. But the next moment I would be appalled as I walked past tourists smiling into cameras with their arms slung across each other outside the chain fence of Ground Zero, as if the footprint of where the Twin Towers fell should be in the background of a photograph like one would see Pyramids of Giza or the Eiffel Tower.

Since the apartment was new, it was very much like the place where Danny lived in Bahrain. It was painted a neutral "off white" color and looked like a cell, albeit a cell that had an entire city in its backyard. During the afternoon, I battled the city to look for everything we needed, from spoons to couches. I e-mailed phone pictures to Danny to get his joint approval before I hauled my selections back to the apartment. Because of the lack of space in the apartment, particularly given the space that Danny was used to in Texas, deciding what to get for our new home was like a weird game of furniture Tetris. But eventually, we made it look more like a home.

After working back in Britain for the month of November, I returned to New York for the month of December. Throughout the month, I was pulled around to various holiday parties hosted by people who worked with Danny. It was the first time in my life that I ever felt that I could be intimidated by business people. Many of these people were high-flying lawyers, bankers, traders, and businessmen, all networking their way through the city. Danny's work as a lawyer entailed complex financial transactions centered on capital markets such as securitization, collateralized debt obligations, and credit default swaps... all of which may as well have been in Latin for all I understood of it. The guests' conversations were as much tongue twisters as they were about life in New York. Well, I say they were conversations, but they were more like interviews.

"Hi, Larry Brooks, I work with Simon."

"So what do you do? Where do you work? Where did you go to school? What area of the city do you live in? Does your company or firm need a…? Here's my card."

Danny introduced me to all of the people I hadn't met during our lunches, some of whom were partners of the law firm or, on occasion, a client of the firm who Danny had nothing to do with. I was as nervous as hell, as I wanted to make a good impression. The strange thing was, I never got the interrogation I expected. Once I spoke, it seemed that my accent immediately put them on guard. After telling me how many people in their family came from Britain, of which they seemed immensely proud despite the fact it was ten generations ago, they would just mingle into another conversation with someone else. Although I was relieved, I thought this was rude, and it began to raise my hackles.

At one party, after being similarly approached and then ignored, Danny and I later found ourselves surrounded by the same group of people, only they'd had three or four drinks and were a little merrier and less tightly wound.

"I have got to say, I love your accent. I'm a little intimidated by the English, I always feel so stupid around them," said one woman. She had given me all of three minutes earlier in the evening.

"Oh my God, thank you! I feel like that too," came the call of another.

With the revelation that the intimidation was actually the other way round, I went on a full charm offensive. By the end of the evening, everyone was so much more relaxed, and we ended up having an okay time. This was mostly due to my discovery that, although these people had frightening intelligence, were at the top of their game in the hardest place to work in the world, and really were the top people in the country, they were all basically a bunch of geeks with little to no social skills at all. Yes, they could tell you how the government was holding in Japan and the latest advancements in technologies in China, the condition of the economy in the United States and how mortgage backed securities had "their problems" in the current economic climate, but they couldn't seem to have a laugh and relate to anyone on a personal level. And, as usual, Danny spotted it before I did.

"Greg, I think we're in a room full of clones," he whispered in my ear as we made our way to a fully attended bar in the living room of one host's apartment. This seemed to be the area in the apartment where people showed off their knowledge of wine and whisky, each coming out with a more obscure name to confirm their superior taste to whomever they were trying to impress.

"Yes, but once they've had a drink and relaxed, they're easier to deal with," I whispered back.

"I am so sorry, baby, but I have to play the game."

Danny played that game beautifully. Where many of the guests in these parties talked so loud to the point of almost shouting to be heard, Danny remained quiet. He knew that the best way to make an impression on these people was not to shout to be noticed, but to listen to be liked. So many of the high flyers who were used to being shouted over or interrupted by other professionals took to Danny instantly, as he would actually listen to them and only offered an opinion when asked. They all seemed to enjoy his company so much more as I think they finally found someone who took a real interest in them by giving them more than a sentence on the ever-revolving soapbox.

We did meet a few rare individuals who were more "our kind of people." Before long, we were being shown around New York to the bars, bistros, and private clubs that I imagine no tourist ever knew existed and that many Manhattan dwellers themselves didn't even know were there.

It was the first year that Danny and I were due to spend Christmas day together, and we were like a couple of excited kids. The city was lit from end to end with twinkling lights and looked like every fairy-tale New York Christmas story imaginable. However, seeing the shoppers on Fifth Avenue with their bags of luxury items, the men and women who came out of Macy's with their fingers and knuckles white from the handles of their full bags cutting off the blood supply, you would never think that poverty was just around the corner.

What most people don't see in these stories are the homeless who sleep on the streets, doorways, and stoops who endure very long and bitterly cold nights. I saw them in the morning, nursing wounds on their legs where they slept on top of subway grates all night to try and keep warm. The grid pattern of the grates was burned into their skin, leaving welts and sores too painful to even look at. I often thought of my trips to Mombasa and wondered if these people's lives were any better.

In Mombasa the poverty stricken were surrounded by others who shared the same anguish, who, at most, would have a little more to eat to show their lives were richer. In New York, the poor were surrounded by some of the wealthiest people in the world, who would sling a coat on their arm that was worth the same amount as two years' worth of begging on the street. I recognized that torment behind their eyes. But unlike the look of desperate starvation in Mombasa, the poor in New York had a look of desperate jealousy. Of course, we had the same thing in Britain, but to me it seemed the British passed by without a look if they had no desire to help—which was also very harsh, as it gave the impression that these people were invisible and not worth acknowledging. But in New York, it seemed that people walked past and made a point of screwing up their noses or muttering something insulting at the homeless, acting as though they were merely getting in the way by blocking the sidewalk as the richer residents power walked past.

On Christmas Eve, I decided that Danny and I should try and help out some of the local homeless. We left it too late to organize volunteering for a soup kitchen or shelter, so instead we improvised the best we could.

We cooked thirty frozen meals in the microwave and oven, wrapped-up rolls, brownies, plastic cutlery, and poured out thirty cardboard cups of hot chocolate. Laden with sports bags and rucksacks, we headed into the streets of Manhattan to spread a little Christmas cheer to the people less fortunate. In hindsight, this was a very good and, some might say, a very Christian thing to do. It was also the dumbest idea I think I have ever had.

At the end of the block where we lived, there stood an old church that held a soup kitchen for the homeless throughout the year. As the most immediate locals seemed to be taken care of we decided to walk a few blocks further into Chelsea before we started handing out the meals, which by this time were beginning to get lukewarm, so that we could find the solitary homeless guys who frequented the subway station entrances.

"You know, baby, this was a great idea, but I don't think we thought this through properly," Danny said to me as we marched through the streets.

"What is there to think through? They are homeless, cold, and need hot food," I said back, as if this was a silly question to ask. "Look, there's one," I pointed out a shabbily dressed black man with a frayed dirty beanie hat on sitting on the pavement in the dark, cuddling his knees to keep warm. It wasn't one of the usual busy streets or main roads but one of the small, dimly lit, narrow crossroads that ran throughout Chelsea.

I walked over to him and smiled.

"Hello there, would you like something to eat and drink?" I asked, smiling.

"Whaddaya got?" he shouted back, as if he was picking from a menu in a diner.

I must admit that I hadn't really expected this. I assumed that most people would be grateful for whatever they got, but what the hell did I know?

"Umm, we have some beef and potatoes in a mustard sauce and roast chicken with a vegetable medley," I answered, remembering the description on the microwave meal box.

I could hear Danny laugh behind me. "You're not on a plane now, baby."

"Beef," the man barked back.

As I laid the bag down to get the food out of the sports bag and Danny pulled one of the cups of hot chocolate out of his bag, there seemed to be a hell of a lot of movement happening very quickly on what was a quiet street. Within thirty seconds fifteen huge men, who looked even bigger in their ten layers of clothing, stirred from every direction. They came out of hidden doorways, from beneath flattened cardboard boxes, and out of old rolls of carpet, all headed in our direction. It was like a scene from Thriller, just without Vincent Price's voice echoing. They began shouting at us, although I couldn't understand what they were saying because the scarves wrapped around their faces muffled their voices. And, for the first time since we arrived in New York, I was truly scared. They picked up their pace, and a couple began to run in our direction.

"Put the bag down, Greg," Danny urged.

"Fuck, fuck, fuck," I whispered quickly.

"Greg, they could have knives or guns under their jackets, and your accent will just tell them that no one will look for your body."

"Fuck, fuck, fuck," I said again much louder, the whites of my eyes giving me away.

"Hey, guys!" Danny called. "Here's some food and some hot drinks. We're just going to head back to the van to get some gloves and scarves for you. It's all here in the bag. We'll be right back."

I put my bag down and, for whatever reason, put my hands up as though I was being robbed at gunpoint and slowly started walking backward. I must have looked like a complete idiot.

"Fuck it. *Run!*" I shouted at Danny. As we sprinted down the street I convinced myself that Danny's quick footsteps were the sounds of a herd of homeless people running after us to rob us. We rounded the corner back onto Broadway, and Danny, gasping for air, looked up at me with his beautiful blue eyes and doubled over in hysterics.

"You see where charity gets ya?" he laughed. "Count yourself lucky that you still have your shoes. One of those guys was practically licking his lips over your sneakers."

"That scared the shit out of me," I said, shaking but seeing the funny side.

"Greg, I'd have paid over a thousand dollars to see you act like that again. Actually, no, that was priceless!"

On the way back to the apartment, Danny's phone rang. As he picked up the phone I saw him smile. It was his mother, and he could not wait to tell her what had just happened. He was laughing as he retold the story, but then his face changed to a frown.

"Momma, it's okay. It's not like I got shot." He paused. "Momma, I was in the Middle East during wartime, and you're freaking out about this?" There was another pause. "What do you mean we shouldn't feed...." He listened for a minute, his eyes rolling to indicate to me that his mother was telling him off. Then he looked like someone slapped him across the face. He shot a warning glance at me as if I was the one having a go at him.

"Right, now stop there. Greg's heart was in the right place," he said. His face had become wild.

"Now, hang on, Momma, there is no need to say...." He looked shocked. "How can you say that when...," he said, his eyes focused so intently on me. There was a longer pause, and Danny's lips began to thin. She obviously had slipped on her charade and said something about me.

"Fine!" he shouted. "Here's Greg."

He thrust the phone forward at me, punching it forward again and again as I waved my hands and mouthed "No way. No. No. No." I knew this wasn't going to be good, as I had never heard him raise his voice to his mother before.

He tossed the phone in my direction, forcing me to catch it, and began marching away.

"Mrs. Taylor?" I said into the phone.

"What were you thinking? You could have gotten Danny killed!" She spat her words with venom. "Next time you want to do something like that, do it on your own and don't involve my son."

"Anything else?"

"This is not a joke!" she shouted.

"Am I laughing?"

"Look here, you selfish, stupid boy—"

"Name calling? How Christian of you."

"Don't you dare—"

I hung up.

I jogged up to Danny, who was still marching with anger.

"What did she say to you?" I asked, preparing to confess being rude to his mother.

He turned on the spot. "I have had it with her. She is out of her fucking mind! If I had told her that story eight years ago she would have laughed, but instead she just said that you were going to get me killed and that you were an irresponsible fool. Just before fucking Christmas! I am so mad right now. Who the hell does she think she is? Don't feed the poor?" He raised his hands and spoke to the heavens and shouted over the traffic. "What would Jesus do, huh? She demanded to speak to you, and I know I shouldn't have passed you the phone, but in some ways I wanted you to say something back to her. I know she's stopped making an effort with you, Greg. I'm not so stupid not to notice it. I just didn't want to point it out to you as you were trying so hard, but she has just crossed the fucking line with that!"

"Danny, I just hung up on her." It was easier to tell him than I thought.

"Good for you. She needs to get back to the real fucking world."

The next morning we woke up, and I expected Danny to be in a very sad and sullen mood. It was not the way I wanted to share our first Christmas together, and I was feeling more and more resentment toward his mother. She had gotten to me again after I had been so careful not to be brought into any kind of conversation with her for the past few months.

But I couldn't have been more wrong. He was in such great spirits when we woke that, at first, I thought he was acting. We sat next to the Christmas tree and opened presents, laughed and joked, and played games all morning. Each time the phone rang, I waited for a dark atmosphere to set in. But the conversations with his sisters and nephews and nieces were light and jokey. There was no mention of his mother or the conversation we'd had with her the night before to either me or his siblings.

In the late afternoon, Danny and I lay on the sofa, stuffed from our Christmas dinner, and began to watch Harry Potter.

"I used to love watching films like this on Christmas Day with the family when I was a kid," he said as he laid his head on my chest.

I looked down. I couldn't see his face, but I imagined that he was sad. Danny reached down and patted the floor, stirring Duke from his dog bed. He cantered over and threw himself onto the sofa and nuzzled into us, laying his head on my stomach far enough up that Danny could reach his arm around and bring the three of us into a hug.

"And I love it even more now watching them with my own family." He broke into a broad, shining smile.

The shift in his thinking was never clearer to me.

"Are you going to call your mum?" I asked, finally pointing out the thing he had neglected to do all day.

"No. Christmas was always a very special time of year for Mom, her favorite season. I thought about it last night before I went to sleep. She needs to feel the impact and repercussions of what she does and says. If she calls, I will speak to her, but I have not and will not let it spoil our day."

"You should speak to your dad."

"He'll understand. And if she calls I'll speak to him then."

The phone call never came.

It was New Year's Eve before Danny had a phone call from George. I was packing to return to the UK, and I left Danny alone in the living room while I sorted out my suitcase in the bedroom. After an hour Danny came in and sat on the bed.

"I hate it when you leave."

"I know," I said, joining him on the bed and nuzzling up next to him. "What did your dad have to say?"

"He knows why we're having issues with Mom, but he lives with her and dealt with her shift in attitude a long time ago. He loves her, and it kills him to see her upset that we are arguing, but insists I should be the one who calls her since he knows she's too hardheaded. She was apparently crying on Christmas Day about the fact that I hadn't called her, but at the same time she was also too stubborn to call me. But she knows that whoever calls the other will be admitting that they were in the wrong, and she wasn't about to do that."

"And how do you feel about it?" I asked, wanting him to talk about it as he hadn't brought it up in days.

"I have always pandered to Mom. My family has always been the most important thing in the world to me. I see what she is like, but I am forever making excuses for her. I don't expect you to understand, since you didn't know her before she became so religious. In the past few years, it's become like an annoying tic that she has where she feels like she has to judge someone out loud and not expect any consequence. She was never like that before. It's almost like when you see the mothers of serial killers being interviewed and they say, 'He was such a sweet boy, so gentle, such a loving son.' I'm the same about her. I see what she's like, but I am forever only remembering what she was when we were younger. And that's the woman I love. It kills me that she was crying on Christmas Day, but she has to learn."

I put my arm around his shoulder.

"I'll end up calling her and sorting things out when you're gone. I think I've made my point enough now. It's easier to speak to her when you're not here, since her opinions seem to rile me one hundred times more when you're around. Honestly, baby, don't think I'm blind. I see your effort."

"Do what you have to, Tiger," I said before kissing him on his cheek. "Just try and sort it out. I put up with your mum because you love her."

"I know," he said simply.

When I returned to New York in February, the city was back to itself, still full of life and bitterly cold, just without all of the flashing fairy lights and overly glittered, dressed shop windows. Danny had to attend a meeting at the Washington DC head office of the law firm and invited me down to do a bit of sightseeing for the day.

Tucker had already moved up to DC for his job with the senator. He had asked us to visit before, but I declined the invitations and insisted that Danny visit him while I was working back home in England. It was my way of saying that my jealousy monster had finally left the building. But since it was only going to be for the day, I agreed to go down with Danny on his work trip.

"You'll love it. You can go and see the White House, the Lincoln Memorial, the Mall, and the museums." he said as he packed a small rucksack for me, stuffed with printed maps of the area, the Metro system, and museum brochures.

"It will be nice to spend some time with you on the train, and I suppose I can check it off my list of places I have been," I said, the last part sounding like I really wasn't that bothered about going.

The journey down to DC was three hours of looking out into mostly wintery landscapes while Danny studied his paperwork, occasionally explaining to me the ins and outs of the case. But, like he did when he was in the Navy, he never actually told me any specifics, which was maddening.

The train pulled into Union Station, and Danny circled the Dupont Circle Metro stop on my subway map to mark where he would meet me for lunch. He checked that I had everything and kissed me like he was sending me off on a school outing and left me to try and figure out where I was going. The Metro system, at first glance, looked like a child drew lines willy-nilly with five different colored pens. I made my way over to one of the guards to get directions to the Mall and was gruffly sent packing down onto a platform and told to "get on the yellow line."

After going in the wrong direction and ending up in Arlington, Virginia, and then getting disoriented at Gallery Place, only to get on yet another wrong train to find yet another identical looking underground station, I finally made it to the National Mall and began my sightseeing.

The White House (from the outside)? Check.

Lincoln Memorial and Reflecting Pool? Check.

The Capitol (from the outside)? Check.

The Washington Monument? Check.

A couple of hours later, I felt I was done with the central attractions and wondered what else I was meant to see. I marveled at the fact that I hadn't realized everything was in one place, so I started looking toward the museums. The only one that held any interest for me was the Air and Space Museum. It was interesting enough, but an hour later I was once again outside looking at my map.

I don't know whether it was because I was alone, or the fact that Washington DC was the home to Danny's previous life, or whether it was the brutal weather, but it all seemed so fucking bleak.

I looked on my sightseeing guide of what to do next.

Vietnam War Memorial. Holocaust Museum. Arlington Cemetery. World War I Memorial. World Word II Memorial. Civil War Memorial. African American Civil War Memorial. Korean War Memorial.

It's not that I don't find these sorts of things interesting, because I do, in moderation. I can sit through a program on the History Channel just as long as the next guy, but that day, standing in the freezing cold, the frigid wind beating around my face, I was in no mood to visit strangers' graves, or read plaques of how horrible war is and the immense loss of lives. There are only so many things you can put a positive spin on by sticking an American flag and a bald eagle next to it and adding the word "proud." I know all about national pride, but it all seemed to be so in your face and vocal here. It was as far away from the British "stoic, stiff-upper-lip, secret pride" as you could get. And in a strange way, they seemed to glorify it that much more by the sheer concentration of the memorials. I understood why, but I found it was just too depressing. So I made my way back toward the Metro station.

"Hey, baby!" Danny called as he shivered his way toward me outside the Dupont Metro station, where I had been standing for thirty minutes, gradually getting colder and colder. He came over and gave me an Eskimo hug and, as was his way, warmed me without doing much at all. Just the look of him still made everything, including my mood, better. "So, did you see everything?"

"Um, yeah, I saw all I wanted to," I said honestly as we made our way down toward a café that we were to have lunch in.

"Do you want me to call Tucker? Perhaps he can show you around some of the areas that aren't so accessible by the Metro."

"Thanks, Tiger, but I think I will give that a miss. Besides, hopefully—" I had to stop and redirect. "Sorry, I mean he's probably at work, and I wouldn't want him to take the afternoon off to show me around this place."

Danny spent the forty-five minutes talking about the head office of the firm and how different things were there in comparison to New York. He seemed to make quite an impression with the DC people with whom he had been working so closely over the phone in the recent months. They invited him down again the following month to sit in on a couple of meetings so he could get more experience. I wasn't too bothered, as I knew that I would be back at work by then so I wouldn't have to accompany him down, and the mandatory Tucker visit could be done without me.

I told Danny that I was too cold to do anymore sightseeing, and after a hint from him that I should see more museums, I told him that I was going to pass the time for the rest of the afternoon looking around the city. The problem was, however, there simply wasn't that much to see. I was so used to accidently finding whole, interesting neighborhoods just by turning down a newly discovered street in New York, I assumed the same could be true of DC. But as hard as I tried to find it, it was never there. Each street I walked seemed equally as bland as the last, and I was getting frostbite searching for this useless piece of information.

By the time I met Danny back at the Metro, I was completely puzzled about why he raved so much about his time in Washington.

"I came here when I was in my late teens, away from small town Texas. This place may as well have been a whole new world," he said as we boarded the Metro to go back to Union Station to catch the train back to Manhattan. "I had a great time here while I studied, so it'll always bring back good memories."

"Uh-huh," I muttered as I raised an eyebrow.

"Not those kinds of memories, Greg. Listen, you were young once too."

"Yes, Danny, but my indiscretions were not in the shadow of the country's biggest phallus." I pointed to the map's image of the Washington Monument.

"Well, at least you can say you've seen it and will know what I'm talking about when I speak of DC."

"Yes, Danny." I smiled. "But I also now know why the aliens always want to attack it in the movies!"

CHAPTER SIXTEEN

AFTER ten months of flying back and forth between New York and London, we finally decided that it was time that I give up flying. We discussed moving to England at some point in the future, but with Danny only at the beginning of a career for which he worked, I insisted that he continue in New York, as such experience would be invaluable on his résumé, before we went down the road of moving anywhere else—whether it be England or anywhere else in the world.

Recent trips had become long and hard, and all I wanted every evening was to curl up with Danny or go out some place and enjoy his company. The back and forth worked out okay at first, but just as I began to settle into life in New York, I had to take off again. I felt that I was letting Danny down when he had to attend functions, parties, lunches, and nights out alone. Although we made new friends, I still felt like I was leaving him to battle the city on his own.

I arranged an appointment with an immigration lawyer in London to discuss my options, although I already had a decent idea of what was going to be said. Sitting in his office, the feelings of anger and frustration crept up on me.

"So, my options are: pay for four years of school in New York to get a student visa, invest a minimum of $100,000 into a company, work for an American company, or marry an American woman?"

"Yes," he replied bluntly.

"Well, if I marry a woman that would be ridiculous, as I would have to live with her and I am known to be gay. That is without even getting into the fact that if anyone found out Danny was involved he would lose his job as well as his license to practice law."

"Yes, and I would never suggest that you do such a thing," he said, covering his own arse.

"If I work for an American company, how does that work?"

"Well, as you are going there specifically to be with your partner, you would have to find a company that has an office in New York, or else there's no point. They usually require you to work for the British side of the company for a minimum of twelve months before they will process your application for sponsorship. But there are a lot of pitfalls with this option. One, it's incredibly difficult to do unless you have extraordinary evidence that your qualifications warrant your demand. Judging by your résumé, your career with the airline simply isn't enough. Besides, it would only apply for employment. Should you lose your job through redundancy you would be expected to exit the country immediately, and, given the economic climate at the moment, that's a serious concern. If they decided to move you to a different office in another state, you would have to follow or else your visa would become invalid."

"If I invest in a business, I have to own at least a fifty percent share in it and hire two Americans, right? I have money, as I have recently sold property."

"Yes, but even if you invest in the business there is absolutely no guarantee that you will get the visa. They could still refuse you."

"They expect me to go there, spend out the money to set up a business, and then apply for a visa? How does that make sense?"

"Well, if it's your own business, then, in a sense, you haven't lost anything since the business is still there. It's just that you would not be able to run it yourself, so the money has not been lost and has created another job for an American. If you buy into a business, you can offer your investment on the condition that your visa is granted. If it's not approved, the money isn't released to the company. So in that sense, you lose nothing."

He saw me considering this.

"Mr. Stephens, I am not trying to put you off this idea, but I must insist that you take into account the incredible number of small businesses that fold within the first year due to their economic climate. And, of all places, New York City is not cheap."

"And the student visa?" I asked, shaking my head.

"Well, they are difficult at the best of times. In your circumstances, as a mature student without scholarship, you would be expected to pay the cost of your education, which could run anywhere from fifty to one hundred thousand dollars, depending on what you study."

"So I have just paid you two hundred pounds for an hour of informing me I am screwed?" I said, only half joking.

"In a manner of speaking… yes. I would suggest the visa lottery, but England hasn't been included in that for many years."

"But Iraq and Afghanistan, the two countries they are at war with, are."

He could only nod his head.

"So what do I do?"

"Well, until they change the gay marriage laws in America, repeal the Defense of Marriage Act, and allow same-sex couples to sponsor their spouses, the only thing that you can do is continue to return to American on the visa waiver system that allows you three months at a time or apply for the B1 visa that allows you to visit for up to six months without working."

"This is ridiculous," I said, perhaps a little more aggressively than I should, apparently giving the lawyer the impression that I blamed him.

"I agree with you," he replied sympathetically.

"So if I met a girl on a Monday and married her on Thursday, I would pretty much be guaranteed a green card by Friday?"

"Well, it would take a bit longer than that, but you would pretty much be granted automatic entry within months."

EVEN though I had a good idea what the attorney would say before the meeting, as both Danny and I had extensively researched all the possibilities online, I felt deflated that my last chance to find some kind of loophole was gone. It was so frustrating. It was as though the whole country was geared up to keep this from happening, like it was horrendous to, God forbid, give gay couples the same rights as straight couples.

I regularly read the news while I was in America and saw the politicians spout off about how their "Christian beliefs and morals do not agree with the idea of gay marriage." They spoke so eloquently of marriage being "a sacred and valued institution between a man and a woman devoting their lives together through the bonds of love in which to raise a family." Meanwhile they had affairs of their own. It was like watching a teacher tell off a schoolboy for bullying, all the while banging his wife's head against the blackboard.

Along with these politicians sat the fine examples of the Catholic Church, an organization with a ridiculous amount of wealth and power, banging on about how homosexuality was a sin. Meanwhile, they covered up their own pedophile priests' crimes and moved them to other areas, giving them a chance to re-offend.

Countless so-called Christian organizations solicited donations for their cause against gay marriage, raising millions of dollars for campaigns on TV, in newspapers, or on billboards. It was money that, quite frankly, could have been spent in a more "Christian" way. These were the same people who said gay marriage was a threat and "harmed the sanctity of straight marriage." Their spokesmen explained that since gay people couldn't have kids naturally they weren't entitled to the protection of marriage, as it is not natural and therefore not God's will. Of course these people were not out picketing or protesting at divorce courts or IVF treatment centers.

Even one of the married political candidates who was running for president around the same time and stood against "same-sex marriage" was found not only to have had an affair with a member of his campaign staff, but he had gotten her pregnant and lied to his wife... while she was battling cancer! How the hell do you argue with such hypocrites?

I knew that none of this was new, and the arguments were not peculiarly American. Politicians throughout the ages had always been two-faced and untrustworthy, regardless of their country. England was no exception, although I never heard an English political campaign in my lifetime rely so much on whether the candidate was religious. But in America it seemed that the practice of Christians hiding behind the Bible and using the word of God as a rock to stone people with was still very much the norm. What angered me the most, what I had never seen on such a scale quite like I did in America, and what drove me to scream and shout at the television or news articles, were the self-loathing gays who made the situation worse.

Politicians, judges, attorneys general, senators, and mayors who were the first to condemn and vote against gay equality issues and who banged on about the detrimental effect gays have on society were caught paying rent boys for blowjobs, having gay affairs with staffers, sending sex text messages and e-mails to young male pages, or soliciting sex at toilets in airports.

Ted Haggard, an American evangelical preacher who was the head of a strong national evangelical group with millions of members, and the founder of The New Life church, took his platform and told thousands of people that they didn't need to have their own thoughts on homosexuality. They didn't need them because it was all written, clear as day, in the Bible. He was credited with rallying millions of Americans to vote for George W. Bush in the 2004 election, a campaign in which anti-same-sex-marriage messages were used to energize conservatives. He boasted publicly about weekly phone calls with the president and how he offered his guidance and support. This married father of four, who made it his business to judge other people and preach to the masses about "how to live a good Christian life," was found to be paying a male prostitute for sex while high on crystal meth. How do you get over homophobia and inequality when even the gay guys are chucking you under the bus?

All of these people who held esteemed positions, whose opinions were listened to, who produced continuous lines of bullshit that were repeated a million times over eventually pushed me to think, "Fuck you all. I just want to be with Danny. Fuck you all. You're not going to stop us."

It was the end of the winter season when I went into the office to hand in my notice. It was so much harder than I expected it would be. Not only was I giving up my job, my friends, and my lifestyle, I was also saying good-bye to some of the best times of my life.

"We thought it wouldn't be long before you went," said Katie, the beautiful airline administrator who had helped me out on so many occasions. "Still, at least you're leaving to go somewhere exciting!"

"Yeah, I know," I said sadly. "But I still have a month left so I am going to make the most of it while I can."

By the end of the month, I had my last roster published, which showed that my final destination would be India with a great crew, including Donna and Jackie. Everyone on the trip knew it was my last flight, and I was looking forward to a fun week in Trivandrum. I couldn't have wished for a better flight crew to end my flying career, so when the time came I was happy to jump on board.

"Right, my gorgeous little winged ones, let's get this next bit over with so we can get by the pool," Jackie said at the end of the safety briefing. "And just so we are all clear, if I catch any crewmember getting a henna tattoo I will personally scrub that filth off them with neat vodka and a grimace. I will not return to England with someone who has anything remotely hippy adorned on their person." She wagged her finger at each one of us.

Donna and I worked the front of the aircraft with Jackie, who was in the cabin, reluctantly delivering a bottle of milk I had warmed to a passenger holding a rather miserable baby. We were only an hour into the flight and were joking and reminiscing about old flights while we set up for the drinks service.

"Don't go," Donna said at the tail end of a laugh that was making her mascara run.

"I have to, babe. I love him."

There was a slight crackle, and the voice of the captain came through loudly in the speaker above our heads.

"Cabin Supervisor to the flight deck." He paused. "Immediately." Donna and I froze and stared at each other. We knew this was the emergency call, only used when something was wrong. The procedures on which we were trained dictated that the person nearest the flight deck and the supervisor were the first people to go in on hearing this call. And, just my luck, I was standing right by the door.

I was laughing with so much nervousness that my cry to Donna of "Nine fucking years flying and I am going die on my last fucking day" could have been mistaken for a sicker joke than intended.

I looked over at Donna as I typed the emergency code into the door, terrified that I was going to find a dead first officer or the captain clutching his left arm. Just as I pushed the heavy door forward I felt a hand on my shoulder. It was Jackie returning to the galley with a serious look on her face.

The captain, the first officer, and a flight engineer sat in the flight deck, all with their fixed oxygen masks positioned over their faces, which made them look, at best, like professionals from the movie *Top Gun*, and at worst, like they were being attacked by the parasite in *Aliens*. Jackie and I moved in, and the door slammed behind us with such a bang that we both jumped. We stood there while the captain finished playing with knobs, buttons, and switches and rambled into his headpiece to someone that I assumed would be either flight deck operations in the UK or air traffic control.

He switched a button on the side of the receiver on his headphones and twisted around in his seat to speak to us, as the first officer and flight engineer had their heads buried in manuals. The fixed mask had a pair of goggles strapped firmly over the captain's head, which prevented us from reading his face. Because of the obstruction of the oxygen mask, the captain raised his voice to a shout in order to be heard, which did nothing for my nerves.

"Two of the oxygen packs have gone out. If the third one goes we will have decompression. We don't know where the fault lies or what the cause is. There is no indication in the cabin that the fuselage has been punctured," he bellowed, his voice muffled but clear enough to understand.

"Nine fucking years of flying and I am going to die on my last fucking day," I thought again as I stood there trying to take it all in.

"We may have to make an emergency landing. I will inform the passengers and tell them that we are preparing the cabin as a matter of procedure," the captain shouted. "In the meantime I want you to prepare the cabin as if it's the real thing, just in case."

Then he said the words that still make me shudder, even though I expected them, as they came word-for-word from the manual that told him that he must inform the crew of certain kinds of crashes, whether they are expected or not.

"There is no chance of a catastrophic impact on water, as we are over ground."

We exited the flight deck to see Donna and half of the crew in the galley waiting to be told what was going on.

"There goes my chances of getting a decent tan," Jackie said with all of the calmness and nonchalance of someone being told their weekend spa treatment was cancelled. "It's all right, guys," she continued, finally noticing the look of the terrified crew in the galley, "just a problem with the oxygen pack. We are going to descend and land back in London. But we must follow procedure and prepare for an emergency landing on ground, you know, just to cover our own arses." I knew that she was saying it to make them feel better and not to scare them, but unfortunately, my face, as usual, gave me away as I saw Donna looking over at me in terror.

The crew went back into the cabin to prepare for the landing while the captain made a PA, which sounded a lot clearer and calmer over the speakers, as the PA system was linked to his headset. Donna and I began securing the cabin for landing, breaking out into nervous laughter any time we caught each other's eye. The passengers had been told that there was an indication of a fault with the aircraft but not informed of the whole problem. Yet, somehow, they still managed to make things difficult by questioning why the seats had to be in the upright position and why the armrests had to be down. Donna, harassed by the same attitude from passengers on her aisle, began to lose her patience.

"Why do we have to have the window blinds open? I am trying to sleep," one burly looking passenger said to Donna as she looked back at him in disbelief.

"Sir, please, could you just pop that window blind up for landing. You heard the captain's announcement. We are heading back to London and will be leaving this aircraft in twenty minutes anyway."

"That's still twenty minutes more sleep I could have," he replied, shaking his head at her as if she was being unreasonable.

I walked to the end of my aisle, across the bulkhead, and back toward Donna on her aisle to save her from the man when I heard her save herself better than I ever could have done.

"Sir," she said with a smile so as to not alert the other passengers that she was getting mad, "As you are aware, there is a fault with the aircraft. Should we need to evacuate this plane we require that all of the window blinds are open. This is so we can ensure that the firemen on the big ladders can look in through the windows from the outside and see if your trapped body is worth saving or whether your charred corpse isn't worth the risk of reentering."

Without another word he raised the window blind and took out the safety card from the seat back pocket in front of him and began to study it.

As we all took our seats for landing, I looked across the galley at Donna, who sat on her jump seat. She looked back and laughed again. I couldn't help but laugh back at her.

Slowly, we began to see the lights of the houses below us turn into the shining roofs of cars in the satellite lots, which gave way to runway lights. Fire engines and ambulances raced alongside us, as was procedure for an aircraft that declared or ran the risk of an emergency landing. I bowed my head and closed my eyes and thought "Please, God, don't let this go wrong." I couldn't help myself.

The wheels hit the tarmac, and we arrived at the gate without incident with an audible sigh of relief echoing from the passengers in the cabin. The airline's agent arranged for a few of the hotels to take the passengers overnight so another aircraft could be shipped in by the morning to take them on to their destination. We were all asked if we needed "to speak to anyone about our traumatic experience," which we all refused and began joking about what had happened almost instantly. I could tell that some of the crew was freaked out, but with the others now laughing at it, they calmed down and joined in. As I headed back to Donna's place for the night my brain started working overtime.

I had always been a little weird about having daydreams of what would happen if a flight I was on crashed and I was the sole survivor. I always wondered whether I could cope as well as Tom Hanks did in *Castaway*. I knew I would have died of septicemia before I would have knocked a tooth out with an ice skate blade.

This time, though, I was thinking about Danny. We had been through so long being apart, and we now finally had the chance to be together, and it could have all been taken away. I knew then I was making the right decision to leave and be with him. The laws in America were not going to change anytime soon, and waiting for them to do so could take years, but all I wanted was to be with Danny. I laughed and nearly cried from fatigue and mental exhaustion as I drove, Donna looking over at me as if witnessing a breakdown.

The following day, all of the crew returned for a second try at the flight, except for two who obviously thought what happened the day before was a bad omen and insisted that they be released from duty until they had the opportunity to speak to someone about their ordeal. The rest of us laughed it off the best we could, and the flight departed, thankfully, without another hitch. It was a long flight, and I was ready to get off the aircraft as soon as we landed.

Arriving at the hotel, the crew went for the usual post-flight drink and quizzed me on what my life was heading toward, whether I would miss the job, and whether I would be able to cope with living surrounded by Americans. I told them I was cautiously optimistic.

"I am gonna miss you, Greg," Donna said as we sat drinking sundowners on the beach on the last day of the trip. She seemed sad.

"I am going to miss you more. But I am only in New York, so you can always come and visit as often as you want."

"I know, but it won't be the same without seeing you at work too. Are you nervous about leaving?" she asked me.

"I am relieved, but at the same time terrified. I won't be able to work while I am there because of my visa, so I am not sure how I am meant to spend my days."

"I can't imagine you being the type of person who doesn't work. Do you think being a househusband is going to suit you?"

"No, not at all. But what can I do? We can't carry on the way we have been. I love the job, but I need to be with Danny. It's not fair on either of us to carry on having this long-distance relationship. It's time to ride or get off the horse, as they say."

"By what you have said, you have been riding something horse-like for three years!" Donna said as she placed the bottle of beer she was drinking between her legs. "I see what you are saying. It's a big step."

"I have my reservations. I am not too sure how I will fit in over there. It's been great being there so far, and it's amazing to live in Manhattan, but I worry about becoming homesick. It's not the same as flying, when you know you will always be going home soon. I miss my friends and my family while I am there, but we have started to meet new people, so perhaps I will get into the swing of things."

"I am sure you will. Just don't come back acting or talking like a Yank and wearing chinos and polo shirts, or I will have to arrange an intervention."

"I doubt there is much chance of that," I said as I held my bottle out for her to clink. "I have had to beat that behavior out of Danny already. I can't have things going backward."

We sat in silence for a moment.

"What about you, Don? Do you think you will ever leave?"

Donna sat in thought. "I think I will be asked to leave before I offer to," she laughed. "Maybe one day when I get myself a husband I will think about it, but for now I am enjoying it too much to give it up."

"They will have to cut that crew bag from your hand, you old hag. You are going to end up like one of those American Airlines hosties, dragging their cardigan-covered old carcasses down the aisle with a pocket full of boiled sweets and wearing blood red lipstick at sixty."

"And I will look fucking gorgeous doing it!"

Donna, Jackie, and the crew arranged a farewell party for me on the roof of the hotel that night, complete with a cake, a mobile iPod disco, and a sash with my name stenciled across it in glitter. I was so grateful, but hated the fact that all of this was because I was leaving. It made it all seem so definite, so real. I welled up as I read the card and cut the cake. It was the end of my last trip, and it was being hammered home with "Wake Me Up Before You Go-Go" playing as the soundtrack.

The flight home was busy, as it was a day flight full of rested passengers. I looked around at Donna and the crew and saw the frustration on their faces when dealing with the usual problems, the expressions of pain after the service, and the aches caused by constantly dipping toward passengers to listen to their requests. I, on the other hand, savored every service and every bell, as I knew it would be the last time. It wasn't the joy I thought I would feel knowing that I would never again have to deal with rotten passengers or problems that were impossible to fix at 35,000 feet.

I was sad. I wondered if the rest of the crew ever thought what it would be like to say good-bye to all of this, to the lifestyle, to the fun, the laughs, the experiences each trip brought and the people we met. Many would wish for a nine-to-five job so they could know where they would be all of the time and would know their weekends and holidays were free, as on occasion I had done. But we all stayed, as we knew that no other job would afford us the life we were living, where we could see the world with people who could bring us to tears of laughter and experience sights that we would probably never have seen otherwise.

I knew I would never actually miss the labor of the job, but I would miss the people terribly. I scanned the cabin and fondly remembered my very first flight, how terrified I was when I started and how I almost wanted to vomit on my first safety demo with the whole cabin looking at me. It was years before, but only seemed like weeks. The countless trips all merged into one long series of suntans, laughs, beer, and shenanigans, and I was left thinking that my grand holiday had finally come to an end.

After my good-byes to the crew, Mr. Parsons, my manager, and Katie, the office administrator, I hurried quickly toward the door before any emotion showed.

"Good luck out there!" Jackie called with a wink. "I'll be praying for you!"

I handed my airside security ID in to the office, and just like that, it was all finally done. That was it, the end of flying. I tried to make myself feel better by thinking that it was to go on to another stage of my life, but it was still very hard.

The following day I went to visit Mum and Natalie. I had already packed up the few possessions I had left after the sale of the flat and reserved this time to spend with the family. I was nervous about seeing Mum, who Natalie said had become depressed recently with the idea of me going. I went in full of beans, with the intention of not making it into a big deal. To my surprise, Mum was prepared to do the same.

"You all ready to go?" she said at me as I greeted her with a hug.

"Yep, all packed and ready for the off!"

"Oh, by the way," she looked at her table and picked up a sheet of paper, "there are a few things I would like you to bring back for me. You're only going to be gone for a few weeks, so you should have plenty of chance to get them."

I scanned the list.

"Wrinkle cream, Whitman's chocolates, Chanel No. 5, Kool-Aid, and Dunkin Donuts coffee. Anything else?"

"Well, if you see anything I might like, just pop it in your bag and surprise me!" Mum said, hunching her shoulders and smiling widely.

"Are you going to be okay?" I asked, more as a passing question rather than the serious manner in which it was meant.

"I will be fine, Greggy. You're not going to be gone that long. I will see you in three months. It's not like you are moving forever and I will never see you again!"

"That's true. And at least this way you still get all of your duty-free. I know how much that was bothering you." I winked.

I could tell she was stretching for conversation with me, asking question after question and barely waiting for me to answer before she asked another. If Mum wanted to deal with it this way, I was prepared to go along with it. It was true that, because of my visa restrictions, I would have to return every fourth month, but I had never been gone for so long since Dad died. I could tell she was nervous, but I assured her that the rest of the family was more than capable of sorting out anything she needed while I was gone.

Saying good-bye, she hugged me tighter than ever and told me to look after myself.

"Of course I will. I will be back soon. Love you, Mum."

Natalie led me to the front door on her own.

"Greg, she will be fine, I promise." She gave me a hug, and I squeezed her tighter to show that I appreciated her trying to put my mind at ease. I left with a view of Mum waving from her window with a tear running down her cheek, which she quickly wiped away. I felt awful.

I had an early flight going out of Heathrow back to New York the following day, so I decided I would spend the night at a hotel at the airport. I was just going through all of my documents for the fourth time when I heard my mobile phone ringing.

"Hey, baby."

"Hey, Tiger. All done. I am on my way!" I said, trying to keep excitement in my voice when I actually felt quite scared.

"Greg...." I could hear a problem in his voice, straightaway.

"What is it?"

"I don't know how to tell you this."

"Just spit it out, Danny. You're freaking me out," I said urgently.

There was a pause. "They're transferring me to the Washington office."

CHAPTER SEVENTEEN

"ARE you kidding me?" I asked, already knowing that he wasn't.

"I'm sorry, baby, but the market is tanking here in New York, and it looks as though most of the first-, second-, and third-year associates will be losing their jobs. The guys in Washington offered me a place in the white collar group. I find the stuff they do so much more interesting, and my job would be a hell of a lot more secure down there."

For the previous few weeks, the news on both side of the Atlantic documented the oncoming collapse of the markets. Danny was privy to a couple of meetings and overheard more than he should have and was trusted with gossip that was all turning out to be true. He was very lucky to be able to stretch his wings when he was seconded to work with the white collar criminal defense practice group in DC. He was a first-year associate, so his mold was still much more pliable than other associates in the firm who had worked solidly for years on deals that would soon become extinct, rendering their "expertise" practically useless. All of these attorneys knew that the deteriorating economy would affect them and the firm directly. They were scrambling, making the atmosphere of the office feel like a death row of cutbacks and layoffs.

"But, Washington? That place?" I said, my tone showing that I wasn't impressed. "Did they tell you that you have to go, or are they giving you the option to stay?"

"Well, they're not forcing me to go, but we've pretty much been told that the shit is about to hit the fan. Baby, I know it's not ideal timing, with you giving up your job and selling your flat, but I've kind of been pushed into a corner and been offered an escape hatch with this position," he said. I could tell he was worried about telling me, as he began to talk in metaphors, which he often did when trying to convince me of something he knew I would be against.

"When do they want you to leave?" I asked.

"There are a few deals I have to finish here in New York, but they want me down in DC no later than six weeks from now, which they believe will be enough time to finish my work here and find a new place to live in DC."

"But, Danny. DC? I don't think I could stand it." My voice became somewhat whiny, to the point that I didn't even like hearing myself.

"You'll love it down there, baby!" he said a little too enthusiastically, considering what he was telling me. "They have festivals, museums, and Virginia is just across the Potomac River. Oh, oh! There's also the cherry blossom festival in the spring!"

"Cherry blossoms, Danny? Are you listening to yourself? There are ways to convince me to go to that damn place to live, but bigging up fruit trees isn't one of them."

He paused. "Greg, I know it's not ideal, and it's not what we planned, but things are changing fast here. DC isn't so bad. It's got a great nightlife, and we'll find a decent place to live."

"With a view of the cherry trees?"

"Greg, I'm sorry. I know you'll miss New York."

"It's not about New York, Danny. I just handed in my ID badge. It's about leaving the first place we were finally able to call home together."

"I know, and I really do feel awful. But I'll make it up to you." He paused and his voice lightened. "But I promise you'll love it in DC. We'll have a great time. We can go trekking in Virginia, tubing down the Potomac, and camping in the Shenandoah Valley!" he added, still with entirely too much enthusiasm. I got the impression that the decision was already made and he thought it was time to rejoice.

"Again, Tiger, your choice in activities is not making this any easier. Say good-bye to the whirly, bustling metropolis that is New York City, say hello to hiking up friggin' mountains at the weekend!"

"It will be like Brokeback!" he laughed.

"I wish I knew how to quit you," I responded, perhaps a little too harshly.

We said our good-byes with Danny treading on eggshells and attempting to keep me lighthearted. I loved living in New York, but what would be the point of being there if we were both stressed all of the time. Danny had taken on the role of supporting us both, and I knew that in itself was a stress. I felt helpless, because even though I was capable of working and helping out financially with a salary, I was banned from doing so. I reminded myself that I made a deal with myself and with Danny that we would do what we had to, so long as we were together. New York was only three hours away by train, so it wasn't as if I would never see the place again.

Five minutes later I slapped my head and remembered Tucker now lived in DC.

The following day, I boarded my flight back to New York. The positive attitude I had talked myself into the night before began to falter a little. I still felt slightly duped into giving up my job, only to find out at the last moment that I wasn't heading toward what we'd planned. But I knew that it didn't matter anymore.

Once in New York, Danny and I spent the remaining free time that we had getting around and doing everything we could and seeing everything to be seen in the city. It was as though we would never return, and it was probably the most fun that we had there. All the things that we spoke of doing but never got around to, either because I was flying or because of the long hours Danny worked, were crammed into the limited time we had left. It all went by in a blur, like a whirlwind weekend that lasted for a month, before we made the trip down to DC to find somewhere to live.

Danny looked on the Internet and contacted a realtor to show us around a few apartment blocks in DC so we could get around more quickly and see more in the weekend that we put aside. It had been a long time since Danny lived in DC, and although he'd had a few short trips back in between, he was unsure of the ever-changing communities and areas in the metro area. Although the apartments all looked very similar to the one where we lived in New York, the buildings themselves were never higher than seven stories, as no construction in DC could be taller than the Washington Monument. The landscape resembled more of a town than a city for its lack of skyscrapers or raised billboards.

After looking at several places in the Dupont, Logan, and U Street areas, the realtor finished her tour with a building that she promised was "the best for last." We pulled alongside a brand new building situated in an area called Columbia Heights. The realtor began her pitch of the building as soon as we left the last place in Dupont, and sold it as "the up and coming, gentrified liberal area of the District."

The new apartment block was only thirty percent occupied and opened only four weeks before our visit. The rent was half what we paid in New York, and we were also given the first two months free on a year-long contract. As Danny and I looked out onto the view from the fifth floor corner apartment, we noticed that the immediate area outside was extraordinarily new. The pavements were clean and chewing-gum-mark free; the Metro station sign below the apartment was still gleaming fresh; the supermarket, small shopping mall, bars and restaurants in the surrounding streets were newly opened or seemed to be coming to the end of their building or remodeling. Most had balloons and celebratory window dresses with large signs announcing their opening dates. It was how I imagined Milton Keynes looked when they first opened the purpose-built town back in England in the '80s. In comparison to what I saw on my last visit to Washington, this area had a much more modern feel to it and already seemed to be busy, despite the fact that the area wasn't yet fully complete. We decided that the extra money saved from the two months free rent would go nicely toward a car, so we signed the paperwork and left the realtor at the building, hopped onto the Metro, and headed back to our hotel.

That night, Danny arranged to meet up with Chris, an old DC college housemate, and Chris's boyfriend, Randy, who was visiting from Boston, where he lived and worked as a plastic surgeon. I was more than happy that my first night in the city wasn't going to be spent socializing with Tucker or one of Danny's old shags, so I was in a good mood when we arrived at one of the more popular bars in town.

At first glance, the gay scene was similar to New York's. The crowd was older than it was back home in Brighton, but much of that was due to the fact that it was outrageously expensive to live, eat, and drink in such cities, and the younger guys simply couldn't afford it. Most of the men were in their mid-to-late twenties or early thirties, and I presumed there must have been other bars with cheaper beer that catered to the hordes of college students who lived within their means while studying in such an expensive city. And again, like New York, the people who frequented these bars obviously were successful in their chosen careers to continue living and drinking in the nation's capital.

As we waited by the bar for Chris and Randy to join us, Danny filled me in on the occupations that the men, many of whom stared at us, were likely to have. He nodded to a couple of guys as we entered the bar, but I didn't know if this was out of politeness, acknowledgement, or recognition of an old shag. I managed to convince Danny that I didn't want Tucker around all night pointing out all of his ex-lovers, and mentioning it now wouldn't have done me any good. Still, I couldn't help it. The jealousy was there.

"Most of these guys are lawyers, government workers, military, campaigners, or lobbyists," Danny said as he released his index finger from the glass in his hand and pointed to the room in general.

As I scanned the room, I was bumped by a guy who had been steadily getting on my nerves for the previous five minutes. He gestured with his hands with every sentence he shouted to his two friends, who were no farther than two feet away. I knew Americans tended to be loud, but it still wound me up the wrong way despite being in their company so long.

"Hey, take it easy, fella," I said as I moved my drink further away from me so the spill fell to the floor.

"Oh, wow, are you British?" he asked as he looked me up and down like he was trying to find the "made in England" mark.

"I am," I said with a polite smile, then turned back to Danny, who was grinning again, clearly getting a kick out of me being accosted once more.

"Hey, hey, come back here. I haven't finished with you yet!" The guy took his hand to my shoulder and tugged as if to turn me around. It wasn't said in a cheeky, endearing kind of way. It was more of an "I demand your attention and you will answer me, dammit" kind of way.

"Excuse me? You haven't finished with me yet?" I said, a little confused and angry at being manhandled.

"So what are you doing in DC?" he asked, almost swaying like a schoolgirl. His forcefulness disappeared at being called out on his rudeness.

"I am just visiting," I said and once again turned my back on him, hoping that the conversation was over.

"Oh, I live here and work on the Hill," he said, assuming I knew what the hell he was talking about or even wanted to know.

"Uh-huh, that's nice for you," was all I could respond.

"What do you do on Capitol Hill?" Danny asked, as if he was saving me embarrassment for not knowing his reference to the Hill.

"I'm a staffer," he responded, not really telling me anything.

"Will your job change when that Obama guy gets in?" I asked casually, realizing that Danny was going to engage the man in conversation whether I liked it or not, so I attempted to join in.

"That's *if* he gets in," he said, with a look if disdain on his face. "You know, it's all still up for grabs, though I think that Ron Paul is a dark horse. He's one to watch, believe me. I wouldn't be surprised if he manages to get in." He spoke like he had some kind of insider information.

I looked around at Danny. "Which one is Ron Paul?" I asked, trying to rack my brain for some kind of recall.

"Are you serious?" The man turned his head and made wide eyes for effect. "You don't know who Ron Paul is?" He looked over to his friends and laughed. "Wow," he added just to punch in the humiliation he was trying to cause, a smug look etched across his face.

I sucked in the side of my cheek and studied him for a moment before I looked over at Danny, who nodded slightly and raised his eyebrows as if to give me permission to attack.

"Ron Paul!" I said as if it had suddenly come to me, "Yes, he is the one that met with the British Foreign Secretary in DC last week, isn't he?"

The guy looked around again to his friends for support or some kind of indication that what I was saying was right.

"Yes, I think so," he replied, smiling. But his hesitation gave me enough to know he had no idea what I was talking about.

"Now," I said, smiling, "what is the name of the British Foreign Secretary?"

He looked like he was beginning to flounder, moving his eyes up and then side to side as he tried to "remember" the name.

"Jack...." I waved my hand forward to encourage him to finish the name.

"Jack Straw!" he declared with a look of slight relief, which was quickly replaced with the same smugness that was there before.

I smiled and cocked my head to one side, looking sympathetic. "No, it's David Miliband. I see you pay as much attention to foreign politics as I do. Wow, and you work for the government. I am embarrassed for you," I said in mock pity.

"Well we have a much bigger system of government here," he said dismissively.

"Sorry, I don't understand your point," I said, shaking my head slowly and looking at him like he was a puzzle.

"Well, I don't look outside of the USA because there are far too many things to follow here."

"Yet you assume everyone else in the world should know about your politics and your politicians' names and parties?" I asked as if I really didn't understand his logic. "Do you expect that everyone needs to know your politics? What is there to learn? If you are pro-life, hate gay people, quote the Bible—in or out of context—the chances are you are a Republican. Anything else, you are either a Democrat or an independent."

"Actually, I am a Republican, and I am gay," he said with a rather weird look of pride on his face. He noticeably puffed out his chest.

"Great, so you're in favor of a government that incites wars, denies global warming, and encourages inequality of gay men and women. Good for you! Hopefully you will never get drafted, care about the environment, or want a husband to go home to," I said, looking at him like he was a convicted sex offender.

He looked back blankly.

"Oh my God, I just love your accent. Are all of you British guys uncut?"

Danny took my arm, laughing as he spotted Chris and Randy, who had just arrived and stood at the opposite bar.

I was still shaking my head in disbelief when I was introduced to Chris and then, in turn, to Randy, who was looking at me oddly.

"You look confused," Randy said

"Greg just had his first political debate in DC, and it ended with him being asked if he was uncircumcised." Danny laughed, soon joined by Chris.

"You poor guy," Randy said sympathetically. "But get used to it. Americans always want what they don't have. And thankfully that keeps me in a job!"

Randy and Chris were a very well-suited couple. Chris was a financial officer at a large bank and was unbelievably laid-back and handsome in an "outdoors man" kind of way. He stayed in Washington after college and had obviously grown accustomed to the attitude without succumbing to it over the previous fifteen years.

Randy, just as handsome as his partner but without the designer stubble that Chris sported, was much more animated but just as down to earth as Chris. Like Danny and me, they shared the same sense of humor, although it was delivered very differently. Chris opted for the back-slap punch line, while Randy went for the edgier, more blatant, dark-humored jokes that are common among healthcare professionals, who deal with some of the harsher realities of life.

It was apparent that they were very much in love. They had been seeing each other for a year, one living in DC while the other was in Boston. It was funny to see the way they interacted with each other, as it mirrored Danny and me in the early days. The way they cherished every minute they had together and held on tight to each other reminded me how hard it was to say good-bye to Danny on so many previous occasions.

The evening passed more quickly than I would have imagined. For a while, I actually forgot where I was. Once I was reminded, the idea of Washington didn't seem as bad as I originally expected. Danny and I spent most of the evening being quizzed by Randy and Chris on how to sustain a long-distance relationship, which I thought was ridiculous because they were obviously so into each other. "You'll make it work" was the only advice I could give them, as it was the only thing I knew with any honesty to be true.

It was odd to talk about so many of the hardships and trials Danny and I had been through in one go, especially with two people who knew instantly what we were talking about. Although the obstacles they faced perhaps were not as high as those that Danny and I endured, I knew that they were going through all of the same emotions that we ourselves experienced. And I knew there were many more to come.

Thankfully, Chris and Randy both remained even-keeled when it came to my jokes about Americans, even when they led to quick-fire sarcastic rounds between Randy and me about the differences in appearance between Brits and Yanks. It had been a while since I allowed an American to get the better of me, and I gave them their dues and respect. Both Randy and Chris made me feel at home, even when I mocked their countrymen.

As we boarded the train back to New York, I was no longer filled with the dread about Washington that plagued me before our trip. I still wasn't thrilled with the idea of moving yet again, but I thought that perhaps DC wasn't the bland, boring place that I thought it was. All I knew was that I was going to have to make a go of it. Danny was going to be there, and, ultimately, that was all that mattered.

CHAPTER EiGHTEEN

WE STOOD at the window of the apartment in New York and waved to the Empire State Building. The moving truck downstairs was illegally parked, and the driver awaited our signature so he could set off to the new place in DC. Grabbing the keys, Danny took hold of me and, damning the waiting removal men downstairs, we danced our good-bye on the bare parquet floor as Duke wove in and out between our legs. It was a glorious, clear day in New York, and the buildings were as bold as ever on the blue sky. It was sad, but after waltzing me to the door, Danny took the edge of sadness away. "I love New York, but everywhere is New York with you, Greg."

After a few weeks of settling in to the area, Danny and I had our first night out as DC residents rather than mere visitors. We headed to a newly opened place in town called Secrets (which, based on the volume of closeted politicians and government workers, was a very apt name). We arranged to meet Randy, who was on his alternate week in DC, and Chris in the upstairs bar. It was billed as one of the best new venues in DC and consisted of a bar, nightclub, drag revue, and strip joint all rolled into a two-story building located near the baseball stadium.

The usual Abercrombie and Fitch brigade were all in attendance, many students from the universities who were there to take advantage of the cheap promotional drinks, as well as many much older men armed with a fistful of single-dollar bills. The patrons must have been starved for the sight of a naked man for many years, judging by the way they salivated over the bar on which the strippers displayed themselves. God only knows how many paper cuts were inflicted that night on the thighs of poor dancers, who endured these old fools running dollar bills up the dancers' legs with their best, and incredibly creepy, seductive looks.

"You should think about having Botox, Greg. It would get rid of those lines around your eyes when you smile," Randy said, pursing his lips as he gave me an unrequested consult.

"Cheers, Randy, perhaps you should turn the needle on yourself and paralyze that nasty tongue of yours."

"Danny has amazing skin for someone his age, but that's because he doesn't smoke." He wagged his finger at me in doctorly disapproval.

"Some of us need a crutch. If I had your personality I would prescribe myself anti-depressants every day."

"It's only a couple of little jabs, and it will take years off you. Maybe even decades."

"Do you do penis reductions? I have a voucher."

"Only on Medicare, and I don't think you qualify. Besides, I only do enlargements. It's my pro bono work. You know I can get you some hair plugs too, to sort out that receding hair line of yours."

"It's distinguished," I said, tracing the hairline around my temple with my middle finger.

"On a man ten years older. Still, I guess your wrinkles go with it. It's like having the pie without the cream."

"Speaking of pies...," I said as I saw the crowd being parted.

Tucker bounded forward after spotting me from the bar. We hadn't seen him in a while, as he had begun a relationship with a twenty-one-year-old who lived in Wisconsin. They had met at a convention in DC, and Tucker gave the impression that he was smitten, using the expression "I think this might be the one," the last time we spoke.

"Hey, guys! It seems like ages since I've seen you." He clearly had been drinking for a while. He looked at Randy as if he knew him.

"We're good. Tucker, this is Randy," I introduced them, and I saw Randy's eyes sweep Tucker's face, silently giving him a consult.

"How's your boy in Wisconsin?" I asked, forgetting the kid's name. "Are you still all loved up?"

"He's not too good. He found out a couple of weeks ago that his mother has terminal brain cancer." He looked sympathetic for a moment before he shrugged.

"Poor kid. How is he?"

"Okay I guess. We've split up, so I haven't really spoken to him."

"Why?"

"I had to end it. He didn't share the same beliefs as me and refused to accept God as divine, so it wasn't going to work out...." He waved his hand as if he wasn't bothered.

Randy studied him for a moment to figure out whether he was joking.

"Tucker, was this before or after his mum got sick?" I asked.

"After. Why?"

Randy looked as though he was still wondering whether this was some big and rather weird inside joke between us and Tucker. My face told him it wasn't. Tucker had no look of shame.

"Anyways, I've been seeing a new guy from the local deaf college," he shouted louder than necessary above the music.

"Deaf?" I asked. "You don't know sign language."

"Aw, I know all I need to know." He clenched his fist to the side of his mouth and moved it from side to side while his tongue poked out his cheek. I looked around, mortified that anyone could see him do this in my direction.

Danny and Chris returned from the bar with our drinks.

"I was just telling Greg and Sandy about my new trick."

"Randy," he was corrected, but Tucker continued, oblivious.

"He's deaf! Have any of you guys ever been with a deaf guy?" he asked excitedly.

"No, I like to tell them when to leave, as I think it's rude to just point to the door," Randy said, grinning from ear to ear and enjoying the entertainment.

"You guys are missing out." He smiled wide and held his hands up and clenched them in excitement. "They are just so primal. They don't demand stuff or do any of that dirty talk during sex."

"What? Like, 'please get off me' and 'stop'?" Randy asked, nudging me.

"They are just so animalistic. It's just so raw. It's how sex should be!" Tucker said, a little too enthusiastically.

Chris, Danny, and I looked at each other and tightened our lips as we all had the unfortunate image in our heads. Randy, however, went for it. "So what kind of noises do they make?"

Tucker moaned and grunted like Helen Keller in a sex tape. I wondered how much mental bleach I would have to use to get the sound out of my memory.

"So, do you have a specific type, or is the only prerequisite that they are deaf?" Randy continued.

Tucker was excited that someone was asking him about his sex life. God knows we never did, even though we were unwillingly updated on a regular basis.

Tucker looked around and pointed up to the bar to a black stripper wearing nothing but white socks. His abs looked like they were hand carved into his stomach.

"I love the chocolate ones!"

"Oh, you like deaf black guys?" Randy cried. "Well, that's nice!"

"Nice? They are fucking hot, and you get to do stuff to them that's different."

"Different?" Randy asked.

And without a hint of shame or worry of being overheard, he responded. "Yes! You can fuck them from behind and call them 'nigger' and they can't hear you!"

Both Danny and I looked away, ashamed to be associated with him.

"Wow, you like the whole plantation owner fantasy, huh?" By this point, Randy was just egging him on to say something else.

What he wasn't expecting was Tucker moving behind him to dry hump his back, shouting "Take it, boy!" in an old-fashioned southern accent into Randy's ear.

"Tucker, what happened to the guy you were seeing in Wisconsin?" Danny asked, desperate to change the subject while Randy bucked himself free and scolded Chris with his eyes for laughing.

"He didn't believe in God," Tucker said simply, as if Danny would understand immediately.

I looked over at Danny and punched two thumbs up in the air and mouthed the word "Christian!"

"Mark!" Tucker suddenly shouted over Chris's shoulder. He moved toward a guy who looked in his early thirties, was stocky, and had a gleaming shaven head, who was talking to a guy he was clearly hitting on.

"Oh, for fuck sake." I looked at Danny for confirmation that it was the same Mark who chastised Danny for coming out to the Navy. He nodded.

Tucker slung his arm around Mark and brought him over to the group. He wasn't what I expected. Either he had suffered from bad acne as a kid or the years hadn't been too kind to him, as his skin was shot to shit. Still, I could imagine him as a young Navy officer being relatively attractive without the pebble-dashed features and the slightly sagging muscles. As Danny introduced Chris to Mark, Randy mouthed, "Who is that?" clearly enough to understand. Not having a great deal of time, I whispered back "Danny's ex-Navy boyfriend. Never met him, but I really don't like him."

Randy eyed me as if he was already on my side.

"Greg, this is Mark!" Tucker said without a hint of realizing this might be awkward.

"It's a pleasure to meet you, Mark." I smiled and bowed my head slightly in polite acknowledgement.

"Oh, you're the Greg that Danny gave up his Navy career for, huh?" he said with a slight sneer.

Before I could even form a comeback in my head, Randy shot ahead of me.

"Hey, I am Dr. Randall Davis, nice to meet you."

I looked over and saw Chris wince. He obviously recognized Randy's tone of voice.

"This is Mark!" Tucker said, pointing to him. "Mark and Danny dated while they were in the Navy together."

"The Navy?" Randy asked.

I tried to get Danny's attention, but his eyes were boring holes into Tucker. He looked like he was about to explode.

Randy reached into his pocket and pulled out his wallet.

"Listen, I do a lot of work with the military. I'm a plastic surgeon in Boston, and my hospital takes many cases of you brave guys who were wounded in action. Since you're a friend of Danny's, I would be happy to try and bump you up the list and see if we can get that shrapnel out of your face, or at least try and hide some of the scars," Randy said as if sincere as he handed Mark his business card.

"I don't have shrapnel in my face." The lights were flashing, but I could tell that his face was getting darker from embarrassment.

"Oh, sorry, when Tucker said you 'were' in the Navy, I assumed that you came out because of your injuries. So, was it like a car accident or something like that?"

Mark turned and walked away, leaving whoever he was talking to at the bar alone. I followed his shaved head until it went out of the door.

"Randy!" Chris began to chastise. "Man, that was just mean!"

"But trust me, Chris, it was well deserved!" I raised my glass.

CHAPTER NINETEEN

THE three months I was allowed to stay in America on my visa was coming to an end, and I was looking forward to short trip back home to England. For the first time in a long while I was beginning to feel a little homesick. I was missing the look and the smell of the sea in Brighton and craved the familiarity of my hometown. I was also looking forward to getting back and seeing Mum. She had remained quite chipper on each phone call I had made while I was in DC, but there were occasions that I knew that this was an act. I felt like I needed to check on her myself, face to face, to make sure she was okay. Danny was busy with work, so there was no way that he was able to join me, but I would have the company of Donna, with whom I would be staying.

I was also looking forward to getting back to feeling like I was in a place that was a little more accepting. My mood and attitude toward some Americans were becoming a little dark as each and every day it seemed that I was reminded that the gay people in the country were being treated like second-class citizens and had to battle each fire that was set by yet another Christian group. With the presidential elections coming up there were more and more debates on hot button issues, one of them being gay rights and gay marriage. Each morning I felt like I was being bombarded or personally attacked by the right wing media, the politicians, the church, or simply by the public who were given time on camera and who expressed their views on opposing gay rights so freely on the television. Then as I would drive Danny to work, I would see the protests down by the mall, some of which were directly aimed at gay people.

"MOM and Dad are coming down for the weekend," Danny said over breakfast one morning before he left to go to the office.

Danny had made an obvious effort recently in not bringing up his mother around me. It seemed that, despite their argument at Christmas, they were back on track.

"Okay, I will make up the spare room."

Danny stared at me, not in mock surprise as expected, but with a worried look on his face. It was the first time I hadn't kicked off when his family was sprung on me.

"You seem to be taking it very well," he said.

"Well, I am going to be in England, so it doesn't really affect me too much, Tiger. Besides, even if I was here I wouldn't mind because I loves ya so much!" I smiled and reached for a hug.

"They are, um, coming this weekend."

"What?"

"Dad arranged it. I think that since it's been so long since I last saw Mom, he thought it would be a good thing. But I only found out about it yesterday. He called me at work and said that he had some frequent flyer miles that he wanted to use up and thought it would be nice to get away for the weekend. I could hardly refuse, could I?"

I had already said that I would endure a visit from his mother, even though I didn't suspect I actually would have to. I had no choice but to concede.

When Mrs. Taylor and George arrived at the apartment, I didn't act as I usually would have. The false greetings, smiles, small talk, and welcomes were replaced by a general "Hi" to Mrs. Taylor, where as George got the whole welcome package. I wasn't trying to make a point, as I was sincerely happy to see him.

"SO HOW do you like Washington DC, Greg?" Mrs. Taylor asked as I pottered around the living room to keep myself busy, trying to avoid any real conversation with her. She was playing pleasant today, but at least her falseness was easier to deal with than any direct confrontation. Unfortunately, Danny and George started a debate about politics, which left me conversationally alone with Mrs. Taylor.

"I am not a fan, Mrs. Taylor. It's not really my kind of town, but as long as Danny is here I am happy."

"Well, I guess you have no interest in history, then," Mrs. Taylor said, raising her nose as if she had smelled something revolting. "History is best left to the intellectual visitors, I suppose."

"I am not a visitor, Mrs. Taylor. And as for history, I have socks in England that are older than this place."

"This is the land of our forefathers," she said, looking offended. "This is where our very nation was built."

"And I am sure you will find it all very interesting. Perhaps on our day out today we can go to the Smithsonian and see if we can find one of those old dunking stalls in which they tried to drown witches. I am sure it will bring back lots of happy memories for you." I laughed to give Danny and George the impression that we were having a fun chat.

"Shall we go, then?" Danny said, standing up and gathering his keys together.

"Oh, this will be fun!" Mrs. Taylor said, taking her husband's arm and following us out the door. "Are the cherry blossoms out at the moment, Danny?"

"No, Momma, not this time of year. They don't come out until around April."

"Oh, that's a shame. Maybe we can visit again when they're in full bloom."

"Yes, you must visit again next year," I said, already working out my visa dates, satisfied that there was no chance I would be in the area.

Although we all walked together, Danny and George were deep in conversation as we ambled around the central tourist area of DC. It was great seeing Danny engage with his dad again. I knew that, like many people, each call to the family home while you were away was usually made up of a brief chat with Dad before Mum took the receiver and proceeded to talk until the cows came home. Danny kept in such regular contact with his mum that I think George felt like he was missing out, only ever hearing things secondhand.

Since Danny had lived in DC before, he was able to talk his way around the various sights with the knowledge of a guide. His dad stopped him to ask random questions on history that probably no one in his life other than Danny would know.

As we traipsed around the Washington monument, Mrs. Taylor took hold of my arm and linked it in her own. "You boys keep going. I am going to have a word with Greg," she called to George and Danny. They both looked at me and walked ahead of us.

"You're not playing your game today, Greg," Mrs. Taylor deadpanned.

"No, I am not playing your game today, Mrs. Taylor."

"Danny doesn't like to see us not get along. I tolerate you now because it makes him happy. Though I must admit he doesn't mention you half as much as he used to when I speak to him on the phone."

"Do you want a repeat of Christmas?"

"You made sure Danny didn't call his momma on Christmas day, and for that I will never forgive you."

"But I thought Jesus taught forgiveness?"

"So you don't deny it?"

"If you maintain that your relationship with your son is so wonderful, I am sure he has told you that it was his decision and not mine."

"Oh, he did," she said, nodding. "But I know he was only saying that to try to protect you."

"Uh-huh. Ever wondered what he was trying to protect me from?"

This was ignored.

"I know it was you."

"Mrs. Taylor. You believe so many things that you have no evidence of. This is no different. So what's the point of trying to argue with you?"

We continued to walk in a silence for a couple of minutes. I noticed that Mrs. Taylor had slowed our pace again.

"Danny has told me you're unhappy here, Greg."

"Of course he has," I said, not even pretending to keep it under my breath. "But that is more to do with the fact that we live in an area where stupid people make dumb laws that make our lives harder."

"What I want to know is, why don't you just go home?" she asked, smiling and cocking her head to one side like she actually cared about my happiness, as though she was a sympathetic school nurse and I was being sent home sick from school. Instead, of course, she was practically telling me to leave. "I know you're leaving next week, but why not go home for good this time?"

"You're right, I think I might leave for good this time," I said, letting out a long breath like I finally admitted defeat.

"I think it's probably for the best," she said. She nodded slowly, like she was agreeing with my wise decision, but the joy on her face couldn't be masked. I decided to knock it off.

"I have things to organize that I can't do from here. Danny and I will head back to England soon enough to live and settle down. We have looked into adoption or maybe surrogacy. We are excited to have a couple of kids of our own. I can't wait to have another little Danny running around! Can you imagine? Thankfully, the firm has an office in London, so it should be sooner rather than later. Then there will be no reason to come back here." It was an utter lie, although we had spoken about it as a possible plan in the future. It was the only thing I could think of fast enough to wipe the smug off her mug.

She stopped dead in her tracks.

"Danny is going with you? You're taking Danny away?" she asked, wide eyed.

"Of course he is. Why wouldn't he?" I asked as if any answer would be absurd.

"But Danny has family here. You want to take him away from his family?" she asked in a flat tone of statement.

"And I don't have family in England? I don't have family that I left? The way things are now in this country, we cannot have a family of our own here. Even if we could, there is no way I would ever raise children here to be influenced by certain people and their beliefs on what is right and what is wrong."

Mrs. Taylor smiled back at me, an all-knowing smile that she couldn't contain. Even after all this time I could still be surprised how quickly she could turn.

"I know my Danny, and he won't leave his momma. I think you are under the impression, Greg, that you are more important to him than his own family. Let me tell you, you are not. You have a lot to learn, young man. Perhaps you should learn it back in England, on your own."

"Let me tell you, Mrs. Taylor, I *am* his family. I am more important to him. And when we have children they will be more important to him. You seem to want to turn this into some kind of competition. If that is the case, then I think that perhaps you should fold now."

"Of course you would compare this to gambling, Greg. But the sin of gambling will always be ended by greed."

"Greed? You think I am greedy?"

"And very selfish," she added.

"You know nothing about me, and what you do know you manage to distort."

"Oh, no, Greg. Not distort. You are crystal clear to me. I've met many people like you throughout my life."

"I know, coming from such a worldly, well-rounded, and diverse place such as Baytown."

"I know your agenda, and I will not permit you to bring my son down with you."

"Bring him down with me? Why do you keep saying that? Where on earth is it that you think I am going to bring him to?"

"Nowhere on earth, Greg. Hell isn't somewhere on this plane."

"I beg to differ, Mrs. Taylor. I am walking around Washington DC arm in arm with you. That's proof enough for me."

"You can joke as much as you like—"

"I am not joking."

"But there will come a day that you will show yourself." She stopped, released her arm from mine, and pointed a finger at my chest like she was some kind of seer.

"I already have. Hopefully there will come a day when you will show yourself too." I walked forward aggressively until her hand drew back.

"We will see. I have faith that Danny will see you for who you truly are. I thought you had come into our lives to test me, but now I wonder whether God is trying to show you something about yourself instead."

"And what would that be?"

"That people who live sinner's lives will not go forth and win the souls of the pure."

"So I am a sinner, sent here to turn your son into some kind of monster, change him into a demon, and possess him and his immortal spirit?"

"My eyes have seen the light."

"It must have been bright, because you're obviously blind."

"Greg, you cannot fool me. You're no different than that Diana woman, sent to break up a family. And look what happened to her."

She walked away from me with her head held high as if she had won a battle, while I held my hands on my head wondering if anyone would ever believe that, at best, she compared herself to the Queen of England and, at worst, hoped that I would be killed in a car crash in Paris.

The weekend finally ended, and Danny was once again happy after a dose of family and Texas cuisine, which Mrs. Taylor insisted on preparing, gracing the table with, among other things, fried chicken gizzards. Now that his family was gone, I planned my remaining days to make sure Danny and I had as much time together as we could before I was to depart. I looked forward to my trip home, but leaving Danny was still hard.

On the day before I was due to fly back to England, I was busy packing my clothes into my suitcase. My documents, passport, plane ticket, and wallet were all laid out on the table so I wouldn't forget anything. I wrote my usual twenty messages of love and sarcastic comments on Post-it Notes and hid them around the flat in books, drawers, kitchen towels, shirt pockets, or anywhere else that Danny would eventually find them. They were my little absent love reminders that would hopefully bring a smile to his day.

Later that morning the phone rang, so I pulled the last shirt off its hanger and threw it toward the suitcase as I walked over to answer.

"Mr. Taylor?" I recognized the voice of the reception lady at the front desk of the building, who only called to announce visitors.

"No, Mr. Stephens," I replied.

"This is Anna from the front desk. I have two gentlemen to see you. I will send them up." And before I could say anything, she hung up.

I had no idea who would be there to see me and would address me as "Mr. Stephens." I waited by the door until I heard the elevator ping. Two men in dark suits walked around the corner, down the corridor, and toward the open door, where I stood looking rather confused. One of the men was shorter and rather dumpy but with a very official look about him. The other was slightly younger and looked much more casual in his stride.

"Hey, sorry, guys, but whatever you are selling you have the wrong guy. Thanks for your time, anyway," I called as I held my palm up and gave my most apologetic face.

"We are not selling anything, Mr. Stephens. You are Mr. Gregory Stephens, I presume?" the shorter one said with direct eye contact.

"Yes, sorry, should I know you?" I asked, confused. For a moment I thought they were plainclothes policemen doing the rounds, as there had been a recent upsurge in gun violence all around the city.

The younger man stepped forward. "I am Special Agent Thame, and this is my colleague, Special Agent Talbot. We are with the Department of Homeland Security, Immigration, and Customs Enforcement."

My heart started beating so fast in my chest that it felt like an angry gorilla was beating against my ribs.

"May we come in?" He made a move forward, as if there was to be no discussion and he was only asking me as a formality.

"Sure, I am just packing at the moment, so please excuse the mess." I waved my hand through politely, the same way I had done a million times at an aircraft door. Duke instantly shot out of his bed and toward the strangers, but I managed to catch him by his collar in time and settle him down.

As they entered they looked around the apartment. They looked at eye level height on the walls and surfaces of the side tables. I immediately knew that they were looking for photographs. Danny and I had spoken about moving to another apartment building as soon as our contract was up, so I hadn't bothered decorating or putting up paintings or photographs, apart from one of Mum and Dad that sat on an end table by the sofa.

"Can I get you a drink?" I asked in my usual manner of airline politeness.

"No, thank you, sir," Special Agent Thame said rather stiffly as I showed them to the sofa where they took their seats.

"I'm sorry, but I am a bit confused as to why you are here," I said, trying to remain calm and casual.

"Mr. Stephens, we have received a phone call regarding your stay in America and were asked to investigate your immigration status," the younger agent said as he opened a file onto his knees and withdrew a pen from his suit pocket.

"My immigration status? I don't have one." I threw in a laugh. "I am not emigrating here. I am just visiting my partner."

"Well, that explains why we have no record of your application," said Special Agent Thame, eyeing me like I was being interrogated. "Do you plan to emigrate here? Have you applied?"

"No, I haven't. I have no intention of moving here full-time or becoming a citizen. I am sorry. I am a bit lost," I answered, screwing up my eyes as I saw him ticking a box on a form that he was careful not to show me.

"Are you going somewhere, sir?" he asked as he looked over toward the suitcase and the documents.

"Yes, I am going back to Britain tomorrow. Would you like to see the ticket?"

He nudged his head in a single nod and took out a pair of glasses to inspect the ticket confirmation.

I turned to Special Agent Talbot and furrowed my brow. "What is going on here?"

"Mr. Stephens, how long have you been here?"

"Three months. Well, almost. I am on the visa waiver program. I have never overstayed my time on the visa and have always followed the rules to the letter."

I reached over and grabbed my passport, showing them the immigration card that was dated for another week.

"Have I done something wrong?"

"Have you worked while you have been here?" special Agent Thame asked, ignoring my question.

"No, I am well aware of the conditions of the visa waiver program."

"May I ask how you have been supporting yourself on such a long stay?"

"I have money in the bank from the sale of property, and my partner is an attorney. Would you like to see a bank statement?" I offered genuinely.

I knew I had to give these guys the impression that I would help with their enquiries any way I could. I had nothing to hide, and I certainly hadn't done anything wrong as far as I knew, but just a dislike toward me could cause these two strangers to recommend that my visa not be renewed, or make a note on my status as I came back into the country. "The face of the nation" immigration officers at border control at the airport were hard enough to deal with, as they had become stern and overly combative in any discussion that they had with an entering tourist, as if each and every one of them caused a threat. Although I knew it was their job, I didn't believe I could ever fit a threatening profile such that they could have reason to speak to me like a suspect in an interrogation unit. These men were calmer than the uniformed border control officers, but they were still just as harsh.

Special Agent Talbot moved forward on the sofa. "No, I don't think that will be necessary. We can see that you are planning to exit the country. Judging by the stamps in your passport and your immigration card, you have not done anything that would warrant a full investigation requiring the expenditure of government funds." With this, he seemed to back down, and briefly changed his manner to someone who was just passing the time of day with a stranger.

"Could I possibly use your restroom?" asked Special Agent Thame, who gathered his things.

"Sure, it's just through there." I pointed toward the bathroom.

As he left the room Special Agent Talbot walked toward the entertainment center and ran his fingers through the DVDs, which I thought at the time was incredibly forward.

"Madonna in Concert, Brokeback Mountain, Oz, and Titan Men." He turned and winked. "We have the same taste in DVDs."

"What is going on? Is this some kind of random thing you guys do?"

He looked toward the bathroom door and lowered his voice. "Listen, I can't tell you anything other than we had a phone call that suggested that you were in the country illegally."

"Someone reported me?" I asked, looking surprised, but my red face of anger showed through. "Who was it?"

"I can't tell you the name. Perhaps she just thought she was being a good citizen."

I closed my eyes and rocked my head to one side. "She?"

Special Agent Talbot pulled in his lips and nodded.

"I am not going to put you in any awkward position. I wouldn't do that to you. But I need to ask a quick question. Did the call come from within the country but outside of Washington DC?"

He opened his file and glanced down the page. "This is a very comfortable sofa," he said, nodding as he spoke.

"Was it from area code 281?" I asked, referring to Baytown's area code.

"Yes, this sofa is one of the most comfortable I have ever sat on." He leaned over and whispered, "Look, I know you guys can't win at the moment, the way things are, but you are playing the game. That's important. Keep playing by the rules, and hopefully the rules will change by the time the game is done. Good luck."

With that, Special Agent Thame returned. "Sorry we disturbed your packing, Mr. Stephens. Please ensure that you obey the conditions of your visa waiver," he said sternly.

"I will."

"I have taken a note of the number on your departure visa form and will follow that up in a few days to confirm your departure."

"Sure."

After almost apologizing to them for having to make the journey to the apartment, only not to find a room full of illegal immigrants, I unnecessarily assured them that I understood they were just doing their jobs. I watched them walk down the hall and get into the elevator before I slammed the door and ran to the bathroom. I held a towel to my mouth to muffle the screams as though they might possibly still hear me.

"*You fucking bitch!*"

CHAPTER TWENTY

I RETURNED to England still seething and, for the first time, considered not returning. The thought didn't last for long, though. Each day back in England, I pined for Danny and missed him more than I ever believed possible. He was working hard on a case that occupied every second of his ever-lengthening workdays, with his client's freedom or incarceration lying in his hands. I did all I could in the weeks leading up to my departure to make sure he was comfortable and that he didn't have anything else to deal with in the way of ordinary day-to-day life. It fulfilled my nightmare that I was to become a househusband that took control of everything domestic or social, but I did it all to make his life easier.

During my time in England, we returned to our regular routine of snatching all the time we could to be together through the webcam. I could see that work was beginning to distress him, and I just couldn't bring myself to tell him about the visit from Immigration. I planned to tell him almost every time we spoke, letting it near the tip of my tongue before I backed off. I knew that, regardless of the long-standing argument that "lawyer Danny" had with himself, it would ultimately boil down to one question: his mother or me?

Since I lost Dad through nothing I could control, the idea of Danny as good as losing his parent was more than I could bear, let alone be responsible for. Mrs. Taylor was still his mum, offering him daily advice and praise as any good mother would. However, her advice now seemed to steer away from any mention of me or our relationship. I couldn't tell whether she was being purposely nice so she could then convince Danny that she had no part in my report to Immigration, or whether the last battle with her son during our Christmas in New York led her not to risk Coventry, to which she would surely be sent again.

Either way, with so much on his work plate, Danny seemed happy enough when speaking of his family that I concluded Mrs. Taylor had pushed things to the limit and failed, so perhaps she finally gave up.

Danny was finally finishing up with his case when I returned to DC and looked physically and mentally exhausted. He was successful in his case, and celebrated with some much-needed time off. As I only had been able to listen to him sound off, rant, and rave during his workdays due to the time difference, he spoke to his family regularly in the evenings.

At some point, Mrs. Taylor convinced Danny that part of his time off after trial should be spent back home in Baytown. During my time in the UK, I had investigated and successfully applied for a B1 visa that gave me the opportunity to spend up to six months at a time in America, though still without work. I knew that such a long stay would, at some time, coincide with a visit back to his home state, but I hadn't expected it to happen within the first week of returning.

We hadn't been to Baytown for over a year, but throughout each segment of the journey—leaving the car in the garage to get to the airport terminal, going through security, waiting for departure, the flight, the arrival, the bus to the car rental—my mood became more and more sullen, and I found it hard to fight it off of my face. As we got closer, the recollection of her last stunt grew clearer and clearer in my memory, along with all the anger that infected me in the days that followed. I passed a lot of the time of the journey trying to convince Danny that we should spend more time with his sisters and the kids on this trip and trying to coerce him into taking a day out of our four-day visit to take his nephew and nieces to a water park in Houston, knowing that it would take up the entire day.

I booked a hotel near to his parents' house, which prompted a short-lived argument that I won quickly with the excuse that the celibacy we suffered while apart could not continue any longer than it already had. I gave up smoking the week before I got back to Washington, and I could hear my cravings loud and clear, making Danny stop short of arguing any point for too long for fear of my wrath, but also to show he understood and supported me.

Before I left the UK, I went to Dad's grave for the first time in years and spoke to his headstone about everything that had happened and was once again cruelly reminded that I dishonored him by continuing to smoke. This only added to my guilt, as every time I returned to America I felt a sadness that took days to shake, as I was leaving not only my living family, but him too. Although I had cut down my smoking considerably since I had met Danny, I knew that Dad would be disappointed in me for not stopping altogether. I was determined to succeed this time.

As we entered the Baytown city limits, Danny drove into a car park in front of a massive Walmart.

"I just want to get Mom and Dad a gift, something small, just to ease the way," he said as he pushed open the car door.

"Sure," I agreed, thankful that our delay meant less time with his mother.

As we walked through the gift aisles, Danny looked over to me. "Baby, I know this isn't your idea of fun, but I hardly ever get to see my family anymore. Don't think I don't appreciate you coming. You know that I love you more than anything else in the world, don't you?"

His words calmed me. I looked at him and knew straightaway that I was being a prick. I got homesick every so often too, and there was no reason why Danny wouldn't feel the same way about Baytown. I had the luxury of going home more often than him, so I bucked up and smiled back.

"It's only for four days, and then we are out of here."

"I know, Tiger. It's just been a long morning already, and I am gasping for a cigarette. I promise I will cheer up. Honestly."

Danny walked over, placed his hand around my waist, and nudged me with his hip while he buried his head into my neck and kissed me gently. As often happened in the past, my silent torment of nicotine withdrawal was replaced by hyperactivity in a moment, and I began to jig up and down. I think the compulsion was a need to do something active with my hands to free them from the longing to hold a cigarette.

"That was quick!" Danny said, remarking on my apparent change of attitude. "You know, we can always use that energy up on other things." He winked at me. Even after all this time, he still managed to turn me on in an instant.

As I put my arm around him I noticed a couple walking toward us. The man was an extremely overweight redneck wearing white shorts and an XXXL T-shirt with an array of freshwater fish printed on the front, pushing a cart full of brightly colored boxes of corn dogs, pizza, and Tex-Mex ready-made meals. His wife, barely smaller than her husband, pulled her peroxide blonde hair back into a vicious ponytail and was trying to pull off a pink-frilled sleeveless top that didn't match the camouflage shorts, which were bursting at the thighs.

The man turned to his wife and nodded toward us. He saw our public display of affection and acknowledged it to his wife with a look of disgust. I straightened up, more out of habit than anything else, and continued to stroll alongside Danny. As they walked past us the man continued to stare forward ahead of him, but said, "Fucking faggots," intentionally loud enough for us to hear and carried on walking, leaning on the cart as a weird walker for obese people.

My mood, which was just starting to lighten, turned and jumped like the back draft of a fire.

"What did you say?" I rounded on him, only eight feet separating us.

He sneered and looked at his wife, whose lips curled into a smile and showed a set of disgusting teeth.

"I said—" He inhaled either for effect or for lack of breath. "Fucking faggots."

Danny stared the man down, took my arm, and tried to usher me away.

"I am surprised to hear you say that," I said, releasing myself from Danny's grip on my shoulder. "I would have thought you would be happy we were gay. That's two less men in the world who are going to fuck your wife!"

While his face turned red with rage, I looked the fine specimen of feminine redneck over from head to Croc-covered toes. "Although, judging by the state of her, every guy at the trailer park has had a chance to hang out of the back of her."

He took a step forward, nudging the cart out of the way. "I'll fucking kill ya!" he shouted.

"You gotta catch me first, chubby!" I said, raising my arms. "Running shoes are in aisle four, but the donuts are in aisle three. I know that's got to be a tough decision for you."

Danny caught hold of my arm firmly and pulled me backward.

"Greg, that guy could have a gun. We're back in Texas. You're going to get us killed," he whispered urgently in my ear as I concentrated a smile on the now fuming hick who was balling up his fists.

"C'mon, chubby, catch me if you can!"

The redneck's wife pulled as he made an attempt to waddle toward me. Seeing that he had no chance of getting a hold on me, he turned his reddened face and made his way toward the back of the store, which incidentally held the glass cases of rifles and ammunition. He shouted abuse at me, which by this time I couldn't understand, as Danny practically dragged me out of the store.

"I have had it, Danny!"

"Greg, this is the reason why I left this place. There are thousands of people just like that in this town. We don't live here; we don't work here. It's only a few days, and I would like to get through it without being murdered."

"Fine," I said, crossing my arms like a stubborn kid as Danny drove out of the car park, far faster than he pulled in. "It doesn't mean that they should get away with saying shit like that." I looked over at Danny. "I will do my best, I promise, but you can't say that fat bastard didn't have it coming."

Danny looked as if I amazed him and laughed. "I have to admit, that was funny. I know you want a cigarette and you're not in the best mood, but if you could temper it, I'd appreciate it."

"I have an emergency packet in my pocket."

"I can't believe I'm saying this, but I'm kinda glad you do. You want to go smoke now before we get to Mom and Dad's?"

"No, I am determined to give it up this time, but thanks for all of your support!" I laughed, even though I was slightly taken aback by his reaction.

For the rest of the journey, I actively tried to elevate my mood. I didn't want to be there, and quite frankly I would have burned down an animal shelter just to inhale some of the smoke. It had been a while since I was with Mrs. Taylor on her own ground, but once again I was comforted knowing that I wouldn't have to be there for too long. I convinced myself that I could treat it as a long chore that, thankfully, I would only have to do once a year if I was lucky.

When we pulled up to the house, I saw Mrs. Taylor and George fussing with keys and locking the front door. Apparently, they were waiting for our arrival in order to depart immediately. Mrs. Taylor looked at me for a moment before her eyes darted away. She stood for a moment looking over the house as if to check if all of the windows were closed, but I knew she was buying time to see if I was going to confront her about the visit from the immigration department. I enjoyed seeing her so uncomfortable. She then started to head toward their car, satisfied that she hadn't been caught and that her call to report me had remained anonymous.

"Hey, where are you going? We just got here," Danny called out of the car window as we pulled into the driveway.

"We're going to church," Mrs. Taylor replied without looking at Danny. "We'll all go in our car."

Danny and I got out of the rental car and walked up the driveway. He threw me a look of apology as I opened the back passenger door of the SUV. I shrugged and got in, pleased that we were headed somewhere I wouldn't have to have to talk to Mrs. Taylor for an hour or so.

As we drove toward the church, Mrs. Taylor continued to act strangely. I knew she was concerned that her beloved son was going to be going to her church with his boyfriend, and it was obviously scaring the hell out of her and, quite frankly, I couldn't enjoy it any more. I was almost giddy watching her squirm, but wondered why she would put herself through it.

"Momma, you know, we don't have to go to church today," Danny said, almost ruining my pleasure.

His mother didn't respond straightaway, instead she looked around as if concentrating on the passing traffic. Finally, she answered him. "Danny, your soul is like…." She paused to search for a comparison. "It's like a truck."

"Is it a big truck?" I asked, not even attempting to mask my grin.

"Is it a four-wheel drive truck?" Danny asked, nudging me.

"Is the truck red?" I asked. "I like red trucks!"

Mrs. Taylor looked severe as she peered at me through the rear view mirror. I returned her look with a menacing glare.

"Danny, your soul is like a truck and going to church is like getting its annual inspection."

"Is that like an MOT?" I asked Danny.

"Yes, they give you a sticker that you put in your windshield."

I raised my hand into the air. "I like stickers!"

Danny stroked my cheek with the back of his hand as if I just got off the special school bus. "Yes, baby, I know you do."

Mrs. Taylor looked out of the windows, and I knew she was terrified that she might know one of the other drivers.

George had not made his usual greeting when we had arrived. Instead we got a brief wave at the door before he walked toward the car with his head down. He hadn't spoken either, though I noticed his fingers were drumming against the passenger door while his wife was driving.

The drive was much shorter than the one we took the last time we went to church in Texas. With Danny not making any comments on directions, I rightly assumed that we were heading to the church where Mrs. Taylor worked. I was surprised and confused that I was now being shown in public. Mrs. Taylor had gone to such extremes to get me out of her son's life that I wondered whether she was taking me for an exorcism or whether she finally succumbed to the unavoidable truth that nothing was going to split us up, so for Danny's sake, she was making an effort.

Once we reached the car park, George finally spoke. "Boys, you go ahead now. We'll be along in a minute."

Danny looked at me and indicated to get out of the car. We began to walk toward the church, stopping just short of the entrance.

"Has your mum forgotten something again?" I asked Danny, who answered this with a look of confusion. "The last time we went to church with your parents your mum pretended like she had forgotten something in the car and sent us ahead so we didn't all have to sit together."

"No. Something is wrong," Danny said, looking over toward the car. Mrs. Taylor sat stoically in the driver's seat while George seemed to be quite animated next to her. "It looks like they're arguing. Dad looks pretty riled."

After a few minutes, Mrs. Taylor got out of the car and walked past us and into the church. George joined us outside the front doors and peered in to see Mrs. Taylor speaking to the pastor.

"Is she running to Brother Thomas now every time you have a fight?" Danny asked George.

George didn't look happy and chewed on his lip. "C'mon. Your momma is waiting for us," he said without answering Danny's question.

Although there were many empty seats in the church as we entered, Mrs. Taylor stood at the end of a row of chairs that was in the middle of the sanctuary. She waved George into his seat first before following, leaving Danny and myself seated to her right. I imagined it was so she could just blend in, but wondered why she hadn't perhaps chosen the empty row at the back in order to make a quick getaway after the service and not risk any kind of scene or chance to be stopped.

Many people that walked past us waved at Mrs. Taylor, George, and Danny. Since we were in the middle of the row they didn't stop to speak, as the remaining chairs had already filled. The reaction to Danny being back in the church was so obvious that you would have been forgiven in thinking that a long-lost child was back in town years after its abduction. Danny, a little confused by the attention, smiled back and also returned the odd salute from a few older gentlemen.

"Wow, you're famous!" I whispered behind a hymnal.

"I know. They keep staring at me. I know it's been a while since they saw me, but it's beginning to freak me out a little," Danny replied.

"You grew up around this church, and your mum obviously speaks very highly of you. They're excited to see you! I think it's nice."

Mrs. Anderson walked down the aisle and gave Danny a huge smile, a wink, and a boney thumbs-up before finding her seat with a group of old women who she blended in with well. They all seemed to know each other and all seemed in such celebratory moods. I could hear Mr. Mayer in the church before I could see him. I looked around to see him at the back of the church with his wife, who was an older version of Marylou. I nudged Danny, who looked around and received a double thumbs-up from Mr. Mayer and a short, excited clap from his wife, who seemed thrilled to see him.

Finally, the pastor came out onto the stage and began his service. Every head turned and settled down. He was just as old and looked just as much like a car salesman as the pastor at the last church and seemed very excited as he delivered a sermon on the "price of freedom" and "the casualties of war." He seemed to direct the majority of his words to the older men and women of the congregation, but his eye often stopped on Danny. The pastor knew his audience well, and they hung on every word he said, only interrupting with cries of agreement.

He stepped to one side and indicated for the choir to sing a hymn that I had never heard before. Once again, I silently mouthed the words to the song in an attempt to show I was joining in. As the choir sang, the pastor left the stage and disappeared through a door on the left. He reappeared moments later, wearing a flowing white robe. I saw George shooting his wife a look and begin drumming his fingers on the chair in front of him.

As the song ended, everyone took their seats again while the pastor raised his hands for attention.

"Now, brothers and sisters, you may recognize a familiar, if not slightly older looking face in our congregation." There was a ripple of murmuring. "Today I would like to welcome back... Daniel Taylor!" He raised his voice and pointed to Danny like a game show host. Every head turned toward us, and I instantly felt uneasy.

"Daniel is back from his job in our glorious nation's capital, Washington DC, where he is now a lawyer, and where he continues his quest to help our less fortunate brothers and sisters with their legal battles."

Danny caught my eye and looked every bit as puzzled as I was. He defended wealthy executives in complex government investigations and was far from a legal Mother Theresa.

"You may also know that our Danny—" He looked at Danny and gave a rather creepy smile as he used his nickname with pride of familiarity. "—also served in the war, where he was a Navy officer in the Middle East during the sad, troubling times of September eleventh."

With this, applause came from everyone, and hands reached over us to grab Danny's shoulders and shake them in an effort to say thanks for his service.

"Stand up, Daniel. Let's have a good look at you."

Danny, now red in the face, looked around and slowly raised himself out of his seat, nodded with a smile, and began to sit back down. But the pastor addressed him once again, and Danny stood back upright and at attention.

"Now, Danny, I would like you to join me up here. And I see you have brought a friend. Did he serve in the military too?" Without waiting for an answer, he added, "Please, both of you come and join me up here."

I shook my head like I was having a seizure at a now baffled Danny, who looked every bit as anxious as I was.

"Greg," he whispered, "we have to go up. Everyone is staring at us. I can't disrespect this man in his own church. Please, we have to go."

With that, Danny made his way past the knees being shuffled to one side to let him through. The owners of those knees looked at me and kept them in place to indicate that the path was clear for me to follow. I looked over again at Mrs. Taylor, still stoic and not even acknowledging her son. She refused to look in my direction.

I followed behind Danny and walked the raised steps onto the stage and looked back at what now looked like hundreds of faces staring at me. I wanted to say I wasn't in the military, but I knew it would cause a scene and raise too many questions, which Danny would have to answer. So, hoping that I was going to get a brief, thoroughly undeserved round of applause, I nodded and took a step to walk back the way I came.

"Danny!" cried the pastor, louder than anything he said up to this point in the service. "Your momma came to me and told me that you would be visiting home again. And we are just delighted to see you." Once again, a round of applause echoed through the church. I stood to one side and smiled, like an actor who announces the Oscar nominees and then stands to one side while the winner accepts the trophy.

Then I noticed Danny's face shift from embarrassment to shock as he looked the pastor up and down, then turned to face his mother in the crowd. There was something going on, and somehow I was two steps behind.

"Your momma, Vivien Taylor"—he pointed to Mrs. Taylor, who still sat with her eyes gazing straight forward while George looked at the floor—"is so proud of you, and when she told me you wanted to be rebaptized back into our church and community while on your visit here, well, I could not have been more thrilled."

I couldn't read Danny's face at first, as he had turned it to look at the blue velvet curtains that were being opened by a young man behind the sitting choir, revealing a small room that held a huge tank of water. Slowly, he turned back around and stared at his mother. He still looked shocked, but I could see the sadness and anger creeping onto his face. I was repulsed that his mother would put him in such a situation where he was forced into choosing between his well-bred manners and courtesy for not disrespecting the church, and telling the truth and ending this bizarre charade. Any amount of faith that Danny, or even I, had left was being tested in that moment. If there was even the smallest residue of faith left in him, how could he lie to a man of God in a church under a stained glass window of a dying Christ?

"Your momma is so pleased to have you home and has spoken from the heart about how truly blessed she feels being able to witness your rebirth back into the church. You may live in Washington DC, but you are and will forever remain part of our flock, only visiting another glorious green pasture." The pastor again looked over at Mrs. Taylor. "Vivien, George, you have raised a fine man," he said as he placed his hand on Danny's chest, where his heart was beating furiously.

"Perhaps his friend would like to join him in being baptized," Mrs. Taylor called back, but this time she was looking directly at me. She smiled and looked around, clapping to encourage others to do the same, until the whole room applauded my acceptance of God and imminent baptism.

I always thought it was a comical effect to have one's jaw drop to show surprise or shock. But amid the thunderous applause, I felt my gritted back teeth relax and separate, my bottom lip lower, and my mouth open wide. I heard a whistle of air as I looked at Mrs. Taylor and deeply inhaled.

I began shaking in anger and nerves. I felt as though boiling water was being poured on the top of my head and running down my body. My face seared, and I knew my features were scarlet as I turned to Danny. Over the cheers and chants, and over the pastor's cries of "Praise the Lord and accept him into your heart," I leaned forward. "I am out of here. Now."

I didn't wait for a response. I took the three steps leading from the stage in a single bound. I landed, pulling myself upright facing everyone in the church.

"No!" I shouted.

The cheers and cries stopped immediately. This was good, as it gave me silence in which to think of the order in which my shaming would begin. Do I announce who I am and tell them all that Mrs. Taylor, the church secretary, has lied and has set this up? Do I shout at the pastor that the same person that he had just applauded for the service to their country is gay and that he is standing in a church that condemns him for it? Do I ask the crowd if those who have an issue with him being gay consider themselves real Christians? Or do I just scream "You are all fucking crazy!" at the top of my voice?

I glanced at Danny. The face of the handsome man I loved and who did everything he could to make me happy looked desperately back at me. There would be no coming back from this. I looked through the stunned crowd at George, whose face I couldn't read, as it was in his hands. I caught sight of Mr. Mayer, who I knew would feel so foolish and betrayed if I were to let out the secret. I heard whispers and turned to see Mrs. Anderson, already gossiping with her cronies. My actions and revelations would be around the city within an hour.

Finally, I looked at Mrs. Taylor. The fear on her face was that of a woman who sees the bus a second before it hits her.

I turned and walked down the aisle. I heard heavy footsteps marching behind me and my name being called, but I didn't stop until I was outside. Danny put his hand on my shoulder, and we both turned to hear the muffled voice of Mrs. Taylor calling "Can't handle crowds," "Iraqis," and "post-traumatic stress disorder."

Danny turned toward the door, waiting for his mother's appearance. "There had better be a new fucking truck at home," he spat at her as he snatched the keys dangling from her purse and walked toward the SUV. He beckoned me to the passenger seat, and I climbed in. He didn't glance back once as he peeled out of the car park.

Danny and I sat in silent fury as we drove back toward the house.

"I cannot believe she just did that!" he shouted and hit the steering wheel with the palm of his hand and parked up in front of the house. "I cannot believe she did that!"

Danny jumped out of the car and paced around the front yard, shaking his head and muttering to himself. I kept my distance and allowed him to let off steam, only getting out of the car when I saw another car pull into the driveway.

George and Mrs. Taylor climbed out of the back seats, and I heard Mrs. Taylor thank the lady in the driver's seat for giving them a ride home. The lady politely waved to Danny, and I heard her say, "I'll be praying for y'all," as she backed out of the driveway.

I expected Mrs. Taylor to be sheepish and run to her son, begging forgiveness. Instead, she walked past him, opened the front door, and closed it behind her, leaving George alone with us outside.

"How could you let that happen?" Danny said to his dad. The hurt in his voice unsteadied George.

"Danny, the first I knew of this was this morning."

"And you couldn't have warned me?" Danny shot back.

"I didn't tell you because in my heart I never thought in a million years she would go through with it. It wasn't until we were at the church that I realized she was being serious. We had a fight, and she finally backed down and told me she was going to cancel it. I thought that was the reason that she walked ahead of us into the church and why she was talking to Brother Thomas before the service."

"There are things that need to be said," Danny said to George, holding up a hand as if to silence any argument.

George raised both palms to shoulder height in submission. "You're right. But remember, she is still your momma."

Danny bolted through the door toward the kitchen with George and me trailing behind. "Why did you just do that? What the hell…."

Mrs. Taylor, who was facing the sink, looking out of the window in the conservatory, rounded on Danny and began to bellow. Not at Danny, but over his shoulder at me.

"Are you happy now?" she shouted.

Danny moved a step to his right, blocking his mother's view of me. "What is your problem?" he shouted back.

Mrs. Taylor took a step closer to her son and began to shout. "You have just embarrassed me in front of the whole church. I have never been so ashamed!"

Danny stepped back, taking in his mother. "What exactly are you ashamed of, Mom?"

"You know what I am talking about, Daniel," she said, moving one step to the side so she could see me again. "But it's okay, isn't it? Because he can just turn around and go home and leave us with all of this mess." She strode past us all and went into the living room where she peered out of the front window.

"What mess?" Danny said, his tone dangerously even. "You just caused that mess." His jaw clenched, and I knew that his mother was reaching the mouth of the volcano.

"What is the church going to say? What are the neighbors going to say?"

I couldn't stay silent any longer. "That's it, enough is enough. I'm leaving." I dug into my pocket and unwrapped the cellophane from the small square box. "Danny, your mother is crazy!" I pulled a cigarette to my lips and began clicking my lighter.

Mrs. Taylor ran at me, her arm swinging as if to strike my face. "Do not smoke that thing in my house!" she screamed as she slapped my hand and cigarette away from my mouth. The paper on the filter took the first layer of my lip with it.

"Momma, what the hell are you doing?"

Mrs. Taylor struggled with her son's grip on her arm while his other held me back. She raised a finger and pointed it at me.

"You are a godless son of a bitch, and I wish Danny had never met you!" she shrieked.

"You're right, I am godless. I know he doesn't exist. Every day my dad was sick I prayed to God that he would get better, that he would be cured, that he wouldn't leave my mother. That he wouldn't leave me. But God still let him die."

With all the malice she could muster, Mrs. Taylor leaned offensively close and spat, "Well, Gregory, perhaps if you had a little more faith, maybe he would still be alive."

CHAPTER TWENTY-ONE

"YOU vile fucking woman!" I screamed, edging forward, every inch of my face now scarlet with rage. "Don't you dare, don't you fucking dare! Who the hell do you think you are?"

George shot forward in his chair, then paused, his eyes darting at Danny to see whether he was going to intervene. Danny moved forward and grabbed my arm, which I shook off. He made a second attempt, which I batted off as fast as the first. I was still wide-eyed with fury at Mrs. Taylor.

"I know who I am!" she said, her voice trembling. She seemed momentarily scared, knowing that she had gone dangerously too far, but returned defiant after seeing her husband and son nearby, both of whom she was sure would come to her rescue. "But I think it's about time Danny saw you for who you are!"

"Danny is well aware of who I am. I am the one who left my family and widowed mother, I am the one who left my friends, I am the one who left my job, I am the one who followed him from Bahrain to Texas to New York to Washington. Danny knows who I am because since we met I have always been there." I punched a pointed finger at her face while spit flew with the shouts. "You know nothing about me because you have never bothered to try and get to know me. You are just a dried-up old woman with nothing in her life except a book telling her what to do, what to think, and what to say every day."

"I have the Lord with me every day. I have His love every day." She pounded the palm of her hand across her chest. "What do you have? I pity you."

"You? Pity me?" A maniacal laugh shook my words. "You see? Instead of saying that you have a son and two daughters who love you and a husband who, quite frankly, must be a saint to put up with you, you go straight for God. Forget about the real people in your life, who support you and do what they can for you. No, put them second place behind God."

"I am a God warrior!"

"Oh, for fuck sake."

"You have nothing if you have no faith!" she declared as if on an altar.

"You think your son is 'nothing'? Are you listening to yourself, lady? I put my faith in your son, not a make-believe zombie do-gooder!"

She gasped and leaned on the wall in a fake attempt to steady herself. She fished a gold cross out of her cleavage and held onto it as if it would give her power to finish.

"How could you say something so evil about our Lord, Jesus Christ?"

I thumped the palm of my hand against my temple in angry frustration. "You're not at church now, woman. You have no one to impress or convince. What exactly is your problem with me? Do you forget that Danny was gay before I met him? Do you think that I turned him? Am I to blame for keeping him gay? Because if that is what you think, then perhaps your belief in someone that you have no proof of is more understandable, because you are obviously off your fucking rocker!"

"Do not deny Jesus Christ in my house!" she screamed.

"This isn't a church. Where's the lightning bolt, huh? You may be a slave to the Word, but you bring everyone into the shackles with you!"

"Now, hang on," George began.

"Greg, what the hell are you doing?" Danny stepped forward and finally came to his mother's defense. "She's my mother. You need to calm down."

264

"Calm down? Are you out of your mind?"

"Greg, I am just as angry as you are, but—"

"No, Danny, you're not nearly as angry as I am." I spun and laughed. "Do you want to know what else your precious bloody mother did, apart from ambushing you into a baptism against your will?"

"What do you mean?" Danny asked, sounding alarmed and confused.

"Are you going to tell him or am I?" I spun back on Mrs. Taylor, who looked as if she was trying to figure out what was about to be let out into the open.

"Well?" I asked.

Mrs. Taylor looked at me and George, her eyes refusing to wander any closer to her son, who stood looking puzzled.

"So you can do the deed, but you just can't confess your sins, huh? Well, I am not that surprised considering that you, Mrs. Holy Spirit, just lied to a pastor."

"Oh, Vivien, what else did you do?" George said.

"What is going on?" Danny demanded, raising his voice.

"She reported me to Immigration, Danny. She called them, said I wasn't in the country legally and I should be investigated. They came to the apartment before I left Washington to go home and questioned me," I said, now prepared to let it all come out. I was already far over any mark of reservation.

It took a moment for Danny to turn toward his mother in disbelief. I could see his mind ticking over as it all began to sink in.

"I don't know what you're talking about," she said, looking directly at me with a slight shake to her head as if she was perplexed. It was almost convincing.

"*God is watching, Vivien!*" I shouted in frustration, pointing to the heavens.

She refused to respond and looked out toward the window.

Danny stared at me, angry. For a moment it looked as if he thought I was lying. He fixed his stare on me like I was the enemy, then asked evenly, "Momma, did you really do that? Momma, is that true?"

Flustered, she looked over to George, who looked just as mad. "I thought if he left, then…."

Danny began shouting. I had never heard his voice sound so hurt, so angry, so desperate. "Do you have any idea of what could have happened? I could have lost Greg. I could have lost my job if they thought I was harboring an illegal immigrant. I would have lost my license to practice law. I could have been convicted if they had decided we were trying to dupe immigration. What on earth were you thinking?"

She rounded back on me.

"I knew you would come between me and my Danny!" she shouted as she moved herself around Danny and out of the way of his damning stare.

"So you're a prophet, now? Is that really possible when you are the one who made this happen?"

"This is a test. You are here to test me. You come here—" She waved a limp wrist in camp mockery. "—with your British ways. Try and charm everyone into thinking that you're something special, but I saw right through you, didn't I? All you British are the same." The look on her face was almost demonic.

"What?" I screamed back "How many British people do you know? How are we all the same?"

"You British lost your ways a long time ago. You Europeans think that you can just live your lives any way you want and there won't be consequences."

"And what consequences would that be? God forbid it should be living happy and free lives. You people are obsessed with sex and the Bible! What you can do, what you can't do; what you can say, what you can't say; who you can be with, who you can't be with. But, hey, so long as you have the good book in one hand and a gun in the other—" I inexplicably began wiggling my stretched out fingers like jazz hands. "—everything is right with the world!"

"You are no good for my son!"

"Not this shit again. Tell me what I have done so bad that you have found it necessary to treat me like a piece of dirt since I have known you."

"I don't need to tell you, you are showing it now, you are evil. Someone has to stand up against you."

"Jesus Christ, you really do believe that, don't you? It's a good thing that you believe in hell, Vivien, because it won't be a fucking surprise when you get there."

She raised her head and stared down her nose in disgust at me. "If you have to address me, I am Mrs. Taylor to you, young man."

"There are plenty of names I think would be an appropriate way to address you, Vivien. Count your blessings I haven't used any of them yet."

"You have changed my son. He was a good boy before you met him. He was decent, respectful. Now I hardly ever hear from him, and I know that is your doing."

"He is a good *man* now. You have to deal with that. So he doesn't call his mommy every single day, you think I am the cause of that? You think I hide his phone and forbid him to call you?"

"I wouldn't be surprised. You are capable of pretty much anything."

"What did I do that is so wrong? Huh? Come on, what is it that makes you feel like I am some sort of threat to your relationship?"

"It is written in the Bible that—"

"Forget what it says in the Bible, as I am sure that I am not personally mentioned in it. So, in the real world, what have I done?"

"But you are mentioned." She took a step back to take in every heathen inch of me. "You are the serpent!"

I pulled at my hair in anger and frustration.

"Stop shaking your fucking tambourine at me and tell me what it is I have done! He is a grown man; he lives his own life. I am not responsible for the way he feels toward you, and I am sick and tired of getting the blame for it. Exactly what magical powers do you think I hold over him? It's you who has chosen to see him differently, and it's you who has the issues. You hate the fact that he can only be happy with another man. Or is it that the other man is me?"

She turned to Danny, who by now was hunched over on the sofa with his face buried in his hands, his elbows dug into his knees. George looked on silently.

She ran the few steps toward him and knelt down in front of him, her hands grasping his forearm, almost pleading with him. Danny made no attempt to shake her off; he just simply remained still and rigid. "This is not what you want from your life, Danny. There are so many different ways to live, happier ways to live. Please, don't stay with this man. He will bring you down! Think about a life that involves the church. They will help you, Danny. They will pray for you."

"Pray for him? Bring him down? Are you out of your goddamn mind? He is a successful attorney in Washington DC, not a drug-addicted rent boy on the streets of Houston. The only thing he needs saving from is the continuous disappointment of a mother who chooses to make snide comments to his partner and conspires to make life difficult for him. You have just made such a scene in front of that church and had the nerve and the audacity to say that *you* were ashamed and embarrassed," I shouted as I watched her pulling at Danny's hands that were pressed in tight against his forehead. "Danny is the last thing in the world you should be embarrassed or ashamed of and the first thing you should be most proud of. But you can't see that, can you? It hurts him when you deny him and who he truly is. He is a proud man, and you do nothing but make excuses for something that he doesn't feel you need to make excuses for!" I brought my clenched fists down hard on the coffee table, causing the china hands in prayer to fall and shatter. Mrs. Taylor jumped at my aggression. "He would never tell you this himself, but he is ashamed of you!"

She looked at her son. She waited for him to say it wasn't true, hoping that he would get up and defend her and join in her chorus of jibes against me, finally ending our relationship. But Danny's silence told her I spoke the truth.

She stood up and faced the wall of photos in which Danny was the main star. The glass, which framed all of the glorious moments that she captured when she was most proud of him, reflected the face of a woman whose son was now ashamed of her. She turned back to me, her eyes brimming with tears.

"You don't understand."

"I don't understand because you can't give me an explanation. You can't tell me, can you? You can't see what I have done for him, how I have supported him and loved him. No, you, in all of your wisdom, decided from the very moment you heard about me to hate me, for no good reason. You are just stubborn. You can't even give me a decent reason why you have been such a vile bitch to me."

"Greg, remember that's my wife you're talking to," George snapped.

"You don't understand!" she cried.

"Don't understand what? Explain it to me. What is the problem?" I said, not lowering my voice from George's warning shot.

"You don't understand!" she looked over, pleading for understanding from Danny, tears spilling from her eyes with a look of a broken woman on the verge of meltdown.

"*Understand what?*"

"I won't have him with me!" she bawled. "He'll be lost!"

"What are you talking about?" I shouted back.

"You don't understand. You don't believe!" she cried.

"What are you talking about?" I shouted again.

"I won't have him with me. I won't have him with me in heaven!"

Mrs. Taylor looked at her son, a dozen emotions pouring from every feature.

I had never seen anybody look so broken, so desperate. Danny and George looked at each other. Despite their knowledge of Mrs. Taylor's faith, they still both looked bewildered by her explanation.

We remained silent as Mrs. Taylor wept on the floor by Danny's feet. George got up to help his wife to her feet, but she waved him away. He returned to his seat and continued the silence.

There was nothing I could say. There was nothing I wanted to say. I took a seat and hung my head. Even though the argument was fought from two corners, I felt as if I was the one that had punched the winning blow by making her confess and leaving her knocked out and weeping on the floor.

Danny finally spoke. It seemed that he had used the silence to think, while I had used it to feel shame.

"You believe that God is love, that God is good. Momma, I am gay. Why would God punish me when He was the one who made me this way? But more to the point, why would God inflict such a harsh punishment on you by not letting you have your son with you in heaven when you have led a good life? When you have helped people you don't know, when you have helped all of us? If family means everything, why would he separate us? I know you, Momma, and I know you believe God loves you, and in your heart you believe He loves me. But, Momma, you have to stop letting other people, regardless of who they are, convince you that He has such a hard heart that he would tear apart a family over something like who I love. Through your beliefs, through your faith, and through your own mind, you know, Momma, that simply doesn't make sense."

Danny grasped his mother's hand a little tighter.

"God didn't make me gay as a constant test of temptation. He made me gay because he knew that there was someone else in the world who could receive my love, and I found him. It's Greg. You've always trusted me and know I am the sensible, levelheaded man you taught me to be. Please stop taking the opinions of people you barely know over mine. It hurts me to think that you can be influenced by people with no knowledge of my life, or faith, or who have agendas you don't know of."

Mrs. Taylor squeezed Danny's hand back in response.

"And, Momma, if there is a separate heaven for gay people," Danny continued with a smile, "well, you'll just have to come visit."

He raised his mother's chin gently with the side of his index finger, forcing her to look at him. "I hear it's on a rainbow, not a cloud, so at least you'll get some color."

Mrs. Taylor smiled and held out a hand to me as if for me to join them, which I did without making eye contact. I sat looking at George, who had a kind of relief etched on his face.

"What I said, about your dad, can you forgive me?"

"Mrs. Taylor—"

"Vivien," she interrupted.

"Vivien, you hit a nerve. I am sorry for shouting at you, and if I scared you in any way I am sorry. My dad would have been mortified if he saw the way I just acted."

"It was nothing less than I deserved."

Danny rose from his seat and indicated for his dad to follow him into the other room and leave us alone. George followed and nodded kindly, with a look of appreciation at me as he disappeared through the door with his son.

"I know more about you than you think I do. Despite all the things I've said and done…." She looked to the sky and offered a short prayer of apology under her breath. "Danny has always told me what a good man you are."

"That's why I couldn't understand what was going on," I replied with a shrug.

"At first, I didn't want to know. What you said was true. To me, you were someone who came into my son's life and were yet another person who would lead him further away from the church. My faith in what people said was God's word told me not to encourage such a thing. The more apparent it became that you were becoming such a large part of his life the more I became confused as to what to do. I couldn't seek any guidance from the church, because in my heart of hearts I knew what they would say."

"That it was wrong?"

"Greg, no one wants to hear that they should turn their back on their son. Not telling them was just delaying the conversation I knew would follow from telling them that he was gay. I couldn't cope with the thought of anyone making fun, ridiculing, or condemning him. But they don't know him like I do. They don't see how wonderful he is."

"Then why not just leave it at that? Why try and ruin our relationship?" I felt sorry for her, but I still thought I deserved more of an explanation.

Mrs. Taylor sat in thought. It was if she had known the reason all along, but had never strung it together before.

"Because I felt guilty lying to the church. If Danny had no relationship, I could have simply convinced myself that he was a single man, so the gay part wasn't an actual issue and the lies I told to the pastor and congregation would no longer be lies."

"So rather than lie, you were prepared to risk your son's happiness?" She began to weep again. I let her cry it out before she answered.

"I know how selfish I've been. Sitting here now and hearing you say it out loud is more than I can bear because I know in my heart that's what I was doing. But the church has very strict opinions on certain things, opinions that are repeated over and over again every day, every week, every year. It became such an issue because I was constantly bombarded and reminded that they regarded my son's life as less than.... And what makes it worse is that I have so many more reasons to be proud of my children than anyone else at that church. But for so long, if Danny's name was mentioned I would shake, knowing that I would have to lie, so I steered the conversation away as soon as possible."

Mrs. Taylor sniffed again and took my hand.

"You don't have children, so please try to understand. You love them more than anything else, more than you could have ever thought possible. Now, just for a moment, try to imagine what it's like to hear a stranger, or worse, a friend, say that your child, who you have loved, cared for, and protected, and who means more than anything else in the world to you is 'an abomination'."

"But...."

"I know what you're going to say. Believe it or not, I've had the same argument with myself so many times. 'Why not stop going to church if you don't believe it?'"

I nodded.

"There are many more, much stricter religions out there, Greg, and you have to find the one that is closest to your own beliefs. Since I started working at the church, it has become my entire life, and I've been so wrapped up in its teachings, as I am expected to know answers when people ask questions. So I did start to believe it. But I have done myself, my community, my church, and my God a disservice. I lied to them all. Your relationship with Danny forced me to face the fact that I was lying, so I resented you for it and used that resentment as an excuse to make things difficult for you and Danny, therefore getting what I wanted, which was the opportunity to stop lying."

"So the more guilt you felt, the more you blamed me. And the more you blamed me the easier it was to ease the guilt?"

She drew a deep breath. "Yes."

"You know how crazy that sounds, right?"

"Yes, I do." She sniffed quietly. "Greg, you have no idea how much better it makes me feel to admit that."

"But, Vivien, the baptism. How did you think that could have helped?"

"After five years, it was obvious that you were going to remain in Danny's life. He was clear about that before he even returned from Bahrain. But, as usual, I didn't want to hear it. I thought it would be my last chance to protect his soul."

She looked sadly at the door. "Danny must be so mad with me. He must hate me."

"Of course he doesn't hate you."

"Then you must."

"I don't hate you. Don't get me wrong. There were times when I was as mad as hell at you. Above all of it I just never understood you. I so dearly wanted to know the woman Danny had described in his memories."

She let out a little sob.

"You know I love your son, don't you?"

"Yes, I know." She drew another deep breath. "And I know that he loves you."

Vivien pulled me into an embrace and spoke into my shoulder. "I believe in heaven, I believe in God—" She came up to face me. "—and I believe that I will apologize to your dad when I meet him one day, because as sure as I am sitting here, he is there taking pride in his son for showing such compassion to this old fool."

"Vivien, my dad is going to kick your arse when he sees you."

Finally, she laughed.

EPILOGUE

"PUT her on speakerphone."

It was two years since the day of the baptism and a year since we moved back to England. Danny, frustrated at the glacial pace of changes, was initially confident that things would change when a "fierce advocate" for gay Americans was elected into the top job.

We stood on the National Mall in Washington DC with a million other people, in the most extreme cold and bitter weather I ever experienced, while Mr. Obama became Mr. President. He practically had the whole country in the palm of his hand during that time, hanging on his every word. Although he had successfully managed to get Don't Ask, Don't Tell overturned, the Defense Of Marriage Act was still alive and well and making our lives difficult to plan. When a position in the London office had come up out of the blue, we had a hurried discussion about the future and Danny, Duke, and I bolted for Great Britain.

"How are you, Momma? Greg's here, but he's driving so you're on the speakerphone," Danny said as we drove toward the huge shopping mall, excited to be making some special purchases that day.

"Hey, Greg! Is my son still making you do all of the driving out there? You should tell him to get his thumb out of his ass and take British driving lessons. He can recite pi to the hundredth digit but can't drive a stick."

"I would love to, Vivien, but he keeps freaking out and screaming every time we reach a roundabout. He jumps out of the car and runs away, abandoning me in the passenger seat," I said, not entirely joking

275

as Danny had done something similar two days before. Despite his vast intelligence, he just couldn't grasp the idea of driving on the left, in a manual car, toward a busy roundabout.

"Danny, you're going to have to learn. What are you going to do when you have kids? You can't expect that poor boy to do all of the running around on his own. You'll have to pick the kids up from school, take them to their little friend's houses, parties, playgrounds, and anywhere else the little buggers demand to go."

Danny and I both laughed at his mother's use of the phrase "little bugger." We had been over to Texas for a two-week visit six months earlier, and his mother picked up on the word when I used it to describe a particularly whiny kid in the supermarket that was not getting his own way and throwing packets of cookies at his mother.

The trip was a dream. It was as though I was being introduced to Danny's mother for the very first time. We spoke regularly on the phone beforehand, and our relationship became one that I never would have imagined. She gave up her job as a church secretary and started work in the small town's only travel agency. She called me regularly when we were still in Washington to get travel tips on various destinations while her customers sat in front of her.

Her whole personality changed. She was so much more relaxed, as if she never even had a shadow of being uptight. She even went as far as to joke about her past behavior, occasionally slipping back into the character she once was to freak me out and make Danny laugh.

The church still called to her every Sunday, which she attended without question. But she no longer came out troubled or stressed. It was as if she'd had a fix of something that could sustain her addiction for a week, a kind of spiritual nicotine patch. On the occasions that I saw or spoke to her after a service, she seemed nothing more than inspired, explaining that she took from the service what she wanted, rather than taking everything so literally.

Our relationship became that of two distant friends who actually enjoyed catching up with one another. Vivien's humor, about which Danny so often told me, was so much more enjoyable and constant than I imagined it could be. But I wasn't the only person to benefit from this change of personality. To me it was new, but George, who seemed so beaten down and resigned to the idea of his lifestyle, also came bounding back. Their marriage now could be viewed by anyone with envy, their love and enjoyment of each other so obvious.

But I was most pleased at Danny's happiness at his getting his old momma back. Even when we said that we were moving to England, which we worried could destroy all of this new found "familiness," his mother gave her blessings, with the added cheeky condition that we spend at least two weeks a year in Texas on vacation. On reflection, that was more than we would have ever spent in twelve months of weekend visits. The fact is, she would see her son more than she ever did before.

"Actually, I am glad you called," Danny said, raising his eyebrows to me as if to ask permission. I nodded back.

"Of course you are. Why wouldn't you be glad to get a call from your Momma?"

Danny could hardly contain himself. "Momma, we're gonna be daddies!"

"You mean...?" Vivien took a deep breath, as if she was too excited to finish the question.

"Yep! We heard from the adoption agency this morning. There's a girl in Essex who is four months pregnant and has selected us to adopt the child."

"Oh, Danny!" she squealed. "I am so thrilled for you both. I am gonna be a grandma again!"

"Yes, and I get three months paternity leave, so we're going to come back to Texas with the baby."

"I can't wait!" she squealed again. "What are you going to call her? Or him? Do you know what she's having yet?"

"A little boy," I said, grinning from ear to ear.

"A little boy! How wonderful! And what are you going to call him?"

Danny and I had spoken about this from the moment we registered with the adoption agency. It was a heated debate, as I was three weeks into my last, and ultimately successful, attempt to give up smoking. We both knew that having me down as a smoker would hurt the application, so I was on the anti-smoking pill Chantix and slowly climbing down the walls. We narrowed the list down to five different names for a boy and six for a girl. We still hadn't officially chosen which one to use. I looked at Danny, shrugged, and then shouted into the speakerphone.

"Christian!"

GREG HOGBEN was born and raised on the South Coast of England, where he spent his school days learning how to get into trouble. But more importantly, he learned how to tell stories to get out of it. Greg is a huge fan of British humor and counts Stephen Fry and Jennifer Saunders among his comedy gods.

You can contact Greg at greghogben@gmail.com.

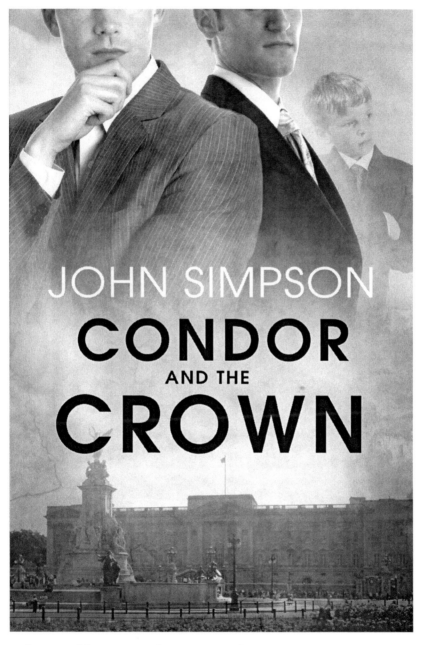

CPSIA information can be obtained at www.ICGtesting.com
Printed in the USA
BVOW041906260912

301492BV00007B/9/P